Beyond the Land of Dreams

Beyond the Land of Dreams

Beryl's Awakening

Susan Bruck

Soul Blossom Living

To my beloved daughters, Rachel and Gabrielle, who fill my life with magic everyday. And to all the children in my life who inspire me to dream and love fairy tales. And to Midnight, Cinnamon, Sky, and Buddy--the cats in my life. You are all purr-fect!

CONTENTS

CONTENTS

Late summer, just outside Xantalon City

Dear People of Floredelis,

Many tales begin with the words, "Once upon a time." But how does the teller know when a story begins?

The tapestry of life has too many threads to count. Pick any thread and follow it back. Does it start when the hero was born? Does it begin with her parents? If she's not careful, the storyteller may find herself back at the beginning of time, or even before.

But this story began with a dream—

From The Book of Jocasta

Beryl looked at the Shadow Man, who towered over her, his tears dripping like rain, called up all her courage, and shouted, "Who are you?"

The rain stopped.

"The Thirteenth. Don't forget me." The voice rumbled like thunder, surrounding her in darkness, so she could no longer see.

"What do you want?" Beryl asked.

"Take care of my baby," he said.

Beryl heard a thin wail in the grass next to her. The darkness thinned. She saw a tiny baby, its face red and distorted from crying. She felt afraid to touch it, almost certain it wasn't real, but her heart went out to the miserable babe. She picked it up, holding it close. It felt light as a feather, lighter than any human baby. Its cries quieted, but it still breathed quickly, gulping in air.

"Don't forget me." The voice and shadow faded away as the clouds lost their human shape and rolled back toward the woods. She held the baby close, rocking it, making sounds to comfort both the child and herself. As the sunlight returned, the baby disappeared, leaving behind only dampness and a sudden silence echoing with tears.

Just moments before—or had it been days? --Beryl had looked up from the Book of Jocasta, reading what Jocasta said about the power of fairy tales for maybe the hundredth time. The feeling in her stomach matched the roiling clouds that she saw blowing in much too fast, considering there was no wind. She glanced back at the *Book of Jocasta*, with its hard brown cover and golden letters, before hurriedly wrapping it in its thick blue felt bag to protect it from whatever was approaching, placing it on top of *Jocasta's Book of Fairy Tales*, her other favorite book. She idly fingered the red flowers she'd embroidered on the sack as she watched the world change from light to dark.

The early fall afternoon grew suddenly cool, even cooler than the water of the stream in which her feet dangled. She didn't see any clouds over Xantalon City in the distance. She could make out the turret of the castle and the top of the stone wall that surrounded the city. She didn't even see clouds over her stone house, built by her moms and the villagers, which was just a stone's throw away, or over the garden behind it, where she could still hear her sweet mamas giggling as they harvested herbs and vegetables.

The darkness that haunted Beryl's dreams had been breaking through more and more into her waking life. She knew the darkness in her dreams reflected the darkness inside her. Ava had told her so. She tried hard to be good, hoping the darkness would fade from her dreaming and waking, that the nights would go back to the comfort of peaceful darkness, stars, waxing and waning moons, the owl's call, leaves rustling in the forest, and the comforting sound of the stream's lullaby singing her to sleep. She remembered just last year, just before her fourteenth birthday, when clouds still meant rain if they were dark or looked like funny animal shapes or fairies when they were white and fluffy. But before Beryl could ponder the nature of clouds further, the roar of the wind behind the clouds had driven away the sound of her parents' voices in the distance, the song of the happy brook in which her bare toes tickled the stones at the bottom, and finally, drove all thoughts from her head.

She sat transfixed, wanting to run away but fascinated at the same time. She had wondered if she could force her body to move while frozen with terror. The wind's had begun to howl, making her curls dance across her face. She recognized his shape and darkness, the Shadow Man. She squeezed her eyes shut tight, trying not to remember how he used to come to her in her dreams when she was just three years old, appearing on the door of her bedroom. "I'm going to fall on you," he always said. And she knew that if he did, he would suffocate her. In her dreams, he always fell just short of reaching her and then disappeared—until the next time. Those dreams had stopped, but when she turned nine, he started coming to her in the night, sitting in the chair by her bed, watching her sleep, or at least she'd find him sitting and staring at her when she opened her eyes in the dark. A shadow in the darkness of light, like a hole or negative space. Today, he'd looked like a storm cloud, darker than the night, with coal-red eyes. A gaping hole through which she could see the blue sky and that looked big enough to swallow her was where his mouth should have been.

When he visited her at night, he spoke to her of evil things, showed her visions of her beloved homeland destroyed, the people and land suffering beyond belief.

"Please, not again," she said to herself as she recognized not so much his shape as the feeling of despair he always evoked. She had been surprised to feel drops of water falling softly, tickling her scalp as they found their way through her burgundy curls. She closed her eyes and prayed to the goddess that this was just a storm and that she just imagined his cloudy shape striding across the land to her. She opened her eyes, hoping to see rain clouds, but it was him, and he was crying, water pouring out of eyes now pink like a cloudy sunset, as fire and water combined. The rest of him looked like a cloud just before the thunder boomed, full of electricity and potential.

And just as quickly as he'd appeared, he disappeared. Her moms still laughed, the house still stood, Xantalon City stood unchanged in the distance. Only she was left wondering what was real.

Later that afternoon, in the woods

"Beryl, are you ok?"

A shadow fell over her, and she jumped, startled out of her reverie. After the Thirteenth left, she'd tucked her Jocasta books into a hollow in the willow tree which stood at the bend in the creek just a short distance from her house, pulled on her brown leather shoes, and ran as fast as she could into the forest. She imagined she could run as fast as those clouds had moved, that she could outrun the darkness that hounded her. But she knew that was impossible because the darkness was inside of her. So she just ran until she didn't have the breath to run anymore.

She had tried to tell her parents—and Ava—about her encounters and dreams a few times. After trying a few times and just getting a pat on the head, like she was still a little girl, she'd given up. She didn't dare tell anyone else about them. Everything and everyone around her was good—except her.

As she leaned against her special oak tree, the one she meditated under, her friend Squirrel sat on her shoulder, nibbling a nut she had brought him. She had been telling him about the Thirteenth. He listened and poked his nose into her pocket looking for more treats. That's someone startled her by calling her name. Squirrel scampered up the tree.

Beryl looked up and smiled. This shadow, unlike the ones that stalked her dreams and now her waking, belonged to her godmother, wise, solid Ava. Beryl often went with her to gather herbs in the woods or commune with nature. Ava had taught Beryl to meditate under this very tree. Beryl thought Ava was very old. Well, Beryl wasn't sure how old she was, but her hair was all white and had been for as long as Beryl could remember. She had eyes the color of a blue jay, and really white teeth with a gap between the top front ones.

"Did you forget I was coming today?" asked Ava, a sparkle in her eyes.

"Oh, no, I remembered," said Beryl, looking away. "Well, kind of... just now. Would you like some tea? I made mint tea this morning and some cookies. My parents were in the garden a little while ago. They'll be happy to see you."

"Thank you, Beryl. I do want to talk to them, but I want to talk to you first. Are you feeling well? You look pale."

"I'm fine," Beryl said. It wasn't exactly a lie, but it wasn't exactly the truth, either. Part of her wanted to tell Ava what had happened that afternoon, but she feared Ava would turn away, they all would, if they knew the truth. Or she just wouldn't believe her, which would be even worse. Maybe she had lost her grip on reality. Even though she loved Ava, she felt really alone. But the Shadow Man, or the Thirteenth as she guessed she should call him now, had been with her for many years, whispering to her about the destruction of her beloved land, showing her violent deaths. The visions—or perhaps hallucinations— of the dead bodies of her beloved king and queen hanging from some kind of scaffolding haunted her. She didn't know why she carried such darkness inside of her, but she knew she had to find a way to protect them. She'd have to figure out how to banish the darkness by herself.

Ava tilted her head to one side. "If you say so. Anyhow, I have a story to tell you."

Beryl smiled, her troubles momentarily fading into the background. She wondered if Ava would tell her a fairy tale. She'd loved fairy tales for as long as she could remember. She'd memorized all twelve in *Jocasta's Book of Fairy Tales.*

Ava sat on the moss that grew soft and golden between the roots of the oak. Beryl snuggled against her, leaning her head on Ava's shoulder. She felt safe and happy.

"When I was just a little older than you, maybe sixteen or seventeen," said Ava, stroking Beryl's hair, "I lived with my parents, but I longed for adventure. I begged them to let me go to the Temple City. They were both farmers, and my mother was a fine weaver, as well. They weren't initiates of the Temple, but they loved the teachings of Jocasta.

"My parents let me go. They knew my calling was different from theirs. I felt sad to leave but excited to begin my life's work, even though I didn't know exactly what it would be. Before I left, my mother gave me a scarf woven with all the colors of the rainbow. Her great-grandmother, one of the original settlers here, had woven it in the Old World. They passed it from mother to daughter as each daughter came of age. When I wore it, I felt the arms of my mother and my grandmothers holding and protecting me. I went to the Temple City, learned, and found my life's path. But I never had any children, no daughter to give it to."

Beryl looked at Ava. "Are you sad that you never had children?"

Ava was silent for a moment. "Yes and no. I chose my path, and I am at peace with the choices I've made. Beryl..."

Ava's eyes looked moist. Beryl wondered if she had asked the wrong question. Ava pulled Beryl closer. Beryl loved how Ava always smelled of lavender. For a moment, they listened to the breeze rustling through the leaves. Beryl tried to block out the memory of that earlier wind, without success. Beryl's big black cat Midnight lay down against her leg. She absently scratched between his ears, and he purred loudly.

"I want you to have this, my dear." Ava handed Beryl a pouch of dark blue wool tied with a pale blue ribbon.

"Oh, you didn't have to...I mean, thank you, Ava."

Beryl untied the ribbon. Midnight batted at it.

"Oh no, that's my ribbon, Middy," she said, rolling it up and putting it into the pouch.

She felt a lot of fabric inside the bag. As she pulled it out, it shimmered with many colors. Ava had given her her grandmother's rainbow scarf.

"Oh, Ava," was all she managed to say.

"You are my goddaughter. Your journey is about to begin, Beryl. May this scarf remind you that you are loved and let you know that you are protected by all the generations of mothers going back to the beginning of time here in Floredelis, and even before that."

Ava hugged her again and kissed the top of her head. Beryl noticed that Ava's attention had wandered. She started toward the house.

"I must go and speak with your parents now. But know that I'm so proud of you, and I love you very much.

Ava headed to the garden to find Beryl's parents.

Beryl hugged the scarf to her chest and breathed in its scent. It smelled like Ava. She wrapped it around her shoulders and over Midnight's head, scratching his chin through the rainbow of fabric.

3

Two weeks later, just outside the Temple City

> *On healing:* True healing comes when body and mind align with the spirit. True health comes when the four elements are in balance. The plant beings will guide our healers and teach them to harvest and prepare herbs to heal those experiencing dis-ease in body or spirit. Healers, share your gifts freely! Always give to those in need.
>
> *From* The Book of Jocasta

Ava felt tired. Every one of her fifty-nine years weighed on her. Every bone in her body longed to lie down and rest. She recalled her excitement the first time she entered the Temple City. The magnificent granite archway hadn't changed in all those years. As she approached, she began to make out the relief sculpture that showed the beginnings of Floredelis. She could already see the twelve-petalled flower, the map of the land, at the peak of the arch. She wished she hadn't sent Eugene into the city the night before. She would like his strong arm to lean on and his warm smile to lift her spirits. Eugene, the first baby she delivered when she moved to Xantalon, had grown into a fine man with a family of his own. He didn't like to leave them, but when the queen asked him to bring a message to the Temple Council, he went without hesitation.

The trip took two days on foot, the best way to travel on the narrow forest paths. Eugene had brought his horse with him, though, so he could carry back supplies from the City. While Eugene entered the city the night before, hoping to deliver a private message to the High Priestess, Ava slept in the forest. Truth be told, she hadn't slept well. She felt every bump and twig beneath her blanket. She couldn't stop thinking about what she had seen that day. On their way to the City, she and Eugene visited the place where she gathered wild ginseng and also the spot where the most potent motherwort grew, hoping to harvest some to prepare medicines for the coming winter. But at each spot they found only holes where the plants should be, with a few loose roots and stems lying on the rumpled dirt. Could this really be the work of Dr. Hami? She had heard his name mentioned by other healers. None of them knew where he came from or who he was. As she lay restless in the dark forest, she touched the crystal she wore around her neck. She tried to clear her mind and connect with Ontihaponati, the great crystal through whom the initiates communicated with each other. She couldn't, again. It had been months since she'd been able to connect with her fellow initiates.

When she tired of worrying about that, her mind raced on. What was going on with the queen? Why on earth would she choose this moment to retire? She was in good health, at the height of her powers, and the people of Xantalon loved her. And if it was her time to step down, why would she choose Beryl to succeed her? Certainly, Beryl's birth signs indicated strong leadership qualities, but she was only fourteen, and a young fourteen, at that. Ava felt it was no coincidence that Lillia wanted to relinquish her queenship at the same time they had lost contact with Ontihaponati. Ava worried about the queen, she worried about Beryl, she worried about the forest, and finally she gave up on sleep and just waited for the sun to rise.

As she neared the City, Ava saw a crowd of travelers standing outside the gate. She pulled her thick white hair back into a ponytail and covered it with the hood of her cloak. Her eyes narrowed as she tried to see over the heads of the crowd to figure out what was going on. The City gates were always open to welcome travelers, but they must not be now, although she couldn't see them through the crowd.

A young woman carrying a baby in a sling stood near her, gazing at her sleeping child. Ava touched her shoulder and asked if she knew why everyone was waiting. The woman replied that the guards were questioning everyone seeking entrance to the City, but if you had money or something else the guards wanted, you could go right in. Ava's mouth hung open in surprise. Could this be true? In the silence that followed, the baby, whom Ava judged to be about six months old, began to wheeze. The woman lifted the child onto her shoulder. When Ava looked at the baby's pale, pinched face, she knew he had a bad case of bronchitis. She reached into her bag and pulled out a bottle containing a tincture of herbs that would strengthen his lungs and ease the babe's strained breathing.

"I am a healer from Xantalon," she said as she felt the baby's head. It felt hot and dry. "My name is Ava. Here, take these herbs for your baby. Give him a few drops in the morning and evening and anytime he starts to cough or wheeze. He should start feeling better in a day or so. Keep him nice and warm and give him...."

Ava's voice trailed off as she realized that the murmuring crowd around her had fallen silent, and the only voice she heard was her own. She had been stroking the child's head and looking into his wise gray eyes. With her hand still on the child's overly warm head, she looked up and saw the mother's face frozen with fear. She noticed the people around them seemed to be purposely looking away; many had actually turned their backs on them. What in the world was going on, Ava wondered. As Ava turned her head toward the sound of a flute, the woman grabbed the bottle of herbs, hid it in her dress, and disappeared into the crowd. Following the sound of the music, Ava saw a man wearing a mask, half black and half white, walking through the crowd playing a wooden flute.

As she strained to get a better look at that strange sight, someone bumped into Ava and grabbed her arm. "Come with me," a man's voice hissed in her ear. He pulled her toward the city wall, toward the mountain called Munin. The people in front of them moved close together, making it difficult for the guards coming toward her to get through. Were they coming for her? They certainly seemed to be. But why on earth would they have any interest in her? She heard one shout, "Out of my way, you idiots. Make way for the Temple guard." Ava let herself be pulled away, hoping she made the right choice.

Soon she didn't hear the guard shouting or the flute playing anymore. The man held her arm tightly. She wanted to look at his face, but he pushed her forward quickly. Her feet no longer felt heavy. She felt almost as though she could fly. Then another pair of hands pulled her into a dark passageway.

4 |

That same day, just outside Xantalon City

Beryl sat by the stream beside her house on another perfect fall day. Today was her fifteenth birthday, but Ava hadn't returned from the Temple City. She always spent her birthday with Ava. Until now. She re-read the passage in the Book of Jocasta that she'd been reading ever since her visit from the Thirteenth, even though she now knew it by heart:

I gathered twelve followers and brought them to this land untouched by human hands. Floredelis, shaped like a flower with twelve petals, each petal a province started by one of the twelve Founders.

After the Twelve and I entered with our followers, Ontihaponati closed the passage. There was no turning back. I strove to bring with me only the good and leave the evil of the old world behind.

There had to be some connection between that passage and the Thirteenth. But Beryl had no idea what it could be.

She wiggled her toes in the water and thought about her fourteenth birthday—which seemed like it had been much longer ago than a year ago. She had been sound asleep when Ava arrived, having one of those horrible dreams about the man called Hamilton. Sometimes in her dreams he was a child and sometimes an adult. Once he had been a baby in his mother's arms. His mother was young and alone, except for him. Hamilton's father had left them.

But that day, a year ago, she dreamt of Hamilton as a grown man who looked like Santa Claus, which is how he always looked when she dreamt of him in the Temple City. In that dream, he met with a man and a woman, members of the Temple Council. Both were short and round and had shoulder-length hair, but the man was bald on top. They looked like brother and sister, but they weren't. She felt Hamilton's contempt for them. He enjoyed manipulating them. The man wanted everyone to recognize his greatness. The woman wanted the man to love her like she loved him. Hamilton convinced them that he would help them become rulers of Floredelis, together. He painted a picture in their minds of them gathering power, supporting each other, saving their people. Hamilton found their fervor to rule—and save— Floredelis deliciously funny, as he contemplated his true plan, which included them dead and Floredelis destroyed. Then Beryl saw younger Hamilton holding his dying mother in his arms and vowing to avenge her. Hamilton kissed his mother's forehead in the dream at the same time that Ava kissed Beryl's in real life, waking her with a start.

Ava asked, "Are you alright?"

"Just a bad dream," she'd replied.

She knew the Shadow Man, the Thirteenth, sent her these dreams. Although he didn't try to fall on her anymore, she saw him, her own shadow side, in her dreams. And right after her last birthday, she'd started seeing him when she was awake. At first, she saw him only in the middle of the night—where she could at least pretend that he was a dream. Then she'd started seeing his shape in the shadows. He'd only spoken to her during the day that one time.

This morning, her fifteenth birthday morning, she dreamt that Hamilton killed Ava by giving her poison to drink. This was the first dream where she saw Hamilton with someone she knew. The Thirteenth was covering her like a shadowy blanket when she awoke. She could barely breathe. But then he faded away. She stayed in bed until Mama A, Anne, called her to breakfast was ready—she made her favorite breakfast, blueberry pancakes with whipped cream and maple syrup and even a few raspberries sprinkled on top. Mama B, Beatrice, her birth mom (another reason she was Mama B), had offered to bring her breakfast in bed, but she preferred to sit in the sunny garden and watch the bees and butterflies visiting the herbs and flowers. Being in the sunshine helped dispel the cloud that hung over her.

She thought about her moms and how different her life was than Hamilton's. She had two loving parents, even though they drove her crazy sometimes. And she had a dad, too, although she barely knew him. He had been friends of her parents back at the Temple school. Her moms still loved each other. She couldn't imagine either of them leaving her or each other for a new adventure, even though they seemed like opposites in some ways. Mama B was dark as the night, but her smile lit up the world like the sun. She loved to laugh and dance and be silly. She got her curly hair from Mama B, although the color seemed to be a combination of Mama B's dark hair and her dad's blond hair. It was a weird kind of burgundy color that made her green eyes look golden. Mama A was plump and soft, with pale blond hair like her dad. She was quiet and sweet, and the kindest person Beryl had ever met. Mama A liked to tell her that Mama B's hair used to be long and wild like Beryl's but when Beryl was born, Mama B cut it all off. She couldn't take care of a baby and her hair, at least that's how Mama A told it. At least her moms were here to celebrate with her, although they seemed rather preoccupied lately. But they'd promised they'd make her a special birthday dinner tonight with her favorites, mac and cheese, salad, and refried black beans. And, of course, a chocolate cake.

Up until now, every year on her birthday, Ava had taught her something amazing—special birthday gifts from her godmother. Beryl knew Ava couldn't be with her today because she had gone on an important journey to find out why the herbs in the forest were disappearing. Beryl cared deeply for the forest and appreciated that Ava was looking after it. She reminded herself that she was grown up now and didn't need to have Ava with her exactly on her birthday. They could celebrate later, when Ava returned. But she still felt disappointed.

Beryl picked up the *Book of Jocasta* and wandered back into her house. The house was built of stones gathered from what was now their garden and from along the stream. Her parents built it together, before she was born, with help from the villagers, when they came to Xantalon to be the Watchers. She still didn't understand what her moms actually did, even though they'd explained it many times. Their job was to watch and listen—to the people, to the land, to the nature spirits—in order to keep things in balance. They often met with the queen to discuss that stuff, and they seemed to be spending a lot more time with her lately.

Behind the front door was a large room which served as the living and dining rooms. On either side of the great room were three bedrooms, her moms to the left, one for Beryl and another for guests down a short hall to the right. Behind the great room was the kitchen, with a wood burning stove, lots of counters and a big pantry filled with shining pots and pans and delicious food. Beryl headed for the kitchen, her favorite place, but Mama A shooed her out. She was preparing a birthday surprise.

After being banished from the kitchen, Beryl ambled toward the village. She kicked stones and picked a few purple flowers for her hair. She picked big ones, because the small ones got lost in her curls, and she disliked picking out the wilted remains the next day. Three figures skipped towards her. She recognized Melanie, James, and Elsa, children from the village. They ranged in age from four to seven. The children ran to her, hugging her all at once.

"Happy birthday, Beryl!" they shouted. James handed her a bunch of wilted violets and perky daisies. "We picked these for you."

"Thank you. Would you like to hear a story?"

Their smiles gave her their answer. She took Elsa by the hand as the boys ran in circles around them like happy puppies, and they walked to their favorite story-telling spot under the weeping willow tree.

"Why don't you ask Mama A for tea and a snack," Beryl said to the children. "I'm not allowed in the kitchen today, but she was busy in there a little while ago. And while you're there, you can give her the flowers; she'll put them in water."

She often baked cookies with the children, and they had tea parties under the tree. As she waited, she wondered why she could get along with people younger than her or older, but not those her own age. She felt like the filling in a sandwich—but she also felt kind of lonely.

Ava promised that when Beryl went to the Temple City, she would easily make friends her own age. Beryl looked forward to that. She wanted to go someplace where no one knew her so she could be the person she knew she could be, the one trapped inside because she felt stuck here where everyone already thought they knew who she was. She wanted to be able to speak of her dreams, even when they were dark, and find out what they meant. She had strength to face the darkness, but it was hard to do here where everyone thought of her as a sweet little girl.

The children returned from the kitchen with tea and fancy little cakes that Mama B had decorated. Beryl poured the tea and began her story. "Once upon a time, long ago, in a place far from here...."

5

That same day at the Temple

On Darkness and Light: We are mistaken if we believe light is good and dark is evil. Evil can come out of too much light as well as too much darkness. We must seek a balance between earth/ matter and spirit. We all lose our balance from time to time. Only through working together can we find the greater balance we seek. Only through working together can we keep this new world on the path of beauty.
From The Book of Jocasta

Selene gritted her teeth but kept her eyes wide open. She made herself watch Solomon thoroughly kiss Zorina while she and Jacob waited. Solomon pulled Zorina close. They were the same height, but that was the only thing they had in common. She was half his age, with straight long black hair, deep brown eyes, and a slim, girlish figure. Zorina, one of the high priestess' acolytes, looked young and innocent in her simple temple robe. She had been Solomon's student. Solomon was round, bald on top, and had a fringe of reddish-brown hair that hung to his shoulders. His eyes were deep with big bushy eyebrows hanging over them, making it difficult to tell what color his eyes were-- or if they were even open. Zorina was Solomon's "lady love."

Selene knew it was just an act, part of the plan. She, Solomon, Jacob, and Dr. Hami had worked it all out. They needed Zorina because she provided them with access to the high priestess. Solomon finally finished devouring Zorina and sent her on her way. Selene's stomach lurched watching him squeeze Zorina's bottom as she turned to leave. Selene thought she caught a grimace on Zorina's face, but she must have imagined it. The foolish girl was totally smitten. She found it disgusting to watch Solomon, the man she loved although she would never admit it, paw that child.

"You seemed pretty enthusiastic," said Selene. She and Solomon looked like brother and sister. She stood slightly shorter than Solomon, but just as round, and her hair, although it covered her entire head, was red, straight, and thin. She wore it cut to chin length, as she felt it accentuated her cheekbones.

Jacob, who towered over both of them, had very prominent cheekbones, regardless of how he cut his hair. His brown locks stuck out in every direction, making him look like he'd just rolled out of bed, which he had. He knew, as everyone did, that Selene was in love with Solomon. Well, he wasn't sure if Solomon knew, but Solomon believed every woman was in love with him.

Jacob said, "Let's get down to business. Selene, you know Solomon is doing what he has to. Zorina is our best way to get to Jenna. Our whole plan hinges on Zorina being in love with him."

"Yes, my dear," said Solomon. "I am making the biggest sacrifice of all. Imagine a mature man like myself falling in love with such a child. I do it for us, and for the future of Floredelis, of course."

"I hear a messenger is coming from Xantalon," said Selene. "I wonder if this will be our opportunity."

"We will make it so, my dear," said Solomon.

Every time he said, "my dear," Selene's heart beat a little faster, and her face felt warm, even though she told herself it didn't mean anything.

"It's time to move forward," said Jacob. "Covering Ontihaponati was pure genius. Now the Watchers and other initiates have no idea what's going on, and we can do as we please, for the greater good, of course."

6

The same day, just inside the hidden entrance to the Temple City

On Karma: The word "karma" literally means "action." But I understand it to be the law of cause and effect. In our many lives as human beings, we learn and grow. Our karma brings us opportunities to change old patterns, our habitual way of living. We have the opportunity to restore our inner balance and grow as spiritual beings living in a physical world.

Much wisdom can be gleaned from nursery rhymes and fairy tales. This nursery rhyme, a favorite from the old world, speaks of karma (and it's also fun as a bouncing game for little ones— even the bouncing archetypally represents the cycles of life). Can you understand the deeper meaning?

The man in the moon came tumbling down to ask the way to Norwich,

He went by south and burned his mouth by eating cold Pease porridge.

Pease porridge hot, Pease porridge cold,

Pease porridge in the pot, nine days old.

Mother Goose

From The Book of Jocasta

"I think we lost them," the deep voice tickled her ear.

"That's great," said Ava. "But who are they? And who are you?"

"You mean you don't recognize me?"

"Oh, great Goddess," gasped Ava. "Is that you, Tobias?"

"At your service."

"And I am his son, Andrew. Pleased to meet you." said a voice in her other ear.

No wonder Ava felt safe. Tobias had always made her feel safe. She had loved him so many years ago. They planned to run away together. But Ava had arrived late for their meeting, days late. Afterwards, she searched everywhere, but Tobias had disappeared without a trace, until now. All her guilt and sadness came flooding back.

"Tobias, I tried...I didn't mean to..." Ava gave up. Here was Tobias and his son!

"Ava, let's talk about the past another time, perhaps when our lives aren't in immediate danger," he said, his voice quiet and gentle. "There are more urgent matters that require out attention, like keeping you from being arrested for the illegal practice of medicine. A very serious crime," he snorted, "at least for the last few months. But you never could resist helping a person in need. Your kind heart gets you in trouble again."

Did he know what happened so long ago, Ava wondered.

"Come with us, Ava." said Tobias, "to our home. You could use our help and we could use yours, too."

"Tobias, Andrew, I would be honored to accompany you to your home. But I don't want to put you or your family in danger. I don't understand what's going on, but it sounds like I'm a criminal."

Andrew replied, "We don't know how much the guards saw, and the Pied Piper gave a good distraction. Really, we are more likely to put you in danger than the other way around."

"And Ava," Tobias said, "There is only Andrew and me. My wife died almost two years ago, an early casualty of the Great Illness."

Ava had no idea what the Great Illness was. She was shocked to see Tobias, to learn that he had a wife who had died and a grown son.

Tobias smiled sadly. "You don't know about the Great Illness?"

Ava shook her head no.

Tobias went on, "I can't believe it. I will explain everything later, if you come. We shouldn't stay here. There are also laws against vagrancy."

Ava accompanied them into the City. The first buildings they passed had shops on the first floor and homes above. She noticed flowers painted on many of these buildings. Some looked realistic, and others looked like they might have been painted by a child. Ava stopped to examine a painting of a vase of flowers and saw a name written on each one.

Tobias' touched her shoulder. "A flower has been painted for every person who died in the Great Illness-- by a group who oppose the actions of the Council. It's highly illegal and dangerous to be part of it." Tobias nodded his head toward the doorway of the building. Ava saw two young men huddled in the shadows. "Those boys are Otto and Fain. Their parents died from the Illness. They are about to lose their home because they can't pay the taxes. The Pied Pipers are helping them, giving them food and a place to stay. But if Pipers are found, they are thrown in prison or worse. The Council offers rewards to those who turn us in."

"The Temple Council?" Ava asked. She didn't want to believe it.

They passed more people huddled in doorways and more flowers painted on buildings. The Pied Piper, she thought it was the same person who had helped her just a little while ago, before her world turned upside down, danced down the street playing the flute. As he passed, people emerged from the shadows and followed him. Andrew and Tobias nodded at the Piper and greeted some of those following him. Ava counted twenty people following, but more kept coming out of the shadows. How many hungry and homeless people lived here, she wondered.

"That song lets the people know it's safe to come out. They follow the piper to where they can get food and supplies. The location changes every day to keep the Pied Piper safe," Andrew explained.

Tobias, Ava, and Andrew stopped in front of a small, dome-shaped house that looked much like the others around it, made of stone from the mountains, Hugin and Munin, like almost all the buildings in the City. Tobias opened the door and Ava walked in. The house looked cheerful and tidy. As she pulled off her boots, Ava remembered being in houses like this as a student. Even though she lived at the Temple then, she often came into the town to visit friends and provide healing. She noticed floor's colorful stone mosaic, with images of flowers, trees, and birds. She had never seen anything like it. A table stood near the hearth. She saw upholstered chairs and a sofa, which marked the wealthier houses in the city. Two inside doors led into the bedrooms, which had fireplaces connected to the one in this main room. In spite of the warm day, Ava couldn't stop shivering. Andrew noticed and dragged the couch next to the fire. He put a couple logs on and stirred the ashes to life. The couch, covered with moss green fabric, reminded Ava of the forest. Andrew invited her to sit down. She felt too tired to protest. It felt good to sit near the fire on the soft couch. It smelled faintly of rose. Was the scent left by Tobias' wife, she wondered. Ava felt sad, old, and alone. Andrew made her a cup of tea and brought her a blanket. Ava sipped the tea, tucked her feet under the blanket, and fell asleep.

She awoke to find the sun in her eyes and her hosts quietly preparing a meal. Ava had slept through the day and night and well into the morning. She lifted her arm to shade her eyes.

"Good morning, Ava. I trust you rested well?" Tobias sat down on the couch by her feet.

"Oh, yes. This couch feels like heaven after sleeping in the forest." Ava sat up, settling as far from Tobias as she could, scrunching herself against the arm of the couch closest to the fire, which had been banked. Andrew poured her some tea and pulled up a chair.

"Thank you, Andrew. I want to find out what on earth is going on here. What can you tell me?"

Tobias told her about Dr. Hami, who had come out of nowhere to become the Temple doctor. He told her of the Great Illness. Dr. Hami was the only one who had medicine to cure it, but there he claimed not to have enough for everyone, so he sold it to those who could pay one way or another. Many people died. After the illness ended, the Temple Council passed laws requiring payment for medical care, previously unheard of in Floredelis, where care had always been given to those in need whether or not they could pay for it. The Council also passed a law forbidding the practice of medicine without a license, which could only be issued by Dr. Hami. That had been Ava's crime.

Ava put her head in her hands. She recalled Jocasta's words "On Healing" that had inspired her as a student and continued to inspire her.

Following the teachings of Jocasta, and their own hearts, healers had always considered it their duty to give medicines freely to those in need. Those receiving help paid as they could, usually with some goods or produce. If they had nothing to give, that was fine, too.

Andrew told Ava about the Pied Pipers. The name stood for "People Interested in Ending Disease/People Interested in Pursuing Equality for Real." They fought the injustices that divided their city into rich and poor, initiated and uninitiated. Some of the Pied Pipers worked in secret within the Temple, while others worked more openly, putting themselves and their families in danger. The Pied Piper, with his mask and flute, had become a symbol of the resistance. Few knew his true identity.

Floredelis had never used prisons. Until recently, the main job of the Temple guards was to help people find their way through the Temple's maze of rooms and corridors. Now, they had become an armed militia, and rooms in the Temple had been turned into prison cells. Many of the current guards had been forced into service to work off debts for medicine they couldn't pay for in any other way.

"How can the high priestess allow this to happen?" asked Ava.

Things were much worse than she had suspected. She knew that Jenna, now the High Priestess, would never allow such things to happen. Ava had been the High Priestess' roommate and best friend when they were students at the Temple School. Jenna had always been an exemplary leader, caring for all with love, wisdom, and compassion. She put others ahead of herself, often to her own detriment. Ava had long ago given up trying to convince her that by taking better care of herself she could better care for others.

"The Temple Council claims the High Priestess is ill," replied Tobias. "They say she only wants to be cared for by Dr. Hami. She rarely appears in public, and when she does, she looks pale, weak, and very thin."

Ava blinked back tears. "How is that possible? I wasn't planning to visit her this time, but maybe I should. I'd hoped to come and go unnoticed. What did you think of my subtle entrance?" She smiled sadly. "Do you think I would be able to see her? Perhaps I could help."

"We suspect the High Priestess is being drugged. Dr. Hami watches her carefully. He seems to have most if not all of her acolytes working with him. Those who refused to comply with his wishes have long ago been dismissed from their positions and sent back to their home provinces."

"I hope to learn about Dr. Hami, too. That's one reason I came. Medicinal herbs are disappearing from the woods of Xantalon. Someone has been pulling whole plants, roots and all. If it doesn't stop, those herbs will be gone forever. I heard that Dr. Hami was selling medicine. There must be a connection. I will see him."

Ava placed her hands in her lap, palms up and looked at them for a long time. "I haven't told you the other reason for my visit." She looked up. "Our watchers and other initiates, including me, have been unable to contact Ontihaponati for about six months now. At first, we thought we were doing something wrong, but it's not us. We fear something has happened to the great crystal. Do you know anything?"

"This is the first I've heard," said Tobias. "I did hear they were repairing some masonry in the caves where she lives and that visitors aren't permitted to visit Ontihaponati's cave while work is in progress. I know you well enough to know that I can't stop you from seeing Dr. Hami, but please be careful. He has powerful support in the Temple. And he's evil. I tried to see him after Clara died, to discuss what had happened, but he had me escorted from the Temple with my feet dragging behind me after he refused to see me. Of course, it didn't help that I wouldn't take no for an answer."

"I would like to go to the Temple as soon as possible," said Ava. She looked down at the rumpled dress she had worn in the woods and slept in for four nights. "I suppose I should clean myself up and try to look presentable, first."

Ava bathed and put on her lavender Temple robe. She put on her initiate's necklace. The round copper medallion showed a tree in relief with its roots wrapped around an amethyst crystal—it represented Ontihaponati, the heart of Floredelis. Around the top of the tree flew birds and in the background the sun shone over the sea. It symbolized the Temple and represented the four elements in harmony. Everyone who completed training at the Temple received such a pendant, with different stones representing different callings. Ava's amethyst represented her calling as a healer. She wore her long hair loose around her shoulders.

Tobias watched Ava put on the pendant and smooth her hair. She fastened her cloak around her shoulders and turned to look at him. "I'm ready, or at least as ready as I'm likely to be. Tobias, I can't believe this is happening. I wish I could close my eyes and open them and find that this is all a bad dream."

Tobias put his hands on her shoulders and looked into her eyes, "Ava, it's hard to believe, but you're even more beautiful now than you were when we last met. Please be careful. I hope this part is not a dream. May I?" Ava nodded, and he put a hand behind her neck and pulled her face close, kissing her gently and quickly on her lips.

Ava blushed. She couldn't remember the last time that had happened—a kiss or a blush. Probably not since the last time she'd seen Tobias all those years ago. She hurried out the door.

7

Ava visits the Temple

> *On Contemplation: Make sure that you find time in your day
> for quiet meditation or contemplation. The Buddha said, "Peace
> comes from within, do not seek it without." Get to know yourself.
> Find the silence within you. Know that you are part of the whole,
> a drop of water in the ocean. But know that each drop is unique.
> Through meditation, you will come to know yourself. By knowing
> yourself, you can know others.*
> *From* The Book of Jocasta

Ava's head spun, her heart pounding like a frightened bird trying
to escape a net. She leaned against the outside of Tobias' front door,
taking a few deep breaths. Too many things were happening at once.
She wished she had kissed Tobias some more. She wished she had at
least said something after he kissed her. She touched her lips lightly and
smiled—he had kissed her. She wished her head would stop spinning,
but she couldn't wait for that to happen. She must pursue the business
that brought her here in the first place and do it now. That situation
was far worse than she had suspected.

Ava chose a circuitous route from Tobias' home to the Temple, just
in case anyone was watching. Even so, it didn't take her long to get
there. She stopped for a moment at the main entrance to the Temple.
She had forgotten how beautiful it looked. The Temple, like most of
the buildings in the Temple City was built of mountain stone. But

here, at the main entrance, the builders had covered the stone with huge wooden panels with relief carvings of the graceful figures of the angels who watched over the twelve provinces of Floredelis. They surrounded another winged figure which represented Floredelis herself. A border of roses swirled around this scene, and they'd painted the whole thing in beautiful soft colors. The roses reminded Ava of the flowers painted all over the city to honor the dead. Still, Ava let herself be distracted from her mission for a moment to enjoy the beauty of the entryway. As she looked at it, she thought she saw one of the angel's wings moving--a shadow caused by a passing cloud, perhaps. But she saw that the sun shone brightly, with not a single cloud in sight. She looked back at the panel and saw another movement out of the corner of her eye, a tear rolling down the cheek of the angel of Floredelis. She reached out her hand to touch it. The angel's cheek felt damp. As she stared at her damp finger in amazement, a guard told her to move along and that touching the carving was forbidden.

Ava glanced back at the carving, now still and dry. She looked at the guard. He looked like a teenager. He had a light down on his upper lip, light brown hair, and stood several inches shorter than Ava. He wore a sword in his belt and a knife, too, Ava noticed. She wondered if all the Temple guards now wore weapons. He cleared his throat, twirled a button on his sleeve, but didn't speak again.

"I'm here to see Dr. Hami," Ava told him. "I'm the healer from Xantalon and am in need of some medicines that he might have."

"I'll show you to his office. Follow me, please," The young man let go of his button, turned, and walked quickly into the Temple. Ava saw many guards as she practically ran to keep up with the young man. Most appeared quite young, all of them armed. She saw a few older guards, including a couple she recognized from her student days, but they did not meet her gaze. It was strangely quiet, considering how many guards wandered the hallways. The clicking of their boots on the wooden floors the only sound. She felt anxious—and nervous-- to meet Dr. Hami. Her escort led her toward the courtyard in the center of the Temple. All the Council members, one from each of the twelve provinces, had their offices around it. The courtyard contained a lovely garden in which grew, among other things, some plants that Jocasta brought with her from the old world. They walked up a winding flight of stairs that led to the council chamber, which also overlooked the garden. The guard led Ava past that room. Ava hadn't known that there were rooms beyond the Council chamber, and she thought she knew this entire building. She'd spent quite a bit of time exploring it with Jenna when they were students. Lost in thought, Ava bumped into the young guard when he stopped in front of a large wooden door. The guard knocked, and a young acolyte wearing a violet robe like Ava's opened the door. Thin and pale, her fine blond hair fell over her eyes as soon as she pushed it back. After Ava stated her business, the young woman let her enter. The room had two plain wooden chairs near the entrance, a low bookshelf crammed full of books, a table stacked with papers and a third chair behind the table. No fire cheered the fireplace, and the heavy, dark curtains were pulled back just enough to let in a sliver of the sunlight that shown so brightly outside. A small oil lamp on the table, precariously perched on top of a stack of papers, provided the only other source of light. Ava's nose twitched. The room felt dusty and smelled of mildew. The young acolyte invited her to have a seat in one of chairs near the door and went through a door behind the table. Instead of sitting, Ava looked at the books on the shelf, mostly tomes of herbal lore from the old world. She wanted to look at the papers on the table, curious about what she might find, but worried about getting caught. She sat down in the chair and tried to breathe through her queasiness.

In a long few minutes, Dr. Hami came out. Tall and slightly round in the middle, with sparkling blue eyes, white hair and a full, well-combed white beard, he reached out his hand to shake Ava's. His hand felt strong and clammy, and his smile, even though it produced many crinkles around his eyes and made his cheeks look rosy and round, seemed clammy, also.

"You must be Ava. I am Dr. Hami, very pleased to meet you. Your reputation precedes you. I've heard about your healing abilities. What brings you here? How can I help you? Come into my office."

The voice sounded strangely familiar. Ava's jaw dropped as she realized who he was. It had been so many years, but the eyes were the same, and so was the scar over his left eye.

"Hamilton?" she asked.

His smile turned into a scowl. "My name is Dr. Hami, and you will call me that."

"It is you, Hamilton. It's been a long time."

He grabbed hold of her upper arms. He squeezed them so hard that it hurt. "I once knew a man named Hamilton, but he died a long time ago. That man was an idiot. Do not mention his name again."

Ava was sure it was Hamilton. What had happened to the kindness in his eyes and the playful smile that had so charmed her all those years ago? The pain in her arms increased as he kept squeezing, but still the images flooded her mind.

She had been on her way to meet Tobias when she answered Ontihaponati's call. She had never seen Tobias again after that, until now. But Ontihaponati had wanted her to come immediately, so she went. She wondered at the time—and still wondered—if it was a mistake to listen to the great crystal instead of meeting Tobias as they'd planned. What would her life have been like had she made a different choice? But she certainly could not have foreseen any of what came after she answered the crystal's call. She entered Ontihaponati's cave and saw a young man, about her age, tall with medium brown hair and a smooth, hairless chest laying on the ground. He wore tightly fitting blue pants unlike any she had seen before. He had a large gash over his left eye and hadn't stirred since she entered the cave. She hurried to his side and put down her brown canvas traveling bag, the one she had packed to take with her to begin her new life with Tobias. The stranger was breathing. The gash over his eye oozed blood, but not a lot of it. She ran her hands over his body to feel if anything else was wrong but didn't feel anything unusual. When she reached his bare feet, she let her hands rest there, feeling his energy, as she looked at his face. He opened his eyes. They were startlingly bright blue, although she found out later that he had little pieces of blue glass in them to help him see better. They weren't quite so blue when she later saw him without them. Those bright blue eyes stared at her. She stared back, amazed. His cough broke the spell, reminding her that this man needed care.

"I'm Ava," she said. "I'm a healer. How are you? You have a cut above your eye, but I don't see any other injuries. Are you in pain?"

"Where am I?" he asked.

"You are in Ontihaponati's cave. She asked me to help you."

He gingerly touched the cut. "Ontihaponati? That's impossible."

"You seem disoriented. Do you know how you got here?"

"Just a minute ago I was being chased by....well, never mind. My name is Hamilton. Is this Floredelis?"

He was obviously disoriented. Ava thought the injury must be worse than it looked, but then she heard Ontihaponati speaking within her:

"He comes from Jocasta's world. He is the one whose coming I foretold to Jocasta. The chosen one. Care for him. Make him welcome."

Ava had never heard of a chosen one coming from Jocasta's world. She had understood the opening was permanently sealed.

"What is your name again?" she asked as she tried to orient herself.

"Hamilton."

"Hamilton, welcome to Floredelis."

"Perhaps you know my father?"

She felt a sharp pain in her face, and tears stung her eyes. Dr. Hami had slapped her and brought her back to the painful present.

"What is my name?" he hissed, his face close and red with anger.

"Dr. Hami," said Ava rubbing her stinging cheek and then her arms.

He smiled. "Pleased to meet you, Ava."

This man was dangerous, and Ava realized that she'd better not argue with him, at least for now. "Pleased to meet you, Dr. Hami." She held out her hand to shake his, but he just walked away.

He uncorked a bottle that he picked up from his desk. He poured some of the liquid into a glass. As he walked toward her, he said, "You do not look well, Ava. Old age must be catching up with you. Drink this. It will ease the pain." He held out the cup. "I made it myself," he added. "I promise it will make you feel better."

Ava felt like she could use something to make her feel better but felt certain that whatever the offered cup held wasn't it. Nonetheless, she took the cup and put it to her lips. She sniffed at the contents. It smelled sweet and sickening. She did not doubt that this draught would ease her pain, in fact, she would probably not feel anything at all if she drank it—she would be dead or at least unconscious. She pretended to take a sip, then coughed and dropped the cup on the ground. Dr. Hami watched with narrow eyes as she bent to wipe up the spilled contents with her handkerchief. Ava didn't think she had fooled him but kept moving anyhow.

"Oh, dear. Your medicine is a little strong for me. Actually, I'm feeling much better. I've come to seek your advice about a patient who isn't responding to my treatment. Also, I require a white rose from a bush that grows in the courtyard to make a flower essence, and I wonder if you might permit me to harvest one of those precious blooms."

Dr. Hami assured her that he would be delighted to assist her in any way possible. Unfortunately, he told her, the roses weren't in bloom just now. Since it was early fall, Ava suspected this was a lie, but if not, she feared for the health of those irreplaceable plants. She hoped someone hadn't "harvested" them like the missing plants in the forest.

Ava described a pretend patient who had mysterious rashes that came and went along with joint pain and swellings. She also mentioned, casually, she hoped, that she hadn't been able to find the herbs in the forest that she would normally use. Dr. Hami sat behind his large desk and smiled. He folded his hands and tapped his pointer fingers together as Ava spoke, nodding his head from time to time. When she finished, he smiled more broadly and told her he knew just what her patient needed and that, luckily, he had some on hand. Ava pulled a gold coin out of her pouch. Dr. Hami waved his hand. "No payment necessary, my dear. Professional courtesy, you know. Perhaps you can help me some day." He winked. Her stomach churned. She was playing a dangerous game, and she didn't know the rules.

"I am at your service, Dr. Hami. My patient will be most grateful."

"My dear Ava, I must go to the dispensary to get the remedy. Please accompany me. I've made some changes to the space since you were a student. I hope you'll approve."

Ava followed Dr. Hami to the dispensary. It smelled of dried green leaves and the alcohol used to make tinctures. It looked much the same as she remembered it at first glance, but as her eyes adjusted to the dim light, she noticed piles of wooden crates in the back of the room. A smell like freshly turned earth wafted toward her from those boxes. She felt sure they contained the missing herbs.

"You see, Ava, I organized the herbs according to their uses, rather than alphabetically. So, for example, you see that mint and ginger are together for stomach aches, while comfrey and arnica are over here for injuries. What do you think?"

As Ava tried to decide if she should actually tell him what a bad idea that was and that all herbs had a variety of uses, a Temple guard hurried into the dispensary. Dr. Hami took him by the arm and walked away from Ava. The men spoke quietly and urgently. Ava strained but couldn't hear what they said. Soon she heard a woman crying in the hall. Another guard peeked in. Dr. Hami motioned him to enter. The crying grew louder as the guard pushed in the woman that Ava had given medicine for her baby the day before. The woman looked at Ava and then looked away.

"I'm so sorry," she sobbed. "They have my baby."

Dr. Hami turned her to face him. "I hear you took medicine from someone without a healer's license. If you tell me who it was, I'll let you go with only a warning this time."

The woman glanced sadly at Ava. "They have my baby."

Her voice was barely audible. "It was her. She gave me the medicine. I didn't even ask her for it." She looked straight at the floor.

Dr. Hami pointed at Ava. "This woman gave you medicine?"

The woman nodded.

"Ava of Xantalon, you are accused of practicing medicine without a license. This is a serious crime. You will be detained until a hearing can take place." He turned to the guards. "Take her away and get that disgusting woman out of my sight."

As one of the guards escorted the mother out of the room, she pulled away for a moment and looked at Dr. Hami.

"My baby. Please can I have my baby back now?"

Dr. Hami nodded at the guard once again without looking at her. The guard dragged the woman away. As they left, Ava noticed two other guards near the door, one the man who had shown her to Dr. Hami's office. Ava looked around. She could see no way out. She felt faint when Dr. Hami said something about her illegally practicing medicine and the punishment for such a crime. Her head spun, and she couldn't focus on his words. He pulled her close, speaking so only she could hear him. "It would have been easier if you'd taken your medicine like your friend Jenna," he said and then pushed her towards the guards. They each grabbed one of her arms and pulled her towards the door.

She pulled her arms back and stood up straight. "I will walk," she said.

Dr. Hami nodded his agreement. She saw the clammy, jolly smile on his face again as she walked out of the room behind the two guards. She followed the two men back toward the center of the Temple. She wondered where the prison cells were. She thought she had known all of the rooms in the Temple, but she had been wrong. She had been wrong about many things.

One of the guards opened a plain thick wooden door with a small window near the top. The wood grain looked to Ava like a giant snake pointing up, waiting to strike. She walked in when the guard stepped aside and jumped as she heard the door slam behind her.

She heard one guard say, "I guess you'll get the reward for capturing the old witch. Maybe you'll be able to go home."

"Yeah," said another voice. "I wonder if I'll really get it."

Their voices faded into the distance, and Ava found herself alone. She noticed a small window high on the outside wall. Beneath it sat a bench with a thin mattress and in the corner stood a small basin. Ava sat on the bed and rubbed her hand over the stone wall. It felt rough and cool. She sat in silence for what seemed like hours. Then a guard, a different one, brought her a bowl of thin soup, a glass of water, and some stale bread. It tasted horrible. She couldn't even tell what kind of soup it was; it tasted like water with a little bit of salt in it, or maybe like dirty dishwater. She tried not to think about it too much. She needed to eat to keep up her strength. At least it didn't seem to be poisoned. She wondered what would have happened to her if she'd drunk Dr. Hami's medicine. After she'd eaten, the guard took away the tray. He gave her a thin blanket and a pillow. She didn't think she would be able to sleep. Her mind kept spinning over the events of the day and of events from days long past, but she finally drifted off.

8

Early the next day, in the Temple prison

Ava awakened to the sound of yelling. It took her a moment to remember where she was. She blinked as her eyes adjusted to the dim daylight that peeked in through the high window, piercing the dark room with a blade of light.

One of the voices sounded like Tobias'.

"I demand that you release her at once." That was definitely Tobias. Her heart beat faster. "She committed no crime. Let me see her. I know she's here."

"You need to leave. The old witch is under arrest for the illegal practice of medicine. Dr. Hami's orders. No visitors."

"You can't hold her without a hearing."

"Oh, yes we can. Dr. Hami's orders are all we need. He has the authority to use whatever means necessary to maintain order in these dangerous times. Now get out of here before you end up in one of these cells, too."

She heard more yelling and finally what sounded like Tobias being dragged away. Hot tears poured from her eyes. She thought of their kiss. Would she ever see Tobias again? What a good man. She felt so ashamed for what she had done to him all those years before. She didn't deserve him. Perhaps she did deserve to be in prison. What would have happened to Hamilton if she hadn't gone to his aid all those years ago? How did he become the person he was now—whoever that was?

Ava sat in the cell for two days and nights after that without seeing or hearing anyone, except for twice daily when the guards brought her the nasty substances which masqueraded as food. She had plenty of time to remember and re-remember her first encounters with Hamilton.

He lay on the ground next to Ontihaponati, looking at her with those impossibly bright blue eyes. She felt half-naked under his gaze like he could see her soul. He watched her look through her bag. She had all her medicines with her, as well as her few other belongings. Surely Tobias would understand that when Ontihaponati called, she had to go. She gave Hamilton a few drops of flower essences for shock and then took some herself, as she had been taught. She felt much better after taking them. Ontihaponati glowed with a pink light. Ava wondered if crystals could fall in love, for that's what seemed to be happening. Hamilton leaned his back against the large crystal and crossed his legs.

"Is Jocasta here?" he asked. He smiled at her in a way that made her feel beautiful.

Ava laughed. "Jocasta has been gone for many generations, although her words live on."

"You know who she is, though, so you must know my father. His name was Hamilton, too."

"No," said Ava. "I've never heard of him."

Hamilton was silent as she took him back to the room she shared with Jenna. She wanted to stitch the gash above his eye somewhere with better light than the cave. She wasn't sure why she didn't take him to the infirmary. She remembered Jenna's surprise when Ava entered their room with a half-naked man. Of course, Jenna had known Ava's plan to run away with Tobias. Ava explained to Jenna what had happened, including what she had heard Ontihaponati say. Hamilton listened but didn't comment. Not only could he not hear what Ontihaponati said, but he also didn't experience her glow. Ava watched with amusement as Jenna also seemed to glow pink in the presence of this stranger. Jenna was beautiful and had been admired by many men, but this was the first time Ava had seen her show any interest. Jenna had always focused on her studies and spent a lot of time meditating. Ava had felt even then that Jenna would become the high priestess.

It took Ava only a few minutes to stitch up the gash over his left eye. It would leave a scar. Hamilton seemed fine after the stitches and more flower remedy, but Jenna insisted that he lie down on her bed and rest while she fetched him something to eat. He seemed quite willing. Jenna returned with soup, bread, and cheese, as well as some men's clothing. In response to Ava's questioning look, Jenna said she had "borrowed" the clothes from the laundry. Jenna had never stolen anything before. Hamilton had an interesting effect on her.

He stayed for only ten days, but those few days changed their lives. They agreed, at his request, to tell no one that Hamilton came from Jocasta's world. He was a physician in that world. He explained how healing was done there, and Ava and Jenna were shocked that they treated only symptoms and not the whole person. Hamilton knew alternative ways of healing, mostly through the use of spiritual energy and the laying on of hands. They spent happy days wandering the forest together. Hamilton flirted with both women, although Ava tried to stay out of the way, as Jenna seemed to be falling for him. Ava showed him the plants she used for healing. He took samples of some of them, although Ava advised him not to. She told him what had happened to the seeds Jocasta had brought from his world to Floredelis. She brought seeds of many plants—grains, vegetables, fruits, cotton, herbs—to plant in Floredelis so they would have food and fiber. The first settlers planted the seeds. The seeds germinated, but soon withered and died. Apparently, plants from the old world couldn't live in Floredelis. The people and animals they brought with them did fine. The only old-world plants that thrived were the flowers and herbs in the Temple garden. The founders discovered that Floredelis had all the food plants they needed, as well as medicinal ones and fibrous ones for clothing. She knew Hamilton wanted to experiment with these herbs, and she worried about that.

But she enjoyed their time together. She found him charming, funny, and attentive. He refused to speak about his father again, however. When Ava asked him how he received the gash in his head, he told them he'd been injured when the husband of a young woman he was healing came home unexpectedly and jumped to the wrong conclusion when he saw Hamilton, shirtless, kneeling over his wife who also had her shirt off, purely for medical reasons, according to Hamilton. Ava wondered if he told the truth but noticed Jenna nodding her head sympathetically. At any rate, Hamilton had taken off running as the husband chased him. He ducked under a tree and ran into a big branch. That was the last thing he remembered until he woke up in Ontihaponati's cave.

He'd read a book his father wrote with Jocasta. It described her first trip to Floredelis. It had been published years before, and he'd found it by his mother's bed. He'd thought a lot about that book and wondered if Floredelis could possibly be real. He wanted to return to his own world. His mother was dying, and he needed to see her. He hoped the herbs from Floredelis might help his mother and others.

Ava barely thought about Tobias during those ten days. After Hamilton left, she spent months looking for him, but he was nowhere to be found. Finally, she gave up and moved to Xantalon, where they needed a healer. She built herself a hut in the woods and settled down to work. How many nights had she spent thinking about Tobias and Hamilton? She thought she'd never see either of them again, and now she had seen them both in one day. She wondered if she would ever see either of them again.

On the third day in her cell, late in the afternoon, Ava heard a woman arguing with the guards. She didn't have to wonder who it was for very long.

"I am the high priestess, and you will obey me regardless of what Dr. Hami says. I will see the prisoner. Now."

The door creaked open, and Jenna entered. Ava went to embrace her old friend but stopped short. The change in Jenna's appearance shocked Ava. Jenna had been so beautiful, her body curvaceous and full. Now she looked like a skeleton, and her hair, which had been thick and brown, lay limp and thin. It looked like it took her a great effort to walk.

"Jenna," said Ava. "Sit down. How are you?"

"Not well. Not well at all," Jenna replied. "I haven't been well since the great illness. So many died; so many were injured. I couldn't help. Thank goodness Dr. Hami arrived. He saved as many as he could."

"I heard you were here," Jenna continued. "I can't believe it, Ava. I told Dr. Hami that you were good, that you just didn't know the rules, but he wouldn't listen. There's not much left that I can do, but I can release you from this prison. Go now, Ava. Do what you can to save Floredelis. Don't speak to me; don't judge me, just go. And be careful, my dear friend."

"Jenna, let me stay and help you." Ava gently embraced her old friend. Jenna leaned on her for a moment and then pulled herself upright.

"Guards, by order of the high priestess, release this woman. Escort her out of the city."

One guard said, "We need to check with Dr. Hami."

"I am the high priestess, and I have spoken. Dr. Hami can speak with me if he likes." Then she spoke softly to Ava, "My friend, I doubt if we will meet again. I will not be in this life much longer. Remember me as I was. I wish I could tell you all, but it's too dangerous. Hamilton blames Floredelis and us for ruining his life and wishes to destroy us and our land. Don't let him. Please. Now go before it's too late."

Ava wanted to run out of the prison as quickly as possible, but she couldn't leave Jenna like this. Or Tobias. "Please Jenna, you need me, and I think Tobias is locked up, too. I can't leave him again."

"Tobias would want you to leave. He can take care of himself. At any rate, you'll be of more use to him, and all of us, outside this cell. Go to the Council of All Beings. Perhaps it's not too late. Please, Ava. For all of us. I'll try to get Tobias released, too."

Ava couldn't argue with her old friend, the sad figure who had come to rescue her even though she could barely stand. She knew Jenna was right—if she was going to help anyone, she couldn't do it from here.

"Go now, Ava."

Ava nodded gravely. She kissed Jenna's papery cheek and forced herself to walk away.

9

Three days after Ava's arrest, in the Council Room at the Temple

In the middle of the room sat an old round wooden table surrounded by thirteen high-backed wooden chairs. The chairs looked plain and uncomfortable, but the table's top was elaborately carved and painted. A golden sun rayed out from the center, and around it circled planets and stars. The earth, in its four seasons, with minerals, animals, plants, and humans, filled the outer ring of the table. An interesting table to look at and touch, especially during a boring meeting. Many meetings took place here in the Temple Council's meeting room.

On this sunny fall day, all the chairs were filled. The sound of children playing came through the window, open to let in the warm breeze. The high priestess looked out the window as she finished reading the message.

"What do you think?" she asked the Council.

The high priestess looked old and tired. She looked much older than she had even a few months earlier. She had stopped taking the medicine Hamilton gave her, yet she kept growing weaker. Her head felt heavy and hard to hold up. But she willed herself to sit straight as she spoke. Her people needed her now more than ever. "Queen Lillia of Xantalon would like to retire to pursue her private interests. Is there a successor to take her place?"

Patricia, the tall, bony representative from Xantalon, spoke, her voice deep and crackly, "I have spoken with Lillia's messenger. There is a child there, on the edge of womanhood, who the stargazers have said would be a good leader. She is named Beryl. She is the daughter of our watchers, Anne and Beatrice. She is just turning fifteen and will need several years of training. She is quiet but has many gifts in the realms of connecting to nature spirits, intuition, and storytelling. Lillia feels strongly the girl is meant to be her successor. She is willing to remain queen for two or three more years while Beryl is trained and then work with Beryl for another two or three years of transition. It seems strange to me that Lillia should step down in her prime, but she is a good and wise woman, and if this is her wish, we should send for Beryl, and, if it seems good, begin her training at once."

Jenna also wondered why Lillia would want to retire at the peak of her power. It was the third such request in the past several months. She looked around the table. No one else seemed surprised or concerned. If only she could think clearly. If only it didn't take so much energy to speak.

Solomon, the representative from Vertumnus leaned forward. He had been gnawing on a cuticle and staring out the window. "Is there more about this girl?" he asked. "There must be more if Lillia wants her to take her place."

"These are challenging times in Floredelis," Solomon continued. "We cannot afford to have children in positions of leadership. There must be more."

Selene, another council member, nodded approvingly at Solomon. She had fallen in love with him the first time she saw him many years ago when she first joined the Council. Now that she and Solomon worked with Dr. Hami to save Floredelis, he finally acknowledged her existence.

He winked at her. Her heart fluttered.

The high priestess lifted her head. She took a deep breath, her voice barely audible, "Solomon, sometimes the spiritual world whispers to us, and we can but trust there's a bigger reason than our small minds can comprehend. Lillia is a trusted colleague and would not make a recommendation lightly. Beryl may lack experience, but sometimes it is through taking on responsibility and meeting challenges that a young person develops her gifts."

"It sounds like Lillia is lazy and living in a fairy tale," said Solomon. "It is well and good to look for signs and portents, but we cannot let our imaginations carry us away. Our decisions must be grounded in reality."

"The voice of the spirit, the still, small voice, is what it sounds like to me. We should support Lillia and this young woman," said Felicia, the representative from Wolpe.

"Do you think it's a good idea to bring her to the Temple now?" asked Solomon. "There is much unrest here. She might be a target for the resistance forces."

"I believe we can keep her safe. Besides, she must be strong if she is to take on leadership at this time," said the high priestess.

"Is there no one from Xantalon who is older and already an initiate who could take on this role?" asked one of the council.

"No," replied Patricia. "None who have the breadth of abilities and the compassion necessary for a worthy Queen."

"All right," said the high priestess, "Any more questions or comments?"

No one spoke. "Then all in favor?" she asked. She rested her head on the table. The wood felt cool and bumpy beneath her cheek. Selene, who always sat at the priestess' right, nodded at the guard who stood near the door. He opened the door, and Dr. Hami brought in a glass filled with nasty-looking brownish-green liquid. He supported Jenna's head while she took a few sips.

All twelve members nodded in agreement.

"Then let us send for her immediately," said Selene. "Queen Lillia's messenger is waiting to bring back our reply. Let the scribe write a letter with our response, and let us send an escort to bring Beryl to the Temple."

"Shall I bring our decision to the scribe so he can prepare a letter for the Queen?" Solomon asked.

"Yes," replied the high priestess, "and then bring the letter to me to sign. Patricia, will you find an escort to accompany Beryl back to us? And let's keep this confidential for the time being."

"Of course."

"The priestess is exhausted," Dr. Hami said. "She must return to her chamber and rest. She is not to be disturbed until midday tomorrow. Perhaps you could sign the letter on the Priestess' behalf, Solomon?"

"Yes, my pleasure."

Dr. Hami offered the priestess his arm and escorted her from the room. Solomon wrote some notes on a piece of paper and hurried out of the meeting room with a bustle of importance.

"Boy," he called to the first person he saw outside the chamber door.

"My name's Randall," replied seventeen-year-old Randall, his hazel eyes sparking with anger.

"Yes, of course, Raymond, take this to the Temple Scribe at once and tell him it's urgent. Wait for the letter and bring it to me immediately."

"Of course, sir."

The meeting continued. The remaining representatives discussed the organization of the kitchen staff and complaints from parents about the Temple City school. Selene went on to talk about forming a committee to plan for the fall equinox festival. Two Council members stared out the window. Shoshi, the quiet representative from Ashkelon, fingered her grey curls and began tracing a flower carved into the table. When

Selene paused, Shoshi spoke. "I remember when we dealt with spiritual matters instead of deciding what's for dinner. Maybe the Pied Pipers have a point. I think it would be good to work with the townspeople to plan our festivals. The festivals seem to have lost their power to awaken us to the change of seasons and our connection to the cosmos. We go through the motions but have lost the essence."

"Perhaps you've lost your essence," said Selene. "The people need us to lead. They don't have the temperament or training to carry the spiritual impulses that keep our world aligned with the spiritual world."

Patricia said, "Let's adjourn until tomorrow. We can revisit Shoshi's concerns when all of us are here and perhaps a bit refreshed." There was agreement all around.

They all stood, pushed their chairs in, which made a lot of noise on the bare stone floor, and stood with their hands at their sides.

They spoke together the verse written by Jocasta that they always said at the beginning and end of their meetings.

"Beings of light, guide us.
Spirits of earth, support us.
Hearts of the people, show us the way,
To guide and protect,
To see and to do,
In accordance with the highest good
For all sentient beings.
So may it be.

10

After the Council Meeting, just outside the City gates

"I leave tomorrow for Xantalon City," said Randall.

"This trip could be a good opportunity for us. Especially since the Pied Piper will be away for a while," said Ian. Ian, the main chef at the Temple, known for the delicious food he prepared, winked and pushed his pale red hair out of his eyes. He was one of the few people who knew the Pied Piper's true identity.

"Maybe you should leave the mask with me, and I could be the Pied Piper, although I can't play the flute as well as you." Ian laughed. He laughed a lot.

Randall smiled. He had sandy hair, blond or brown, depending on the light, and a sharp beak of a nose. "Ian, you are one of the tallest people in the city, and with that red hair and your round belly, every-one would recognize you even if you wore a mask. Besides, you have a family, and it's too dangerous."

"Yeah, I was joking about the mask. But I'm serious about doing something besides flowers and flutes. It's not enough."

"We've helped a lot of people. We feed them and help them find a place to stay. Eventually, we'll prevail because we are right. Besides, what are you suggesting?"

"I'm not suggesting you harm anyone. You're a charming fellow. Perhaps you could convince this girl, Beryl, to be our ally. If not, maybe you could delay her arrival until we can get some concessions from the Council, if you know what I mean."

"Do you mean kidnap her?"

"Well, kidnapping sounds harsh, but I suppose that is what I mean."

"If I did that, what would we ask for in exchange for her release? And what would become of the Pied Piper? I could never return here. Someone else could wear the mask, but this is my home."

"It's a lot to ask. But if we don't do something big, nothing will change. We would never hurt the girl. There are some others I wouldn't mind giving a good thrashing to, though," Ian laughed. "Seriously, I can't keep watching people die for lack of medical treatment, starve, and lose their homes while the schools program our children to be servants to the initiates. We need to do something to make the Council listen."

"But we're supposed to be the good guys," said Randall.

Ian sighed. "We are the good guys, but we're losing. I don't want to resort to violence, but many others are angry enough to do so. This would be more of a trick; no one would get hurt. Maybe the girl would even be on our side."

"I don't have a good feeling about this plan, and I'm not making any promises. Do you know anything about the messenger from Xantalon?" asked Randall

"His name is Eugene, and he loves his queen. That's all I know. But you have a long journey. You'll have plenty of time to get acquainted. Back to the kitchen for me—See you." Ian gave Randall a quick hug and left.

As they said their goodbyes, Randall and Ian nodded at Solomon, the Councilman, as he walked through the Temple gates with Zorina, his "Lady Love." They made an odd couple. Solomon, old enough to be Zorina's father, wore green pants tied around his ample waist and a yellow tunic that laced at the top. His reddish-brown chest hair bushed out from inside the laces. Zorina, taller than Solomon and slim, with straight dark brown hair and pale, gray eyes, wore a simple yellow gown. Jocasta had spoken of colors associated with the energies of each day of the week. Solomon always dressed in the color of the day, and Zorina had taken up the same practice since she'd started seeing him. Neither Randall nor Ian could understand what Zorina saw in that man.

Solomon watched the men walk away. He leaned close to Zorina and whispered loudly, his breath smelling of stale ale, "They've chosen a mere girl to become Xantalon's next queen." He put his arm around her shoulder, squeezing her close. Zorina pulled away and took his hand.

"Oh," she replied.

"I don't understand why they would choose an untrained girl when we have fine acolytes at the temple ready to serve," he continued, staring at her so she would know he meant her.

Her cheeks grew pink.

"I'm going to Xantalon myself to meet this child and see if she's acceptable. I cannot believe she would be better suited than you, my dear. Why the high priestess herself has chosen you to serve her. You were my best student."

Zorina's face grew hotter. "You shouldn't say such things. It's not proper. And besides, it's not your decision who will be the queen of Xantalon."

"Don't forget, my dear, that I am part of the Council, and no appointments can be made without my approval. The high priestess respects my opinion. One word from me and the little princess will be history. Besides, it's a long, dangerous journey from Xantalon to the Temple. She might not even arrive."

Zorina gasped.

"I'll send for you to join me as soon as I can."

"I don't like it when you're gone." Zorina pouted. "I feel lost. I count on your guidance in all things."

Solomon stroked her delicate face with his pudgy hand, drew her close, and kissed her. "Don't worry, my love. It won't be long until we're together again."

"What if you like her more than me?" Zorina looked up at him through her lashes.

"She's a child. I'm not interested in children. Well, I was interested in you, but I waited until you were grown and no longer my student before pursuing you. Don't worry, my darling. I have your best interests at heart, as well as the best interests of our beloved country. Now I must go to Xantalon in service of the greater good, even though it breaks my heart to leave you. The messenger leaves tomorrow. I leave tonight. Do not mention this conversation to anyone. Be good while I'm gone and try not to miss me too much."

11

Later that night, in Dr. Hami's room at the Temple

As the sun set, Dr. Hami lit a candle. He wondered where that boy was. Lucas played him for a fool, and Dr. Hami liked that. At sixteen, Lucas was still a foot shorter than Dr. Hami and moved quietly as a mouse, or more like a fox. It amused him to let Lucas get away with his annoying, manipulative habits, but he needed to be careful that the boy didn't outwit him. Dr. Hami put his mirror next to the candle and began trimming his beard. He didn't hear Lucas enter and nearly knocked the candle over with the scissors when Lucas put a hand on his shoulder. Dr. Hami glanced at Lucas in the mirror. He could barely see Lucas' dark skin in the dim light, but his brown eyes flashed as he pushed his dark bangs out of his eyes and laughed. Dr. Hami smiled.

"Lucas, I have an important job for you. I'm sending Solomon to follow the messenger to Xantalon. Solomon intends to make Zorina the new queen of Xantalon. You know Zorina, don't you?"

Dr. Hami knew the answer to that question. He had encouraged Lucas to charm Zorina so they could use the girl to get to the high priestess. Lucas also convinced her to pretend she liked Solomon so he would help her become queen of Xantalon, where she would rule under the direction of Dr. Hami, and Lucas.

"Zorina? Yes, I believe we've met."

Dr. Hami smiled. "I want you to go with Solomon and make sure he doesn't get lost. He's expecting me to send someone to him tonight. I don't want Randall to reach Xantalon City. Take the gun and use it. Do you understand? I've instructed Solomon on what to tell Queen Lillia."

Just past midnight, Lucas left Dr. Hami's room. He knocked on Solomon's door. There was no answer. He knocked harder and put his ear to the door. He heard snoring, so he went in. Lucas whispered, "Rise and shine, Sunshine" in his ear and grinned when Solomon practically jumped out of bed.

Solomon's breath smelled of alcohol. He was fully dressed, except for his boots. Lucas wondered if he had dressed to prepare for their journey or just fell asleep that way.

"It's time to go, sir. We'll leave by the back gate so we won't be seen, but we must get moving. Can I help you with your boots?" Lucas despised Solomon, but Dr. Hami insisted he was necessary to the plan, and Lucas knew how Solomon liked to be treated. Solomon offered his feet to Lucas.

"I know where the messengers are likely to camp tomorrow night," Lucas told him as he struggled to get Solomon's boots on. He'd spent some time in the woods of Xantalon. "We must stop Randall from reaching Xantalon. I'll take care of him, and you can take care of Queen Lillia—Dr. Hami said you know what to do."

Lucas hoped Solomon could move quickly enough for them to arrive at the campsite while Randall and Eugene slept tomorrow night. He doubted Solomon could move very fast on his short stubby legs. Maybe it would be easier to roll him through the forest. Randall smiled at that image. Still, they should have enough time; they were leaving before the messengers and needed to arrive after them.

They saw no one as they left the city, and once they reached the forest, they stayed off the main path. Lucas knew these woods well from his herb-gathering excursions with Dr. Hami, as well as preparing the way for Solomon, although, until tonight, he hadn't known when this part of the plan would be put into action. As they walked, Lucas told Solomon the rest of the plan. Lucas had gathered some men who were holed up in Ava's empty house in the woods. He'd promised them food, drink, and a roof over their heads come winter if they would serve Solomon, the eminent council member. Solomon's chest puffed with pride at this title. Lucas had promised these men that all criminal charges against them would be dropped if they cooperated. He also threatened to send them to jail for a very long time if they didn't help. They seemed convinced, but Lucas knew that desperate people were not difficult to convince—but they also were not likely to be loyal. Still, they should give Solomon whatever help he needed during his stay in Xantalon. Ava's house would be the perfect spot for Solomon to stay—hidden away in the woods, but close enough to Xantalon City to get there quickly when he needed to.

Unfortunately, the high priestess had released Ava that very afternoon. Lucas had been sure she would be stuck in her cell indefinitely after Dr. Hami had her arrested for practicing medicine without a license, a new and useful crime for someone asking too many questions. Lucas had a wanted poster made. It had a likeness of Ava's face and her description. He would leave it with Solomon's men on his way back to the Temple City, promising a reward for her capture. He would instruct them to lock her in her own cellar if she showed up—that would be an amusing turn of events.

Dr. Hami thought that Queen Lillia was confused enough by his manipulations that when Solomon delivered the message that the Council wanted to replace her with an acolyte from the Temple— because Beryl was too young and totally unprepared-- she would accept it. Lucas wasn't sure how Dr. Hami had gotten her to want to resign, but he suspected the Doctor used Ontihaponati. He had a special connection with that stone. At any rate, he hoped Doc was right because he had little faith that Solomon could handle anything. Nor was his confidence bolstered as he guided the stumbling, half-drunk council member through the woods.

Earlier that same night, in the Temple kitchen

Randall and Eugene, Queen Lillia's messenger, met for dinner-- delicious Harvest Soup with homemade bread and chocolate cake for dessert, all prepared by Ian. They discussed their journey. Eugene had made this journey twelve times for the queen, delivering messages, and gathering news from the Temple and supplies from the Temple City. He used to enjoy it, but now that he had a wife and two young sons, he preferred to stay home. He was glad to have Randall's company. Especially since he had received the message from the Temple Council that Ava would be spending a few more days here in the City. A companion would help to pass the time, and he felt safer traveling with a companion. In the past, he enjoyed spending time alone in the forest, but the woods didn't feel right on this trip, and he felt uneasy. He'd heard men were hiding from the law in these woods, although he hadn't seen them yet. After learning of their circumstances while on this trip, he felt more sorry for them than afraid.

Just after dawn, Randall approached the gate and found Eugene on his horse waiting for him. "Good morning, young sir," Eugene said. "Are you ready?"

"The blush of the morning is still on the cheeks of this day, so let's be on our way before age and sorrow catch up with us. I know the lovely Isabella and your little ones are anxious to have you safe at home," said Randall.

A guard opened the gate just wide enough for their horses to pass through. It creaked shut behind them. No one would be admitted to the City for hours, but already a dozen or so people stood outside waiting to enter. The horses walked slowly through the waiting people, but their pace quickened as they left the city behind and passed fields in their harvest glory. The damp air smelled of fertile earth and green leaves. The path through the woods from the Temple to Xantalon, not traveled much, had become overgrown. They would walk the horses once they got into the woods.

When Randall saw the edge of the woods in the distance, he said, "I'll race you to the woods."

Without waiting for a reply, he urged his horse forward. Eugene let his horse break into a gallop and follow Randall at its own pace, wishing the horses could go that fast all the way home.

"You won," laughed Eugene when he caught up with Randall.

Randall let Eugene lead the way. The forest was dark, lush, and cool, with occasional bare spots. They stopped mid-day for lunch in a clearing next to a pond. Pink and white flowers grew all around. Three large rocks that looked like a table and two chairs stood close to the water. They led their horses to the water, allowing them to drink and graze on the sweet grass. Randall pulled a flat rectangular picnic basket out of his saddle bag. He put it on the table rock, opened it, and found sandwiches filled with fresh cheese, roasted peppers, fresh basil, and tomatoes. He also removed two beautiful cupcakes, each with a candied violet flower on the top. Eugene smiled.

"Ian takes good care of me," said Randall. "The initiates aren't the only ones who can do magic. Have you heard about the unrest among the serving people at the Temple?" he threw in, casually, he hoped.

"I've heard a little here and there. Dangerous business that. I hope you're not involved. I hear the council has ways of knowing who goes against their edicts."

"The Council would like us to think they know a lot more than they do. But one who finds himself involved in such goings on had best be careful."

"What do you think about this girl, Beryl? Will she be able to deal with all this unrest?" asked Randall

"Well, she's a quiet one, little Beryl. But she's strong. And she loves to cook. She and Ian could have fun together," said Eugene

"But if she's queen, she won't have much to do with a commoner like Ian, even though he's a most uncommon man. She won't have time to cook either."

"Yes, I suppose you're right. Let's get going. I want to reach our campsite before dark"

They walked until dusk, stopping only once for a snack and to give the horses a short rest. Because the trees grew so close together in the forest's heart, it grew dark well before sunset.

"We're almost there," said Eugene. "See the break in the trees up ahead, where off to the left a tree was split by lightning. Just past is a sheltered spot with soft moss and pine needles where we can rest. I hope Ian packed us another delicious meal because I'm ravenous. As soon as we get the horses settled and build a fire, let's eat."

They started a fire, more for light than warmth. They cared for the horses, ate what did turn out to be another delicious meal, and slept deeply, tired from the exertions of travel and lulled by the song of cicadas.

13 ▍

Early the next morning, in the woods of Xantalon

It was still dark when Randall awoke to what sounded like a loud explosion followed by people yelling and horses whinnying. It took him a moment to remember where he was. He'd fallen asleep near a toppled tree. Eugene slept next to the same tree, closer to the fire. As his eyes focused, he saw a man standing over Eugene.

The man poked Eugene with his foot and said, "You got the wrong one."

Eugene didn't move. Randall wondered what had happened to Eugene. Then it dawned on him; if Eugene was the wrong one, they must be looking for him. But why? Who were they? They apparently hadn't seen him yet. He was glad his clothing was dark brown, like the tree. The light was gathering, and if he moved, they would hear and see him. Yet he couldn't just lay there, waiting for them to find him. The two men walked around the fire. When they turned around, so they faced away from him, he quickly scrambled over the log, which was almost as tall as him, and ran.

"Get him, you fool," he heard. Then he heard running and swearing behind him. He turned his head to see if they were close and stumbled over some low vines. As he scrambled back up, he heard a loud cracking sound and felt a burning sensation in his foot that he felt all the way up his leg. He made himself run, despite the pain. The forest seemed to close behind him. Soon he couldn't hear his pursuers. Some branches opened in front of him and revealed a hollow in a tree. He crawled inside, and the branches sprang back up to cover the opening. Inside was dark and cool and hidden. He wondered if Eugene was dead or just injured. He wondered who on earth was chasing him. Even if someone knew he was part of the resistance, why would they want to kill him? Had they heard him and Ian talking about the kidnapping? Obviously, they intended to kill him, as it would have been very easy to capture both him and Eugene as they lay sleeping. But what weapon had they used?

As he caught his breath, he became aware of the burning pain in his foot. Whatever weapon they'd used, it worked from a long distance. He had taken his boots off to sleep and wore only his socks, now torn to shreds. He examined his foot. It looked like a bad burn. The sock had burned to his foot. He carefully peeled it off and saw that his skin had also burned away in a hole three fingers wide. The wound was open and very dirty. It should be cleaned and wrapped. He wondered if he could find clean water nearby. This wound wasn't caused by any weapon he knew of; perhaps it was magic. He'd heard stories of evil magicians who used their power to maim and kill but hadn't believed they were true. Whatever the cause, now that he had stopped running, the pain felt very intense and very real. His foot hurt and his head pounded. He couldn't think anymore. He felt young and frightened. He tried to picture the girl, Beryl, thinking about what he had been contemplating doing to her and how it would make her feel, and then, thankfully, he fell asleep.

14

Early afternoon of the same day, outside Xantalon City

> *Dreams can mean many things. Some foretell the future. Some are caused by eating too close to bedtime or sparked by things that happened during the day. But most of all, dreams tell about our unconscious. They connect us to archetypes. We can learn much from our dreams if we pay attention.*
> *From* The Book of Jocasta

Beryl sat by the stream on another perfect fall day. Her parents had left early to meet with Queen Lillia. They spent much more time at the castle than they used to, but they wouldn't tell her why. She knew it was something important. But of course, there were things she didn't tell them, either. She'd dreamt about Hamilton again. This time he showed another man, whose face she couldn't see, how to use a strange, curved piece of dark metal that he called a gun. Hamilton showed the man how to use this horrible thing. He pointed it at a tree and moved his finger to a little piece of metal that stuck out. A loud sound exploded from the straight end and left a big hole in the tree.

The nature spirits fled. The other man practiced using that thing; he killed a deer with it. Hamilton cut up the animal. It was bloody and horrible. They cooked pieces of the dead animal on sticks over a fire and ate the flesh. That was when she knew her dreams had no connection to reality. Who would create a weapon like that, and why would anyone slaughter and eat one of mother earth's creatures? Still, it had been terrifying. She kept remembering when Ava said dreams were projections of your inner self. She couldn't believe how much darkness was inside her if she could create these horrible images. She wondered when the darkness would grow too strong for her to control. Beryl dangled her fingers in the water, enjoying the plinking sound as she flicked the water onto itself. Then she saw someone approaching from the forest on horseback. As he got closer, Beryl saw two horses and one rider. She wondered if it was Eugene returning from the Temple. From the way it moved, she could tell it was Eugene's horse even before she could see it clearly.

She ran toward the road-- barefoot, wearing a light brown dirndl skirt and a simple white blouse, her curls wild and uncombed-- waving her arms to welcome Eugene. She stopped. She couldn't see the man's face yet but could tell by his shape that he wasn't Eugene.

The horses and rider approached Beryl at a leisurely pace.

"Hello, young lady," said the man, who was Solomon, although Beryl hadn't met him yet. "Could you kindly point me in the direction of Queen Lillia's castle? I come to her on most urgent Temple business."

What a pompous man, thought Beryl. He talked down to her and not just because he sat on a horse. Besides, it was a ridiculous question. There was one road, which he was on, and it led directly to the castle, the spires visible from where they stood.

But she didn't see any point in antagonizing him until she knew who he was, so she smiled and nodded politely. "The castle is just ahead, sir," she answered. "Stay on the road, go through the gate, and you will find the castle in the center of town." Looking more closely at his face, she thought he looked familiar, but she couldn't imagine where she might have met him.

"Thank you for your kindness to a passing stranger," said Solomon. "This is for your trouble." He threw her a coin, which she caught without thinking.

It made her nauseous to touch something he touched. His energy disgusted her. Without saying goodbye, the man urged his horses to a gallop and disappeared.

Very curious, thought Beryl. Why was he suddenly in a hurry, she wondered. She combed her fingers through her hair, tied it back with an emerald-green ribbon, pulled on her green shoes, and headed toward town. The man would be halfway to the city gates by now if he kept up that pace, she thought. It would take her almost an hour to get to the castle. By then someone could tell her who he was and what he wanted.

15

The same day, at the Temple

Ontihaponati, the great crystal who is the heart of this land, is unlike any crystal I have met before. She is so alive, pulsating with love. I seem to be the only one she communicates with, so far, but I trust there will be others in the future with whom she will speak and share her wisdom. Already, all of the rulers of the 12 provinces can communicate with each other through her. She has given each of them a piece of herself to wear, and it connects them. In the old world, we had machines, we called them telephones, that allowed us to speak across a great distance. This is much better!

From The Book of Jocasta

Dr. Hami thought about the day returned to Floredelis, just over two years ago. Back home, dying from an illness he had picked up in Central America, he'd been staying in a cheap motel just north of the U.S. border. He had no money left to pay for the room, let alone food-- not that he could have kept it down, anyhow. He didn't expect to live long enough to be thrown out. He had been taking aspirin, the only medication he had. It didn't help the fever or the pain as far as he could tell. But he somehow felt comforted to feel the light weight of it against his chest and the pills rattling against each other as he coughed, so he kept it in his shirt pocket. He'd stashed his gun under his pillow. Someone knocked on the door, identifying himself as the police. Hamilton sat up, pulled out the gun, and picked up his bag of ammunition. He had no intention of opening the door; besides, he didn't think he could walk that far even if he wanted to. As he sat up, the room began to spin. As everything whirled around him, he clutched the gun in one hand and the ammunition in the other.

He felt like he was being pulled through a tunnel. This is how it ends, he thought, hoping to see the light and maybe his mother and not some version of Hell. Then he felt hard ground beneath him. The cool, damp air smelled familiar. As his eyes adjusted to the dark, he saw Ontihaponati. She had saved him again, even though he wanted to die. She had ruined his life; wasn't that enough? He wondered what would happen if he shot the crystal. He closed his heavy eyes. Within a few minutes, Jenna arrived in the cave, summoned by Ontihaponati. It took her a moment to recognize him; he knew he looked older and shrunken and pale from the illness. She wanted to get help, but he shook his head. He put his hand on the stone and pictured people bringing a stretcher to the cave. They arrived shortly. He never heard the stone speak as the initiates could, but he could communicate through her— she passed along his messages. He remembered Ava telling him the first time Ontihaponati had brought him there that she thought the great stone had fallen in love with him. She told him how the stone glowed warm and pink in his presence, even though he couldn't see or feel her. He quickly learned he could manipulate people by sending his thoughts through that ridiculous, apparently besotted stone. After he recovered, and the great illness he had brought with him from the old world had spread, Dr. Hami covered the crystal with black wool. It had the same effect as putting a cloth over a bird's cage. The great stone slept or at least remained inaccessible to anyone but him. He used her to suggest Lillia retire, among other things. He had felt pleased when the Queen's request to retire came to the council—more proof of his power and that his plan was working. He wondered how things were going in Xantalon with Lucas and Solomon.

16

Later that afternoon, at the castle in Xantalon City

Solomon arrived at the castle, both horses out of breath from the short but fast gallop from Beryl's house.

He told the servant who opened the door, "I must speak to the queen immediately. I am a member of the High Council and bear an important message from the High Priestess."

"May I have a groom take your horses?" asked Stephan, the servant who had answered Solomon's impatient knock. He looked at Eugene's horse and wondered where Eugene might be.

"Yes, yes, but hurry, you fool, this is urgent," spluttered Solomon

"Of course, sir." Stephan meandered to the stable. Solomon followed. Stephan spoke to the young woman brushing a mare. "Some horses here need tending," he said loudly, and then softly, "One of them is Eugene's, but he's not here."

"I'm coming," said Leanne, putting down the brush and patting the horse affectionately.

Eugene's horse whinnied softly when he saw Leanne.

"There, there, Stormy," she said, stroking his cheek and putting her forehead against his. "Welcome home. And what's your name, beautiful?" she asked the other horse.

Solomon's already narrow eyes narrowed further. He wasn't pleased that these people knew the horse. To him, they all looked pretty much the same—people and horses.

When it became clear she would receive no answer from man or horse, she took the horses' reins and led them away.

"I'll tell Queen Lillia you're here," Stephan said. "May I tell her your name, sir?"

"Solomon, of the High Council."

Stephan walked to the Queen's study, where she sat with Beryl's moms and Ava, who had just returned from the Temple City. Ava had traveled all night, not stopping to rest or eat until she arrived at the castle.

The others sat in stunned silence as Ava described her experience. She omitted a few details, like the kiss and her former acquaintance with Dr. Hami.

"He arrested me for the illegal practice of medicine. I would still be in that cell if Jenna hadn't set me free. Tobias tried to rescue me. He's part of a group called the Pied Pipers..."

Just then, Stephan entered and told the queen that Solomon demanded to see her immediately and that he had arrived on Eugene's horse, but without Eugene.

"Oh, dear," said Lillia. "What does this mean? Show him in, Stephan. Thank you. Ava, is there more?"

"Yes. The high priestess is very ill. Also, as I was leaving, I saw a poster with my face on it saying I was wanted for the illegal practice of medicine and offering a sizable reward for my capture. I came straight here. But we can talk more about this later."

Anne, Mama A, asked, "Would you like to speak with Solomon alone?"

"Please stay," she said. "I could use your support. But be careful what you say to Solomon. Have you met him?" They had not. "I've known him for a long time, and I don't trust him."

Ava nodded her agreement. "I should probably leave. I suspect Solomon may be behind the wanted poster—he certainly knows about it. At any rate, I suddenly feel exhausted, and I'd rather not see him. We'll speak more later."

Usually, the library's curtains remained closed to protect the books from damaging sunlight. Candles in sconces on the wall, well away from the books, offered the only source of light. Books made in Floredelis, either handwritten or on the letterpress Jocasta brought with her from the old world, as well as the precious books from the old world, were irreplaceable.

But in preparation for Solomon, Queen Lillia opened one set of curtains, flooding the room with light. She wanted to see him clearly. The light streamed all around her, making her long blond hair glow like a halo. When Solomon strode in like he owned the place, she offered him her hand.

"Solomon, what an unexpected pleasure." She smiled.

He drew her hand to his lips and kissed it. "Lillia, you look lovely, as usual. But as pleasant as it is to meet, I bring sad news." He looked around, noticing the others for the first time, even though he had walked right past them. "I think we should speak alone," he said in a whisper loud enough for everyone to hear.

"Solomon, let me introduce you. These are our watchers, Beatrice and Anne. They are also Beryl's parents. I assume you bring the

Council's response to my request? They have my full confidence and can hear whatever you have to say."

"As you wish, your highness." Solomon bowed. "Let me get right to the point. As perhaps your servant told you, I rode your messenger's horse, but he is not here. I regret to inform you that he was killed by the resistance forces, the Pied Pipers, in the woods. He traveled with a messenger named Randall, a high-ranking person in the resistance. Shortly after they left, my source informed me there was a plot afoot. I left immediately, attempting to intercept them. But, alas, I arrived to find your messenger dead and that villain, Randall, standing over his body. I tried to detain him, but he escaped."

Solomon felt quite pleased with himself for coming up with this new story. That fool, Lucas, killed the wrong man, and Solomon needed to use his wits to keep the plan to save and rule Floredelis on track. He watched to see how the Queen responded to his news.

Lillia sat down. "Who is Randall? I'd heard about the unrest in the Temple city, but not that there was violence. Why didn't you bring back Eugene's body?"

"I'm sorry, Lillia. I am a man of words, a man of science. I lacked the physical strength to lift the body. I pursued the villain who murdered him, but lost him, and was lucky to find my way to you. I think I can find his body again if the wild beasts haven't eaten him. Your man was still wrapped in his blanket, murdered in his sleep."

Lillia didn't know how much of the story was true, but something horrible had happened to Eugene, and as queen, it was her responsibility. "Solomon, don't trouble yourself. My people will find him. Stephan will show you to your room."

"I would, indeed, welcome a rest, but I have one more piece of news...regarding your request to the Council," he said in a stage whisper, glancing at Anne and Beatrice. "I bring a letter, signed by the High Priestess, who, by the way, sends her regards. The Council believes it is possible that the girl, your daughter," he nodded at Beryl's parents, "can replace you in time, my dear. But the Council recommends appointing an interim ruler. The council recognizes that someone younger and stronger than you would best serve Xantalon in these difficult times"

Anne and Beatrice gasped audibly, but the Queen shot them a glance, and they remained silent.

Solomon continued without pause, "Someone with more training and experience than little Beryl, however. Also, I believe your daughter may be in danger. The reason I pursued Randall was because my informant told me that Randall planned to kidnap the child. I didn't know he planned murder, as well, or I would have brought some of the Temple Guard. I suggest we find a safe place for Beryl until this is all sorted out."

"Does the council have someone in mind for the interim ruler?" asked Lillia

"Yes, a gifted young initiate by the name of, uh, Zorina. She is the best student to come through the Temple training perhaps since you were there, your highness." He looked at his thumb, which he lifted to his mouth, nibbling on the cuticle.

The Queen looked pale, except for a bright red spot in the middle of each cheek. She took a deep breath. "This is most unusual, Solomon." She said slowly, weighing each word before she spoke. "She is not from here."

"She is from Rabican, your highness," Solomon replied, examining his thumb.

"The Council has never done such a thing before. Do they believe no one in my province could carry on until Beryl is ready? I am willing to continue until a suitable replacement is found.

"Also," said Anne, "do not underestimate the child. She is quite capable."

"I asked the same questions, Lillia, and I trust your choice implicitly, but this is the Council's decision. I am but the messenger. You may read the letter yourself."

The queen looked weary as she took the letter. "This is a lot to think through, Solomon. I'll read the letter, and we can talk in the morning.

But Beryl's safety must be seen to at once. Solomon, she doesn't know I have suggested her as my replacement. I think it best if she not know any of this yet."

"Yes, I quite understand. Would you like me to arrange for a safe place in my province for her? I could say she is a long-lost cousin come for training with the master." Solomon put his hand on his chest, ensuring they knew to whom he referred.

"No," said Lillia. "I want her closer, and with someone she knows and trusts. I'm sure her parents would agree."

"Yes," said Beatrice. "We can discuss this matter further, Lillia, but perhaps we should see to Eugene...to Eugene's...." Beatrice began to sob. Anne wrapped her arms around her and wept, too.

"So sad to lose such a loyal man," said Solomon as he ran a hand over the spine of a large black book.

"Do you think Beryl is in the city? I'd like to see her, and make sure she's alright," said Lillia

"My guess," said Anne, smiling through her tears, "is that she's not too far away. She has a nose for trouble. Try the kitchen."

Stephan found Beryl in the kitchen carving radishes into roses for the dinner salad. The kitchen, a large room with grey stone walls, had a large stove and a fireplace for cooking. It overlooked a garden overflowing with vegetables and a smaller garden filled with kitchen herbs. The room smelled of tomatoes, garlic, and basil.

"I know," Beryl was saying to Sadie, the chef, "Food must be beautiful to the eye as well as the taste buds. You say that every time."

"The Queen would like to see you in the library," said Stephan, popping a radish rose into his mouth.

"Hey, take the ones I haven't carved yet. Those things take a long time. What's going on?"

"A lot is going on," Stephan replied. "First, Ava's back from the Temple City. She was in jail there—for practicing medicine without a license! And there's some pompous guy there, Solomon, from the

Temple Council. Everyone's crying, except Solomon, and they all want to see you."

"What?" asked Beryl. But she ran out of the kitchen before Stephan could answer.

Beryl flung open the library doors and rushed in, then stopped. She loved this room almost as much as the kitchen. Most of the curtains were closed, as usual. But light streamed in through one window.

Queen Lillia sat slumped over in the bright sunlight, her head resting on a golden oak table. The light streamed all around her. Beryl paused to catch her breath and let her eyes adjust to the bright and dark lighting. She curtseyed politely to the queen before running to her and throwing her arms around her. Then she noticed Solomon standing beside the queen. He still chewed on the side of his thumb as he stared off into space.

Behind him, through the window, Beryl watched a shadow pass across the sun in the cloudless sky. She made out the shape of a man.

"It has begun," the Thirteenth voice whispered in a breeze so soft it wouldn't have moved a candle flame.

Beryl's jaw dropped. Queen Lilla hadn't moved, and Solomon still stared at his thumb. No one else noticed, she thought. An old dream flashed before her eyes, and she remembered where she had seen Solomon before—plotting the overthrow of Floredelis. Then she noticed her moms standing in the shadows by a bookcase, weeping. She ran over and hugged them.

The queen said, "Solomon, this is Beryl. And Beryl, this is Solomon, the Council representative from Vertumnus and an old friend, as well. He brings news about Eugene."

Beryl didn't trust this man. Why was everyone else weeping and why was he here?

"And news about why you were riding his horse?" she asked.

"Beryl," the Queen said, "He tried to help Eugene.

"I apologize, sir," Beryl said. "When I saw you earlier, I noticed you riding Eugene's horse. Please forgive me, and welcome to Xantalon."

"I accept your apology, child. Have we met before?"

"You asked me for directions to the castle and gave me a penny," said Beryl, speaking through the tightness in her chest.

"Ah, I remember. I mistook you for a peasant girl. Allow me to beg your forgiveness, as well, my dear."

Beryl glared at him, her arms still around her parents. She took a deep breath, counted to three, and said, "No offense taken." It was moments like these that she appreciated the calm she had learned from her meditation practice and the power of three breaths.

The queen said, "Beryl, Solomon brings us news of Eugene's death. He was killed in the woods this morning." The queen began weeping again.

Solomon now examined a page of the black book in the light of the window.

Beryl said, "I think it's time for you to leave. You have done enough for one day."

Solomon laughed. "I like a girl with spirit. She reminds me of my own daughter. She would have been about your age." A tear came to his eye.

"Beryl is right, Solomon. I mean, you have been through a lot today, and it is time for you to rest. And we must find Eugene." Lillia pulled a cord and Stephan appeared. "Stephan, please give Solomon a room and bring him some supper."

"As you wish, Your Highness, but there is yet one more matter that must be addressed immediately." Solomon turned to Beatrice and Anne. "As I mentioned earlier, we have reason to believe your daughter may be in danger. I followed Randall because my informant told me he planned to kidnap the child, and now he is at large. I suggest we find a safe place for Beryl until this is all sorted out."

"Why on earth would anyone want to kidnap me?" Beryl asked. But her heart pounded out the answer—maybe they know the truth about the darkness that seeps through me. Maybe they want to stop me.

No one answered Beryl's question. No one even looked at her.

"We will stay here tonight," said Beatrice. "Beryl will certainly be safe here. And then we can make some longer-term decisions tomorrow. But now we must take care of Eugene...his body...." She began to sob again.

"This way, sir," said Stephan. "I will show you to our best guest room."

"May I take this book with me?" Solomon asked. "It's quite an intriguing tome."

He took it and left without waiting for an answer.

After Solomon left, Beryl said, "I don't trust that man. Do you think he's telling the truth about Eugene?"

She couldn't believe he was dead—murdered. These things didn't happen.

"I don't know what to believe anymore," the Queen sighed. "Let's find Ava. She's been through so much, but she'll never forgive us if we don't give her this news immediately."

*

Ava cried as Beryl stroked her hair. "He was the first baby I ever delivered here, a beautiful child and a fine man. I'll retrieve the body. I'm sure he camped at the spot I showed him when he was a boy, when he helped me gather herbs. I helped him enter this world; I would like to help him leave."

"I thought you'd say that, Ava, and I know you won't rest until you see him. Take a few of my men with you. Have them bring their swords in case Randall, or whoever killed Eugene, is still around. And while they get ready, please eat something."

"Lillia, I don't think we'll need weapons, but if it makes you feel better, I'll have the men bring their swords. I will definitely take you up on your offer of food. Thank you." At the mention of food, Ava realized how hungry she felt. It had been days since she'd eaten anything other than the horrid food in the prison. The last meal she'd had was with Tobias and Andrew. Was Tobias still imprisoned, she wondered.

"Of course, my dear Ava," the Queen replied. "There has never been death by violence in Xantalon, until today. And I still can't believe you were put in prison! I have failed my people."

Anne gave her a reassuring hug. No one believed the queen was responsible, but they knew her well enough not to argue.

"I'll go with you," Beryl said to Ava.

They told her all the usual things-- that she was too young, that Ava and the soldiers could do it, that if someone was trying to harm her, she would be safer staying in the palace. But in the end, when she threatened to sneak out and follow them anyway, and if they said yes, at least the guards could keep an eye on her, the adults finally agreed to let her go.

17

That night, in the woods outside of Xantalon City

Oh, Moon, great daughter of the night. You teach us of the cycles of life, and the cycles of women, especially. You hold the power of new beginnings when you grow large and the power of fruition when you are full. I love watching you shine over the mountains, Hugin and Munin. I wonder if you are the same moon that shines on the old world.

From The Book of Jocasta

When the full moon rose, Beryl and Ava set out with six guards. The guards wore their short swords, which did prove useful for hacking through the underbrush. They also brought a stretcher made of cotton canvas sewn onto long wooden poles.

The trees glowed gold in the moonlight, as a cool breeze caressed and comforted the wanderers.

"I've never seen the woods this bright, even during the day," said Beryl.

"That's Ava's magic," said a guard.

"It's not my magic. The trees have moved their branches to let the moonlight our way. I hear the trees' song telling us to take courage and that all is not as bleak as it seems. It's hard to tell what that means, though. Trees have such a different perspective on life. But I'm glad for the light and their song. It won't be long until we reach our destination."

As they approached the campsite, Beryl wished she had stayed at the palace. She feared what she would see. But she steeled herself to face the darkness. She demanded that her recalcitrant feet keep moving. Just ahead, fireflies formed a luminescent cloud. Their shimmer made the forest look even more magical, but they didn't distract Beryl from what lay ahead.

The glowing creatures gathered like a tornado of light around a fallen log.

"This is the spot," said Ava. And there, on the other side of the log, lay Eugene's body, just as Solomon had described, still wrapped in his blanket. He also sparkled in the fireflies' light. Beryl sat on the log and forced herself to look at him. Ava knelt next to him, tears in her eyes. She put a hand on his forehead and one on the center of his chest. There was a hole in his chest about the size of a finger.

"He was not killed by a blow from a human hand or any weapon I have ever seen, although I seem to remember seeing an injury like this in a medical book from the old world. But how could it be?"

She reached underneath and felt the hole in his back. It was sticky with blood beneath him, but it was not fresh. Strange, she thought. His body didn't feel stiff as it should if he'd been dead since morning.

Ava barely breathed as she continued her examination. "Oh, my," she said.

"What is it?" Beryl asked.

"Eugene is still alive, but barely. We must take him home immediately. I hope the journey doesn't kill him. But if he stays here, he will surely die."

"Beryl, you gather some sphagnum moss to pack the wound—you should be able to find some near those decaying logs. George, give me the bands that bind the stretcher; those will serve as bandages." Beryl gathered the moss, thanking its spirit for its gift, and relieved to have something useful to do. Ava placed it over the holes in Eugene's chest and back, binding the wounds tightly with the straps from the stretcher. She put some flower essences on his lips. She silently thanked the Goddess that whatever injured him missed his heart and lungs. She ran her fingers around the moon of his face. What a fine man he had become.

"Move him gently; we will wrap him to keep him warm and as still as possible." The men lifted Eugene as tenderly as if he were a newborn baby.

"While I finish getting Eugene ready, look around and see if there are signs of a struggle or anything that might help us figure out what really happened here."

Beryl examined the bloody hole in the ground under where Eugene had lain. His blood had mostly soaked into the ground. It looked like rust in the firefly light and smelled like iron—like his iron will that had kept him alive so far. She grabbed a stick and started to poke around inside the hole, feeling she'd find something important there, maybe whatever made that hole.

The guards gathered Randall's shoes and blanket. They found the saddlebag and the remains of the campfire. Another man found some blood on the log near Randall's things. They put everything moveable into the saddlebag.

"Look," said Beryl. "What do you think this is?" She held up a piece of metal shaped like a flower. It was about as long as one joint of her pointer finger. "I found this in the hole."

Ava examined it. "I wonder," was all she said.

Then, "My dear friends, not a word of this to anyone except the queen. Eugene will be safer if whoever did this doesn't know he's alive —if he stays that way."

The guards carried Eugene on the stretcher, careful not to jostle him. Their hearts and steps were lighter, knowing Eugene was alive. The trees now blocked out the moon, but fireflies lit their way to the forest's edge.

They arrived at Eugene's house after midnight. Leeann had come earlier to tell his wife, Isabella, of Eugene's death. Isabella sat by their sons' beds, gazing at their peaceful, sleeping faces. She always thought she'd know if something happened to Eugene. She couldn't believe he was gone.

Ava knelt by the grieving woman, while Beryl stood behind her and looked at the sleeping boys. Ava took Isabella's hands in her own and spoke quietly, but clearly. "Eugene is outside. He's not dead, but he is gravely injured. I don't know if he'll survive the night."

"What?" Isabella pulled her hands away and rubbed her eyes. "Can I see him?"

"Yes," said Ava. "We'll bring him in. He's unconscious. I have no idea who would have a weapon like the one I believe injured him. So, for now, it's best if people believe he's dead."

"Let me see him now, please. I'll do whatever you want."

18

Very early the next morning, back at the castle

The time between midnight and dawn is a time of quiet and mystery. For us humans, it is a time for rest and rejuvenation. But many creatures awaken during this time. While our angels watch over us, the large-eyed creatures of the night hunt and play. It is good from time to time to stay awake in the small hours and observe. There is something magical about being awake in the quiet of the night. But don't do it too often—we need to sleep and dream!

From The Book of Jocasta

It was well after midnight when Beryl and Ava returned to the palace, having left three of the guards at Eugene's house. They found Beryl's parents and Lillia in the kitchen, by the fire, sipping chamomile-lavender tea. King Jyrym, Lillia's husband, had returned from helping some people dig a new well just outside the far side of the city wall.

Seeing Jyrym's kind brown eyes and curly greying brown hair made Beryl feel better. In two strides with his long legs, he crossed the room and scooped both Beryl and Ava into his strong arms.

"He's alive," Beryl said.

"But just barely," said Ava. "There's a chance he'll survive. I've done what I can for him. Isabella and her neighbor will care for him tonight."

"Show them the flower," said Beryl.

Ava opened the saddlebag clutched in her arms. She pulled out a handkerchief and unwrapped the cylindrical piece of metal with the flower at one end. "This is what injured Eugene. I believe it's a bullet. There was a weapon in the old world called a gun. It propelled small pieces of metal at high speed. I read about the injuries it caused in an old medical text."

Beryl gasped. "Does it have a round part that looks like a barrel and then bends around to a handle which has something you pull back to make that thing come out?"

"Yes, that sounds right," said Ava, "but how...?"

Beryl looked at the floor. "I saw one. In my dream. It was horrible and loud. I didn't think it could be real."

"We should talk some more about your dreams," said Ava.

Beryl's parents nodded.

"But not tonight," said Jyrym, "tell us quickly about Eugene. And then we all need some rest—especially you, Ava!"

"This piece of metal went into his chest and came out his back, but it missed his heart and lungs. He lost a lot of blood. I can't imagine who would have such a weapon, if that's really what injured him. Until we know who did this, I don't think we should let Solomon or anyone else know Eugene is alive."

Ava had an idea about where it might have come from, but she kept it to herself. Beryl thought about the Thirteenth and the darkness. Was she somehow responsible for Eugene's injury?

"Beryl, while you were gone, we talked about where you might go," said her mother. "We know you have been planning to go to the Temple City in the spring, but we would like you to wait at least until we understand what is going on. In the meantime, we thought you might like to stay with Ava when she returns to her house. It might be good for both of you. If Ava agrees, of course."

Beryl looked at Ava who smiled and nodded her agreement.

"Yes," said Beryl with a tired smile. "I'd like that."

This had been the longest day of Beryl's life. As she snuggled into her bed at the palace, exhaustion hit her, but she couldn't stop thinking about Eugene and the gun and Ava in prison. She felt someone watching her, but when she looked out the window, she only saw the full moon. Then she saw two more golden moons watching her. Her cat, Midnight, sat on the window ledge. He meowed a couple of times and jumped onto the bed. He curled up on Beryl's chest, purring loudly. They both fell asleep. Beryl sometimes wondered what Midnight dreamt about when she watched his nose and paws twitching in his sleep. But tonight, Beryl didn't wonder. She was busy dreaming herself.

She stood by the ocean, the water dark and still, the sky gray and heavy. Everything completely silent except for the soothing sound of waves caressing the shore. She gazed at the horizon, trying to see where the water ended and the sky began. She wore a brown woolen dress, warm and loose, with sleeves that covered her wrists and the skirt touching the sand, which felt cool and rough beneath her bare feet. Many other women stood with her on the shore, wearing the same brown robes. They were priestesses. She had no memories of where they came from or why they were there.

She had been chosen as a sacrifice to the sea. She walked toward the water, a priestess on either side. The sand changed from cool and dry to hard and wet as she approached the water. The water flowed between her toes, wetting the hem of her dress. She walked until the water reached her chest. She stood on a ledge. She knew the next step would be into deep water, over her head. She hesitated, suddenly afraid. The sea sent a wave to help her. It washed her into the water, under the water. She let the water carry her further and further away from the shore, deeper and deeper below the surface. She held her breath for a very long time until she could hold it no longer. She had to inhale.

She expected to die.

She inhaled. The water felt warm and nourishing in her lungs. She could breathe!

Beryl woke up, her heart pounding, breathing fast. She was at the castle. Her bed felt safe and dry. Outside she saw the first pink rays of the sun peeking into her cozy room. She wanted to tell her moms about her dream, curl up between them like she did when she was little, but she didn't want to disturb them. She saw Midnight's pale green eyes watching her from the foot of the bed as he washed his face. Beryl still felt tired but knew she wouldn't sleep anymore. She thought about Solomon's warning but didn't believe she was in danger. So, after letting Stephan know, she headed for home, Midnight trotting beside her.

19

A few days later, in the Temple City

Lucas spread Solomon's story about Randall killing Eugene throughout the Temple City. Dr. Hami agreed, having Randall be a murderer was even better than having him dead. Soon Jocasta's letterpress was printing posters offering a reward for Randall's capture, dead or alive.

The brothers, Fain and Otto, looked at Randall's poster.

"Do you think he did it? Did he really kill that guy?" asked Otto.

"I don't think Randall would hurt anyone, except maybe in self-defense. They're trying to frame him because they think he's a trouble-maker. After all, he doesn't follow their rules. I bet he's hiding in the woods now. A lot of people are out there."

"Maybe we should go, too. Anything would beat staying here. We're going to lose our house soon, but really, I can't stand being there anymore since, you know," said Otto.

Fain put an arm around Otto. "Yeah, I know what you mean."

Their parents had both died in the Great Illness that had swept the Temple City. They had begged at the Temple for someone to help their parents before it was too late, but they were too young to serve as Temple Guards, and they had nothing else to offer. They had been fed and cared for by the Pied Pipers, following the sound of the flute to safe places where they were given food. And they still lived in their family home. But now it had a notice nailed to the front door saying that the Temple Council would confiscate the house if someone didn't pay the taxes. And they weren't going to pay; they had no money. Plus, every moment they spent in the house reminded them of their dead parents. They decided to go—the Temple City held nothing but danger and bad memories for them.

They packed up their few belongings and headed for the woods. With the mild weather, they didn't need a tent, which was good, because they didn't have one. They did bring two wool blankets to sleep in and some warmer clothes for when the weather changed.

They wandered into the woods searching for Randall, without success. Soon their meager food supply ran out. They ate raspberries and wild blueberries but didn't know what else was edible. After wandering in the woods for about a week, they met a man staying in a deserted cabin in the woods—Ava's house-- with some other fugitives. Ava hadn't returned yet. She had remained in Xantalon City so she could more easily care for Eugene. The man invited Fain and Otto to join them, telling them that Lucas promised to feed them and give them back their homes if they worked for Solomon and helped save Floredelis.

When Fain and Otto arrived, the five men already living there still had plenty of food because Ava had left a good store of food in preparation for winter. But the men soon ate almost everything she had left. Her garden was filled with the bounty of fall, but these men had lived their entire lives in a city, and none of them were gardeners, so they didn't know what was within their reach. They did pick some strawberries and raspberries from the garden and found an old sack of flour with which they made pancakes, but even those supplies were running low.

Lucas had promised to feed them, but they didn't know how to find him or when he would return. They had no idea when—or even if—Solomon would arrive. They were all wanted men. If they went home, they might be thrown into prison. They didn't dare go into Xantalon City, although they knew it was close by, because they didn't know how they would be received. At this point, they had low expectations. They stayed because they feared going home and had nowhere else to go.

But finally, the dwindling food supply sent them out of the house to search for food. Fain, Otto, and four others followed the path toward Xantalon City. The first house they came to was Beryl's. They watched through the windows with hunger and longing as Beryl and her parents ate their evening meal by candlelight, cleaned up, and went to bed. Otto began to cry. Fain put his arm around him, managing not to cry himself.

One of the men suggested breaking into the house and stealing their food. The other three nodded in agreement. Fain and Otto didn't want to, but they were hungry. They also feared what would happen if they didn't go along with the plan, for they had nowhere else to go, so they agreed. In the end, they decided not to break in that night. They would take turns watching the house and go in when no one was home.

20

Two days later, outside of Xantalon City

Beryl woke to a bright morning, a cool breeze blowing through her open window. She pulled her summer quilt up to her chin. Soon it would be time for her heavier comforter, although she wouldn't be staying here by then. She jumped out of bed, put on her new red wool slippers that Mama A had made for her birthday, and wrapped the rainbow scarf around her shoulders. Her moms had told her they'd be going to the castle early that morning, and they'd left already. Beryl would join them later.

The smell of fall permeated the air and put Beryl in the mood to bake. She made her favorite apple cake with the first apples of the season. They weren't the sweetest, but they were good for baking. The kitchen filled with the smell of baking apples, butter, and cinnamon.

She thought of how her moms would smile when they came home to that delicious scent. Since Eugene's injury, her parents spent even more time at the castle. Today she would see Eugene for the first time since he'd been so gravely injured. Ava told her he had opened his eyes the day before and seemed to recognize his wife and children. Although he still couldn't speak, he showed the inkling of a smile before closing his eyes again.

From the kitchen window, Beryl saw the road from the castle to the forest sparkling in the sunlight. Fairies danced among the flowers, and the fish in the stream splashed and played. Beryl felt glad the cake had almost finished baking. She wanted to be outside. She sighed as she brought the mixing bowls to the sink. She didn't like washing dishes, but Mama A and Mama B insisted that if she made a mess, she should clean it up. They had been so preoccupied lately that Beryl wanted to cheer them up with a delicious treat, not annoy them with a sink full of dirty dishes. When she'd finished the dishes and set the cake out to cool, she would enjoy her walk to the city.

The cake smelled done. The top looked brown and bubbly. She touched it with her finger; it gave a little and popped right back. Beryl smiled—perfect! She put it on the counter to cool, closed the kitchen window so her little friends from the forest couldn't help themselves to a taste, and set out for town.

She thought Eugene smiled at her when she approached his bed, but it might have been a twitch. Isabella looked exhausted, so Beryl offered to watch the boys while Ava sat with Eugene. They shooed Isabella out with instructions to spend some time outside and go to a friend's house for supper. Isabella did as she was told, returning home that evening to find her boys sitting on the edge of their father's bed, all three of them listening to Beryl tell them the story of "Little Red Riding Hood." Isabella looked refreshed, although she still had dark circles under her eyes. She smiled to see her boys so content.

Beryl and Ava hugged the boys and Isabella goodnight. They returned to the castle in time to have dessert with Beryl's parents and the queen. It was late, so they decided to spend the night. Beryl thought wistfully of the apple cake. She hoped it would still be good tomorrow.

When she fell asleep, she found the Thirteenth waiting. "Remember me," he repeated over and over. "Take care of my baby."

"Who are you?" Beryl asked.

In answer, she saw a woman in labor in a messy bedroom in the old world. Another older woman sat by her side. The pregnant woman cried. "I thought he would come back. How could he leave me, leave us?" She stroked her belly. On the bedside table, Beryl saw a picture of a man. He looked like Hamilton, but he wasn't. He must be the baby's father.

The older woman held a book. "I told you that woman was trouble."

Beryl saw the title of the book, *The World of Floredelis: a new beginning for you and me* by Hamilton Sperry and Jocasta Reed. The old woman opened the book. Beryl read the handwritten inscription, somewhat smeared. It said, "You are my Lucky Thirteen."

As Beryl tried to decipher the signature, the young woman yelled and the baby crowned. The book fell to the floor. Beryl woke up. If the baby was Hamilton, how could the father be Hamilton? She'd seen pictures of Jocasta and neither woman was her. So how was Jocasta involved? It didn't make sense. "Lucky Thirteen"—was the father the Thirteenth? She felt like she was underwater and couldn't breathe.

21

That same night, while Beryl dreamt of the Thirteenth, outside Xantalon City

While Beryl slept at the palace, Fain, Otto, and the others walked to her house. One of the men had checked a little earlier and found no one home. They watched darkness fall and saw no candles shining and no smoke rising from the chimney. It seemed they'd gone out for the night They left one man to keep watch by the road, to give a warning if anyone headed their way. The doors in Floredelis didn't lock, so after making sure once more that no one was home, they just walked in. Some of the boys cheered when they found the apple cake, but Fain hushed them. Otto found the well-stocked pantry, and they took as much food as they could carry. Like all families in Floredelis, Beryl's family preserved food to eat through the winter. And since the harvest had begun, they had already begun to fill their pantry for the winter, both with their own harvest and foods brought in from other provinces. The men found grains and beans, coffee and tea in bags— imported from provinces further south, and canned fruits, vegetables, and jellies lined up in neat rows on the pantry shelves. They didn't leave much. They headed back to the cabin with their feast. That night, they all ate their fill, with plenty left for tomorrow.

*

Beryl left the castle early, asking Stephan to tell her parents to come home for breakfast. She stopped at the castle kitchen to get some eggs. She practically ran home, wanting to check on the cake and make a special breakfast for her parents.

When she approached the house, she noticed the kitchen window stood open. She remembered making a point of closing it before she left. As she came around the front, she also saw the door standing open. She stood in the doorway, unsure if she wanted to enter. She had probably just forgotten to close it, or maybe a friend had come to visit and decided to make themselves at home, but that's not what it felt like. Cautiously, she went inside. In the kitchen, she looked at the open window. She looked at the towel that had been under the apple cake. She put the basket of eggs on the towel and walked to the pantry. The shelves, yesterday filled with bountiful food, stood practically empty. Loose barley and two broken jars of strawberry preserves lay on the floor, smelling sweet and covered with swarms of flies. Beryl sank to the ground. She wanted to cry, but no tears came. Midnight wandered into the pantry, curled up on her lap, and purred. That is how her parents found them when they arrived home an hour later.

22

The night before, at Ava's house

Lucas couldn't wait any longer for Solomon to leave the Temple City. That idiot was supposed to go straight from Xantalon City to Ava's house in the woods. But he claimed he had tried and gotten lost in the woods. Lucas didn't believe him. Who knew how long those men would hang around with no one to tell them what to do or to bring them supplies? If there was one thing that Solomon was good at, Lucas thought, it was telling everyone what to do, and he liked to cook, too, Lucas had been told. After Lucas shot Eugene, Solomon shared the story of Eugene's death with Queen Lillia and left to return to the Temple City shortly after, acting like a puffed-up hero. Lucas saw him for the fool he was, but the Council lauded him for his bravery. The time had finally come to begin the next part of Dr. Hami's plan to take over Xantalon, which involved putting the men at Ava's house to work. Lucas decided to go there himself while Solomon strutted importantly around the Temple. He brought food and a keg of ale. But when he arrived at Ava's house to "prepare the men for Solomon's arrival," the house looked dark and empty. Lucas feared they had gotten tired of waiting for Solomon and wandered off.

Once inside, Lucas could tell the house hadn't been empty for long. The fire had been recently banked, blankets and pillows lay on the couch and floor, and the dirty dishes weren't moldy. He went back outside in time to see the men return with sacks and armfuls of what had to be stolen food. He watched them from outside, through the window, until they finished feasting, then he knocked on the door. They let him in, thinking he sought shelter. He reminded them that he was the man who had hired them. He told them they had put not only themselves but the entire future of Floredelis in danger by their reckless behavior. He showed them the herd of footprints and food droppings leading to the cabin. The soldiers of Xantalon would soon arrest them for stealing, he said. Solomon would arrive shortly, and he relied on their help. They could go home before winter set in if they did what Solomon asked and stayed out of trouble. But for now, they needed to lay low for a few days.

They knew Lucas was right. They didn't want to go to jail. They didn't want to be hungry. They longed to go home, but they had no homes to return to unless Solomon helped them. They put the remains of the stolen food and their meager belongings into sacks they found in Ava's pantry. Lucas had two men walk behind the rest of them and taught them to use a leafy branch to sweep away their footprints.

By the time Jyrym arrived at Ava's cabin the next day, following the footprints and crumbs from Beryl's house, the robbers had disappeared without a trace. When he arrived, he found Ava's house looking like a tornado had blown through it. All of her belongings were strewn over every surface except the dining table, which was crusted with dirt and dried food. Every dish that Ava owned sat out on the table or floor or in the sink, also encased in dirt and food. And in the middle of the table, he found the pan from Beryl's apple cake—her favorite white ceramic one with blue flowers. It looked like it had been licked clean.

Jyrym asked two guards to stay in case the thieves returned and asked them to start cleaning Ava's house in the meantime. Jyrym thought that since they only took food, they must have been hungry. He would let the people who lived nearby know what had happened and have them notify the guards if they saw any signs of hungry strangers. If they showed up again, he could help them. He had heard that people from the Temple City who had lost everything lived in these woods now. Perhaps they would like to settle in Xantalon. There was plenty of work and an abundance of food.

Jyrym returned to Xantalon City. He told Ava what had happened. She wanted to go home immediately. Eugene was on the mend, although it would be a long time before he fully recovered. She had shown Isabella and a couple of her neighbors how to care for him so she didn't need to be with him daily. Jyrym encouraged her to wait until the guards finished cleaning her house and until they could gather food, supplies, and clean linens for her. They had already restocked Beryl's family's pantry. Reluctantly, Ava agreed to wait. Even more reluctantly, she agreed to let a couple of the Queen's guards stay with her when she did return. Although she'd wanted to stay in Xantalon City while Eugene needed her, she longed for the privacy and comfort of her own home. She looked forward to having Beryl stay with her, but not the guards. Nevertheless, she knew Jyrym was right. It was better to be cautious, especially now that she was a wanted woman.

One of the guards returned from Ava's house the following evening to let Ava know they had cleaned and organized her house as best they could. They had burned the sheets and towels but managed to clean the handmade heart quilt, made for her by a grateful patient, that Ava kept on her bed, as well as her small pink round woolen rug with roses around the edge. She would need new dishes; most of hers were cracked or broken besides being disgusting.

Early the next morning, Ava left with Jyrym and a couple of guards leading horses laden with food and household goods. Ava felt relieved when she saw that her garden had remained relatively undamaged, although it needed some serious weeding. She gathered fresh vegetables and herbs and made a quick stew for the men and herself. Her house looked clean and neat, but she would need to fill it with her own energy again. She could feel the neglect and fear of those who had stayed there in her absence.

After lunch, Jyrym and the guards, except for two, headed back to the city. They planned for Beryl to join Ava in three days. In the meantime, the guards slept in Ava's second bedroom.

All remained quiet for two days as Ava reestablished her home and weeded and tended her garden. Two guards arrived, telling Ava they had come to relieve the two who had been with her. Ava didn't recognize them, but she was too preoccupied with setting up her house to pay much attention. They told her Lillia had brought in new guards from Vertumnus so they would have enough men to protect the city's outskirts. That made sense to Ava, and the departing guards, happy to watch over Ava, were even happier to return to their families.

Unfortunately, everything was not as it appeared. Minutes after Lillia's guards left Ava's house, some of Dr. Hami's men, waiting in the woods, arrested them for harboring a wanted criminal-- Ava. The men tied up Queen Lillia's guards, threw them on the backs of horses, and took them to the Temple prison to await a trial unlikely to happen anytime soon.

Lucas smiled as he watched Xantalon's guards taken prisoner. Everything was going well again after a few minor mishaps. Soon Solomon would arrive, and the hired men would return to Ava's house. He had brought fresh provisions to feed Solomon and his men. The new "guards from Vertumnus" would lock Ava up in the cellar until they were sure they didn't need her anymore and then get rid of her for good. He wouldn't botch the job this time. He had shown the new guards the wanted poster with Ava's face on it and promised them the reward when they brought Ava to the Temple after their work for Solomon was done. Lucas had become, or maybe always had been, an excellent liar. They believed everything he said.

23

The next day outside of
Xantalon City

"Mama B, it's not like I'm really leaving. I'll just be at Ava's. I've been there tons of times."

"I know, Beryl, but I'll miss you. And after everything that's happened, I can't help worrying. I keep expecting someone to tell me all of it, the robberies, Eugene's injury, and Ava in prison were a bad dream. I want you to go, I know it's best, but it's still hard."

"I know what you mean. Everything feels different now. You're right; we live in strange and unsettling times." She hugged her mother.

"Sometimes the biggest journeys don't cover much physical distance," said Mama A, watching Beryl stuff her red house slippers into her full pack. She kissed the top of Beryl's head as she bent to her task.

"I love you, Mama," said Beryl.

"I love you too, Peaches. I hear Jyrym's and Lillia's horses approaching."

"I wish you'd let me make breakfast," Beryl said. "You know I love to cook."

"This is your goodbye party," said Anne. "Your mother and I are the hosts, and you are the guest of honor. I know we don't cook as well as you, but you'll have to make do. Besides, we'd best learn to manage without you." She hugged Beryl again. "Now get that pack closed up and come greet your guests. It's really full. Did you put Midnight in there?"

Beryl walked the newly arrived horses into the gated pasture where they could drink from the stream and nibble the grass while Lillia and Jyrym went into the house.

"I hope we're doing the right thing by not telling her," Anne said, watching Beryl in the distance.

"I think it's best," said Lillia. She didn't want to tell Beryl that she had asked the Temple Council to name Beryl as the next queen. She had made the request, but something didn't feel quite right. Why would she not want Beryl to know if it was the right step, she wondered? No sense in getting Beryl's hopes up if the Council said no, she explained to herself.

She knew Jyrym didn't agree. He thought they should have told Beryl a long time ago and had told Lillia so. And even he didn't understand her choice. But now he kept his own counsel. He rarely disagreed with his wife in public.

Everyone exchanged hugs. They enjoyed wild blueberry pancakes, the blueberries picked early that morning, smothered in maple syrup and whipped cream, and washed down with cool rose hip tea. As they ate, they chatted, as people often do when big changes are coming, of nothing much, but they spoke words filled with love and kindness and best wishes until they met again.

"This is for you." Lillia handed Beryl a white cotton pouch on a sturdy string. Beryl found a clear quartz crystal inside. "It's a piece of the stars," said the queen. "When you hold it, know you are not alone--that your star will always guide you."

"Thank you. I'll keep it close to my heart, where I hold you." Beryl placed the cord over her head and tucked the pouch into her blouse. She hugged Lillia, who stroked her hair and whispered, "I will miss you, Beryl. Don't forget us."

Jyrym cleared his throat. "Young lady, I also have a small token for you. It's a gift I received from my godfather when I first left home. I believe it will fit into your pouch." He handed Beryl a finger-sized brown twig. She examined it, then looked up at the king, puzzled.

"It doesn't look like much, but it acts like a compass. But instead of pointing north, it will point toward the direction you need to go. Look closely, one end is a little pointed. Hold it in your palm. Keep your hand flat; ask it where you need to go and see what happens."

Beryl did as Jyrym instructed, although she felt silly talking to a stick. At first, nothing happened. Then she felt an odd sensation in her arm. The twig quivered. It spun around three times and stopped. The sharper end pointed toward the path into the woods.

"Amazing," said Beryl, staring at the twig.

"It's even more amazing when you don't know what path to take."

"Thank you. I'm honored to be entrusted with such a treasure." She held out her hands and the King took them. He held her at arm's length.

"You've grown into a fine young woman," he said.

Beryl kissed his whiskery cheek and held him close. His arms felt strong and his broad chest felt safe and warm. "I'd like to accompany you part way to Ava's if you don't mind," he said.

"I'd like that," Beryl replied.

"I guess it's time," she said, "unless you want me to wash dishes first?" Her parents stood side by side, holding hands, as they often did. Their eyelids looked heavy, and they both had wrinkles that Beryl didn't remember seeing before.

"We also have some gifts for you." Beatrice handed her a small scroll that she had painted. Beryl loved her mother's paintings. This one showed Beryl leaning against the willow tree next to the pond, one of her favorite places, her feet dangling in the water, a bird perched on her shoulder, and a squirrel on her lap. The forest and flowers bloomed around in their summer glory. Magnificent! The scroll even smelled like her special spot.

A tear escaped Beryl's eye. Several more followed. "I'm sorry. I hate to cry. But this is the most gorgeous thing I've ever seen. Mom, you're amazing."

"Then you must take after me. You're amazing, yourself."

Anne handed her a pair of scissors she had made. They were copper colored and shaped like a hummingbird flying out of a flower.

"Mama A, thank you." She put the scissors in her pouch, feeling the comforting weight of the gifts resting near her heart. Her parents hugged her between the two of them. They used to call it a Beryl sandwich when she was little. For a moment, she wished she weren't leaving, but only for a moment. As hard as it was to say goodbye, it was time.

"Goodbye," she said, "I love you. Thanks for the gifts and for everything."

"Goodbye, dear Beryl. We love you."

When she retrieved her backpack, she found Midnight lying on top of it. He opened one eye and looked at her grumpily. She picked him up and held him close. "I'll miss you, too," said Beryl, placing him on the floor. When she picked up the pack, he stalked into her bedroom without looking back. Beryl smiled.

The king took the pack from her. "I'll carry this for a while," he said as they started down the path. After they had walked for about an hour, Jyrym said, "I'll leave you now. But I won't be far away if ever you need me. Goodbye, dear Beryl." He gave her another hug and watched her continue down the path. She walked a short way, then turned and waved. He waved back and headed for home.

24

In the woods, that same day

Little Red Cap set off for Grandmother's house but wandered off the path to gather flowers. She may not have followed the path already laid out, but she did follow her heart (and the wolf's advice, too—who was the wolf? We'll get to that soon, but first--)

On Finding Your Path: I truly believe that everything that happens to us and everyone we meet all have a higher purpose. There are no accidents; we're all each other's teachers and students - if we choose to honor the lessons life offers us. Trust your intuition, and do not be afraid to take risks. Don't wait for fortune to find you. You won't create a life you love if you sit around and wait for some miracle to come knock on your door. Answer the door and find out if it's someone bringing you sweet cakes and wine or the wolf come to devour you.

Live your life as a great adventure.

Trust yourself, your inner knowing, and take one step at a time. You may end up where you thought you were going, but you may find yourself someplace you never even imagined. I never could have imagined coming to this new world. What discoveries await you who come after me?

From Jocasta's Guide to Fairy Tales

Beryl felt alone and very young after Jyrym left. But she'd arrive at Ava's house soon. She decided to pick some flowers for Ava along the way.

She remembered the story of Little Red Cap,

Little Red-Cap raised her eyes, and when she saw the sunbeams dancing here and there through the trees, and pretty flowers growing everywhere, she thought: "Suppose I take grandmother a fresh nosegay; that would please her, too. It is so early in the day that I shall still get there in good time," and so, she ran from the path into the wood to look for flowers. And wherever she had picked one, she fancied that she saw a still prettier one farther on and ran after it, and so got deeper and deeper into the wood.

Wearing her traveling cloak, she felt like Little Red Cap, except instead of wolves, there might be hungry men in the woods. She'd never seen one, but they'd stolen the food from her house. She stayed alert but didn't see or hear anyone. She also didn't stray too far from the path. In another hour, Beryl arrived at Ava's flushed, happy, and hoping for a warm meal, holding a bunch of wildflowers in all the colors of the rainbow. As she approached the door, she felt shy and unsure. Should she knock or just walk in? She knocked. This would be her home for a while, but she still felt like a visitor. She waited for what seemed like a long time. She knocked again, harder. Smoke curled from the chimney, so Ava must be home. Ava knew she would arrive today. The guards should be there, too. Beryl counted to herself to make sure she was waiting long enough for Ava to answer the door. Perhaps she just needed more patience. When she'd counted to fifty, she opened the door and peeked in. She didn't see anyone, so she slipped inside. As her eyes adjusted, she saw someone lying on the couch. The person was shorter and rounder than Ava. Beryl moved closer, then rubbed her eyes and blinked hard, not quite believing what she saw.

Solomon sat up, his eyes barely visible under his prominent brow. His open shirt showed his very hairy chest. Beryl felt excitement combined with nausea. She felt like running away, back home or anywhere but here.

"Ah, Beryl," Solomon yawned and scratched his chest. "I've been expecting you."

As he stood, he tied the drawstring in his pants. "Come in; you must be tired after your long walk. Let me take that." Solomon walked behind her, shut and latched the door, and pulled her pack from her back, leaving her holding the flowers.

When he said, "So good to see you again," he leaned so close that she could smell the alcohol on his breath.

"Where is Ava?" gasped Beryl, trying not to inhale.

Solomon replied, "She's out. Wise woman business. I waited for you. You must be hungry. I've made supper."

Beryl remembered feeling hungry a few minutes ago, but not now. Something felt very wrong. "When will she be back?" she asked.

"Who?" Solomon queried. "Oh, Ava. Tomorrow, or maybe the day after. Come, I'll show you your room."

"What about the guards?" Beryl asked.

"They went with her to guard her, of course," Solomon replied. Beryl thought he was getting annoyed with all of her questions.

Solomon took her pack and walked through Ava's bedroom door. Beryl looked at the cheerful yellow walls, the patchwork quilt on the bed, and the drawings of plants on the wall. It smelled like Ava, of lavender, roses, and pine.

"But this is Ava's room," Beryl said. Immediately she wished she hadn't spoken.

Solomon smiled at her, his yellow teeth showing. He put his arm around her shoulders and squeezed a little too hard.

"Of course it is. Very perceptive of you. You will share Ava's room. I'm using the other bedroom. You'll be quite comfy, don't you think."

"Oh, yes," said Beryl stepping out of Solomon's grasp. "It's lovely." She didn't like being alone with Solomon, especially in Ava's bedroom.

"I'd like to rest a few minutes before I eat if you don't mind," she said.

He scratched his chest thoughtfully. "As you wish. But don't be too long. I'm so hungry I could eat a bear."

She wanted to tell him to eat without her, but her voice wouldn't co-operate, so she nodded. He stood there long enough that she wondered if he would leave. He finally did. She closed the door behind him and leaned against it. The door had a lock with a key in it. She would check later to see if there was a key in the lock on the other side. She wanted to lock the door but didn't want Solomon to hear. She took the key out, slowly and carefully so as not to make a sound, and put it in her skirt pocket. She told herself that even though this wasn't what she expected, everything was fine. Ava would return in the morning, hopefully. And Solomon was a council member, a respected leader. She had wanted an adventure, and she was getting one. She wished she could relax and enjoy it. She put the flowers into a cup of water sitting on the little bed-side table. Her hand felt stiff. She hadn't realized how tightly she'd been holding them.

She sat in the darkening bedroom, watching the sunset colors dance across the yellow walls. She wanted to crawl under the covers and not come out until morning but felt that she should go eat with Solomon. She removed her cloak, feeling even more vulnerable as the air touched her arms. She opened her pack and took out her red felted slippers. Only a few hours ago, she had stuffed those slippers into her pack, imagining putting them on in her new home. That felt like a different lifetime.

Beryl put the slippers on and patted her hair. As usual, several wild tendrils had escaped her ponytail. She tucked one behind her ear and left the rest. She touched her pocket, making sure she still had the key, took a deep breath, and walked into the main room.

Solomon sat at the table, his shirt still undone, reading a book. She tried to read the title, but he closed it when he saw her and put it down on the bench.

"Beryl, come sit by the fire, and I'll bring you your dinner."

He'd set the end of the rough wooden table closest to the fire with two woven green and blue plaid placemats. The table could easily seat eight people, but one spot on the bench nearest the fireplace had worn down a little. That's Ava's spot, thought Beryl, feeling the comfort of

Ava's presence when she sat there. Solomon brought two plates of stew. It smelled wonderful. Suddenly, Beryl felt ravenous.

"I made lentil stew with fresh vegetables from Ava's garden."

Beryl smiled politely and took a bite. "Thank you," she said, "It's delicious."

As the stew warmed her inside and the fire warmed her outside, she relaxed a little.

"I'd like to hear about your life and why you're here, if you care to talk about it, of course," she said, looking up from her bowl.

He smiled at her. He did have a nice smile.

"We'll have plenty of time to get acquainted," he said. "Tonight, I want you to eat and go straight to bed."

He poured himself a big glass of wine and took a long drink.

"In the morning, we'll begin our work, with or without Ava."

He seemed kind. Why had she felt so suspicious? She felt warm and sleepy as she watched the flames dance in the fireplace.

"Would you like some wine?" he asked. "It might help you sleep."

"No, thank you."

Solomon drained and refilled his cup. Beryl found it strange that Solomon drank so much alcohol. Her moms taught her that people on the spiritual path lived lives of moderation and rarely drank alcohol because it dulled the senses.

As if reading her thoughts, Solomon said, "I didn't indulge in the fruit of the vine for many years, but I find that it does not affect me."

"Oh," said Beryl and kept eating. After she finished every drop of stew, she washed her bowl and put it away. "Well, good night. Thanks for dinner."

"Good night, dear, sweet dreams," said Solomon. He sat by the fire, put his feet on the bench, and poured himself another glass of wine. As Beryl went into Ava's room, she noticed a keyhole on the outside of the door, but no key. She pushed the door shut. She turned the key very slowly in the lock. It locked with a soft click. Still, she decided to sleep in her clothes.

The rattling sound at the window startled her as she took off her slippers. She held on tight to the one slipper still in her hand, expecting to see—what? Solomon? But then she smiled and opened the window.

"Midnight!" She picked him up off the ledge and hugged him. "I'm glad to see you."

The big black cat rubbed his head against her cheek, put his paw across her arm, and purred. Beryl crawled into bed. Midnight curled up between her arm and chest, his head on her shoulder. Surrounded by Ava's sweet smell, with Midnight purring at her side, Beryl fell asleep.

25

The Temple City, the day after Beryl arrived at Ava's house

> *Once upon a time, there was an old goat. She had seven little kids and loved them all, just as a mother loves her children. One day she wanted to go into the woods to get some food. So she called all seven to her and said, "Children dear, I am going into the woods. Be on your guard for the wolf. If he gets in, he will eat up all of you, even your skin and hair. The villain often disguises himself, but you will recognize him at once by his rough voice and his black feet."*
>
> *From Jocasta's Guide to Fairy Tales*

After sitting alone in his cell for many days and nights, wondering what had become of Ava and how Andrew fared, Tobias had lost track of the time. He felt surprised and suspicious when the guards brought him to Dr. Hami's bedroom.

Dr. Hami held his hand out to Tobias. Tobias took a deep breath, tamping down his revulsion at the thought of touching him, and grasped it. Dr. Hami's hand felt cold and clammy, like his smile. "So good of you to come," said Dr. Hami. Tobias laughed. They both knew he hadn't had a choice. He didn't trust himself to speak.

"I had your friend Ava released," Dr. Hami lied. "It was just a simple misunderstanding. She didn't intend to break the law. I asked her to leave the Temple City, however, for her own safety. A lot has happened since you've been, um, out of communication."

"Like what?" asked Tobias.

"Do you know Solomon, the council representative from Vertumnus?"

Tobias nodded yes.

"Solomon tried to kill your friend Randall," Dr. Hami said with a smile that made Tobias' stomach turn. "Instead, he killed Queen Lillia's servant and tried to make it look like Randall did it. Randall is in great danger as many believe Solomon's story. Also, I heard that Solomon captured Ava and is keeping her prisoner in her own house."

"Why are you telling me this?"

"Let's just say that I'm a lover of justice, and I want to see these wrongs righted." The smirk never left Dr. Hami's face.

"Yes, but why tell *me*?" Tobias repeated.

"I thought you'd be interested."

"A guard told me that the queen's man was killed using magic."

"Not exactly." Dr. Hami pulled his beard.

Tobias knew that Dr. Hami wanted to manipulate him, and it seemed to work. Ava and Randall, two of the people he cared most about, seemed to be in danger. But he didn't trust Dr. Hami.

"You're a trustworthy man," Dr. Hami continued. "I'll tell you how Solomon did it, but you must promise to tell no one else." Without waiting for a response, Dr. Hami bent his head closer to Tobias and whispered, "He used a weapon from the old world called a gun. It propels small pieces of metal at very high speed, so fast that it can cut through flesh and bone and anything else in its path."

"I've heard there were terrible weapons in the old world. But how would Solomon get one?" asked Tobias.

"That is a very good question and one which I cannot answer. But he showed it to me. I imagine he's hidden it somewhere in the healer's house. If someone found it, they could use it to help those wrongfully detained, don't you think?"

Tobias wasn't sure what to think, and he certainly wasn't going to share any of his thoughts with Dr. Hami. All he said was, "Thanks for telling me."

"You're free to go," said the doctor.

Tobias spent the night at home. The next morning, he and Andrew left for Ava's house. He only wanted to, he told Andrew, check in on Ava, but Andrew knew better.

26

Ava's house, the morning after Beryl's arrival

Beryl ran as fast as she could to escape the man trying to kill her. She tried to get to the public square, hoping she could lose herself among the crowd. She kept running through alleys, into the front door of someone's house, and out the back. She saw no other people, only the man with the knife. He kept getting closer. She heard his raspy breathing, and it tickled the hairs on the back of her neck. She ran into a garden with a high wall around it. There was no way out. The man laughed as he drew near, knife raised to stab her.

She awoke, heart pounding, to find the sun shining. Midnight had left, but a little white cat sat on the windowsill, staring at her with big topaz eyes. Beryl recognized Crystal, Ava's cat. Crystal disappeared as Beryl felt someone else watching her. Solomon smiled at her from the foot of the bed.

"That must have been quite a dream," he laughed.

She had locked the door. How had he gotten in?

"Time to wake up, Beryl; we have a busy day ahead." He walked to the head of the bed. His breath smelled like old wine mixed with half-digested food. Beryl felt ill and confused. And afraid. She needed to stay calm and observe. She reminded herself to breathe. In and out, slowly. But it was difficult to think or breathe with Solomon's warm, sour breath so close and his reddish chest hair puffing out of his shirt and tickling her shoulder.

"Ava will be wanting her breakfast—she had no supper last night."

"I didn't hear her come in. Where did she sleep? Where is she?"

"So many questions first thing in the morning," Solomon said. He continued in a falsetto, "Where is the great and mighty Ava who will teach me so I can be a watcher like my Mommies or a witcher like Ava, or maybe I will be Queen one day. Wouldn't I look fancy in those queen dresses?"

"Well," continued Solomon in his own voice, "Ava is my prisoner— and so are you, dear. I suggest you do as I say and stop asking so many questions."

Could this be true? She must see Ava. Beryl held the covers up to her neck even though she was fully dressed.

Solomon smiled again. "You needn't worry about your virtue. I'm not interested in children. Besides, my beloved will arrive shortly. Now be a good girl and bring Ava her breakfast. It wouldn't do to have the old bat starve, at least not yet."

"Please, can you give me a moment? I'll do whatever you ask. I just need a moment." Beryl didn't know what she was saying. Her head spun, and she couldn't feel her legs. She wasn't sure she could stand and didn't want to collapse at Solomon's feet. What had happened to the Queen's guards who supposedly were guarding Ava? Had Ava really been here last night without Beryl knowing it?

"Don't take long," said Solomon. "I don't like cold eggs." He walked out, leaving the door open.

Beryl pressed her treasure pouch against her chest so she could feel the hard edges of the star crystal the queen had given her. She silently asked her moms and the king and queen for help and asked the goddess for guidance. She took a few slow, deep breaths and swung her legs over the edge of the bed. In a minute, she felt strong enough to stand and went out to face Solomon.

Oddly enough, Solomon had prepared a delicious breakfast--eggs seasoned with fresh dill and basil, sprinkled with goat cheese, and strong coffee with milk. He apparently didn't intend to starve anyone into submission. Solomon divided the food and placed it onto three plates. He put two of them on the table and put one by the fire to keep warm.

"Eat," he said. "You'll need your strength."

He ate with gusto.

I guess the food isn't poisoned, thought Beryl as she gingerly put a small bite in her mouth.

"Eat up, girl," he said. "We have a lot to do. I need you strong."

Beryl knew she should eat. She tried another bite. It tasted delicious. He put sugar and more cream into her coffee, although he drank his black. She'd never tasted coffee before. It tasted bitter, sweet, and creamy, very pleasant. It seemed odd to be enjoying food under the circumstances, but she didn't know what would come next, so she figured she might as well enjoy this moment.

"I like it so strong a spoon will stand up in it." Solomon gulped the steaming coffee. "This stuff'll put hair on your chest."

Beryl felt bewildered. How could he joke so casually? Maybe he had been joking about Ava and her being prisoners. She felt like crying and wished she could hide under the table. But Beryl didn't want Solomon to know how shaken she felt. She forced herself to look directly into his beady grey eyes. He winked. Then she got angry. How dare he act so smug? If he wanted something from her, she wouldn't make it easy for him to get it. She could use her anger to help her focus. She wished she had trusted her intuition and left yesterday. On the other hand, if Ava needed her help, it was good that Beryl was here. But where was Ava?

Again, as though he could read her thoughts, Solomon said, "Ava is locked in the cellar. So is her cat. I hope that scrawny cat of hers is a good mouser so she doesn't have too many mice for company. Let's bring the old bat some breakfast, shall we? I don't want you alone with her, but I don't suppose you'll believe she's here unless you see her. I wonder if the seriousness of your situation has begun to dawn on you."

"What do you want from me?" demanded Beryl.

"I don't want anything. Let's go."

Solomon picked up Ava's plate of food and pulled a key ring from his pocket. "The keys to the kingdom," he joked. Beryl noticed he found himself very clever. "Let's see, which one opens the basement door? This one, I know, is for the bedroom," he said, holding a key identical to the one she had in her pocket. "I will take its twin, now, if you please." He put the plate down and held out his hand expectantly. Beryl stared at him, not wanting to give him the key. He grabbed her wrist and twisted her arm, forcing her to kneel. "Perhaps you didn't hear me. I want the key. I can't believe I didn't notice it before you arrived. I thought I had prepared everything so nicely."

She reached into her pocket and handed him the key. "Here," she said angrily. "Now, let me go."

"Yes, of course, dear." Solomon pushed her as he let go, knocking Beryl to the floor, smiling all the while. "Do as I tell you, and we'll get along fine. Just remember, I always get my way."

He put the key into his pocket and picked up the plate. "Now, where was I? Ah, yes. I believe this is the key." He selected a big rusty metal key. He walked out the front door and around to the side of the house. On the ground by the outside wall was a flat double door with metal handles in the middle of each door. Below was Ava's herb cellar. Beryl had visited there many times, watching Ava work when she was little and, when she got older, helping her prepare the herbs they had collected. Now, she saw a padlocked chain wrapped snugly around the handles. Solomon handed Beryl the plate, unlocked the padlock, and threw the chain on the ground. He pounded on one of the doors.

"Ava," he yelled, with a snort, "I hope you're decent. Ready or not, here we come."

He flung back the right-hand door. It was dark inside. "After you, my dear," he said to Beryl. She walked carefully down the steps, holding onto the railing with one hand and balancing the plate with the other. Four narrow windows high on the wall let in a little early morning light. Drying herbs hung from the ceiling; shelves covered with jars containing medicines lined two walls, and a pile of big wooden boxes sat on the floor. It smelled like the woods in fall. In the middle of the room sat Ava, tied to a wooden chair and gagged.

"Good morning, old girl," said Solomon. "I trust you rested well. I brought you some breakfast." He removed the gag.

"Go ahead and feed her," he told Beryl. "Bon appétit."

Beryl didn't move. Ava didn't look hurt, but she looked angry.

"Give her some food before I get tired of standing in the dark," said Solomon. Beryl gave Ava a forkful of eggs.

"Don't you girls have anything to say to each other?"

"Beryl, I'm so sorry. Despite how it looks, I'm fine. Don't worry about me. Take care of yourself. And please look after my cat, Crystal."

"All right, enough blabbing. Eat up; it's time to move on."

Ava ate a little, with Beryl's help. Then Beryl watched Solomon tie the cloth around Ava's mouth. While he did, Ava looked directly into her eyes and nodded. She was alright.

"Please don't put that on her," said Beryl. "Even if she yelled, no one would hear her but us."

"True, there isn't anyone else around, for now. Still, better safe than sorry." He smirked and tightened the cloth. "Take the plate and follow me."

Beryl kissed Ava's cheek. She would find a way to get them both out of this. Solomon wasn't as clever as he thought. He was too full of himself and wine. Beryl needed to stay calm and pay attention. She must be ready to act quickly when the time was right.

As Solomon walked up the steps, he reminded Beryl not to do anything stupid like trying to escape. If she did, Ava would pay the price.

"Now what?" Beryl asked after they washed and put away the dishes.

"I thought we'd work in the garden," he said. "I want to gather some herbs and vegetables. My lady love will arrive tonight, and I want to prepare a feast for her. While we work, I will share some wisdom with you. I know a lot about the plant world. Even though you are my prisoner, there's no reason why a bright young lady like yourself shouldn't learn something. Besides, it will help me prepare the course on nature spirits I will be teaching next spring."

"They will never..." She was going to say that they would never let him teach after this, but it occurred to her that he didn't intend for anyone to find out what he'd done, which could only mean that he planned to kill Ava and her. "I mean, I could help you —to cook. I'm a good cook."

Beryl found comfort in spending time in Ava's garden. The echinacea flowered pink, purple, and white, and tomatoes, eggplants, and peppers looked like a vegetable rainbow ready for harvesting. The smell of lavender and mint wafted from the herb garden. Solomon lectured her about the medicinal properties of garden plants. He definitely enjoyed the sound of his own voice. Perhaps he intends to talk me to death, she considered. She wondered if he was this boring in the classroom. He clearly had no connection with the plant spirits.

Crystal the cat wandered into the garden. She lay down next to Beryl, who twirled a twig of oregano between her fingers, pretending to listen to Solomon and hoping there wouldn't be a test. She absently stroked Crystal's ears. Crystal turned her head so Beryl could scratch her chin. Beryl felt something hard there. Crystal purred.

Solomon looked at Beryl and the cat. "Don't care much for livestock, myself."

Beryl nodded as Solomon went back to talking about the healing properties of sage. Beryl felt a string tied around Crystal's neck, attached to the hard thing. She loosened the string, looking at Solomon and pretending to listen. She pulled it into her hand as she kept petting Crystal. It felt like a tight roll of paper. She put it in her pocket, pretending to smooth her skirt.

"Well," said Solomon, after talking non-stop for what seemed like several hours, during which time they picked a small basketful of vegetables, herbs, and berries, "this work certainly gives one an appetite. Let's warm up last night's leftovers. That and a cool glass of ale will be just the thing after a hard morning's work.

They ate lunch, ending with a long belch from Solomon. He scratched his chest. "I could use a little postprandial snooze. Off to your room, young lady, and stay out of trouble."

Beryl walked into Ava's bedroom. She was anxious to see what she had retrieved from Crystal. Her head swam; she longed to rest but needed to use this time away from Solomon wisely.

She heard the lock catch and heard Solomon try the knob. She didn't know how long she had but judging from his condition yesterday and also from the two large glasses of ale he drank with lunch, she might have a couple of hours. She sat on the bed, waited a couple of minutes to make sure Solomon wouldn't come back, then retrieved what did turn out to be a little scroll tied tightly with a bit of white thread. Beryl snipped the thread with her hummingbird scissors.

She read it. "Get him to lock you in the basement."

It was Ava's writing. Beryl turned it over, but that was all it said. How did Ava write this with her hands tied? How did Crystal get in and out of the cellar? For that matter, how did Ava know Beryl would find the note? Beryl ripped the paper into tiny shreds and threw the pieces out the window. They fluttered like snowflakes to the ground, disappearing in the long grass.

Beryl wrapped the rainbow scarf that Ava had given her around her waist. It wrapped around twice and was so lightweight that she didn't think it made her look noticeably bigger. She felt better with it next to her skin. Besides, she didn't want Solomon taking it for his "Lady Love." Her other gifts remained hidden in her pouch. Beryl felt satisfied that her precious things were as safe as she could make them. They were all she had left of her home and family. She wondered if she would ever see them again. She took out the stick Jyrym had given her and held it flat in her hand. Her arm tingled, and then the stick spun around. When it stopped, the pointed end pointed at her. She sighed. "I knew it," she said to herself, "I need to look inside." She put the stick away. Then she put her pack in front of the door and threw some clothes on the floor, hoping the mess would slow Solomon down when he came in.

She pulled out her crystal. It grew warm in her hand, and she felt calm settle over her. She didn't like meditating with Solomon so close but knew she would hear the key turn and have a moment to stash the crystal and compose herself if needed while he dealt with her mess. Her heartbeat slowed, and her breathing eased. If he came in, she would pretend she was asleep. Something jumped onto her lap, although she hadn't heard a sound. It was Crystal. She heard a thud and saw Midnight, too. Both cats settled on her lap. She rested her hands on their backs, holding the crystal between them, glad for their company. Both cats started purring. She quickly entered a meditative state. She asked her angel to help her, to tell her what she needed to know. Images started flashing through her mind. Her angel must be in a hurry, she thought. First, she saw Eugene lying in bed, his wife by his side. She saw him smiling and talking! She wondered if it were true and wanted to see more, but her vision moved on.

She found herself in another room with one large window that let in a dim light. Many people, including Solomon, sat around a table covered with colors, stars, planets, and other things. This must be the Council meeting room. She tried to listen, but she couldn't get close enough to hear everything. She heard them saying something about Queen Lillia asking for a replacement. That scene also faded away until only Solomon remained. Now she saw him with a girl not much older than Beryl. He held her close and kissed her sloppily. It was revolting, and Beryl almost lost her concentration, but she felt the comforting weight of the cats on her lap and the warm stone in her hand. She took a deep breath. The scene faded away, but Solomon remained, now much younger. He sat by the bed of a girl who looked like she was nine or ten years old. A pale, beautiful woman with long dark straight hair came in. She put her hand on Solomon's shoulder and asked, "How is she doing?"

"I believe she is getting better, Mother."

"I wish you would let me call the healer," the woman said.

The girl looked extremely pale, with the same dark straight hair as the woman, her forehead moist and her breathing shallow.

"Trust me, my dear. I will take care of her. The higher beings will guide me."

As the scene faded away, she heard the woman's cries of anguish and saw a sheet pulled over the face of the dead child.

Then she found herself in a cold place where darkness swirled around her. She felt alone and vulnerable. "Is this what lives inside me?"

"No, but like all humans, you carry darkness and light."

"Then where am I?" she asked her angel.

The reply echoed in her heart. "This is how the world feels for lost souls like Solomon. They see the physical world but not what stands behind it. It is a lonely and frightening place."

"May I leave this place now?" Beryl asked.

She heard a clicking sound. It took her a moment to realize that it was the key turning in the lock. She jerked herself back from her meditation and put the crystal away. Both cats jumped off her lap and hopped out the window.

"Well, it looks like you had a little rest, yourself," said Solomon, moving her bag and kicking her clothes out of his way.

Beryl rubbed her eyes, took a deep breath, and said nothing.

She helped Solomon prepare dinner. The fresh vegetables and herbs from Ava's garden smelled good and felt full of life. As she chopped, Beryl wondered about her meditation. She could feel darkness swirling around Solomon. It made her sad. And it made her angry that she and Ava had to experience the fruits of his darkness. At some point, she thought, he must have made a choice, probably not a conscious one, to go down the dark path.

This led her to a startling realization--she hadn't chosen the darkness, at least not yet, although she had that possibility in her just like Solomon. What she had thought was her own darkness was something else, but she wasn't sure what, and this wasn't the moment to figure it out.

"Solomon, do you have any children?" Beryl had worked up the courage to ask. She thought she remembered him saying something about a child that day she met him in the castle library.

After an uncustomary silence, Solomon replied, "That is a subject you will never mention again. Do you know how to make bread?"

When she told him she did, he instructed her to make a dozen loaves. Good thing she had spent time helping in the castle kitchen. She never made that much bread at home.

They prepared the rest of the meal in silence. She wanted to ask why they were making such a large quantity of food. Was his Lady Love a giant? But she held her tongue. She had never made so much bread at once by herself, and it required all her concentration and arm muscles.

As the sun set, Beryl heard people approaching Ava's cabin. They made a lot of noise. Solomon didn't notice. He kept cooking and drinking wine. The first half of the bread baking filled the house with a lovely smell.

"Have to keep the chef lubricated." He winked at Beryl and drained his glass, his narrow eyes bloodshot.

Soon Beryl saw a man and woman. The man led two horses. They came to Ava's door and entered without knocking. She felt pretty sure that the girl was the one she had seen Solomon kissing in her meditation. As Beryl looked out the door, she saw a string of dirty, raggedy men—maybe seven or eight of them—following the pair.

"Hello, Zorina, my dear." Solomon wiped his hands on his pants and walked over, a little unsteadily. He embraced her, kissing her the same way Beryl had seen earlier. Beryl looked away. When he finished, he continued, "Lambert, leave the horses in the shed."

"My name is Lucas," said the man. Solomon paid no attention to his reply, gesturing in no particular direction toward a shed that didn't exist.

Beryl would have liked to look at Lucas longer, however. He was handsome, tall with dark skin and thick black hair that cast a shadow over one of his big brown eyes.

"You men set up camp over here," said Lucas. "You're not staying in the house this time, but supper should be ready soon." Beryl watched the men walk toward the clearing by the stream until Solomon closed the door and told her to finish making dinner for him and his Lady Love.

When Lucas left, Solomon gave Zorina another big hug and kiss. Beryl thought Zorina recoiled, just a bit, from his touch.

"How kind of you to come, dear one," Solomon said, caressing her cheek. "I've missed you."

"And I you," said Zorina. She looked outside toward Lucas.

Beryl went back to cooking but kept glancing at Zorina. She was definitely the girl Beryl saw in her meditation, but she looked even younger in real life.

"Who is that?" asked Zorina, pointing at Beryl.

"Forgive my rudeness, dear one. This is Beryl. And Beryl, this is my dearest love, Zorina. Dinner will be ready shortly, my dear. Why don't you sit down and rest. You must be weary from your long journey."

"I am," pouted Zorina. She talked like a little girl who wants to wheedle something out of her father. "Where is Lucas with my bag?" she wondered, staring at the door.

Solomon put his arm around her and led her to the couch. "Come, rest with me for a few minutes. I'm sure Larry will be right back with your luggage." He pulled her onto the couch. Zorina kept glancing toward the door as Solomon stroked her hair. The whole thing made Beryl nauseous.

"Lucas, thank you," said Zorina, sitting up straight, out of Solomon's grasp, as Lucas brought in her bag. Beryl didn't recall seeing him in any of her visions. She noticed his long, curled his eyelashes. She felt electricity between Lucas and Zorina when her hand brushed his as he handed her the bag. This should be interesting, Beryl thought.

After Beryl served dinner, Solomon gave her a plate of food and sent her to her room. She listened while Solomon locked the door and tested the handle. Beryl had experience listening at keyholes from her childhood, when her parents sent her to her room so they could have adult conversations. She kneeled by the keyhole, leaning her forehead against the cold knob. She couldn't hear everything but surmised that Solomon intended to have Zorina replace Lillia as queen of Xantalon.

She heard Solomon explain to Lucas that he and Zorina had a karmic love connection, which was why he left his second wife for her. He waited until Zorina completed her training, however, as it would be improper for him to have a romantic relationship with his student. Solomon, once again, did most of the talking. His was the only voice Beryl could hear clearly through the keyhole. And it grew louder as the evening progressed. Beryl occasionally heard Lucas or Zorina offer him more wine.

Late in the evening, Solomon suggested that it was time for bed. He apologized to Zorina that the accommodations were not fitting for the new queen. But when he offered to share his bed with Zorina, she flatly refused. She told Solomon that it wasn't proper for a queen to sleep with a married man. Her voice grew shrill. She would have her own bed. She wanted Ava's room. She didn't care what Solomon did with the girl. Zorina didn't understand why he treated Beryl so nicely when they would just have to get rid of her eventually.

"Put her in the basement with the old witch," Zorina demanded. "You can take care of them both in the morning."

Beryl held her breath. She hadn't figured out how to get herself locked in the basement. It seemed almost as if Zorina wanted to help-- except for the getting rid of them in the morning part.

In a few minutes, she heard the key turn in the lock and watched the door open. Solomon took a few steps, unsteady on his feet, his cheeks and nose looked red and veiny, and she couldn't tell if his eyes were open.

He grabbed her roughly by the arm. "Come on. Now."

She didn't see Zorina or Lucas and wondered where they had gone. Solomon pulled her out of the house and around to the cellar. He pulled out the keys and dropped them on the ground. He pawed through them, unable to find the right one, even though it was much larger than the rest.

He handed her the keys, his face close to hers. His breath reeked. "Open it. And no funny business. You're lucky I'm here to protect you. They want to kill you. Hurry."

Beryl could have escaped if Ava hadn't been imprisoned below. Solomon was strong, but she was quicker and knew the woods better. She hoped Ava had a plan. Beryl's hands shook as she fumbled with the keys.

"Hurry." Solomon grabbed her arm so tightly that it hurt. She used both hands to open the lock, especially difficult with Solomon holding her arm. When she opened the padlock, he grabbed it, with the keys still in it, and hung it over the top of his pants. He pulled off the chain. Then, still holding her arm tightly, he threw the chain onto the ground. He flung the door open with a bang, turned Beryl to face him and pushed. Beryl knocked her head on the top of the door and fell backwards down the stairs.

27

The same day, continued

> *Every day the poor girl had to sit by a well next to the high-way and spin so much that her fingers bled. Now it happened that one day the reel was completely bloody, so she dipped it in the well to wash it off, but it dropped out of her hand and fell in. She cried, ran to her stepmother, and told her of the mishap. She scolded her so sharply and was so merciless that she said, "Since you have let the reel fall in, you must fetch it out again."*
>
> *Then the girl returned to the well and did not know what to do. Terrified, she jumped into the well to get the reel. She lost her senses. And when she awoke and came to herself again, she was in a beautiful meadow where the sun was shining, and there were many thousands of flowers. She walked across this meadow and came to an oven full of bread. The bread called out, "Oh, take me out. Take me out, or I'll burn. I've been thoroughly baked for a long time." So she stepped up to it and, with a baker's peel, took everything out, one loaf after the other.*
>
> *From "Mother Holle" in* Jocasta's Guide to Fairy Tales

Beryl lay on the ground, stunned. She'd landed on her back, one arm pinned beneath her. The door slammed, and she heard Solomon swearing as he looked for the chain. What kind of initiate was he? He didn't know the simplest magic, like creating a light. At any rate, he found the chain. She heard it slam against the door, then heard him howl with pain. He swore again and started looking for the padlock.

Beryl gingerly rubbed her head with her free hand. She felt something warm and wet. The back of her head really hurt. She moved her hand further back and felt a lump. She decided to wait another minute before trying to move her pinned arm, although it was starting to hurt, too. Her legs seemed alright. Solomon kept stomping and swearing above her. She heard another man's voice. It must be Lucas. He was yelling, too, telling Solomon to shut up, telling him that Zorina said he could stay outside and guard the cellar. She didn't want him near her right now. Then Lucas pointed out the padlock hanging from Solomon's pants and started laughing. Beryl heard the padlock hit the wooden door and the click of it locking. Solomon yelled a little longer. He had some choicer names for Zorina than "Lady Love," it seemed. She didn't appreciate all he'd done for her. She'd be nothing if he didn't help her. She was nothing until he molded her. Would he never stop? Beryl's head pounded almost as loudly as Solomon's yelling. She longed for silence. Suddenly, he stopped talking and started crying. He lay down on the door, whimpering. A few minutes later, she heard him snoring.

Beryl tried moving her limbs one at a time. She couldn't move her left arm, which was still underneath her. It really hurt. Her other arm felt fine. Her back and legs felt bruised but didn't seem to have anything seriously wrong with them. Her head throbbed, and her neck hurt.

Ava's quiet voice by her head startled her. "An arm isn't meant to bend like that. Beryl, can you hear me?"

"Ava," Beryl's voice sounded hoarse. "How did you...? I thought you were.... I'm so glad to see you." Beryl started crying. Once she started, she couldn't stop. Every time she sobbed, her arm and head hurt intensely. Ava held Beryl's uninjured hand and spoke soothingly. Hearing Ava's voice made her feel better. Eventually, her sobs subsided, and she lay quietly on the floor. Ava helped her to turn on her side. She felt Beryl's arm. "It's broken."

Ava laid the broken arm on Beryl's chest. The pain burned so intensely that Beryl saw bright lights exploding inside her eyes.

Ava gathered herbs and bandages. "Rest as best you can, Beryl. Don't try to speak. I untied myself with a little magic." Ava gave Beryl a flower essence to keep her from going into shock and took some herself. Beryl's head felt clearer after she swallowed the drops, although the pain kept getting worse. Ava covered Beryl with a blanket, slipping it gently under her injured arm. "Good thing we're in my medicine room. Normally I'd give you something to help you relax while I set your arm, but I need you alert. We have a long journey ahead of us tonight. While I work on your arm, I'll tell you what I know. This ointment will ease the pain. It will still hurt, though, when I set the bone."

Beryl had many questions but didn't speak. Ava must know some way to get out of this basement, or she wouldn't have asked Beryl to get herself here.

"Any other injuries?" asked Ava, "Besides the bump on your head, which I can see even in the dark."

"Just a few bruises, as far as I can tell. Mostly my arm and head hurt."

Ava gave her another sip of the flower essences. Ava rubbed some sweet, medicinal-smelling herbs on her arm. It hurt intensely when Ava touched it, but Beryl forced herself to lay still. The ointment eased the pain a little. Ava placed her hands on Beryl's arm. "I'm so sorry, Beryl, but this will hurt. Take a deep breath and hold it. Turn your head away." Beryl did.

"Here it comes," said Ava. She grabbed Beryl's forearm just above her wrist and just below her elbow and twisted. Searing white pain shot through Beryl, and she felt a sickening sensation of bone moving against bone. She watched Ava expertly put a splint on her arm. Then Ava wrapped the splint and arm with bandages dipped in plaster. As the bandage hardened, the pain eased a little. Ava gave her some herbs. They tasted horrible, but Ava assured her they would ease the pain without making her sleepy. Ava cleaned the blood off Beryl's head, rubbed something on the bump that made it feel numb, and tied on a cotton bandage.

"Rest for a few minutes while I get us ready to leave," said Ava. "Your job is to listen for anyone coming. Why don't you try to sit up? You can lean against this crate." Ava pushed a big wooden box next to Beryl and helped her sit up.

Ava made a sling for Beryl's arm out of the rainbow scarf, which she untied from Beryl's waist. "It would be better if you could rest, but that will have to wait. We must leave as soon as possible."

Ava began moving more boxes. Beryl wanted to help but knew she couldn't. Just sitting up was hard enough. She made herself stay alert and listen. All was quiet outside. With the sound of boxes scraping across the floor, she couldn't hear Solomon snoring. She didn't know if she would hear him if he moved either while Ava made all that noise. She scooted over to the stairs, so she could hear better and watched Ava work. Crates had been piled three high and stacked three or four deep against the inside wall. Ava moved them one at a time, dragging and pushing them under the window. Beryl wondered if Ava planned to climb out the window. The windows looked too small for either of them to fit through. Then she saw that Ava had uncovered a door with a rope handle in the floor. She had never seen that before.

"Is everything quiet?" Ava asked.

"Just snoring," Beryl replied. She could hear Solomon again now that Ava had finished moving boxes around.

Ava pulled on the rope handle, opening the trap door. Beryl felt a rush of cold air as the door swung open. "I wish I could put the boxes back over this door after we leave, but my magic isn't strong enough to do that. I think I can remove the ladder when we get down, though." Beryl wondered how they would get out again if they took down the ladder, but her head hurt too much to ask questions.

"I thought this was a well when I first saw it," Ava continued, "but it was dry when I moved in here. We built my house over it. I later learned that it's a portal of sorts. Hopefully, we'll have enough of a head start that they won't catch up with us. This is an old rope ladder, and it has been many years since anyone used it, but it seems strong. I'll go first, and you come behind me. I know this will be hard with only one arm. But we must get out of here."

Ava knelt by the hole and examined the ladder. When Beryl stood up, she felt nauseous and light-headed. She tried to hold herself up by grabbing a beam on the stairwell, but her hand slipped off as she touched something wet that smelled like iron—her own blood from where she'd hit her head, she realized. Holding onto the wall, she walked slowly toward Ava and sat down next to her, carefully hanging her feet into the opening. The rope ladder was tied onto two large hooks embedded in the bricks that lined the well. The hooks looked sturdy, the rope intact if a bit slimy, at least at the top, which was all that she could see. Beyond that, all she could only see darkness.

Ava tapped the cast, which sounded hollow. "It's hardened. Let's go. We'll drop our shoes down first," said Ava. "It will be easier to find the rope with bare feet." Ava pulled off Beryl's boots and dropped them into the hole. It took a long time until Beryl heard their soft thunk when they hit the ground. Ava dropped her shoes down.

Ava pushed the rope handle on the door through to the bottom side. "They will find it, but it will be harder to see and to open like this." She started climbing. She hadn't gone far when she told Beryl to join her. "You'll have to close the door behind you." Beryl took her arm out of the sling. She was afraid to use her broken arm, but she had no choice. She hooked it around the top rung of the ladder, wondering if she could do this. She reached up with her good arm and pulled the door over so it rested on her forehead. It would close as she descended. The door was heavy and hurt when it touched the bump on her head, but it would close soon, and she tried to let it rest on the front of her head.

"I'm right behind you," said Ava. "Take your time. As soon as you close that door, I'll call for some light. It's completely dark in here."

Beryl held on with her good hand and unhooked the broken arm. She wrapped the injured arm around the side of the rope ladder, using it to steady herself without putting too much weight on it. She hoped she wouldn't fall and knock Ava down. She wondered what they would do when they got to the bottom of the well. Being stuck at the bottom of a well didn't seem all that much better than being trapped in the cellar, but she trusted Ava, so she kept going. She could ask Ava questions later. As she stepped onto the eighth rung, the door closed. What a relief! Then a soft glow surrounded them. Beryl didn't want to look down but was grateful to be able to see the ladder right in front of her. Even though the rope felt a little slimy, it was rough enough to get a good grip, and it got dryer as they went down. Beryl was sweating and breathing heavily from the exertion of climbing with one arm and the pain of her injuries, even though the inside of the well felt cool and a gentle breeze blew from below.

As they kept climbing down, Beryl wondered if they would go to the center of the earth. She remembered trying to dig through to the other side of the world when she was little. She had wondered if people walked upside down on the other side of the world. She also wondered if her parents would discover what had happened to her but couldn't imagine how they could. She hoped they were safe and well. Her head began throbbing even more. Her arm, too. Still, they went down.

"We're almost there," Ava called her back from her reverie. After five more steps, she said, "I've reached the bottom. The ground is soft and mossy."

Then Beryl reached the bottom. She sat on the damp moss and looked around. They were still in the well, but she saw a tunnel on one side. She looked up. The well went very far up, with mossy red bricks scaling up into the dark, but she couldn't see the top. This spot where she sat felt soft and cozy. She wanted to go to sleep.

"You are a strong, valiant girl, Beryl. You must be exhausted. But before you get too comfortable, move a little. I want to see if I can convince the ladder to come down. That will make it harder for anyone to follow us"

Beryl dragged herself a short distance away. She sat down again and rested her head on her knees.

"A little further, Beryl. If that ladder does come down, I don't want it falling on you."

Wearily, Beryl stood up. She moved into the opening of the tunnel. She crouched as she entered the tunnel and then gasped. At the end of the tunnel, she saw a forest. It looked and felt different from anything she'd seen before. She leaned against the arch that led into this new world and slid down to the ground, staring with her mouth open.

She heard a loud thud behind her. "Yes!" came Ava's triumphant voice. "Now, let's be on our way. Here are your shoes."

*

Tobias and Andrew had a hard time finding Ava's cabin in the dark. When they finally did, it was the middle of the night. Several men slept outside the house next to a dying fire. Father and son skirted around them toward the house. Following the sound of loud snoring, they found a man sound asleep on a cellar door. They recognized him-- Solomon. The smell of wine wafted off him. They wondered if anyone was inside the house. Andrew, the taller of the two, peeked in the window. He recognized Zorina. She sat by the fire, laughing with a man he didn't recognize. Zorina touched the man's arm as she spoke.

"Hey, what's this? What are you doing here?" Andrew and Tobias both jumped.

"We're lost and looking for shelter. We saw lights in the house. Do you live here?" asked Andrew.

"Well, sort of. We work for the man who's snoring over there. And we sleep outside under the stars. My name is Fain. You're welcome to join us by the fire. There's a bit of food left if you're hungry. I'd stay away from the house, though, if I were you."

"Fain, thanks for your kindness. I didn't recognize you in the dark, but we know you from the city. I'm Tobias, and this is my son Andrew. We're friends of Ava's, the woman who lives in this house. Is Otto here, too?"

Otto was still asleep by the fire, Fain told them. And because Ava was a wanted criminal, she was locked in the cellar until she could be transported to the Temple City for trial. He told them about Solomon and how he had hired them to help with important Council business. Well, actually, that man inside the house, Lucas, hired them to work for Solomon. Lucas had promised them the reward for Ava's capture when they brought her to the City. Fain hadn't seen Ava; he and the others had been away gathering herbs and food and just returned this evening. Tobias seethed with anger when he heard that they held Ava prisoner in her own cellar but kept his feelings to himself. He knew Fain believed he was doing the right thing, and it would be better to be kind. Tobias and Andrew could use his help. Andrew and Tobias gratefully ate the food Fain brought them and listened to his stories. The boy felt frightened and confused—just trying to survive. Fain found them blankets, and they slept for the sliver of night that remained. At least they knew where Ava was. Maybe they could also discover what had happened to Randall when the new day dawned.

*

Ava gently placed Beryl's arm back in the sling. Then she rested her hand on Beryl's knee.

"Where are we?" Beryl asked.

"We have entered the realm of Brother Earth. We've gone through a portal into his realm of reality. I think you will understand better once you see it—and after you get some rest. I don't think Solomon will be able to follow us here, even if he does manage to get to the bottom of the well. Brother Earth will close the door to all whom he does not welcome. To Solomon, this would likely appear as swirling blackness, a vast wasteland, a dark and terrifying place."

Like in my meditation, thought Beryl.

"Brother Earth?" she asked.

"Yes, Mother Earth rules in our physical realm, but Brother Earth rules here."

Beryl was so taken aback that she couldn't even think of any questions.

"But you can see for yourself," said Ava as she stood up and smoothed her dress. "Here he comes."

Beryl struggled to her feet. Soon a green man, taller than any man she knew and surprisingly broad across the shoulders, stood in front of her. He wore a white toga that came to just above his knees and went over one shoulder, with a braided golden belt tied at his waist. His curly brown hair framed deep brown eyes that sparkled green. They reminded Beryl of the moss-covered bark of an old tree. The sweet green scent of the forest surrounded him.

"Ava," he said, his voice soft and deep but filled the world at the same time. "Welcome. It's been too long. I sense that your need is great and the journey that brought you here long. We will go to my home. It's not far." To Beryl, he said, "We will care for your wounds and let you rest. I'm glad you came. Are you able to walk, child?"

Beryl felt incredibly weary; her arm and head throbbed. But even though she never even imagined that a place like this existed, she felt safe. She wondered if he would pick her up and carry her if she said she couldn't walk. She definitely wasn't ready for that.

"I think I can make it," she said.

He assessed her with a scrutinizing eye. It made Beryl feel young and vulnerable.

"You are hurt and weary." He let out a soft whistle.

A cart appeared, pulled by two short green men with long white beards wearing pointy caps. They must be gnomes, thought Beryl, although they looked different from the gnomes in Xantalon.

"Have a seat, child," said Brother Earth. "You need hold yourself up no longer."

"Thank you," stuttered Beryl. The cart fit her perfectly. Like a wheelbarrow, it had two wheels and two handles, but it also had a bench. It was painted with bright red and yellow flowers on the outside and plain blue on the inside. The gnomes put down the handles, making a little ramp for her to walk up. When she sat down, they each took a handle and trotted after Brother Earth.

As she passed through the woods, Beryl's opened her eyes wide, trying to see everything. But somehow, she fell asleep, for the next thing she knew, she found herself in a rough wooden bed covered with crisp white sheets and a warm feather comforter. Her rainbow scarf lay on top of the comforter. The room had a dresser, a wash basin, and a chair next to the bed. The curtains were drawn, but light peeked around the edges, so she knew it was daytime. She tried to remember where she was. She definitely wasn't home. She tapped her arm and found the cast still there. That part hadn't been a dream. Then she must be in Brother Earth's house. She sat up, suddenly awake. Every part of her body hurt when she moved.

28

The next morning, in Brother Earth's Land

Early that morning, while Beryl slept, Ava put on the new clothes she found by her bed and went outside to find Brother Earth waiting for her.

"Shall we walk?" he asked. "It's a lovely morning."

Ava smiled. "It's always lovely here. Yes, I would love to walk with you, dear friend."

"How are you, Ava? You've been through a lot."

"These are strange and difficult times," Ava replied. "Our land is having growing pains. I hope we will come out stronger and more mature. Physically, I haven't really suffered. Beryl got pretty banged up, though. I'm hoping you'll let me take her to the healing bath."

"Of course. Ava, you know that as leader of the Council of All Beings, I have promised not to interfere in human affairs, but you are the only human member of the Council, and there are things you need to know to help our land to grow and heal. What I'm about to tell you will only confirm your intuitions, I'm sure."

"Thank you, Brother Earth. We humans can use all the help we can get right now.

"As you know, Dr. Hami came from Jocasta's world. He brought with him the worst of that world. You must forgive yourself for the past and deal with the present."

Ava sat down under a tree. She'd spent so long guarding her own secret that her knees felt weak when she realized Brother Earth knew. He joined her.

"I didn't think anyone knew about Hamilton's first visit except for Jenna. But of course, you know. Did Hamilton bring a gun this time?" she asked.

"Yes. There's something else you should know about him. His father was one of the founders of Floredelis. The father fell in love with Jocasta and followed her here. His name was also Hamilton. He left behind, in the old world, a young wife who carried his child, the Hamilton you know. The young Hamilton didn't believe Floredelis was real until Ontihaponati brought him here the first time, when you met him. He blames Floredelis for destroying his family and killing his mother. She never recovered from the elder Hamilton's desertion."

"Why haven't I heard of him, the father, that is?"

"I cannot tell you, for that is Beryl's secret to uncover. But I can tell you that Dr. Hami has covered Ontihaponati with layers of wool, making her unable to communicate."

"Oh, dear," said Ava. "That explains a lot."

"There is more, and it gets worse." Brother Earth put his large hand on Ava's shoulder. His strength flowed into her, and she received it with gratitude. "Dr. Hami can send messages through Ontihaponati. He has been planting seeds of doubt in some and greed in others. He is adept at finding weaknesses in his fellow humans to manipulate them."

"Is that why Lillia suddenly decided to retire?" Ava asked. But she already knew the answer. She felt as though a veil had been lifted. Had Dr. Hami manipulated her, too?

"Yes, but in some provinces, the rulers are more susceptible to greed, and Dr. Hami has begun awakening that desire in them. We believe he intends to take over Floredelis. He has torn out many of our beloved healing plants and has been heard saying he will break Ontihaponati into little pieces and sell them to the tourists who come from Jocasta's world."

"Brother Earth, I cannot believe this. How can I help?"

"First, you need to forgive yourself for what you did in the past. Continuing to blame yourself holds you back. Because of your relationship with Dr. Hami, the Council of All Beings requests that you make sure he returns to his world when the time is right. It will be dangerous, but you will have help. We will reopen the passage through which Jocasta entered, but we can only hold it open for a short time. You will have to work quickly lest you become trapped there."

"Brother Earth, I trust you and the Council. I will do as you ask. I would do anything to help this land. I will try my best to transform my relationship to the past. Do you know when we need to take him back?"

"Not exactly. Beryl holds the key. But she can know nothing about this conversation, for she must act out of her own free will. Your friend Tobias and his son will join us soon. They will help you with Dr. Hami. But you must trust yourself to know when the moment is right."

Ava leaned against Brother Earth's green chest. "I feel that we have kept too many secrets from Beryl, but I will trust you on this," she said.

He put his arm around her. She closed her eyes and focused on her breath, reminding herself that in this moment, everything was fine, and this moment is all there is.

After a few minutes, Ava smiled. "At least I'll see Tobias," she said. "Can we go back now? I'm starving. It's been a long time since I ate. I want to check on Beryl, too."

As they walked, Ava asked, "Will getting rid of Dr. Hami solve the problems in Floredelis? I think he's just picking up on issues that were already bubbling beneath the surface of our society."

"You're right, Ava. Our problems go back to the formation of human society in Floredelis. That which is present at the formation lives in the society until it is consciously changed. Jocasta was an extraordinary human being, but she was, as all humans are, shaped and limited by her past—which she never shared with anyone. Dr. Hami brings to the surface what was already here, but he must be stopped. He is doing his best to destroy Floredelis because of his own past. It will be hard to heal this land in any event, but even harder while he remains. Beryl could play a key role in this healing."

Ava started to ask about Beryl, but Brother Earth interrupted her, "I'm sorry Ava. I've already said too much. You humans have free will. I cannot tell you what Beryl could do if she chooses, for it might affect her choice."

Brother Earth's Home, Later that morning

Ava walked into Beryl's room feeling rested and relaxed. She wore a shimmering tunic of pink, orange, and gold, colors of the sunset, with Ava's face and silver hair glowing above it like the rising moon.

"Good morning, sunshine," said Ava. She pulled back the curtains, letting in the abundant light. The light here reminded Beryl of looking at the sun through a crystal. She put her hand to her throat. Her treasure pouch still hung there. It comforted her to have those things with her in this strange place. She missed her moms.

"How long did I sleep?"

"All night, and now it's almost noon. While you slept, I prepared a healing bath for you. This place holds much magic, and we'll use some of it to get you well. Can you walk?"

Beryl put her legs over the edge of the bed. Ava put slippers onto her feet.

"The stone floors are cold," she said.

She offered Beryl her hand. Beryl grasped it with her good arm and pulled herself up, letting Ava take some of her weight. Somehow, they had changed her clothes. She wore a plain white nightgown. Between being shoved down the stairs, the long climb, and the long sleep, Beryl could barely bend her knees. But she felt a little better as she moved, and as she looked around, she was too interested in her surroundings to pay much attention to her aches and pains.

The rounded walls felt smooth to her touch; this must be some kind of a tower, she thought. They went down two sets of spiral stairs that hugged the walls, the building becoming wider as they descended. Suddenly, it dawned on Beryl.

"Are we inside a tree?" she asked Ava.

"Yes, a very large tree. Wait until you see it from the outside. It's the best tree house ever, and the best is still coming." They went down another flight of stairs, going deep beneath the earth. The hallway walls, made of packed earth with tree roots winding through, left a narrow passageway with an uneven ceiling.

"Ouch." Beryl bumped her head on a root hanging from the ceiling. After that, Beryl bent down to avoid bumping her already sore head. Lights glowed on the walls of the dark hallway. Beryl couldn't tell what they were made of. The ceiling got lower as they went along. Beryl wondered if they would have to crawl soon and wondered how she could do that with one arm. She smelled water.

The passageway suddenly widened, and the ceiling became tall enough for Ava to stand up straight. In front of them, Beryl saw a wooden doorway, mostly closed, but a sliver of light shone through. Ava pushed the door open, and Beryl saw a large stone cavern filled with light. Stalactites made of many colors of crystals sparkled on the ceiling. The light, which came from above, danced through the crystals and made rainbows all over the room. Mosaics of sparkly stones in the shapes of plants and animals covered the floor. The unicorn mosaic in the center of the floor looked so beautiful and alive that tears sprang into Beryl's eyes.

Beryl slid off her slippers so she could feel the smooth stones beneath her feet. The ground felt warm. The bath had an irregular rounded shape, like a natural pool. Water poured in from a small waterfall that came through the outer wall. The water in the pool churned pleasantly, and she could see the bottom of the pool, also lined with mosaic stones, although through the swirling water, she only saw dancing colors. She wrinkled her nose as she smelled sulfur coming from the bath.

"There is a hot spring under this room. It keeps the floor warm and the water, too. Let's get you in there. Brother Earth has whispered to the waters and asked them to heal you. We'll take your cast off in a few minutes."

Ava pulled out a small knife. Beryl jumped a little at the sight of it.

Ava laughed. "Don't worry; I've removed many casts and haven't cut off a single limb yet. Now, let me help you out of this nightgown."

Ava frowned as she looked at Beryl. "You're a walking bruise. I'm glad I didn't know how banged up you were when we left the herb cellar. Well, get right in."

Beryl felt the water with her toes. The temperature seemed just right. Stairs went down into the water and led to a bench built into the pool wall. Ava held Beryl's uninjured hand as she walked down. Beryl sat on the bench, and the water came up to her shoulders. She held the cast up in the air, trying to keep it dry.

"You can put it in the water; it'll be easier to remove if it softens a little," said Ava.

Beryl put her arm down and let the water swirl around her. Her aches and pains swirled away. Could the water really be dissolving them?

"Let's see your arm, then," said Ava. The wet cast felt heavy as Beryl used her other arm to lift it out of the water. She rested it on the mosaic floor and looked away, watching the water flow from the waterfall. She trusted Ava but didn't want to watch. She felt the pressure of the knife cutting through the cast, and soon she felt cool air on her arm. "All done," said Ava.

Beryl's arm looked terrible—bruised yellow and purple and very pale in the parts that weren't bruised. It hurt to move it. Ava lowered it so it rested on the water. The pain began to ease. Still supporting Beryl's injured arm with one hand, Ava scooped up water with her other and poured it over Beryl's arm. Beryl watched the bruises fade. Ava removed her hand. Beryl let her arm sink into the water. She couldn't believe her arm could heal right before her eyes. She hoped this wasn't a dream that she would wake up from and find herself at the bottom of the stairs in Ava's herb cellar or even back at home, although she longed to see her parents.

Ava took off her slippers and pulled her gown up over her knees. She slid her feet into the water with a small sigh of pleasure. "You might want to go all the way under or pour some water on your head," suggested Ava. "That bump still looks pretty big, and so is the gash next to it."

"The key," said Ava so quietly that Beryl wasn't sure if she really heard it.

"What?" said Beryl.

Ava spoke softly, a dreamy look on her face. "You hold the key."

If she looked at Ava, she would either burst into tears, overflow with questions, or probably both, so Beryl pretended not to hear. At this moment, she knew she needed to relax and heal more than she needed to learn more about herself that she didn't want to know anyhow. She took a deep breath and lowered herself under the water. She watched the waterfall flow and swirl from underneath. She stayed under until she felt as though her lungs would burst. She wondered if she should try to breathe, like in her dream, but let herself float up to the surface instead. The air felt warm and delicious in her lungs. Maybe these healing waters would wash away the painful memories inside her. Maybe she could stay here forever. She closed her eyes and floated with her ears beneath the water, listening to the moving water and her heartbeat and the air going in and out of her lungs.

In a short time, all her aches and pains floated away. She saw that the bruises and bumps had disappeared, too. Most amazing of all, her broken arm seemed fine. Her memories, however, remained. Ava handed her a big soft towel, and she dried herself. Beryl slipped an emerald green gown over her head. The fabric felt smooth and light. She hadn't noticed it when they came in, but it must have been there. A matching ribbon for her hair lay atop the gown, but she decided to let her hair dry without tying it up. It took days to dry if she tied it back wet. Suddenly, Beryl realized she was starving. She hadn't eaten for almost two days.

Ava smiled. "Come, let's get something to eat. You must be famished. Then, if you feel up to it, we'll talk. Brother Earth wants to speak with you, too. He and I had a lovely chat this morning while you slept."

They went back through the low passage, up many flights of stairs, then through a door. Beryl was surprised to find herself outside on a tree branch, a wide, flat limb about one story above the ground. The wide branch held a dining table set for two. Beryl noticed that green leaves, the color of springtime, covered the tree/house, but acorns grew on it also. A light breeze smelled fresh and green, although the air felt a little chilly to Beryl after her warm bath. Ava pulled out Beryl's rainbow scarf and wrapped it around Beryl's shoulders.

"Come sit down," said Ava. "Our food should be right out."

Two little green men--the same ones that had given her a ride last night? —carried out trays of food.

"Your supper, ladies," said one with a smile. The other one, looking rather grumpy, put a tray in front of Beryl while the cheery one put his in front of Ava.

"Don't mind him, child. He has a good heart. I'm Ivy, and he's Buttercup." Ivy giggled. Buttercup mumbled something. Apparently, he wasn't fond of his name.

"Anyhow, we're glad to see you up and about. You were in pretty bad shape last night. After you eat, we'd love to show you around. Right, Buttercup?"

Buttercup grunted, then winked at Beryl.

"I would love that," said Beryl. "How shall I find you?

"We'll find you when you're ready. Now we'll leave you to enjoy your meal."

The tray held a big bowl of soup filled with vegetables and beans, dark bread with butter, and a mug of tea. Everything smelled wonderful. Beryl blew on a spoonful of soup and started eating. After a few minutes, her bowl empty, Beryl put down her spoon and looked around.

"Ava, this place is like a dream. It's amazing."

"Yes, it is. I've been here a few times. It's a privilege to be allowed to enter Brother Earth's kingdom. He's been watching you for a long time and is quite fond of you. Enjoy your time here. Learn as much as you can and build up your strength. Drink your tea; it will help you get strong again. We won't be able to stay here long. We're needed in our own world."

30

In Brother Earth's Land, later that afternoon

The Four Elements: Air—The breath of life. Our first action upon entering the world is to breathe in air, and when our life ends, our last act is to exhale. Breathing brings balance connecting our inner world with the outside world. We bring the world into ourselves as we inhale and release ourselves into the world as we exhale. In Hebrew, the word "Ruach" means both breath of life and spirit, as well as wind.
From The Book of Jocasta

After supper, Ava showed Beryl a ladder made of thick vines going from the dining branch down to the ground. Beryl wasn't sure she wanted to climb a ladder again, ever, but with Ava's encouragement, she did this once. They sat on cushiony moss beneath the tree castle in the strangely sparkly late afternoon light of Brother Earth's forest.

"Beryl," said Ava. She drew in a long breath and released it slowly. "There is something you should know about—we probably should have told you long ago, but we had hoped to protect you."

"What is it?" Beryl asked. "You're scaring me." She pressed her back against the warm hardness of the great tree, feeling its life force nourish her.

"Queen Lillia has decided she would like to give up her queenship."

Beryl started to speak, but Ava held up her hand to stop her.

"And—she requested that you replace her."

Now Beryl found she couldn't speak. Thoughts raced around inside her head so fast that they became all jumbled.

"That is why Lillia sent Eugene to the Temple City," Ava continued. "Apparently, the Council disagreed. They recommended that an acolyte named Zorina replace Lillia."

A coherent thought formed in Beryl's head that she managed to form into words.

"Why send Eugene? Why not ask Ontihaponati?"

Then another thought formed in Beryl's whirling mind.

"I met her." And in answer to Ava's quizzical stare, she continued, "Zorina, his Lady Love."

"Too many secrets," said Ava as she stared at her palms. "I wonder what else we don't know."

Beryl felt painfully aware of her own secrets but not quite ready to share them. Ava could go first.

"We have been unable to communicate through or with Ontihaponati for some months now. My friend Tobias, the one who rescued me from the guards when I first arrived at the Temple City, told me that the High Priestess ordered the passage to Ontihaponati's cave closed so the hallway and entrance to the cave could be repaired. That happened several months ago, so no one has visited the Great Crystal for a long time. And none of us have been able to contact her for months. We suspect a connection, although what could have happened to her, I have no idea. I miss her, though. She and I have been connected since I started my studies at the Temple. She has been my guiding light and friend, really."

"But where on earth did you meet Zorina?" Ava asked after a long silence.

"At your house. She's Solomon's 'Lady Love,' although she's not much older than me. But I think she's just pretending to like him. She and Lucas...I don't know who he is," she sighed aloud as she pictured his dark brown eyes, "but he brought Zorina to your house...seem to have a, um, romantic connection, I guess you could say."

Then she told Ava everything that had happened to her from when she arrived at Ava's house until Solomon pushed her down the stairs.

Beryl stopped talking to stare at a young hazel tree. She watched the tree turn into Brother Earth, with his green skin and curls, which today looked more like spring leaves. Beryl and Ava started to rise to greet him.

"Please, no formalities. You are my most welcome guests. Ava," said Brother Earth, lowering himself cross-legged to the ground across from the women, "Have you told Beryl about our conversation?"

"Not yet. We were catching up. Would you like to tell her?"

Beryl groaned. She didn't think she could stand any more news. More had happened in these last two days than had happened in her whole life before.

"Certainly. Beryl, your world is in great and imminent danger. The members of the Temple Council have lost their connections with spirit and nature. The people who rely on them are suffering. There is a man from Jocasta's world who desires to destroy Floredelis. He has brought the worst of that world with him. He is using everyone he can manipulate, including Solomon. They will destroy Floredelis if we don't work together to stop them."

"I can see that Solomon and this person from the old world have chosen the dark path, but what does this have to do with me?" asked Beryl.

"Ah, dear one, you hold the key to healing Floredelis. You can listen beyond what is spoken, listen to those who have no words to speak. Even though you are young, you can see the bigger picture and have compassion for all beings, even those who seek to harm you."

"Like Hamilton," said Beryl.

Brother Earth and Ava looked at her in surprise.

"The man who is trying to destroy our world is Hamilton," she spoke softly. "Is he real?"

"Yes, but how do you know about Hamilton?" asked Ava

"I thought he was me. I've seen him in my dreams for years. You told me that dreams reflect what is inside, our unconscious..." She looked at the moss, and ran her fingers over it, unable to look at Ava or Brother Earth. She felt their eyes on her.

"Oh, Beryl, I'm so sorry. You have suffered because of my thoughtless words. Hamilton is very real," said Ava.

"Beryl, let me help you understand. Please give me your hand," said Brother Earth

Beryl held out her hand without looking up. Brother Earth scooted closer to her and held her palm to his heart. Waves of energy and love washed through her. She closed her eyes and breathed deeply. She saw herself as a child sitting by the stream with squirrels, fairies, and fish frolicking around her. She saw her parents and Ava, their love surrounding her. She saw her quiet, happy childhood and saw herself leaving her childhood behind.

She felt the forces of darkness rising and blotting out the light, but she saw that they didn't emanate from her as she had once feared but that she somehow connected the darkness and the light. They both lived within her and around her. She saw a possible future where the children who were born after her no longer lived in joy and freedom as she had. If the balance wasn't restored, Floredelis would become that place of swirling darkness she'd seen Solomon in from her meditation at Ava's house. The darkness didn't need to be destroyed but rather kept in its proper place. She saw rays of light coming into her from above and a cloak of red light surrounding her. The strength of the earth flowed into her through her feet—a different kind of light. She stood at the portal between darkness and light, keeping them in their own realms. She remembered her dream about the ocean, and how it felt to be carried by the water. She remembered her lungs aching for air and then finding that she could breathe the water.

"Beryl... Beryl." Someone called her name from far away. She remembered her body and came back. Her body felt small and cramped after her journey. Brother Earth still held her hand. She opened her eyes and let them focus. She saw her hand in his and looked into his eyes. She saw all the places she'd been in them. He put his arm around her. He smelled of leaves and forest; he felt of love. She breathed deeply, taking it all in—the place, the feeling of safety in his embrace, the strength that flowed from him into her.

"How did you do that?" Beryl asked.

Brother Earth touched her cheek and turned her face toward him. A small tear gathered in the corner of his eye and rolled down his green cheek. He looked at Ava.

"She has no idea," he said.

"No," said Ava. She took Beryl's other hand between her hands. Beryl felt more warmth and love pour into her. "Go further," said Ava.

Beryl looked at her quizzically, sighed, took a deep breath, and closed her eyes again. She saw Ava as a young woman setting off for the Temple City. Her mother asked her to visit her grandmother on the way to drop off some medicine. Ava felt excited about her journey. As she walked, she met a man who made her blush and giggle. His name was Tobias, and he was also going to the Temple City. They walked together, laughing and talking. She forgot all about her grandmother. When she arrived at the Temple, she found the note and medicine still in her bag.

Ava pulled her hand back as though she had touched fire. Beryl looked at her.

"I'm sorry, Beryl. That's a painful memory. I never saw my grandmother again, and my mother was very angry with me. I'd forgotten all about it. But I never forgot Tobias."

"What just happened?" Beryl asked. There must be darkness in her after all; otherwise, she wouldn't make Ava so sad. "I didn't mean to hurt you. I didn't mean to do anything."

"You looked into my heart and called forth a hurt that never healed. You helped me find a place where I'm stuck in the past. It's good that I remembered, even though it's painful. Now I have the opportunity to heal. This is one of your gifts, to stand with compassion in the face of darkness; you can learn to use it."

Beryl rested her head in her hands. She didn't like making Ava feel pain and didn't understand how it could be a good thing.

"It's your gift." Ava stroked Beryl's hair. "Don't try to understand it with your head. Let it come through your heart. It will take time. If it frightens you, acknowledge the fear, and breathe. But enough for today, don't you agree, Brother Earth?"

"We'll talk again before you leave in a few days," he said. "Now, there are some gnomes who would like to give you a tour of our kingdom."

31

Brother Earth's Land, that same afternoon

As if waiting for their cue, Ivy and Buttercup appeared. Beryl smiled. "Ava, are you coming?" she asked.

"No. Brother Earth and I have more catching up to do. I'll see you later. Enjoy!"

Ivy and Buttercup took off their hats and bowed in unison. Beryl curtsied, and they each lifted a hand. She took the offered hands, still smiling. The gnomes were about the same height as her young friends back home, although their skin was rougher and their hands bigger. She thought about Melanie, James, and Elsa, their shining faces and little pink hands offering her wilted flowers. She would do whatever she could to make things right for them.

"Come, Beryl," said Ivy. "This land is filled with wonders. But for today, we'll take you to our favorite place. We know you went to the healing bath. That's a wonderful place."

"If you like getting wet, that is," snarled Buttercup. Beryl saw a smile crinkle at the corners of his eyes.

"Tell me about your life," she said. "Do you have families? Do you live in a village or in the tree castle? What do you eat? How old are you? Are you brothers? You do look so alike. What is it like living here? Have you ever been to my world? Have you been to other worlds? Are there really other worlds, like Jocasta's world? What are they like?"

When she paused to breathe, Buttercup said, "This young human has a good supply of air, does she not, brother?

"Indeed, she does, brother. Too bad my memory can't hold so many questions. We'll be happy to tell you what we can of our world. We've been instructed to show you only the good and beautiful today. But know that there is darkness here, as well, and do not stray from us."

"Thanks for the warning," said Beryl. "But your company is delightful enough to keep me from straying. Where are we going now? What..." She caught herself about to start another string of questions and laughed. "I'll try to ask one question at a time."

Ivy said, "We're taking you to the crystal cave, a place sacred to the gnomes. Few humans have seen it. We are wood gnomes. That's why we're green. But crystal gnomes have pale skin, and their hair is white. They care for the crystals that grow in this cave. They sing to them of light and stars, which nourishes the crystals as food nourishes us. Perhaps you'll hear them sing. It's beautiful, is it not, Buttercup?"

"Indeed, if you like such things," growled Buttercup.

"As you so astutely observed," continued Ivy, "Buttercup and I are brothers. He's the eldest. Gnomes live a long time compared to humans. We're still young, despite our grey beards. We live with our mother, Gloria, who also has a beard. All female gnomes have beards. In fact, it's considered a mark of beauty for a female to have a full, lush beard. When our mama or sisters get dressed up, they decorate their beards with bows, ribbons, and braids, just as human girls do to the hair on top of their heads. We've been to your world many times. We can easily pass back and forth, for our forms are not as dense as yours. That's also why humans generally cannot see us." Ivy stopped walking, and so did Buttercup. Beryl took a few more steps before realizing the gnomes had stopped.

"Here's the cave. Enter quietly. Follow us, and don't step on the baby crystals. It won't hurt them, but the crystal gnomes are very protective."

Beryl watched the gnomes turn sideways and squeeze through the split trunk of an old tree. She followed; it was a tight squeeze. Inside, the cave was big as Lillia's palace. Even though there were no windows, the room was bright and filled with colors. She saw several gnomes with pale skin, all dressed in dark blue robes. Each wore a dark blue hat with a yellow star attached to the top. The gnomes walked along trails between what looked like garden beds, but instead of plants, they contained crystals. Some of the crystals were tiny, and some were larger than Beryl. She watched a gnome stop before a crystal, lift his hands, and sing. As he did, rainbows of light surrounded him. The gnome pulled out violet light and directed it into the crystal. The crystal glowed violet.

The voices of the gnomes were high and sweet. She felt peaceful listening to them, although she couldn't understand their words. As they sang, their voices shaped and directed the light, sending different colors into different crystals. She bent down and touched a crystal. It was the color of the first spring violets. It glowed more brightly as the gnomes' song reached its peak.

"I'm surprised that you could hear the crystal speaking." One of the crystal gnomes stood next to her. "I heard it calling you. You must be Beryl. We heard you were coming. This crystal would like to go with you. It will help you communicate with our world when you return to your own."

The gnome touched the crystal, and even though it had felt firmly attached to the ground when Beryl touched it, it came off in his hand. He held it up to the light and whispered. A beam of clear light danced around the crystal and then filled it, so it glowed from within. The gnome bowed slightly and placed it in her hand. It felt warm.

"Thank you," said Beryl. She held the crystal next to her heart. She searched through her treasure pouch, pulled out the scroll her mother had painted, and handed it to the gnome. "And here is a gift for you. My mother made it."

The gnome took the scroll and unrolled it. "Thank you," he said. "It's beautiful." All the gnomes gathered to look. They discussed where they should put this precious gift. It generated some disagreement among them. Beryl thought it sounded funny to hear them arguing in their sweet, soft voices.

Buttercup took her hand, and the three of them left the cave, leaving the crystal gnomes to their decision-making.

"There is one more place we want to show you this afternoon," said Buttercup as Beryl squeezed back out through the tree trunk. "Then we will go back and give you a tour of the castle before dinner."

They walked along a pleasant path, and as they walked, Buttercup and Ivy told Beryl about their lives. After what seemed like only a few minutes, but Beryl wasn't sure she trusted her sense of time here, they came to a clearing in the woods. The beautiful flowers, in glorious colors, reminded Beryl of the colors in the crystal cave, only sweeter smelling.

Ivy pointed at a hill covered with mist, rising in the middle of the field. "That's where we're going next."

"What is it?" she asked.

"It's the home of the forest fairies. They like to live near Brother Earth, for they are very fond of him. They are green, too. And their home is quite amazing. I believe that they are expecting us. Come, here is the door."

He led Beryl to the door. Beryl had managed to squeeze through the entrance to the crystal cave, but she had no idea how she might fit through this door. It was about big enough for Crystal the cat to go through. She didn't even think Midnight would fit. She looked at Ivy and Buttercup, who looked back at her expectantly.

"Well, go on already," said Buttercup. "We haven't got all day."

"Well, perhaps I should just peek in through the door," said Beryl, crouching by the little door and trying to figure out what to do.

"Well, she does have a point," said Ivy as he looked at her.

He knocked on the door. A green fairy about the size of Beryl's pinky opened the door.

"Welcome," she said in a voice so small that Beryl could barely hear her.

Ivy nodded at Beryl, and the fairy tapped her gently on the forehead. And then, suddenly, the door was just the right size, and the fairy was about half of Beryl's size.

"You will regain your ordinary size when you leave our home," said the fairy, who Beryl could hear quite well now.

"I am Solara, and welcome to our home, Beryl. Oh, and you, too, Buttercup and Ivy, but try not to break anything," she said, giving them a look that let Beryl know it had happened before. The two gnomes had shrunk to the same size as Beryl, too.

"Come, I will show you around. And the queen of the fairies, Sunbeam, would like to meet you, as well. I will bring you to her."

Beryl wondered where all the sparkly light that filled the fairy hill came from. Then she looked up and saw that not only were there many windows that let in the sunlight but that the ceilings were also covered with chandeliers made of what looked like gold and covered with glowing crystals that seemed to amplify the sunlight.

As they went from room to room, Beryl noticed that the walls glowed with bright rainbow colors that seemed to dance. Beryl wondered if they'd somehow painted the walls or if they somehow reflected the crystals that hung everywhere above them.

She saw lots of little shiny things on the walls and the furniture that sparkled in the sunlight, like hundreds of tiny mirrors. The mosaics that covered the floor, made of glass, also sparkled and looked like the field of flowers outside.

Many fairies flitted through the house. None of them seemed to touch the floors. They looked so delicate to Beryl, even now that she was only twice as big as them. Most of them wore flowers in their hair, and much of their clothing looked like it was made out of brightly colored flowers or leaves. The whole place made Beryl feel like she was in the middle of thousands of dancing butterflies.

Beryl remembered hearing fairy tales where fairies stole human children, never to be seen again. It would be easy to forget about home in this enchanting place. Even with her small size, Beryl felt heavy and awkward surrounded by the graceful fairies who flitted weightlessly from place to place and didn't have to stay on the ground. Beryl touched one of the chairs gently as she passed, for the fabric looked like it might tear if she touched it too roughly. But to her surprise, it felt quite sturdy.

"The spiders weave for us," said Solara. "In your world, you brush cobwebs away. In our fairy world, we gather them carefully and stitch them into fabrics. Of course, our spiders weave them tightly for us; they're not using these webs for luring their dinner, after all." Solara laughed, and it sounded like little bells tinkling. Beryl couldn't help but smile at the sound, even though she didn't understand the joke.

They walked through room after room, all of them large and airy. Some contained trees that looked huge to Beryl in her present state but could not have been very tall. Many little fairies sat in these trees, talking to each other and drinking from dainty little teacups. She saw stairways that led to nowhere, as far as Beryl could tell. But why she wondered, would fairies need stairways when they could fly? Solara must have noticed her looking at one stairway that wound up in the middle of the room and then made a kind of bridge up across to a room up above, which she couldn't see.

"We like the way they look. They're mostly just for decoration, although sometimes it is fun to climb them. Especially the fairy children like to climb up the stairs and then flutter down to the ground," said Solara.

"Come carefully up these stairs now. This staircase we built for you." she said, "I will show you to the queen's sitting room now."

They went up the stairs. Beryl walked carefully up the narrow staircase, which had no railings. And it went very high. She went as quickly as she could, for Solara reached the top in a twinkling and floated at the top with her arms crossed, waiting for Beryl to finish climbing, occasionally saying things such as, "The tea will be cold by the time you get up here."

Finally, Beryl got to the top of the stairs, where she found herself face-to-face with a mirrored door. Solara opened the door; on the other side, she saw an enormous room filled with many wonders. First, Beryl focused on the bed that looked like a giant clam shell, covered with exquisitely embroidered pillows shaped and embroidered to look like real flowers that sparkled as though covered with morning dew. Beryl noticed a vanity with a mirror encrusted with stones around the outside, also shaped like a flower. A large picture window overlooked the woods with a sitting area in front of it where one could enjoy the view. The chairs looked like fully opened red roses, the center of which was the seat, with wooden legs underneath that looked like the thorny branches of a rose bush. The settee was covered with the most glorious little embroidered flowers in every color Beryl could imagine. There were more flowery things in the room, but Beryl was so enchanted by the furniture in front of the window that she forgot everything else. She touched the couch. It felt soft like velvet, only lighter. The little table looked like the stump of a tree, all covered over with dark green moss. It had a vase of flowers on it and a teapot shaped like a pale pink peony.

Beryl jumped when she heard a voice behind her.

"I do love flowers." The voice sounded like a songbird.

Beryl turned around. She knew this must be the queen. She wore a pink gown made of thousands of tiny pink flower petals, and a ring of flowers made of jewels encircled her head. Her golden hair flowed in waves down her back and made a halo around her face.

She peered at Beryl with eyes so green that Beryl felt she was resting in the soft, cool grass. Beryl thought she was the most beautiful person she had ever seen.

She gasped as she realized that she was staring, and then remembered her manners and curtsied.

"Your highness," she said.

"Oh, dear child, let us not stand on formalities. Please call me Sunbeam, and I shall call you Beryl. Now, let me look at you."

The queen lifted her hand and touched Beryl's face. She studied her for a moment.

"Ah, you are quite lovely. And I would venture to guess that you have some fairy blood in you from the color of your eyes."

Beryl felt herself blushing and didn't know what to say. No one had ever said anything about fairy blood. She thought that just happened in stories. And while she'd seen gnomes before in her world, she had never seen a fairy other than as a ball of light.

The queen invited her to sit down on one of the rose chairs.

Beryl sat well forward on the rose chair to avoid being scratched by the thorns. The queen sat on the loveseat, for although she was small, her full, flowing dress filled the entire seat. They drank tea together, and Beryl ate little cookies that tasted of rose and lavender. As she ate and drank, Beryl felt filled with good, warm magic. They chatted about their lives and the worlds that they lived in, although Sunbeam knew much more about the human world than Beryl did about Brother Earth's world.

Beryl sensed their visit coming to an end. The queen moved closer to Beryl and put her small hand on the back of Beryl's hand. It felt like being touched by the breeze of a butterfly's wing. The queen's touch filled her mind with blooming flowers. The queen looked into her eyes and smiled. "This is my gift to you," she said. "Not something for you to carry with you in your pouch, for we fairies like to travel light, but something for you to carry within your heart. You are like a flower about to open. You have much beauty and love within you. And it is love, not strength, that will win the battle you are about to face. Leave the fighting to others. Your blossoming will save us. Close your eyes for a moment."

Beryl closed her eyes. She could feel the fairy's light touch on her hand again. This time, Beryl saw another vision, a bonfire in a clearing in the forest. People danced silently around the fire. When she got closer, she saw that the fire was made out of flowers and the people out of flame. Something took form in the center of the fire. It looked like a key. Beryl went closer to get a better look at it. The flame-people continued dancing as Beryl wove through them to get to the fire.

Then suddenly, she found herself in the center of the fire. The touch of the fire felt so light, like the touch of Sunbeam's hand. She looked out at the fiery dancers, who took no notice of her but kept dancing to music she couldn't hear. She watched in amazement for a few minutes, or maybe it was just a moment, then she saw something shiny by her feet. She bent down and picked it up, a golden ring. She put it on her little finger and felt like it was burning through it. She took it off again, and the burning stopped. She heard the Queen's melodious voice, "Now, you must return. Brother Earth needs to speak with you."

Beryl opened her eyes. She felt calm and filled with wonder.

"Thank you," she said, and she knelt by the queen. The queen looked into her eyes.

"Godspeed to you. And know that you are in our hearts."

And the queen kissed Beryl on her forehead.

"You have the fairy mark on you now. It will protect you. Now off you go. And thank you for the picture you shared with me just now."

Beryl touched her forehead. "You are welcome, although I am not sure exactly

what I did. And thank you, Sunbeam. It has been a pleasure and an honor to meet you."

Solara came back with Ivy and Buttercup. Beryl hadn't even noticed them leaving. With

one final glance back at Sunbeam and her flowery room, Beryl left. She walked carefully down the stairs, keeping to the middle. They are not nearly as long as that ladder Ava and I climbed down, she reminded herself, but she didn't want to break her arm again, even if it could be healed in the magic bath. Solara led them back to the door and bade them farewell. Beryl walked out and took a deep breath. Everything swirled around her for a moment, and then she realized she had returned to her normal size. Suddenly she felt quite tired.

"Good thing we brought the cart," said Buttercup. "This youngster looks worn out."

"Yes, she does," replied Ivy.

Beryl didn't remember them bringing the cart but gratefully sat down and let her friends cart her back to the castle. Once again, she fell asleep on the ride home, but this time Buttercup woke her up by the front door, saying, "I'm not carrying her up those stairs again."

32

The woods outside Xantalon City, a few days earlier

> *The Four Elements: Balance—While each one of us comes with one or two predominant elements, which shape our temperaments, our goal should be to create balance among all four. If we can master the elements within us, then we have a choice as to how to respond in any situation—from the everyday to once-in-a-lifetime experiences. But as in all things, we must accept that we are not perfect and forgive ourselves (and others) for our (their) failings. But remember, mastering the elements within ourselves is the basis for magic, which is really not more than controlling the elements around us and bending them to do our bidding.*
> *From* The Book of Jocasta

Randall woke up to find a small, wizened woman bandaging his foot. With the light behind her, she looked like the gnarled roots of the tree in which he rested. He vaguely remembered coming here before passing out from the pain in his foot, which he now saw covered with green slimy stuff. He watched the old woman, then rubbed his eyes, unsure if he was awake or asleep. The woman looked up, startled at his movement, but said nothing. She finished wrapping his foot in a brown bandage, picked up the old gnarly stick she used as a cane, and hobbled away. Randall watched her disappear into the light.

He wanted to say "hello" or "thank you" or "who are you?" but was so startled and groggy that he hadn't managed to say anything before she vanished. He scratched his head and moved his foot a little. It seemed well-wrapped and not too painful. He peered out through the branches that covered the opening of the tree. He wondered how a woman with a cane could walk so quickly through the brush and not leave any broken branches.

Night was falling. He must have slept through the whole day. He had never known the forest to be so silent. Usually, he heard the call of the owls, the song of birds saying good night, and the occasional howl of wolves or the rustling small animals scurrying through the bushes. And always the breeze rustling through the trees. Now he only heard his own breathing and the beating of his heart.

Then he heard a small rustling sound. A little gnarled man, who also resembled tree roots, appeared. He carried a steaming bowl in one hand and a pair of shoes in the other. He nodded at Randall, put the things down, and disappeared, again before Randall could speak. When he smelled the food, Randall realized he was ravenous. He wondered how long he'd been here. He felt as if he'd always been here, like he was part of the tree. He lifted a spoonful of the steaming liquid to his mouth and took a bite. It tasted like carrots, onions, and herbs. It tasted as delicious as it smelled. He ate quickly, and when he finished, found a water skin and a blanket next to him. Even a pile of moss shaped into a pillow had been placed beneath his head. Eating made him feel sleepy again. He took a few sips of the sweet water, pulled on the blanket, and went back to sleep.

He awoke the next morning to find a very small tree person, greener and less gnarled than the others, staring at him with big brown eyes. The little one held out a bowl of porridge, which he took.

"Thank you," Randall said. "Do you speak?"

"Oh, yes, sir, I do. Too much for my own good sometimes, so says my ma."

Randall laughed. "Then you and I have something in common. My name is Randall. Who are you, and why are you helping me?"

"My name is Acorn because my ma says I'm a little nut, but someday I may grow into a big oak. The Great Mother asked us to look after you when you landed in our tree, so of course, we are. She says you're in big trouble, but you haven't done anything wrong. She says you hold part of the key, whatever that means. Oh dear," he said, "I guess ma was right. I do talk too much. All the grown-up tree folk are too shy to speak to you, so they sent me. I'm mighty glad to meet you, Mr. Randall, sir."

"Please call me Randall. Have you had breakfast, Acorn?"

"Oh, yes. Besides, I don't eat people food. Please eat while it's still warm. Otherwise, I'll be in trouble, and that will be the third time already today."

Randall laughed and ate his porridge. "Still nice and warm. It's just what I needed. Please tell your mother that I'm grateful for the food and for all the kindness you have shown me."

"I sure will," said Acorn.

"And by the way, who is the Great Mother? Is that your mother?"

"Oh, goodness, no, sir. I speak of the Great Mother of the forest and us all, Mother Earth. Do you not know her?"

Randall had heard people talk about Mother Earth but always thought it was a figure of speech. "I'm not sure. Will she speak to me?"

Acorn frowned. "Well, I don't know. She doesn't speak to persons so much, at least not directly. But perhaps I could convince my Grandma to come and explain to you. She has never spoken to a human before. In fact, she doesn't say much to anyone."

"If you think it would help, you could tell her I've never spoken to a tree person before, except you, of course."

"I hope she'll come. They aren't all like me, you know. They are quiet and serious and very, very wise. I'm sure they could help you get out of trouble. Maybe if you listen to them, it would help you. I listen to them sometimes, and it always helps when I do."

Randall reached into his pocket and pulled out a shiny copper coin. "I would like you to have this. I appreciate your kindness, as well as your delightful company."

Acorn turned a brighter shade of green.

"Here, take it. It's a little gift for you," Randall urged.

"Thank you, sir. You are too kind. I will keep this forever and remember you always when I look at it. What do you call this shiny thing?"

"It's called a coin."

"Oh, thank you. I'll go find my granny now. Oh, I almost forgot to tell you. You are welcome to stay here as long as you need. We'll feed you. You are safe."

"Goodbye, Acorn," said Randall. "Come visit again soon. I don't think I can go anywhere until my foot heals a little. I'd be happy to have your company anytime. You can talk as much as you want."

33

Outside Ava's house, the morning after Ava and Beryl arrived in Brother Earth's Land

"Look," said Fain, pointing with his foot. "New guys arrived last night. That's Andrew. I went to school with him before..."

"Hey, Andrew," said Otto, "You and your Dad better get up. It's time to get to work."

Andrew and Tobias hadn't slept much or well. They hadn't found Ava during the night. All they found was Solomon snoring on top of the cellar door and a bunch of men sleeping around a dying fire. They decided to lie down with the men, hoping not to be noticed and maybe to get a little rest. Lucas woke the men early. He sent them to raid a wheat field on the far side of Xantalon City, instructing them to bring back as much grain as they could. They didn't need grain, but he wanted them out of the way until nightfall. He noticed Andrew and Tobias. He thought he recognized them from the Temple City but didn't pay much attention. They could use the extra help.

Andrew and Tobias wondered if they should try to rescue Ava and Beryl themselves or go to Xantalon City for help. When the other men took off, Andrew and Tobias followed for a few minutes, then circled back to Ava's house. They'd decided to look around a little more and see if they could figure out what was going on and then decide what to do next. They arrived in time to see Solomon wake up.

Solomon awoke to find the sun painfully bright. He wasn't sure where he was. His head hurt. The events of the previous night were rather blurry. Why was he sleeping on the cellar door? He vaguely remembered putting Beryl in the cellar. Had he tied her up? What was going on with his woman? He rubbed his head, leaving his longish ring of hair pointing in many different directions. He smoothed it down with his hand but missed a couple of spots. His clothes were all askew. Solomon prided himself on his appearance. He wasn't the best-looking man around, but his mother had taught him to present himself well, which meant being clean, well-groomed, and well-dressed. He was far from it today, but since all his clean things were in Ava's house and he wasn't, he would have to straighten himself out as best he could before going in. He walked to the little stream, splashed his face, and rubbed the cold water on his head. He felt more awake now and somewhat presentable, although had he looked at his reflection in the water, he would have noticed that he'd wet his hair into a point on top of his head. He walked up to the door, turned the knob, and found it locked. He banged loudly.

"Open up; it's the big, bad wolf." He found this quite amusing. Zorina opened the door. She seemed much happier to see him than he remembered her being last night.

"Oh, Solomon," she said. "I missed you. Thank you for standing guard all night. Is everything alright out there?"

"Yes, indeed," Solomon replied, feeling much cheerier. "Well, I haven't seen the prisoners this morning, but the lock is secure, and I didn't hear a peep out of them all night."

"You couldn't have heard anything quieter than a stampede of horses with your snoring," said Lucas as he joined Zorina. "Did you hear the boys leave this morning? I sent them off to Rabican to, um, acquire supplies."

Solomon mumbled something no one bothered to try to understand. He prepared another hearty breakfast for himself, Lucas, and Zorina, including a big pot of strong coffee.

"When will Jacob arrive?" Solomon asked.

"He planned to leave this afternoon after the Council meeting. He wants to talk to the old witch and the girl. Maybe after that, we can get rid of them," said Lucas.

"Yes, quite so. Such a bother," said Solomon. "I'll bring them a little breakfast."

Solomon returned a few minutes later, still carrying the tray of food, his hair still pointing skyward. "The cellar is empty."

34

Outside Ava's house, later that same morning

Let us work in partnership with nature. We can co-create our reality. Remember that energy has form and organization, just like physical matter. In fact, physical matter is mostly energy and empty space. It is an illusion that we and the world around us are solid. All that is solid melts into air
From The Book of Jocasta

Andrew and Tobias watched Solomon perform his morning ablutions. When he went into the house, they peered into the cellar windows. It was dark inside, and they couldn't see anything but some bundles of herbs hanging in the window. They decided to hide and watch, at least for a few minutes more, although Tobias was anxious to do something. They watched Solomon unlock the cellar door and enter carrying a tray of food. They saw him come back out a minute later, still carrying the food, which looked and smelled delicious to the hungry men. He left the door open.

"Let's go," said Tobias, nodding toward the door.

"But, Dad, they'll be back soon. Something's going on."

"I have a feeling Ava's not there anymore, and I think I know where she is. Come in, and I'll tell you a story—the short version, for now. But the end of the story is that I know another way out of the cellar."

Andrew knew his father desperately wanted to save Ava and sometimes acted without thinking things through. But he seemed so confident that Andrew decided to go along.

The cellar looked empty.

"Ava, it's me, Tobias. Are you here?"

There was, of course, no answer. Andrew and Tobias hid behind some boxes under the stairs and waited.

Tobias spoke quickly and quietly. "Before I met your mother, Ava and I were going to elope. We planned to meet at noon on the appointed day at our special spot. I arrived early and eager. I waited a long time, impatient, and when I couldn't stand waiting any longer, I climbed the tree to look for her. Of course, with trees all around, all I could see were more trees. I climbed higher and stepped onto a thin branch. It broke. I tumbled to the ground and lost consciousness. I don't know for how long. My last thought as I fell was that it would serve Ava right to find me in this condition. I woke up in a strange place being cared for by little green people. I thought I had either died or was hallucinating. Then a tall green man came in. He introduced himself as Brother Earth. He told me he knew Ava and that any friend of Ava's was a friend of his. They cared for me, all these green beings, large and small. They took me to a healing bath. They had to carry me because I was too broken to walk. But I tell you, Andrew, that bath healed my bones and bruises. It healed my body but not my soul. I still felt angry. I spent a long time with Brother Earth. The gnomes taught me to make mosaics, and to thank Brother Earth, I did a mosaic on the floor of that bath. I made a similar one for our home after your mother and I married— my wedding gift to her. But that's not what I wanted to tell you. After many months, I healed, at least as much as one can heal from a broken heart, and returned to our world. I arrived near your mother's home, and that's where we met. Before I left, Brother Earth gave me this to use in a time of need." Tobias held up his wrist. Andrew saw the heavy silver chain Tobias always wore.

They heard loud, angry voices coming. Andrew felt amazed by his father's story. He thought of the beautiful floor his father had laid in their house. His father never told him where he'd learned to make mosaics. Until now. Tobias pulled off his bracelet.

"If we use this, hold my hand, understand?"

Andrew nodded.

They heard the voices clearly now.

"You old fool," said Lucas. "Zorina, I told you we couldn't trust him. They had to have hidden, probably behind those boxes, and he didn't see them. Now that you left the door wide open, they're gone for sure."

Solomon didn't respond.

Solomon, Lucas, and Zorina searched the cellar. The windows and door appeared intact. They found dried blood at the bottom of the stairs, but that didn't tell them anything useful. After a while, they found the trap door. They opened it and decided it was an abandoned well. There were hooks at the top, but no ladder. Even if there was, why would anyone go down an old well? That would be even worse than being locked in a cellar.

"Perhaps they used magic to escape," suggested Solomon. He felt perky after his pot of coffee. "Legends tell of elevated ones who could move themselves and even others through solid objects..."

"Oh, shut up. You are so full of..." Lucas' cheeks glowed red; his hands clenched by his sides.

"That's what I was waiting to hear," whispered Tobias. "Take my hand."

"Hey," said Lucas, "Did you hear that? They're still here." He walked toward where he'd heard a voice.

Andrew took his father's hand as Tobias breathed onto the chain. He heard Lucas start to speak but didn't hear the end of his sentence as the room disappeared.

Lucas looked behind the stairs, where he felt sure the voice had come from. He felt a breeze but saw nothing.

"That's strange," he said. "I was sure I heard voices back here. And how could there be a breeze here? It's all closed in."

"You seem a little jumpy, Luther," said Solomon.

"You idiot, how dare you...."

Zorina put a hand on Lucas' arm. "That's enough, boys. When the others come, we can send a scout to see if they've returned to Xantalon. If not, and they're alive, they'll eventually turn up. If they're dead, they'll turn up eventually, too, and that would solve two problems. Either way, we'll find them." Zorina led the men out of the cellar.

Late that night, Jacob arrived at Ava's house.

"Solomon, you drunken fool," he bellowed when he heard that Ava and Beryl had escaped.

"Alcohol does not affect me. I have evolved past that," said Solomon. "I can't be responsible for the magic of others."

No one responded.

Before dawn, they sent a man into Xantalon City to see if the missing women had returned. If he found them on the way, he was to kill them—by order of the Temple Council and for the greater good of Floredelis. Ava and Beryl knew too much. The rogue Council members had planned to kill them anyhow. They would claim they had been killed by Randall, the wanted murderer, and enemy of the state.

"There has to be some clue as to how they escaped." Lucas held a lantern aloft in Ava's herb cellar. "People don't disappear by magic, regardless of what that idiot, Solomon, says."

Zorina placed a hand on Lucas' shoulder. "What difference does it make?" she said, "They're gone. Besides, Solomon is busy in the garden, and everyone else is out looking for them. Let's not waste our time in the basement." She stood on the trap door and leaned in to kiss him, but he pushed her aside. He opened the trap door. "Look, there's a scrap of cloth on the edge of the door, the same color as the girl's skirt."

"Why do you remember what she was wearing?"

"Look at the hooks. The metal is lighter here. A ladder was attached not too long ago, I'm sure of it. I'm going down there. This is not just an empty well."

Lucas found a large coil of rope. "Just what I need."

"Don't you dare go and leave me here," Zorina said.

"You can come if you want."

"I'm not going down an old well hole. And if you go, I won't be here when you get back."

"As you wish. Get out of my way. Hold the lantern while I tie this rope onto..."

Zorina didn't hear the rest of what Lucas said as she ran up the stairs and slammed the cellar door behind her, tears streaming down her face.

35 ▐

A few days later, just outside Xantalon City

When Eugene finally became strong enough to talk, he still didn't have much to say about what had happened to him. He remembered being awakened by a loud explosion and then feeling a searing pain in his chest. The only other thing he remembered was seeing Randall lying very still. He heard yelling but didn't think he'd heard Randall's voice. He'd wondered if Randall was dead, and that was his last thought, except for thinking of his wife and sons. The next thing he remembered was being home in bed. But he definitely saw Randall lying where he'd fallen asleep the night before, so he knew for certain that Randall hadn't tried to kill him.

So far, the walls of Xantalon City hadn't been breached by the men in the woods, although the watchers' house had been robbed, and two fields on the other side of the city had been stripped of their grain. The men didn't harm the farmers, but they did tie one farmer to a tree when she had chanced upon them plundering her field. The folk who lived outside the city walls felt uneasy and now often spent their nights in the city with friends and family. Lillia and Jyrym also welcome anyone who wanted to stay at the castle. Winter would soon arrive, and Lillia worried about having enough food for all her people if the robberies continued.

All this was upsetting enough, but then things got much worse. Queen Lillia walked through her village every morning just after sunrise. She greeted the citizens, often stopping to check on someone's health, bring a birthday gift to a child, or sit down with a resident for a cup of tea. She liked to stay connected to the people and the land itself, so she would know if there were matters needing her attention. She loved her people. This ritual brought her and all the residents in and around the city great joy. She always went alone. When the raids started, Jyrym urged her to bring guards with her. She refused. She felt the towns-people would feel more reassured if she carried on as usual, although she did promise Jyrym that she would stay within the city walls.

One fine fall day, not long after Ava and Beryl's disappearance, but before anyone besides Solomon and his company knew they were gone, the Queen went for her morning walk. Near the village gate, she heard a strange noise coming from the other side. She paused to listen. She heard a muffled sound, like a child crying. She remembered her promise, but she told herself she wouldn't go out of the gate. She just wanted to know what was going on.

She heard, "Momma, momma, help me!"

She walked just a few steps out the gate toward the sound, her promise to Jyrym less important than a child in distress. She heard the gate close behind her and turned to see what had happened. The gate shouldn't close by itself. Someone grabbed her arms and pulled them behind her; someone else pulled a bag over her head. She felt a sharp blow on her head, and everything went dark.

When she came to, she panicked because she felt like she was suffocating. When she tried to move, she found her hands tied and her body prone on the floor. She remembered the bag and calmed herself. At least she understood why she couldn't breathe well. Her head ached. She wondered where she was. The air on her hands felt cool on her hands, and the space was quiet. She felt the cool smoothness of a dirt floor beneath her. The air smelled of herbs. Could this be Ava's root cellar? Indeed, it was. But after their last experience with prisoners, Solomon and his cohorts decided to keep a guard on Lillia at all times. As she wriggled, trying to get loose, she heard a chair scraping the floor and footsteps moving toward her. Her body stiffened as she felt hands on her neck.

Thankfully, they removed the bag from her head. The room was dim, but it was much lighter than the inside of the bag. The air felt cool and delicious in her lungs. The man was sixteen, maybe younger. His brown hair looked as though it hadn't been washed or combed for a long time, and his clothes were dirty. He wasn't from Xantalon, or Lillia would recognize him. He watched her. She couldn't read his expression. He reached out his hand and gently touched the part of her head that hurt. She winced and gasped at the sharp pain.

"I'm sorry, ma'am. Looks like they hit you pretty hard," said the young man. "Would you like a drink of water?"

"Yes, please," said Lillia. Her voice sounded far away to her. It must be from the blow to her head.

"Who are you, and where are we?" asked Lillia, trying to keep her anger out of her voice. Anger was good, though; it helped her focus.

"I'm called Otto. We're in a house in the woods that used to belong to some old witch who is a criminal. Can I give you something for your head?" He helped her sit up, leaning her against a pile of wooden crates, and tipped the cup so she could drink.

After she drank, Lillia felt much better. She looked around. "I'm sure Ava, the old witch you mentioned, has some herbs here that would help me. See the jars under the windows?" Otto nodded. "Look for one labeled comfrey."

Otto managed to find it. He also found a pile of bandages. He soaked a bandage in the tincture and laid it on her head. It burned, but the pain and burning subsided quickly.

"Thank you for your kindness," said the queen. "May I ask why you brought me here?"

"Well, it wasn't my idea, ma'am. I'm just doing what they told me. They sent three men to bring you back. I'm to guard you. If I don't do as they say, they'll hurt my brother. He's tied up upstairs. I'm supposed to keep you all bagged up, but I can't do it. When they come down, I'll have to put the bag back on you. I'm sorry. I probably shouldn't talk to you either, but I haven't talked to anyone in a very long time, and I'm worried about my brother. Truth be told, I don't know why you're here. They don't tell me anything."

"You seem frightened, Otto. You can talk to me. It won't do any harm. Tell me why you're here. How did you end up so far from home?"

Otto told her about his life and how he and his brother were about to lose their house, and that they missed their parents every day. He told her of Lucas' promise of food, shelter, and redemption if they worked for Solomon, who was supposedly working to save Floredelis. But Otto didn't know he would be asked to do something as horrible as helping kidnap a queen. Solomon had fed Fain and Otto, as he had promised, but didn't seem to intend to send them home anytime soon. When Fain told Solomon that he and Otto wanted to leave, Solomon threatened to send them to prison. Solomon kept Fain as a prisoner to ensure Otto would do as he was told. So Otto had to do what they told him for his brother. He was sorry.

Queen Lillia watched the sad figure sitting before her. She knew he felt ashamed. They heard a chain rattling at the door. "They're coming," Otto said. He picked up the sack.

"Don't forget to take the bandage," the queen said. "And don't worry about me. I'm stronger than you think."

Solomon came in with Zorina. The queen leaned against the crates, hooded and hands tied behind her back.

Solomon roughly pulled off the hood. He looked quite pleased with himself. Lillia knew he was showing off for the young woman.

"Well, Lillia," he said with a smirk, "Fancy meeting you here. I want to introduce you to your replacement. What with your being kidnapped by the Pied Piper and all, someone will need to step in immediately. Good thing we happened to be nearby when this tragedy occurred."

"Solomon," said the Queen, "How do you think you can get away with this?"

"Lillia, you don't like to lose, do you? You were always jealous that I did better than you in school. I always knew you fancied me. Too bad you missed your chance and got stuck with that hick of a husband. You were such a pretty thing in your youth."

"You pig," spat Lillia. "You won't get away with this. Your head is full of hot air, and your heart is empty."

"How dare you speak to me that way," said Solomon, "I think you are jealous of my beloved."

Lillia said, "She's as big a fool as you if she thinks she can be Queen of Xantalon."

"Do not insult Zorina," said Solomon. His face turned red. He slapped Lillia's cheek hard.

"You're a brave man, aren't you," she said, "hitting a woman, and one who is tied up, at that."

"Don't speak to me again. If you do, I cannot be responsible for what happens next."

He turned to Zorina. "I'm so sorry, my dear, that you had to see this. Let's put this little bird back in her cage."

As he bent down to put the bag on, he paused to leer into Lillia's face. Lillia reached out her arms, which she had untied with magic, grabbed him by the knees, and knocked him down. She grabbed the board that formed the top of Ava's workbench. Jars of herbs went crashing to the ground. "Sorry, Ava," she muttered under her breath as she hit Solomon on the back of his head with the board. He fell and didn't move. Zorina backed into a corner, edging toward Otto, whose mouth hung open. Lillia leaned against the board. "Come with me, Otto. You can stay at my castle for as long as you like"

Otto hesitated. "You're very kind, your majesty, but I can't leave my brother."

"Of course."

"I can help," Zorina said. "I know where he is, and they will release him if I tell them to."

Lillia's eyes narrowed. "Why would you help us?" she asked.

"I want something." She stepped closer to the queen but not so close that Lillia could reach her with the board.

"I'm listening," said Lillia.

"Take me with you. I can't stay here anymore. I will go as your prisoner."

"Come closer to me," said the queen.

Zorina hesitated, looking at the board.

"I won't hit you unless you attack me first," said the queen lowering the board. Zorina walked closer, and the queen looked into her eyes. She saw fear. She saw a young girl who had given in to promises of power and love and didn't know how to back out.

"You may come if you help us get the boy," said Lillia. "But you will be my prisoner."

"I'm a prisoner here, too." Zorina looked at Solomon as a soft moan came from his mouth. "Let's go."

The queen nodded. "Follow me, then. And Zorina, if you make a sound to call attention to us, then, as your boyfriend said, I cannot be responsible for what happens next. Do you understand?"

Zorina nodded.

"Good," the queen said. "Where is the boy?"

"He's in the garden. I don't think anyone is even guarding him now since Lucas ..." Zorina didn't finish.

Zorina suggested they padlock the cellar door. She took Solomon's keyring and handed it to Lillia.

They didn't see anyone on their way to the garden. There they found Fain tied and gagged. He leaned limply against a post but sat up when he saw his brother. Zorina and Otto untied him, and gave him water and a moment to get steady on his feet before they left.

It was a long walk back to the village, and night was falling. Lillia wondered how long it would take Solomon's men to notice him missing. Or for Solomon to call for help. His followers didn't seem very loyal, so perhaps they would be pleased to find him a prisoner.

She suspected that Solomon, too, was being used. He was a fool but not so foolish as to devise this crazy plan. She would send her guards back to take Solomon and his men prisoner. But now, she just wanted to go home.

As they approached the city several hours later, the queen saw her guards.

"Sam, Wiley," she called.

"Lillia," they came running. "Are you all right?"

"Yes, I'm fine. Please take us home. These men are my guests; the older one is Fain, and the younger is Otto. This woman, Zorina, is my prisoner. She can stay in a guest room, but the windows must be locked and a guard posted outside the door and window at all times."

"Of course. Let's get you home. Everyone's been worried about you."

Everyone felt happy and relieved that she was back. She told them briefly what had happened and promised to tell them more in the morning. She was unbearably tired, and her head hurt. Jyrym brought her supper while she soaked in the tub. He fed her, although she certainly could have fed herself. He dressed the wound on her head. He is a good man, thought the queen, as she drifted to sleep in his arms.

36

The next day, in the woods
outside of Xantalon

Randall found himself lying in the woods, his water flask by his side. His food pouch was there, too, although he hadn't seen it since he left Eugene at the campsite; he wasn't sure how long ago that was. The pouch was full—bread, cheese, apples, dried fruit and nuts. Had the tree people been a dream? No, here were the boots they'd given him. But he didn't see anything resembling the tree trunk he thought he'd stayed in. His foot seemed healed. He had a bright green sock on one foot, which didn't match the brown one he wore on his other. He pulled the boots on. They fit perfectly. He sat and ate some bread and cheese. His head felt a little clearer. He must be in the woods of Xantalon—either still or again, he wasn't sure.

Even though he didn't know where he was or where he might be heading, he decided it was better to walk than to sit and wait for something to happen, or for nothing to happen, which would be even worse. He heard a rustle from the bushes, then a flash of green sped past him. It looked like Acorn, although Randall never imagined the little fellow could move that quickly. He followed the green flash and eventually came to a path. He decided to head west now that he could see the sun since that was the direction he'd been traveling in with Eugene. He wondered if Eugene was alive. He wondered if anyone had noticed he was gone.

He walked for a long time. As dusk approached, he felt happy to see a cottage in the woods. With his hand raised to knock on the door, he saw Solomon, with a bandage around his head, walking toward the cottage carrying a basket of vegetables. Solomon's face looked red, and he was talking loudly about the illegal use of magic, although Randall didn't see anyone nearby to whom he might be talking to.

"Hey," Solomon yelled when he saw him, "Aren't you supposed to be looking for the queen with the others?"

"I've been looking everywhere. I thought she might have come back here," said Randall, hoping that would make sense to Solomon.

"Yes, you could be right. Carry on. I'm roasting some vegetables for supper. When you see the others, let them know dinner is at 9:00. I take good care of my boys." Solomon lurched toward the house.

That man is drunk, thought Randall. He remembered seeing Solomon with Zorina the day before Randall left the City. Then Randall had a flash of Solomon standing over Eugene's still body in the woods.

Randall refilled his water pouch in the stream. He leaned against a tree, out of sight of the house but near enough to see anyone coming or going. Something strange was going on. Maybe he could figure it out if he observed for a while.

Night had fallen by the time Solomon's men returned—about eight of them. They built a fire and sat around it. Someone lit a lamp in the house, and Randall now saw two people inside. One was Solomon, but he didn't recognize the other. The men outside grumbled. They mentioned Fain and Otto. Both had disappeared, as had the queen, Solomon's woman, and Lucas, although he often came and went without telling anyone. The men found it amusing that Zorina had disappeared and speculated as to whether she had left with Lucas.

Solomon carried out a big tray filled with food. "I don't know why I bother feeding you. You're all worthless. I should send you back to the forest where I found you. Maybe your leader, Randall, will take care of you if you can find him. Here's some supper, made with fresh vegetables and herbs from my garden. Eat and shut up. We're meeting inside, and it's hard to think with all your carousing. Here's some wine, too. But don't get drunk. We're leaving tonight."

Solomon carried down a small barrel of wine.

The men ate in grumpy silence.

"Where are we going? I'm exhausted. We've been walking all day looking for the queen. Thank goodness we didn't find her," said one.

"I heard that tall skinny one say he knew a place we could hide. Since the queen escaped, he thinks they will send someone to arrest whoever was responsible for taking her—they'll blame us, for sure. The Council members won't get blamed for anything."

"Randall," Randall heard one of them say, "I hope he starved to death in the woods. A lot of good he did us. I was better off at home."

"It's not his fault, man. He didn't ask you to come. We all came of our own free will. We were just stupid, that's all."

"Not stupid so much as desperate," said another.

"You can say that again. I hope my family is alright."

"We all do. Hey, did you hear something in the bushes over there?" He pointed toward where Randall hid. Randall's heart skipped a beat. He'd been sitting very still and didn't think he'd made any sound. Something scurried past Randall and ran into the woods.

"It was just a squirrel," one of the men laughed.

Randall breathed a very quiet sigh of relief.

"I wish we could sleep. I'm worn out by these wild goose chases. I'll bet the queen is home now in her nice warm bed."

"Yeah. I wish I were with her."

They lay down by the fire to rest until it was time to leave. Randall watched as, one by one, they dozed off. Light reflected in one of the cabin's windows. He thought he could listen beneath it without being seen or heard. Carefully he inched his way over. No one seemed to be standing guard. He almost fell into a cellar door, which looked like it had been chopped open with an ax. Randall wondered why they hadn't opened it the regular way. When he finally got to the window, he heard men's voices.

Randall gasped as something rubbed his leg--a big black cat. When Randall scratched its ears, it purred loudly. This is great, thought Randall. I won't be able to hear anything over that sound. But the cat, as if reading Randall's thoughts, stopped purring and curled up on his lap.

Inside, the two men started yelling. Randall appreciated that, as he could hear them much better. One was angry at the other for letting someone escape and then getting trapped in the cellar. They would never take over Floredelis if he kept messing up. They mentioned Randall's name. He wondered again if they were talking about him. They planned to blame Randall and his men for the queen's kidnapping. Randall was already a wanted man, as Solomon had told the queen that Randall killed Eugene.

At this point, Randall knew they were talking about him. Did they know he was the Pied Piper? His heart pounded so loudly he could hardly hear. They thought the queen must have returned home by now but weren't sure if Fain, Otto, or Zorina were with her. And they had no idea where Lucas could have gone. Solomon felt sure that Zorina had either been destroyed by magic or taken prisoner. Nothing else would tear her from his side.

The cat, Midnight, stood up. He bit Randall's hand gently and trotted away, pausing to look back at Randall before continuing. Randall decided that was his invitation to follow. He crawled on his hands and knees to stay out of sight. Midnight led him to some raspberry canes in full berry. The cat disappeared through a hole in the bushes, only to poke his head out and look at Randall. Randall heard footsteps coming from the house and dove into the opening, ignoring the scratches from the brambles on his face and arms.

"Someone was here. The grass under the window is still warm," said Solomon.

Midnight sauntered over to the men. He hissed at them and lay down in the spot where Randall had been.

"It's a cat," said Solomon. "Get out of here, you little beast."

He kicked Midnight in the stomach. The cat casually stood up and sauntered into the bushes.

"Solomon, you're a fool," laughed the other man.

"Better safe than sorry," said Solomon.

"Look, the men are sleeping," said Jacob. He began kicking them, shouting, "Wake up, you idiots, we have to get out of here."

There was a little cave inside the raspberry canes, with just enough space for Randall to curl up without being scratched by thorns. He heard the men get up and put out the fire. He heard them talking and Jacob telling them to be quiet. Jacob reminded them that Lucas, wherever he was, had taught them to move quietly and without leaving tracks. Soon they left, and the woods grew still. Randall stayed where he was. Why were they all talking about him? Why blame him for killing and kidnapping? Who wanted to take over Floredelis?

The ground prickled with old raspberry branches. Randall wondered if he'd be able to sleep. He kept replaying the overheard conversations in his head until they got all jumbled. He jumped again, scratching his arm on the brambles, when something rubbed against his back. He turned over and saw a sweet-faced white cat glowing in the moonlight that filtered through the branches. She curled up against him and fell asleep. He scratched her head, ate a handful of raspberries, and fell asleep, too.

He woke just before dawn when a cold nose poked his cheek. Two cats, one big and black and one small and white, stared at him. He sat up.

The cats kept staring.

"I don't suppose you'd like to show me where to go?" he asked.

As though he'd asked the right question, the cats walked out. Randall grabbed his things and followed. He felt that someone besides the cats was watching over him, maybe Mother Earth. The cats led him to a road. They trotted ahead of him, tails high and ears twitching. Randall listened, too, although he didn't know what for. If he was still in Xantalon, Eugene, if he still lived, was the only one who knew him. Perhaps he would help. But what if Eugene was dead or thought Randall tried to kill him? He reminded himself not to get ahead of himself. After all, his best plan seemed to be following two cats to who knew where. Maybe they were taking him to a mouse nest to get some breakfast. Or maybe he was the mouse.

He saw the walls of a city ahead. This must be Xantalon City, he thought. The gates opened, and a group of men came out.

Dawn rubbed against Randall's leg, then walked away. Midnight jumped onto a low branch and disappeared, leaving Randall alone. He considered running away but didn't see much point. He'd done nothing wrong and could use some help and a safe place to stay, not to mention some food. The group stopped in front of Randall.

"Greetings, friend. What brings you here?" asked the leader. He had a broad chest, deep voice, and kind eyes.

Randall replied, "I'm a stranger, lost and unarmed. I seek shelter."

The man looked him up and down. "Welcome, stranger," he said. "I'm Jyrym, king of Xantalon. What is your name, and where are you from?"

"I'm from the Temple City. But I was attacked in the woods and have been lost for I'm not sure how long."

He took a deep breath, unsure how the king would respond. "My name is Randall."

"Welcome, Randall. I know who you are. One of my men will take you to the castle. The Queen protects all in need here."

"Thank you. After what I've heard said about myself, I worried about what kind of reception I might receive. Are you looking for the queen's kidnappers?"

Jyrym nodded.

"I know something that might help."

Randall told Jyrym what he'd seen and heard, although he didn't know where Solomon and his men had gone.

When Randall arrived at the castle, Lillia came down to meet him.

Randall felt overjoyed to learn that Eugene had survived the attack. He also felt relieved that she didn't think he had tried to kill Eugene.

The queen told Randall about her kidnapping and about the three guests that had returned with her. They would speak more later. First, Randall was given a room, a bath, and food. Midnight joined him in his room. Randall felt pleased to have his company and happy to have him purr as loudly as he liked.

37

Later that day, in Xantalon city

Is seeing believing, or is it only through believing that we can see what is real? The world is more complex and wonderful than we adults often remember. That is one way that fairy tales help us—they remind us of the magic all around us.

Here's another favorite quote: "It is only with the heart that one can see rightly. What is essential is invisible to the eye." Antoine de Saint-Exupery

From The Book of Jocasta

Beryl's moms felt wild with worry about Beryl and Ava. When they went to check on them, they found Ava's house empty. No one knew where they had gone. It seemed like they'd disappeared from the face of the earth. Anne and Beatrice consulted with Lillia and Jyrym. They considered what Ava had told them about the strange and terrible things happening in the Temple City. They wondered what had really happened to Eugene in the woods. They hadn't heard Randall's whole story yet, but that seemed very strange, too. Somehow everything must fit together, but they needed some missing vital pieces of information to figure it out.

Jocasta had warned of the danger of a few individuals holding too much power. She wrote about people in her old world destroying Mother Earth in their quest to accumulate material wealth and power, forgetting that the earth was a living being. Anne had been shocked and saddened when she first read about this tragedy in the Book. She thought something like that could never happen in Floredelis. But now it seemed likely it had already begun.

Anne, Beatrice, Lillia, and Jyrym decided to go to the Temple City together. Perhaps they could find out something about Beryl and Ava. If, as they feared, Ava and Beryl had both been imprisoned there, hopefully, they could get them released. At least they would be doing something besides worrying and waiting.

Once they decided to go, the queen met with Zorina to tell her. She asked Zorina what she knew about Solomon's plan.

Zorina said, "I want to help you, but I'm confused about what's happening, too. Solomon wanted to make me queen so he could tell me what to do. He would have been the real ruler of Xantalon. I loved Lucas, but Lucas used me to control Solomon. Maybe he would have been the one really in charge. I don't even know. By the time I realized I was in over my head, I didn't know how to get out. Until you came along. I can't thank you enough for helping me get away from those men and their lies and manipulation."

"Tell me what you know," Lillia encouraged.

"I know that Selene and Jacob were also involved with whatever they were doing. And that there's more going on than just their plan to make me queen. Solomon and Jacob were boyhood friends. They both felt they hadn't gotten their fair share of wealth or recognition. I didn't know Jacob well, so maybe he is the brains in this plan, but Solomon doesn't seem smart enough to devise a plan like that."

"I agree," said Lillia.

Zorina continued, "Jacob should have been at Ava's house with Solomon and the men when your friends went to look for Beryl and Ava. I don't think anyone staying at the house could have taken them to the Temple City. We were all at the cabin when Solomon discovered they'd gone missing. I just have no idea where they might have gone or even how they got out of the cellar"

"You worked for the High Priestess. What was going on with her before you left?"

"All I know is that since the Great Illness, she's seemed like she was drugged or maybe under a spell." Zorina looked away as she said this last part. Lillia felt sure she was hiding something, but let it go. The girl was young and confused. She had been used, and whatever true power she had remained untapped. Thank goodness she hadn't become Queen. She was nowhere near ready, and maybe she never would be.

Zorina didn't want to stay in Xantalon without the queen, but she didn't want to go back to the Temple City, either. What hold did Solomon have on her, Lillia wondered? Clearly, it wasn't love or even lust. The thought of Zorina and Solomon together disgusted Lillia. Or maybe Lucas, whoever he was, was the one who had planned to make Zorina queen? What had made her vulnerable to him? And why were the queen and her watchers oblivious to the trouble in the Temple City? She hadn't known anything was amiss until the men in the woods became desperate enough to steal food from her people. Even then she hadn't paid much attention.

Lillia worried about leaving Zorina behind. What if Solomon or Lucas found out she was here? Jyrym hadn't found Solomon and the others. Lillia doubted Solomon felt a real affection for the child, but he wouldn't hesitate to use her again.

Eugene would watch over Xantalon city while they were gone. They decided Zorina would stay at Eugene's home while they were away. She could help tend the garden and care for the children. She might find it healing to work with the land and spend time with little ones, and she would be safer there since it seemed an unlikely place for anyone to look for her. Eugene's wife agreed, as did Zorina. Randall would stay at the palace with Fain and Otto.

With all the confusion, one thing troubled Lillia more than the rest. She felt as though she was waking up from a dream, like someone had planted a seed of doubt in her mind, urging her to give up her crown. Why had she felt the need to retire at the height of her career? Lillia felt someone was trying to control her, and she didn't know who or why, or how. She remembered Ava talking about the strangely powerful Dr. Hami, although it hadn't sunk in at the time. She hoped to meet Dr. Hami when they got to the Temple and maybe get some clarity. Now that she'd woken up, she couldn't imagine stepping down as queen when Xantalon needed her more than ever, and she loved her work and her people.

38

Two days later, in Xantalon City

The day before they left, Lillia said, "Let's gather the townspeople. I'll ask the children to sing for us and charge my stone with their love. Maybe it will give us strength on our journey. Goddess knows we could use some."

The Queen's Stone was a round diamond about the size of a quail's egg. On state occasions, she wore it in her crown, but most of the time, she wore it on a chain around her neck. It held the love of the people and the wisdom of the land. Lillia remembered receiving the stone after the people of Xantalon blessed it and imbued it with their love on the day she took over the queendom. She remembered wearing her crown for the first time with the light of the people shining out of it and sending rays of warmth through her body. Not so many years ago, but it seemed like another lifetime now.

Everyone gathered just before dawn to bless the stone and their queen and her companions on their journey. The children sang about dawn and the return of the light, and everyone prayed for the success and safe return of the travelers. The travelers carried enough provisions to see them to their destination. They carried nothing else, no weapons, no tools of magic. They would rely on their senses, their intuition, and each other.

The first night they slept in a big old willow tree that they called the wisdom tree or Grandmother Willow. This oldest tree in the forest grew near a deep, clear pool. And people came to sit beneath it or in its branches, often finding answers to questions they couldn't figure out on their own. Just a few feet off the ground, the branches grew close together, forming a kind of giant hammock. They could all sleep comfortably there, hidden by long branches still covered with golden leaves. The weather was mild, although they all felt the chill in the air, a foreshadowing of winter. They wrapped their brown wool capes closer and, snuggled together and cradled by the wisdom tree, they slept well after their long day's walk despite their worries.

They arrived outside the Temple City the following day just before dusk. They climbed a hill outside the city gates to observe before they entered. But as the four sat on the hill, eating the last of their bread and cheese in the dimming light, the gate closed. The only reason the gates had ever closed before was to keep wild creatures from wandering in. A woman pounded on it, begging to be let in. A guard holding a spear opened the gate. He knocked the woman down with the stick end. Then he went back inside and shut the gate. After seeing that, none of them had the stomach to finish their simple meal.

The woman leaned against the wall crying. Eventually, she became still. The four travelers tried to rest a little before what was likely to be a long night.

The wall around the city had three hidden entrances. They would try to enter through one of them. They waited until just before midnight. The city fell quiet, although from high in a tree, Beatrice could see guards patrolling inside the wall. The travelers walked to the first hidden entrance, the one Ava and Tobias had used. Anne went in and returned quickly.

"It's been walled off. We can't get in."

They went to the back of the City, near the Temple. This entrance stood close to the Twin Mountains, Hugin and Munin, which marked the end of Floredelis. The path ended there, and the only place to go was either into the City or back the way they came. No one knew why there was an entrance here. The others were more convenient and even more discreet if discretion was desired. Jocasta wrote that this entrance existed before she came to Floredelis. She saw it on her first visit. But since no humans had lived here before she arrived, that didn't seem possible. The old door, made of thick heavy wood and round at the top, had a black doorknob in its center. At least this entrance didn't look boarded up, from what they could see.

As they stood by the door, Queen Lillia got a sick feeling in the pit of her stomach. "Something's wrong. I think we should go back to the forest and come back in the morning through the main gate. I doubt anyone would recognize us, but ...."

"You would be surprised who might recognize you," a man said. "Welcome, my Queen, to the Temple." A pair of rough hands grabbed her. She signaled with her eyes and mind for the others to run. Beatrice grabbed Anne and pulled her against the wall, deep into the shadows. Jyrym would stay with the queen no matter what, but there was no sense in all of them being captured.

Anne and Beatrice stayed out of sight, waiting and listening. They heard men shouting. that they had captured the Queen and King and were taking them into the Temple. How did the guards know they were coming? Why were they waiting at the gate? They had more and more questions. When would they find some answers?

The men who dragged Lillia and Jyrym into the city looked like Temple guards, but their language sounded rough and crude. They didn't have the uprightness and gentility that the guards used to be known for.

"What're we going to do with them?" asked one of the men.

"It's late now, but he'll want to see them first thing in the morning. Let's put them upstairs."

They dragged Lillia and Jyrym upstairs and locked them in a room. As their eyes adjusted to the dark, they could see the room only contained a bench attached to the wall, a high window above it, and an empty sink in a corner. Neither of them had ever seen this part of the Temple. But it had been used recently, for both Lillia and Jyrym could smell fear emanating from the walls.

"I guess we made it to the Temple," said the Queen, attempting a smile.

Jyrym laid his traveling cloak on the floor. "Your bed, my lady," he said.

"Your blanket, my lord," said Lillia removing her cloak. Jyrym rolled up his heavy vest to use as a pillow, and they managed to sleep a little in the comfort of each other's arms.

39

In the middle of that same night, in a cave in the mountains of Euterpe

> *On the use of alcohol and other mind-altering substances: Especially for those on the spiritual path, these kinds of spirits can adversely affect your connection with the spiritual world. On the other hand, the experience of using these substances can be enjoyable and relaxing and add to celebrations large and small—only in moderation, however!*
> *From* The Book of Jocasta

Solomon and Jacob had taken the men to a cave in the mountains of Euterpe, a long night and day's walk from Ava's house. Jacob used magic to shield the cave from sight, but Jyrym hadn't searched that far, anyhow. When they left Ava's house, Solomon discovered, to his surprise, that the men had only finished half the cask of wine he'd given them with their supper. He gave it to one of them to carry, but he didn't offer it to them again. A couple of days later, Solomon finished the barrel himself in the middle of the night and started thinking about Zorina. He wanted her back. He peeked at Jacob, who appeared sound asleep. It would be easier to do what he wanted if Jacob stayed that way.

Solomon woke up the four men sleeping furthest away from Jacob. "Find my woman and bring her back," he ordered in a stage whisper.

"That old queen and her guard dog, the king, have her held captive in their castle."

A couple of men looked at him sleepily while the others pulled their blankets over their heads.

"Now!" he growled. "Go now! "

"But Solomon...," one of the men began.

"If you ever hope to go home instead of to prison, I command you to rescue my lady love."

The men grumbled. They didn't think the lady wanted to be rescued. It was a long walk to Xantalon City. Solomon either didn't hear or ignored their comments. He stood at the opening of the cave with his chest puffed out. The men disliked him and thought him an idiot but felt compelled to obey. They still had a small hope that he would keep his promise to give them back their lives. They rubbed the sleep from their eyes, pulled on boots and coats, and headed toward the city.

"Shouldn't we have a plan?" one of them asked.

"Nah, we'll sneak into town, go to the castle, and take the girl. How hard can it be? The queen will probably offer us dinner," said Keith, who, although the youngest among them at fifteen, had appointed himself their leader.

"What about guards, or what if the doors are locked?"

"Don't worry. Even if they put us in prison, at least we won't have to sleep outside or listen to that arrogant jerk." Keith said. "I don't know how much longer I can take this. Living outside, hiding from –whoever we're hiding from. Pretending like we're the good guys and like Solomon will help us go home. I hate this. I hope those guards want to fight. They deserve to suffer, and I need to hit someone."

"Yeah, they probably never had to fight. We could beat them easy," the others agreed.

They trudged through the night, grumbling and joking and arguing. Late in the morning, they stopped to rest. They left again at nightfall. As they approached the city, they stopped talking. They tried to walk silently, as Lucas taught them but were too tired to care. Besides, they didn't see anyone. They found the gate locked. They boosted one man over the gate. Inside, all was quiet, as it should be in the middle of the night. He unlatched the gate, let the others in, and they all headed for the castle.

Keith said, "All these soft people sleeping in their comfortable beds. Someone should teach them a lesson. Why should their lives be so easy?"

"Calm down, Keith," said another. "Let's find the girl and get out of here. These people haven't done us any harm. It's not their fault we're living this crazy life."

"Shut up," said Keith. They carried the long, curved knives that Solomon had given them in their belts. Keith pulled his out and brandished it. "Or you'll be first."

The man backed away. As they approached the castle, the rest of the men pulled out their knives, too. Keith tried the door, but it was locked. He pounded on it. A sleepy Fain opened the door. Keith grabbed him and held the knife to his throat.

"If you help us, you won't get hurt," whispered Keith. He looked more closely. "I know you. You're Fain. You deserted us, you traitor! I ought to teach you a lesson. Give us Zorina. We know she's here. We won't leave without her."

"She's not here," Fain stuttered. "She was, but the queen sent her away. I don't know where she is."

"He's lying," said Keith.

Otto entered the room, followed by Randall. When Otto saw his brother being held by a man with a knife, he tried to run to him, but Randall stopped him.

"He's not lying," said Randall.

"I don't have time for this," said Keith. He drew the knife across Fain's throat and let him drop to the floor in a pool of blood. Otto screamed, running to his brother.

"He's dead. You killed him. Oh, Fain."

Otto wept loudly.

"Shut up, or you'll be next," said Keith, but the other men held him back.

Randall recognized these men. He'd seen them by Ava's house. He thought quickly.

"She's not here," he said, "The queen thought someone might come looking for her, so she moved her to a safer location. You're welcome to her. She's nothing but trouble if you ask me. I'll take you to her. Leave these people alone."

The men conferred.

"All right, take us, but we aren't in the mood to fool around. Do you understand?" asked Keith

Randall looked him straight in the eye. "I understand very well."

Randall led them through town and out the gate.

"Where are you taking us?"

"She's in the watchers' house. They're out of town, but they have 2 guards there with her. They're probably sleeping."

"Yeah, we all should be sleeping. We walked right by that place."

"Well, how were we supposed to know she was there? The place was totally dark."

They walked to Beryl's house. Randall walked with Keith, keeping his distance from the bloody knife, while the rest of the men walked several steps behind in shocked silence. When they got to the door, Randall stopped. "Well, here you are, gentlemen."

"You're coming with us. You're not leaving until we get the girl," said Keith, waving his gory knife.

"Alright, let's go," said Randall. Keith grabbed him by the collar and shoved him through the door first.

"If the guards wake up, I want them to see you first," he whispered. "One of you come with me, and the rest can wait here"

Randall tiptoed in slowly and quietly. He had visited the watchers' house once before. He was glad both bedroom doors were closed. "This is her room," he whispered, walking toward Beryl's bedroom, "and the guards are in there." He pointed toward Anne and Beatrice's door.

He walked into Beryl's bedroom, shut the door, and kicked the rug in front of it. He figured he'd have a few moments before the men followed him. He jumped out the window, closed it from the outside, and ran toward the forest. The men would be after him in no time. He hoped the forest folk would help him again.

He saw what looked like a huge firefly. It circled his head and headed off through the forest. Randall followed, maybe this was his help, and if not, he didn't have a better idea. The light paused until he caught up. As Randall ran as fast as he could, he thought about the strange ways his life had been both threatened and saved in this forest. In the distance, he heard Solomon's men crashing through the brush. The flying light led him into thicker woods. His clothing tore, his face and hands got scratched, and his lungs felt like they might burst, but he didn't slow down. The light came to a tree and spiraled to the ground before disappearing. He stooped to look for the light. It had disappeared, but he did see an opening in the tree. Could this be the same tree that sheltered him before? He heard the men coming closer. He didn't think he could run much further, so he crawled inside, hoping for the best. Once inside, he couldn't hear his pursuers. His chest heaved from running so hard. His lungs and legs ached. He began to feel the scratches on his face and arms. But he focused on his gratitude for the help he'd received once again. He gasped out his thanks to the tree people and Mother Earth and promised to help them in any way he could. As his breathing quieted, a feeling of peace washed over him. He was safe, at least for the moment. He knew another battle was coming, bigger than this one, but for now, he could rest. And he did.

40

Late that night, in Brother Earth's Realm

Beryl felt totally exhausted, more from her meeting with Brother Earth and Ava than her time with the gnomes. How could they think she could save anyone? Lillia had wanted her to be the next Queen? Hamilton was a real person and not her dark side or a figment of her imagination? It was all too much. She couldn't think anymore. She found her way to her room, rinsed her teeth, threw on a nightgown, and even as she wondered how she would be able to sleep, she did.

In her dream, she swam in the ocean. She wore an orange swim outfit. A handsome man swam up to her. He looked familiar, but Beryl couldn't remember who he was. His short, dark hair curled around his ears and over his forehead, and his eyes sparkled blue like the water. He said, "Let me introduce you to Beryl." Beryl, now naked, didn't want to meet anyone. She took a deep breath and went straight down into the warm blue water. Even though they stood near the shore, she swam impossibly far below the surface. The man dove with her. He pulled her close and kissed her. The kiss felt warm and delicious. When they rose to the surface, she could barely see the shore, but she could touch the ocean floor. She put her arms around the man. He put his head on her shoulder and cried in the safe circle of her arms as she held and comforted him.

Then she was in a city, now dry and clothed. Hamilton approached. She had never been in a dream *with* him before. He stood very close to her. His smile looked painted on. He spoke with a strange accent. "I am Hami, the meditation man."

He wrote something on a piece of paper, crumpled it up, and handed it to her. "Pick a number between one and ten."

She said, "Four."

He wrote "four" on a different piece of paper.

"What's your favorite flower?"

"Peony," she said.

He wrote this down, as well.

"How old are you?"

"Fifteen"

He wrote that down, too. He told her to blow on the crumpled piece of paper three times, then hold it up to her forehead. She did.

"Read it."

She smoothed it out and read, "Four, peony, fifteen."

He said, "God loves you. This is a propitious time for you. Your stars are aligned, and Jupiter smiles on you. Expect good things. But beware of friends who are not true."

He asked her to give him many coins so he could pray for her. She dug into her pouch to find some, but couldn't find any coins, although she felt sure they should be there. Instead, she felt something shaped like a tube, moist at one end and soft on the outside, hard on the inside. She pulled it out. It was a finger. Beryl recoiled. That's not what she wanted to give Hami. She put it back and felt some more. This time, she pulled out something large, round, and hard. She handed Queen Lillia's jewel to him. As she handed it to him, she knew she shouldn't, but she did it anyhow. He thanked her and said he would pray for her. The piece of paper blew out of her hand. She bent over to pick it up, but it was gone. When she stood up, Hamilton had disappeared as well.

She woke with her heart pounding. It was the middle of the night. She knocked on Ava's door, sorry to disturb her, but needing her dear godmother. She found Ava staring out the window.

"Come sit with me," Ava said.

They both sat on the bed. Ava put her arm around Beryl and smoothed the hair from her sweaty forehead. She took a good look at her.

"You had a dream, then," Ava said.

"Yes," sighed Beryl. She felt better being with Ava. She described her dream. Ava listened. Ava knew better than to interpret it, though. Especially not after the suffering she'd caused Beryl with her careless comment about dreams reflecting your inner life.

Ava told Beryl what she knew about Dr. Hami but didn't reveal her past with Hamilton, although she knew she should tell Beryl everything. The time for secrets—if there had ever been such a time—had passed long ago. Beryl listened intently, fitting together what Ava told her with what she'd seen in her dreams. She tried to understand her connection to him. He'd tried to kill Ava. He instituted laws that prevented people from receiving health care. Many had died because of him. And it seemed he intended to take over all of Floredelis. She needed to piece together all she'd learned in her dreams, but not tonight when she couldn't think straight.

"I don't know how or why you keep dreaming about him, Beryl, but I do know that you will play an important role in restoring balance. You are stronger than you know."

"I hope so." All Beryl wanted to do was pull the covers over her head, fall asleep, and wake up in the morning in her own house to the sounds of her parents' laughter. She almost wished this was a dream.

"Why don't you stay here tonight?" Ava said. "I'll make you some tea to help you sleep. You can see the moon through the trees from my bed. She looks full and lovely tonight. I'll make some tea for myself, too. You may have noticed—I wasn't sleeping either."

Ava hadn't dreamt about Hamilton, but she couldn't stop thinking about him. He had become an angry, bitter man since his last visit to Floredelis—and a dangerous one, too.

Beryl crawled under the covers. She felt a chill in the air. The seasons were changing, at least in her own world. Everything was changing. She looked at the moon. *I want to enjoy this lovely evening,* she thought. *Who knows when, or even if, I will see another full moon?*

Ava returned with two steaming cups of lavender-chamomile tea. She handed one to Beryl and climbed into bed with her mug. They drank in silence, snuggled together.

"I miss my moms," said Beryl sleepily.

"I know," said Ava kissing Beryl on the forehead.

They drifted into sleep. While Ava dreamed sweet dreams of Tobias, Beryl dreamt about Hamilton as a young man. He walked through the woods with two women, laughing as they picked herbs. One of them was Ava, only much younger. She didn't recognize the other one. Hamilton made notes and stuck small pieces of leaves in his notebook, putting more herbs in his sack. Young Ava warned him that the herbs might not work in his world. The other woman pulled him behind a tree and kissed him. She assured him that Ontihaponati loved him and would do anything for him.

Then she saw Hamilton in a dingy room with his ill mother. He started telling her about his trip, but as soon as he mentioned Floredelis, she screamed and hit him. He pulled her into his arms to try to comfort her. She backed away and pulled out the book she thought she had hidden from him. She hadn't wanted him to know the truth. His father didn't die in a car accident. Hamilton didn't tell her he'd read the book many times. She told him his father wrote this book with a crazy woman named Jocasta. She planned to create a utopia someplace, and Hamilton, Senior, who had fallen in love with Jocasta, wanted to help. After disappearing for a whole month, Hamilton, Sr., returned home to tell his wife he was leaving her for a new world with Jocasta. She begged him to stay. She was pregnant with Hamilton, Junior. All she'd ever wanted to be was his wife and the mother of his children. He disappeared without a trace. Hamilton held her while she cried, which ended in a coughing fit.

He prepared the herbs from Floredelis, referring to his notes, and gave them to her. She died the next day.

Next, Beryl saw a sick woman coming to him for healing. She wasn't deathly ill, but she was in terrible pain all the time. He filled a small brown bottle with medicine he'd prepared from herbs he'd gathered in Floredelis and told her to take twelve drops three times a day, as Ava had done for a man with similar symptoms. The woman died, too, within days. Everyone thought Hamilton killed her. He tried to explain about the herbs from Floredelis. They thought he was crazy. Not guilty by reason of insanity, they locked him up and destroyed his medicines. When they released him, he no longer wanted to help people. He hated Floredelis, blamed it for ruining his life and killing his mother.

41

The next morning, in Brother Earth's realm

> On Solitude: Our soul is a deep pool. In order to draw on its strength and wisdom, we sometimes need to withdraw from the company of our family and friends for a time. Listen to your inner voice. When it becomes garbled or confused, consider taking some time alone, preferably near trees or water (or both). Take time to draw from the well of your own wisdom both for yourself and those you love.
>
> From The Book of Jocasta

Beryl woke up sad and tired. She thought about her dreams and everything that had happened yesterday. She couldn't shake the vision of Hamilton changing from wanting to help others to using them, his joy in discovering Floredelis turning to hatred. She needed to walk and clear her head. She remembered the gnomes warning about the dangers in this place but promised herself she wouldn't go far and would stay on the path. She drank the little bit of cold tea left in the bottom of her mug. She moved quietly so she wouldn't wake Ava, went back to her room, and dressed quickly. Shoes in hand, she walked downstairs. She didn't see anyone, although she heard sounds and smelled bread baking in the kitchen. She resisted the urge to grab something to eat, even though she felt hungry. The front door wasn't locked; in fact, it didn't have a lock on it. She slipped out into the fresh morning air.

Beryl pulled her rainbow scarf around her shoulders, as the morning air felt cool, and put on her shoes. The birds sang, and a light breeze ruffled the trees and her hair. What an amazing place. The darkness that weighed on her during the night faded. She saw a path in front of her. If she walked straight in one direction, she should be able to find her way back. She wondered if Jyrym's stick would work here. She dug it out of her pouch and laid it flat in her hand. It hadn't been long since Jyrym gave it to her, but it felt like that day he gifted it to her happened in ancient times. She asked it to show her what direction she should go. It spun and pointed toward the path. After walking a minute or two, she asked the stick to show her the way to Brother Earth's palace. Thankfully, it pointed back the way she had come. She continued walking, although nothing felt familiar. She thought about turning back but then thought that if she was powerful enough to save the world, she should be able to go for a walk by herself.

Suddenly, she heard a different sound, not the birds or the wind in the trees. Unsure what it was, but curious, she asked her stick to point her toward the source of the sound. It directed her to a boulder, twice as tall as her and as wide as it was tall. She put her ear on it. The sound, a muffled cry, came from inside.

"Hello," she said.

The sound stopped.

"Hello," she spoke louder. "Is someone in there?"

"Help me!" A man's voice spoke from inside the rock.

Beryl walked all around the rock but found no opening. The cries for help started again. Finally, she found an indentation. It wasn't an opening, but Beryl remembered the entry to the crystal cave. She turned sideways and tried to squeeze in. She didn't fit but managed to get her hand and arm inside.

She put her mouth against the opening. "Are you in there? I can't get inside, but if you can see my hand, take hold, and I'll try to pull you out."

"I can't see anything. It's too dark. But you made the wind stop." She heard the voice more clearly now. It sounded familiar, but she couldn't place it.

Then a hand grasped hers so tightly that it hurt. Beryl pulled. First, a hand emerged; Beryl was relieved that it was human. She reached in and found shoulders and, putting her hands beneath his armpits, pulled as hard as she could. One shoulder came out, then his head, followed by the other shoulder. The rest of him slipped out after. The man lay at her feet curled into a ball and shaking. He looked familiar and appeared uninjured. Beryl thought he must be frightened if he'd been trapped inside a rock. She covered him with her shawl and sat beside him, speaking softly and rubbing his back. After a few minutes, he stopped shaking so much, and she could see his face. Lucas! She looked again. It was definitely him. In a few minutes more, he sat up, looked at his surroundings, and then at Beryl.

"How did you get here?" Beryl asked.

"I don't know where here is. Was I inside this rock?"

Beryl nodded yes.

"Last thing I remember was climbing down a rope in a well in the basement of the old witch, I mean, Ava's house. I came to the end of the rope, lost my grip, and I've been falling ever since. I don't know how long that's been, but it would've been a lot longer if you hadn't rescued me. Thank you." He smiled his beautiful smile, pushed his hair out of his eyes, and gazed into hers.

Beryl's face grew red. "Let me take you back to Brother Earth's palace. We are in his land. It's a long story, but come with me. You can have something to eat and drink, and maybe even take a bath in the healing waters."

"No!" Lucas spoke sharply, startling Beryl. He immediately softened his tone, "I mean, I don't think I would be welcome there. I've done some bad things." He paused and smiled. "Besides, you're all I need to soothe my nerves. Is there somewhere else where I could rest? I don't want anyone to know I'm here—at least not yet."

"I don't really know what's around here. But maybe…" She pulled her stick out of her pouch and held it flat. It spun and pointed. "Let's try it and see. It led me to you. Can you walk? Maybe I should go for help. Everyone is very kind here. I'm sure they would help you no matter what you've done."

Lucas struggled to his feet. He leaned against the boulder for a moment. Beryl looked at him with concern. He touched her cheek. "Beryl, I'll be fine. Not everyone is as good-hearted as you. Perhaps I can hold your arm until I'm steadier on my feet."

Beryl waited while Lucas took hold of her arm. He leaned on her heavily and they started walking. His hand felt strong and warm on her arm. His touch made her feel special and even a little beautiful. She glanced at him. He smiled and ruffled her hair. I must look a mess, she thought. She hadn't even thought about her hair when she left the palace. She put her free hand to her head.

Lucas laughed. "Don't worry; I didn't muss your hair."

"I wasn't worried about that. I just remembered that I didn't comb it this morning. I must look a mess."

"You look beautiful and wild, like a wood nymph."

Beryl knew he was just being nice, but she liked it.

"Let me know if you need to rest," Beryl offered. But Lucas wanted to continue. He said it felt good to feel the ground beneath his feet again. After a few minutes, they came to a hill with an opening in it. "I think this might be the place."

"I don't think I can be inside a stone right now," said Lucas. "Maybe I could stay beneath this tree."

"You'll be cold if you stay outside."

"You could bring me back a blanket and some food."

"I will, but on one condition."

"Anything you ask, my princess and savior."

"When I return, I want you to tell me everything you know about what's happening in Floredelis."

"Of course. First, I'll rest a little. Will you tuck me in?" He lifted a corner of her rainbow scarf. "I promise to return your shawl when you come back."

Beryl felt her face turn red again. Lucas lay down under the tree. He slid the scarf off her shoulders and handed it to her. She covered him as best she could with her little scarf, especially considering that she couldn't stop her hands from shaking.

"Rest well." She gave him a quick kiss on his forehead and ran off.

42

That same morning, in Brother
Earth's realm

On Home: In the Old World, they said, "Home is where the heart is." But I would say the opposite is true. Where your heart is, you are home. Be like the turtle and carry your home on your back. If you love yourself, you will always be at home no matter where you are. Follow your heart. It will lead you home to yourself.
From The Book of Jocasta

With the help of her twig, Beryl easily found her way back to the tree palace. Now she was ravenous, and she needed food for Lucas. As she stood thinking, she heard laughter and looked up. Ava sat on the tree branch dining room with two men, one older and one younger.

"There she is," the older man said.

"There you are, Beryl. Come up. I want you to meet my friends," Ava said.

Beryl climbed up the ladder. She said hello to Andrew and Tobias, who had somehow arrived here in Brother Earth's realm. She thought she should be curious about the new arrivals, but she couldn't keep her eyes off the food or her mind off Lucas. They'd set a place for her. Ava put food on her plate, and she ate. Her plate empty again, she looked at Ava. She saw a glow of happiness on her godmother's face that she had never seen before. She looked at the men curiously. The younger one looked like the one she had seen in Ava's vision of the woods from long ago, but that didn't make any sense. "This is my friend from the woods, Tobias," Ava said with a wink, nodding at Tobias, "and this is his son, Andrew."

Beryl had never kept a secret from Ava before. Well, she knew that wasn't exactly true. She hadn't told Ava about her dreams, but she longed to tell her about Lucas. Ava was her only connection to the world she'd known before, and she longed to tell her everything—but she had promised. And Ava looked so happy. It was obvious that she was in love. Ava hadn't mentioned that part when she told Beryl about her trip to the Temple City. Beryl realized that she wasn't the only one who kept secrets. It made Beryl feel even more distant from Ava—and sad, too. She noticed Ava's flushed face and how she smiled at Tobias. Tobias didn't take his eyes off Ava. Beryl wondered how all this had happened without her knowing anything about it. She wondered if she looked like that when she looked at Lucas. Was she falling in love with him? She wished he had come back here with her, but when she tried to picture Lucas sitting here, she knew he didn't belong, although she wasn't sure why.

"It's been nice to meet both of you. Ava, would you mind if I packed a picnic and spent the rest of the day in the woods? A lot has happened in the last few days, and I need to be alone for a while."

Ava looked at her, but Beryl couldn't bear to look her in the eye and quickly looked away. Ava said, "Of course. Why don't you go to the kitchen and have them pack something for you? Are you sure you're alright?"

"Yes, I'm fine. I didn't sleep well last night, even after the lovely tea you made me. I wonder if there's a blanket or something I could use to sit on."

"You're not planning on sleeping out in the woods, are you?" asked Tobias with a laugh.

Beryl felt like running away as fast as she could, but instead, she said, "Oh, no. Just a picnic. I've been walking in the woods this morning and found the loveliest spot. I want to go back there and ....” She examined her fingernails. What should she tell them she wanted to do? She hadn't had much practice in lying. But she had to say something. She could feel all three of them looking at her waiting for her to finish. “... and be alone in the beauty of nature.” She looked at them but couldn't read their expressions. She mostly felt the blood rushing to her face as she tried to look serious and honest.

“You run along then,” said Ava. “We'll talk later.”

As she left, Beryl heard Ava saying, “I hope she's alright. I've never seen her like this.”

“Do you suppose it's because of us?” asked Tobias.

Beryl didn't hear Ava's answer as she hurried to the kitchen. She saw no one to ask, so she grabbed a sack and started throwing in food—bread, fruit, cheese, and part of a cherry pie. She grabbed a skin of ale, as she supposed Lucas would like that. She found a pile of blankets in the corner of the laundry room and grabbed two. As she left, she hoped she wouldn't have to talk to Ava and the men again on her way out. She glanced up and saw that Ava and Tobias were still sitting up in the tree, holding hands across the table and gazing into each other's eyes. They didn't notice Beryl.

“They're cute, aren't they?”

Beryl practically jumped out of her skin.

“I decided to leave them alone,” Andrew said. “I don't think they noticed that I left. Would you like some company? Or help carrying your sack? It looks heavy.”

“No thanks, Andrew. I want to be alone. And I'm really hungry. I must be having a growth spurt.”

She met his eyes. He looked nice. She smiled. “Thanks for the offer, though. Maybe another time.”

“Sure, just let me know.” She waited until she was out of sight before pulling out her magic stick. She thought she remembered the way back to where she'd left Lucas, but the bag was heavy, and she didn't want to carry it any further than she had to—and she couldn't wait to see Lucas again. He is in a lovely spot, she thought. At least that part was true.

43

A short walk later, in Brother Earth's land

She found Lucas sitting up when she returned. He must have found water because his hair was wet. He wore no shirt. She saw it dripping on a branch of the tree he sat beneath.

"Just cleaning up for you, princess," said Lucas.

Beryl felt a flutter of fear and wondered if coming here alone had been a good choice. Perhaps she'd jumped in over her head.

"Please don't call me that. It makes me feel strange."

"As you wish. It looks like you brought some food. Let's eat. I'm starving."

"Me, too. I haven't eaten yet today."

She wondered why she had lied. Beryl didn't feel like herself at all. She felt a sharp pain in her little finger. She flashed to her dream, finding a finger in her pouch instead of gold. She handed Lucas a blanket which he spread on the ground while she pulled out the food. They ate, and as

Beryl had hoped, he'd have enough food left for a few more meals. She felt relieved, after her time with Solomon, to see that Lucas drank only a few sips of the ale.

Lucas lay down on his back, bent his knees, and placed his hands behind his head, his chest still bare. Beryl sat on the far edge of the blanket. She thought he was smiling at her discomfort. Her face turned red again. Thankfully he put his dry shirt back on. But then he moved very close beside her. He smelled good, like fresh air and sunshine. The white shirt, still warm from the sun, brushed her shoulder. Had he done that on purpose? It felt good and scary at the same time.

"Alright, now for my part of the bargain. What do you want to know?" he asked, his warm voice tickling her ear.

Lucas told her he had loved Zorina, but she hungered for power and left him for Solomon when he promised to make her queen. He'd stayed near her afterward to protect her because, despite himself, he still cared for her even though he knew they'd never be together.

"I'm sorry for the pain I caused you." As he said this, he put his hand over hers.

Beryl felt a sense of revulsion. She remembered what Ava and Brother Earth had said about her abilities. She needed to focus, although it was hard with Lucas so close and so beautiful. She let him leave his hand on hers. He kept talking, but she listened now to her inner voice, which spoke of danger. She wanted to believe everything was fine and he liked her, and she could help him be a better person. But her deep inner voice insisted that he lied and wanted to use her—to seduce her.

Well, that felt kind of exciting; no one had ever done that before.

But she had to keep her focus. She felt danger emanating from him and knew without a doubt that she needed to get away now.

He stopped talking. Had he asked her a question? His big brown eyes stared directly into hers. She could swim in those eyes. But his eyes weren't the color of the ocean like the boy in her dream. She forced herself to smile. He kept looking at her. Maybe her inner voice had made a mistake. Maybe she feared surrendering to love, taking another step toward growing up. His face moved closer. His hand rose and touched her cheek. He started talking again, but his lips were so close that she couldn't concentrate. What was he saying?

"You saved me. I am forever in your debt. I would do anything for you."

His lips grazed hers. They felt soft and warm. Her first kiss, at least in her waking life. Beryl backed away. She put her hand on his mouth. She wanted to act grown-up and sophisticated, but she felt young.

"Please, Lucas, I'm not ready for this. It's too fast."

His eyes filled with anger; instead of the warm ocean, she felt ice. He pulled her hand away from his mouth and held it so tightly she couldn't move it.

He pushed her down on the blanket, rolling on top of her, pushing his face towards hers.

Somehow her free hand found its way into her pouch to the clear crystal that contained starlight. She hit him hard on the back of his head with it.

He rolled off her and grabbed his head. Beryl jumped up and ran as fast as she could. She heard Lucas yelling. As she turned to look behind her, an arm reached out and grabbed her. The other hand went over her mouth.

She raised the crystal, which she still held in her hand, ready to strike, when a voice whispered in her ear.

"It's me, Andrew. I'm here to help. Please don't hit me."

He pulled her into a cave. Beryl handed him the crystal and let him put his arms around her. She was too out of breath and full of tears to speak.

"I had a feeling you might need a friend," he said. "But you did a pretty good job by yourself. Two green friends of yours told me where to find you. I believe they've captured your attacker."

Andrew poked his head out of the cave and whistled. A whistle came back.

"Come on out, Beryl. It's safe."

Beryl peeked around him when she heard familiar voices. Ivy and Buttercup pulled their cart, and in it sat Lucas, tightly bound. When he saw Beryl, he started swearing, but before he could say much, Ivy tore off a piece of the picnic blanket and tied it around his mouth.

"Let's head back," Andrew said. "We'll let the gnomes go ahead, so you don't have to see that man."

But Beryl didn't want to go back. She had lied to her friends. She'd let herself be swayed by Lucas' sweet words and pretty face. How could she face everyone?

"Come on," said Andrew. "We all make mistakes. Think of it as a test that you passed. Brother Earth knew. He knows everything that goes on in the woods. Everyone loves you. It will be alright."

He took her hand. On the way back to the palace, he made her laugh by telling her about the time he bought some magic beans—like in Jack and the Beanstalk, but these didn't even sprout when he threw them out the window. At least he hadn't traded the family cow for them.

44

That same day, in Brother Earth's realm

For a long time, she did not know that she had had brothers, for her parents took care not to mention them to her. However, one day she accidentally overheard some people talking about her. They said that she was beautiful enough but that, in truth, she was to blame for her seven brothers' misfortune. This troubled her greatly, and she went to her father and mother and asked them if she indeed had had brothers and what had happened to them.

Her parents could no longer keep the secret but said that it had been heaven's fate and that her birth had been only the innocent cause. However, this ate at the girl's conscience every day, and she came to believe that she would have to redeem her brothers.

She had neither rest nor peace until she secretly set forth and went out into the wide world, hoping to find her brothers and to set them free, whatever it might cost. She took nothing with her but a little ring as a remembrance from her parents, a loaf of bread for hunger, a little jug of water for thirst, and a little chair for when she got tired.

She walked on and on -- far, far to the end of the world. From "The Seven Ravens" in Jocasta's Guide to Fairy Tales

At Brother Earth's palace, everyone treated Beryl with extra kindness. They understood and forgave and agreed with her that Lucas shouldn't be put back in the stone no matter how badly he had treated her or the other wrong things he'd done on the earth. But Beryl didn't want everyone to act so nice to her. She felt angry at herself for being tricked and guilty about lying. She felt angry at the others, too, although she couldn't say why. She wished they would yell at her so she could yell back.

Ava wanted to talk, but Beryl couldn't bear to spend time with her.

"Ava," she said, "You are so kind. But I really need to clear my head. I want to walk in the woods and be alone for a while. This time, I really want to be alone. I mean...I don't know who I am anymore."

"I understand." Ava felt disappointed in Beryl, but even more, she felt deeply disappointed in herself. She should tell Beryl and the others about her relationship with Dr. Hami, but she didn't have the strength —or perhaps, the courage.

"Of course you can go. Buttercup and Ivy will accompany you; I'm sure they'll give you plenty of space."

Beryl lowered her head. Ava didn't trust her. She tried to tell herself that was fine, but it wasn't. She'd really messed up. She didn't even trust herself anymore.

"Alright," she agreed with a sigh.

"When you come back, I'll show you how to cleanse your crystal. It may have picked up some negative energy when you clocked Lucas with it." Ava gave her a little smile. "I also have something to tell you that I should have told you earlier."

"Thanks, that will be great," Beryl replied without emotion. She hoped she would feel like talking with Ava when she got back. "See you later."

Beryl didn't use her magic stick. She just walked. She didn't worry about getting lost with Buttercup and Ivy nearby, and she didn't really care if something bad happened to her, although she doubted the gnomes would allow it. Rather than enjoying the woods, she walked as fast as she could, looking at her feet. She almost ran into the big stone hill, which seemed to have appeared out of nowhere. She stared at it, then leaned against it and slid to the ground. The sharp rock hurt her back as she slid, and the pain somehow made her feel better. As her breath quieted, she noticed a breeze coming out from the rock, although she saw no opening. Holding up a hand, she found a small hole where the breeze came from. She knew by now that openings and solid rocks were not always what they seemed in Brother Earth's Land.

When she stood to take a closer look, she heard singing inside, a woman's voice, high and faint. As she peered into the hole, she didn't hear Ivy shouting at her to step back, for as she looked, she was inside.

But now she heard the voices of Ivy and Buttercup. They sang, "Beryl, come back. I told you we should have stayed closer." What a lovely melody. It seemed to twinkle in the darkness of wherever she had landed. Had she fallen into the place of swirling darkness, like Lucas? Had she left the path of light? But this darkness sang and didn't swirl, and lights sparkled further in. She tried to berate herself for messing up again, but the lights entranced her. The gnomes' song faded away, replaced by a new song. Many voices sang, but not in unison. "Beryl, Beryl, Beryl." They sang her name again and again. "She holds the key." "The key." "The key."

Beryl put her hand to her throat. Her pouch was gone. She hadn't taken it off. All alone, she didn't have anything or anyone to help her. She felt her pulse pounding in her throat. She felt dizzy. Goose bumps rose on her arms. Was she cold? She wanted to float away on those voices that kept singing her name. They soothed her, but she feared being lost forever if she followed them. She looked around. It looked like the inside of a hill, which didn't surprise her, since it looked like the outside of a hill on the other side. She thought again about the stories of people stolen away by fairies, never to be seen again. But this place was nothing like Solara's home.

She thought of the story of the seven ravens, where the little sister went to rescue her brothers, who have been turned into ravens by their evil stepmother. She lost the key the stars gave her to enter her brothers' home, so she cut off her little finger and used it to open the door. Why was she thinking about that? The pouch in her dream—the finger inside. The finger? Why was she singing about that? No, she wasn't singing. The voices were still singing about the key, but she had no key, and she saw no lock. She felt her thoughts drifting away. It would be so easy just to let go.

"No!" she said loudly.

"No," she said again.

Her voice sounded strange, but it was louder than the singing, and that helped her stay present. She crossed her arms and squeezed her upper arms with her hands until her arms and hands hurt. She took a deep breath.

"Hello," she shouted. The sound of her own voice startled her and perhaps startled the singers, as silence surrounded her.

"Hello," she said, more quietly this time. "Who are you? What do you want?"

The only sound Beryl heard in reply was her own breathing. She concentrated on it, in and out, in and out, in and out, slowly to the count of 3 each way. She felt a little calmer. But the eerie silence seemed full of ears. Maybe she could get out the way she had come in. Beryl looked for the opening but saw only the curved wall and the sparkling lights. She walked toward the sparkling lights. They didn't look far away, but as she walked, she got no closer to them, nor did she seem to get closer to the opposite wall. The singing started again. "Beryl, Beryl, Beryl, Beryl," again and again.

She covered her ears.

"Stop," she screamed.

She heard laughter. Then she got mad.

"Stop," she screamed again.

Cautiously she removed her hands from her ears; silence. She should have talked to Ava. She should have stayed at Brother Earth's tree palace. Maybe she should have never left home in the first place. Things kept getting worse and worse. Would she ever get out of whatever this place was? Could Ivy and Buttercup help her? She couldn't need rescuing. Not again; not so soon. She'd find a way out and then stay at the tree castle with Ava and everyone and be good if only the Goddess would help her find her way back.

But maybe she'd found her way here for a reason. Maybe something good could come of this. Maybe the lights and voices wanted to help her—or needed her help. Perhaps she should try being nice. She calmed herself and spoke kindly to the voices.

"Hello," she began, "I'm Beryl." That was dumb, she thought. They know my name; they've been singing it. But she continued. "Please tell me or show me who you are. Can you help me? I don't know where I am or how to get home."

In the twinkling of an eye, the sparkling lights surrounded her. They felt safe and warm. The voices started again, but this time they spoke to her.

"Welcome, Beryl. We've been waiting for you. We have a gift for you."

"What is it?" Beryl asked.

"Jocasta's journal."

"What? We already have the Book of Jocasta."

"This is different. Jocasta wrote the story of her life in her journal. She hid it here until the time it might be needed by the humans in this world. That time is now, and the person to whom it belongs is you."

"Who are you?" Beryl asked.

"We are the Grandmothers, guardians of Floredelis. We have been here since the beginning. Before Jocasta, before Brother Earth, and even before Ontihaponati. Come, you have no time to waste. We will show you where the journal is, but only you can take it. You must use your key."

Beryl had no idea what she had that might be a key; she had nothing with her except her clothes. The lights that sparkled around her made her tingle. They urged her forward. Her body stiffened, resisting, but she made herself relax. If she listened with her whole body, she could feel where the light wanted her to go. She still could see nothing but the inside of a big hill, and the walls remained the same distance away no matter how many steps she took, but she felt as though she were winding through paths and climbing up and down hills. She grew weary, but she didn't stop.

Just after Beryl's disappearance, in Brother Earth's land

> *Mineral Kingdom: The gnomes work with stones and crystals, and also the soil. They help roots find their way through the earth. Some of you will be able to see them. Children often can. But strangely, gnomes cannot see human children until they turn three—until then, the children are too close to the spiritual world, not fully here on earth. Gnomes love to hear stories about small children, and they think it's funny to hide your things. If you ever need their help or suspect they are hiding something you're looking for, tell them a story about a baby and be amazed when whatever disappeared suddenly is right in front of your eyes!*
>
> *From* The Book of Jocasta

Ivy and Buttercup raced back to tell Brother Earth what had happened. They found him sitting beneath a tree with Ava and Tobias. The humans stopped talking and laughing when they saw the gnomes.

Ivy twisted his beard, and Buttercup examined the tassel on his cap. The three humans watched with puzzled amusement. Finally, Brother Earth asked, "Where is Beryl?"

Buttercup burst into tears, and Ivy's eyes threatened to overflow.

"You had best tell us what happened," Brother Earth said.

Buttercup spoke through his sobs, "She's in... That is, she is in.... We've failed. We will never forgive ourselves."

Ivy's lips quivered. He blurted out, "She's in the Hill of the Grandmothers." Then he, too, burst into tears.

Father Earth put a hand on each of their shoulders. "Good gnomes, this is troublesome, indeed, but don't blame yourselves. If the Grandmothers wanted Beryl, there is no way you could have stopped them. I'm sure you cared for her well. Come sit with us and calm yourselves."

They sat down and eventually stopped crying after much reassurance from the humans and Brother Earth.

"I hope she will be alright. Dear Beryl, we love her." Ivy said.

Ava and Tobias looked at Brother Earth.

"You want to know what is happening," he said.

They nodded.

"The Grandmothers have been here since before time began. They were here before I came to Floredelis, which was long ago. They live inside a hill. But none can enter unless the Grandmothers want them to. Few humans have gone in, and even fewer have returned. But I feel certain that Beryl will come back. Jocasta did."

Brother Earth looked at the worried faces of Ava and Tobias and continued, "The Grandmothers won't harm her, but she will have to face her demons before she can leave. She won't be the same when she returns."

"Can we help her?" Ava asked, although she already knew the answer.

"No, she must do this on her own. I'm afraid all we can do is wait."

"And pray," said Ava. "I will pray for her."

"I will, too," said Tobias. " I will stand by you, Ava. I know how much you love Beryl. She is strong, and you've taught her well."

"Thank you, Tobias." She took his hand. "I'm so thankful to have found you after all these years." She kissed him. "I think I've finally gotten my priorities straight."

"Ava, your priorities were always fine. I was young and impatient. We're both lucky to have a second chance. Maybe this time we can work together. We make a good team." He held Ava close.

46 |

In the Hill of the Grandmothers

Beryl rubbed her eyes. She lay on the ground, surrounded by darkness. She didn't remember falling asleep; she remembered walking a long time and going nowhere. Was that a dream? Was she still dreaming?

"Need some help?" Lucas stood over her, smiling and holding out a hand. Where had he come from, and why would he want to help her?

"Hey, you saved my life. Even though you whacked me on the head, I still owe you."

"You don't owe me anything, and I don't trust you."

"Look," Lucas said, looking more beautiful than ever, "the way I see it, you don't have a lot of choices. You're stuck inside a hill. You can stay here until you die of thirst, or you can let me help you. Here, have a drink; it's water."

A wineskin appeared. Lucas took a long drink, then offered it to her. Beryl realized she felt very thirsty. She took the skin and tipped it toward her mouth, then suddenly remembered the story of Persephone —because she ate one pomegranate seed, she had to spend half of every year in the underworld. She returned the wineskin to Lucas without drinking. "No, thank you," she said. "I'm not thirsty."

Lucas cocked his head and grabbed her wrist, pulling her to her feet. "Suit yourself," he said, still holding on. The wineskin disappeared. He pulled her close and kissed her hard. She stomped on his foot and pulled away. "No!" she shouted. He still held her wrist. Then he was no longer Lucas but Andrew. "You know you like me. I'm a nice boy, and I saved you from that horrible Lucas." Andrew pulled her close; Beryl put her hand in front of her mouth. Andrew pulled her hand away. She turned her head to one side, and when she turned back, Solomon stood in front of her. "I'm not interested in little girls," he said, "but you are now a woman." He pulled her close by both of her elbows. She thought of Poseidon, the god of the sea, who could change forms, and how Hercules held on to him until he gave up and returned to his true form. She didn't know who this was, but it wasn't any of the men she was seeing. Next, she saw Dr. Hami. Would this ever stop? More men appeared before her, mostly ones she knew, all trying to take from her what she wasn't willing to give.

Then he was there. The shadow man. The Thirteenth. He didn't touch her, although he stood as close as the others. She had never seen him so clearly before. He looked like Dr. Hami and yet different, dark and shadowy, like looking at someone through dark water. Tears ran down his face. She longed to reach out to him but felt afraid to touch him. She wanted to talk; she had many questions but couldn't find her voice. His tears fell silently. She felt his pain and could bear it no longer. She opened her arms and held him close. His tears showed no signs of stopping. "Why are you so sad?" she asked.

"In the beginning was the word."

"What?" she asked.

"The land of Floredelis wouldn't exist without my words and my love. I have been forgotten. There has been no one to hold me, to hold my pain, no one who could even hear me until you."

Beryl tried to understand, tried to think of something to say, but he was gone.

"You passed the first test, Beryl. You listened to your inner voice and didn't give in to lust or fear, but you did offer compassion to one in need. Let's continue our journey."

Who said that? What happened to the Thirteenth? She felt dizzy. "May I sit down?" she asked.

"Of course," came the answer. "Your journey will take you nowhere but into yourself, so you can travel just as well sitting down."

"Thank you," Beryl said. She saw a chair next to her. Although it hadn't been there a moment earlier, it felt solid, so she sat down. She concentrated on counting her breaths and soon felt calmer. She thought of the story of Mother Holle and how the good stepsister helped her after she fell down the well. She wondered if the Grandmothers needed her help.

"Grandmothers, is there something I can do to help you?" Beryl asked.

"Yes. Take Jocasta's journal back to your world and put the wisdom it contains to good use. But first, you must learn to distinguish truth from illusion, and then you must find the key."

"Can I touch you? It helps me understand."

"We thought you'd never ask." A very old woman sat next to her in a rocking chair, her face all wrinkles with wisps of white hair on her almost bald head. She was shorter than Beryl and looked pale and weak, but her green eyes sparkled like the lights Beryl kept seeing. She looked so strange that Beryl found it difficult to touch her. Still, she reached out her hand, and the old woman offered hers in return. Beryl looked at it. Almost as wrinkled as her face, with large blue veins running through the back, when she turned it over, Beryl saw that her palm was smooth. Beryl took the old woman's hand between her two hands and rested them on her knee. The woman's skin felt as thin as paper, and yet her hand contained great strength. Beryl closed her eyes. From the woman's hand, she felt life flowing like a river, she felt flowers blooming and trees dancing their stately dances from birth to death. She felt like a drop of water in the river, separate yet part of the whole. She felt infinitely big and infinitely small at the same time. This being, the Grandmother, neither good nor evil, encompassing everything. She let herself flow into the Grandmother. She could stay and live in that flow, a life of bliss, a life without hardships. She wanted to. Life seemed too hard, and this, her vision, so blissful. She could breathe this water.

But then she thought of her parents, of Ava and Brother Earth. She wasn't ready to leave them. She loved them, and they needed her. Now the river tasted like tears. The sadness of the Thirteenth called her. She pulled back from the river, said goodbye to endless peace, and found herself back in her body. "I will stay here," she said. She opened her eyes and let go of the Grandmother's hand. The Grandmother looked different. Many of her wrinkles had plumped out, and she had some color in her cheeks. Her hair, though still white, was now covered her entire scalp in soft curls. She patted Beryl on the knee. "You have chosen well, my daughter. Your time to flow into me lies far in the future. You have passed the second test. Now you may rest, and when you awaken, you must find the key."

The Grandmother disappeared. Where her chair had been stood a little bed. Beryl felt so tired she could have slept in her chair. But the bed looked inviting. She picked up the comforter and shook it, laughing with delight as the feathers flew, just like in "Mother Holle." She quickly fell into a deep, dreamless sleep.

Brother Earth's Land, evening of the second day after Beryl entered the Hill of the Grandmothers

> *The wisdom of our ancestors—both our familial ancestors and those to whom we are connected spiritually: Never forget that not only do the angels and archangels want to help us, but also our ancestors who watch over us from the other side. You can connect with them through meditation or prayer—and even in everyday life.*
>
> *From* The Book of Jocasta

Beryl had entered the Hill of the Grandmothers two days ago. Ava tried unsuccessfully not to worry. She and Tobias walked to the forest's edge to watch the sunset. They sat under a tree and looked at the glorious colors. The moon rose early and passed the sun as it headed toward the horizon. Both planets seemed to pause for a moment as they met.

"I really appreciate your support and your friendship," said Ava. "I couldn't bear to lose you again." She looked at the moon. "I have prided myself on being an independent woman, able to care for myself and others. But I find myself longing for something else. With you."

"Ava, I have no intention of letting you go unless you want to go, of course. I had a good life with my wife. We brought a wonderful son into the world. But I never stopped loving you. I don't know if we'll survive whatever is coming, but whatever time we have left, I would like to spend with you." Tobias cradled her face in his hands and looked into her eyes. Ava felt like she was melting. She couldn't believe Tobias loved her, too.

"Ava," Tobias said, his lips almost touching hers, "Will you marry me?"

Ava gasped. Tears sprung into her eyes. "Oh, Tobias, if we survive...."

"I don't want to wait. Brother Earth has agreed to perform the ceremony. Let's get married as soon as Beryl returns."

"I've never felt the way I feel with you-- happy, loved, vulnerable, strong. The vulnerable part scares me, but that's alright. Nothing would bring me more joy than to spend whatever life I have left with you. Yes, I will marry you. I love you, too."

Ivy tiptoed up to Tobias and handed him a ring. He had tears in his eyes. "I thought you might like this. It's a gift from the crystal gnomes."

Ava and Tobias laughed. They didn't know they'd had an audience. Tobias placed the ring on Ava's finger. Its stone glowed pink.

"Thank you, Ivy," he said, "and thank you, too, Buttercup, wherever you are."

Buttercup appeared, dabbing his eyes with the end of his beard.

"Come, brother," he said, "We must prepare. We've never had a human wedding here before."

The gnomes ran off, leaving Tobias and Ava to enjoy the moonlight and each other.

In the Hill of the Grandmothers, the third day

Beryl had entered the Hill of the Grandmothers at least two days ago, as best she could tell. She woke up, unsure if it was day or night, as it was always dark here. At least she felt rested and knew where she was. The Grandmother sat in her rocking chair by the bed, knitting something very long. Beryl watched her knitting needles working and listened to their comforting clack.

"What are you making?" she asked.

"You're awake. I'm knitting a blanket to keep Floredelis warm through the long, cold winter." The knitting dissolved. "But you must get started, for today, you must find the key."

Beryl rubbed her hands through her matted hair, pulling out a couple of stray leaves. "What key?"

The Grandmother held a box in her lap. "This box contains Jocasta's journal," she said. "The key will open the lock so you can remove the journal and return with it to Brother Earth's house."

Beryl sat up. The Grandmother sat so close to her bed that their knees almost touched. She handed Beryl the box. It felt heavy. She heard something sliding around inside but saw no opening or keyhole. She started to ask how it opened, but when she looked up, the Grandmother was gone, along with her rocking chair. Beryl wasn't particularly startled. She no longer expected that anything or anyone would stay where or even who they were in this cave.

She put the box down and rubbed her head. There was nothing in this place besides this bed and now the box. How could she possibly find a key for a box with no keyhole in this empty place? She picked up her pillow, still warm from her head. She hugged it, curled herself into a little ball, and cried. She sobbed until her tears were gone. That's what Mama B used to tell her, "Let the tears come out. When they all come out, you'll stop crying." She missed her mothers.

She wiped her eyes on her sleeve. She hadn't eaten since she arrived, but she wasn't hungry another strange thing. She walked around for a long time, never reaching the walls. She looked up and down and all around but didn't see anything resembling a key. She didn't see anything but space and rock. She walked back to the bed with the box still sitting on it. She looked under the bed and searched the mattress and covers but didn't find a key.

She looked under the bed a second time and, this time found a hand mirror. It hadn't been there before. It had delicate lacy metalwork that framed the glass like a flowering vine around a still pond, and many intertwined vines formed the handle. In stories, mirrors sometimes spoke.

She cleared her throat. Her voice sounded surprisingly loud. "Mirror, do you speak?" Beryl waited for an answer. She noticed her face in the mirror. She looked like a wild thing. She saw streaks in the dirt on her cheeks where her tears had fallen. Her eyes looked red and swollen. They sparkled green, like the eyes of the Grandmother. The mirror didn't speak. She could think of nowhere else to look.

Then she noticed that the handle of the mirror was loose. She wiggled it, and it got looser. She pulled, and it came off to reveal a thin, very sharp knife. The knife frightened her. She put it down on the box and sat as far away from it as she could. She stared at it. She picked it up again and looked at it some more. Maybe it was the key. She poked the box with the knife. Nothing happened. She pushed the knife hard into the side of the box, hoping to cut it open. It slipped and cut the palm of her hand, causing her intense pain. Tears sprung into her eyes. She watched her blood drip onto the box.

Beryl watched in amazement as, starting where her blood had dripped and going all around the narrow edge of the box, an opening appeared. In her amazement, she forgot about her hand and the knife for a moment. She tried to open the box, but her hand hurt too much, and the blood dripping from her wound made everything slippery. She used the knife to cut a strip of fabric from the bottom of her skirt. She put the knife down carefully. The fabric was dirty, but it would have to do. She wrapped it around her hand and tied it tightly. It felt much better.

She wiped her blood off of the box with the comforter and picked it up. It still had an opening, and now it had a lock, too. The lock looked about the size of her little finger. She stuck her finger in the hole. It fit, but the lock didn't turn. She knew what she had to do. Her breathing became ragged, and her eyes blurred with tears. She put the box on her lap, put her injured hand on the box, put the knife against the bottom joint of her little finger, and pressed.

49

Later that same day

"Beryl, can you hear me."

Beryl heard her name from far away. She wished the Grandmothers would stop singing. She didn't want to listen; she just wanted to sleep. She felt a hand on her shoulder. "Beryl, please wake up." That wasn't the Grandmothers. Something dripped onto her face.

She heard a man's voice. "She's injured, Ava. Look at her hand. Oh, dear goddess!"

That voice definitely came from outside of her. Did it say 'Ava'? A breeze tickled her cheeks. She forced her unwilling eyes open. Everything looked blurry, but she saw Ava's face. Tears dripped from Ava's eyes, but she smiled and stroked Beryl's face when Beryl opened her eyes.

"Thank the Goddess, you're back," she heard Ava say before she passed out again.

When Beryl's eyes closed, Ava looked at what Tobias had seen. In her many years as a healer, Ava had always remained calm and professional. But this was too much. Beryl's left hand, wrapped in a bloody bandage, obviously made from her tattered skirt, looked badly injured. In her right hand, she clutched an old black book. Tobias held another bloody piece of Beryl's skirt that he'd picked up from the ground next to her. When he'd unwrapped it, he'd found a severed finger. Ava sat back and put her head between her legs. She looked at Beryl, all dirty and covered in her own blood.

"Ava, we must get her back to Brother Earth. Perhaps he can...," Tobias paused, looking for the right words. He worried about Beryl, and he worried about Ava, too. She looked like she might faint. "Perhaps he can put her back together. Ava?"

He put his arm around her. She leaned against him heavily and then pushed away, standing straight. "You're right," she said. "Time is of the essence."

Tobias wrapped the finger back up and put it in his pocket. He tried to take the book, but Beryl clung to it so tightly that he couldn't remove it from her grasp. He picked her up. She felt light. Ava looked anxiously at Beryl's face, and then, with no more words, she and Tobias hurried back to Brother Earth's house.

Brother Earth reattached Beryl's finger, although she would always have a scar. The cut in her palm had become infected. She had a high fever. Ava cared for her, bathing the hand in healing tea to cure the infection. The hand started looking better quickly, but the fever raged on. Beryl occasionally opened her eyes but didn't seem to recognize Ava or know where she was. Ava gave her drops of water so she wouldn't get dehydrated. She wouldn't leave Beryl's side even though Ava was exhausted. Tobias insisted she get some rest and promised to stay with Beryl. He promised to wake Ava if anything changed and promised to keep giving Beryl water. Ava, who could barely sit up anymore, finally agreed.

Tobias looked at the girl. Ava had cleaned her face, but her hair was matted. Her cleanly bandaged hand rested over the covers. She wore the same dirty clothes they'd found her in, and she still held tightly to the book. Tobias had watched Ava clean Beryl's feet and legs and wrap her feet in cool, wet bandages soaked in lemon water to help bring her fever down. He checked the bandages on her feet. They felt dry, so he removed them, soaked them in the lemon water, and wrapped them back up. Even in her exhaustion, Ava couldn't rest. She worried about Beryl. She came back to ask Tobias a question but stood in the doorway and watched Tobias care for Beryl, although Tobias didn't notice. Her heart filled with love as she saw his tender care. Finally, she surrendered to sleep.

Ava was sound asleep when Tobias woke her. It was dark and quiet, as only happens in the middle of the night. "Beryl? Is she alright?" Ava sat up, instantly wide awake.

Tobias put a hand on her shoulder to calm her. "Her fever is breaking. She's waking up. I hate to wake you but know you want to be with her now. And I'm sure she would rather see your face than mine when she wakes up." Tobias longed to kiss Ava; she looked so beautiful in the dark, warm from sleep.

Ava hurried into Beryl's room. Beryl's cheeks were flushed, and her whole head was sweaty. Ava watched her eyelids flutter and then open. She watched as they went from unseeing to focused. When those green eyes met hers, she smiled. "Beryl, you're back. Praise the Goddess."

Beryl's lips could barely move her parched, cracked lips. "Ava, I'm so thirsty," she croaked.

Ava helped her sit up, and Tobias brought some cool tea. He handed it to Ava, who offered Beryl a sip. Only then did Beryl realize she was holding something. "The journal," she said, her voice still hoarse. "I can't let go of it."

"You've held onto it since we found you almost two days ago. Let me help." Ava massaged Beryl's arm and hand. In a few minutes, Beryl released the book. Ava set it on the bedside table. She gave Beryl more tea, as Beryl's one hand was too stiff to use and the other wrapped in bandages. After sipping some tea, Beryl felt hungry. "Could I have something to eat? I'm famished."

"Of course. Tobias, will you get some soup for Beryl while I bathe her?"

"Ivy and Buttercup are on their way up with warm bath water. They're anxious to see you, Beryl," said Tobias

He kissed the top of Ava's head. He hugged her from behind. Beryl watched curiously as Ava put her hand on Tobias' arm, squeezed it, and smiled. She noticed the ring on Ava's finger. Ava followed her gaze. "I'll tell you all about it while I bathe you."

Tobias held the door for the gnomes. Ivy carried a tub of steaming water, and Buttercup came behind carrying firewood. Buttercup built up the fire while Ivy put the tub near the foot of the bed. They both gazed at Beryl.

"We're glad you're feeling better," Buttercup said.

"You don't have to talk," said Ivy. "We just wanted to see you. We'll come back when you're stronger."

Ava gently removed the tattered dress and bathed Beryl. When Tobias arrived with the soup, she sat in her clean bed wearing a warm, clean nightgown. The soup smelled delicious. Beryl still couldn't move her unbandaged arm, so Ava fed her. It felt wonderful to be cared for. Beryl smiled to see how happy Ava and Tobias looked together, even though smiling made her lips hurt even more.

50

In Brother Earth's house, the next day

The next day, after more food and rest, Beryl decided to look at Jocasta's journal. Her fever had gone, although her body still ached, especially her hands and arms. At least her right arm had relaxed enough that she could use it. After lunch, she found herself alone for the first time since her return from the cave. Ava left her a bell to ring in case she needed anything and went to plan her wedding. Beryl shook her head in disbelief. Ava and Tobias, long-lost lovers, reunited. She wavered between thinking it was the most romantic thing she'd ever heard and being totally disgusted by two old people being in love.

Beryl looked at the black book. She touched it gently, feeling the rough texture of the cover. She sighed and picked it up. She wondered what it contained that could be so important that she had to endure so much to bring it back. Propping it on her legs, she opened the cover.

"Journal" was handwritten on the frontispiece. Was that really written by Jocasta, the woman who found and created Floredelis? The writing didn't look special. It wasn't particularly beautiful. It wasn't even written in a straight line. She flipped through the pages; they were all written in the same hand.

She turned to the first page and began:

August 18: Today, I had a hard day at work. Nothing came out right. The people I work with drive me crazy. What have we done to this world? People have forgotten who they truly are. Are there still places where people live in joy and community? Places where people recognize that the true gifts of life are not material? I long for a new beginning for myself and humanity. I am a social being. I don't want to live by myself in a cave. I want a fresh start. I want to return to Eden and start again. Maybe we can learn from our mistakes and not repeat history. I wonder if it's possible. I wonder if someday I will have the courage to write about my past. I wonder if I have the courage to create a new future.

Beryl wondered if Jocasta had really written this in the old world. She wasn't sure she even believed in the old world. It sounded like a scary fairy tale. She rubbed her bandaged finger. She'd only read the first page, but it certainly didn't seem earth-shattering or world-changing.

September 21: In my meditation this morning, the most amazing thing happened. I saw a place that was pristine and pure. It had forests and mountains, prairies, and oceans, all alive with the spirits of nature. The being of the place spoke to me. She invited me to visit. She told me that this is the place I seek. This place longs for humans to join their family. She heard my heart's call for a new beginning, and she offers me an opportunity. Could this be real? It felt real. But it's impossible. I hope I'm not losing my mind. Well, since I don't know how to get there, I guess it doesn't really matter. The rest of the day flew by. Everything flowed at work. I can't wait to see what happens next.

October 7: Ontihaponati is her name. She is the heart of Floredelis, which is the name of this world. Her physical form is a large quartz crystal. "And I will remove your heart of stone and give you a heart made of flesh." But I have found a heart of stone, and I feel that a whole new life is about to begin for me. A joining of heart of stone and heart of flesh. She promised to show me the passage from my world to hers. She invited me to look around and decide if I would like to live there. I have been meditating for so many years now, probably 28, give or take a few, and never have I experienced anything like this. Even if it isn't real, my life is changing. I am filled with joy and love, even for my co-workers—which is truly a miracle.

December 15: I am taking the next two weeks off. I had to take my vacation anyhow or I would have lost the days off. I packed a backpack with clothes, matches, a small empty pouch (which Ontihaponati asked me to bring), and some food. I will put my journal in, too, as soon as I finish writing. I am excited and scared at the same time. What if I am really losing my mind? What if I think I'm in Floredelis, and I'm really wandering around downtown muttering to myself? Well, life is nothing if not an adventure. I told no one about this for fear that they would have me taken to the loony bin if such a place really exists. Ha—all sorts of imaginary places for me to visit. But I am just avoiding the next step now because I'm really nervous. I asked Ontihaponati if I had to go somewhere special to find the passage. She laughed and asked me where I would like to go. Then she told me that she could open the portal wherever I wanted. So here I sit in the living room of my apartment, backpack on my lap. All I have to do is enter my meditative space and tell her I'm ready. Here goes nothing—or maybe everything.

December 15, but how could it still be? —Floredelis—Oh dear God, I am really here. I am sitting under a tree in the woods, breathing the sweet, pure air, and I tasted the water, amazingly sweet and nourishing. Each sip filled me with life and hope. I am watching the sun set behind the twin mountains, Hugin and Munin. This morning, I sat in my chair and meditated. I found Ontihaponati, and she opened a passage for me. It felt like going through the tunnel of light that people describe when they have near-death experiences, except at the end, I arrived in a cave filled with light and mostly filled with the largest crystal I have ever seen. Love emanated from her. I touched her and felt filled with golden light. She gave a piece of herself to me. I put it in the pouch she told me to bring and placed it around my neck. Her warmth still fills me. She sent me out to see the land. First, I saw a flat grassy place. I pictured a city here, with homes and a temple built of stone from the mountains. Next, I came to the woods. It took me 2 or 3 hours to get here, as best I can tell. My watch doesn't work here. I wish I had the words to describe what I see. Everything feels new. The air seems alive. I want to live here. I hope it's not a mistake to bring people here. What if we bring evil with us? How will I find others who want to come? Who else would believe such a place exists? I can't imagine how this will happen, but Ontihaponati promised to help me. Now I must rest. May all this be done in accordance with the highest good for myself, Floredelis, and all sentient beings.

Beryl wondered what Floredelis was like before people came. She wondered what it would be like to move to a new world. She also wondered if it was right to run away from one's problems rather than face them. She wondered what had happened to Jocasta to make her want to leave her world.

January 5: Back to the "real world." Everything feels heavy here. The buildings, the sidewalks, even the air feels heavy. But I must still spend a little more time here so I can prepare. Ontihaponati assures me that the people who are meant to come will find me. I am to publish a book. She said I will find a man who will help me write it. She told me to sign up for a writing class at the community college, and I did. Classes start next week.

January 23: What does one bring to a new world? What is essential? It depends on what we want to create. Ontihaponati has a vision for her world. I have a vision for humanity. Together, we can co-create a vision for the society we will form in Floredelis. I must remember that I don't have to do all this myself. I couldn't. It would be like growing a baby if I had to figure out how to make all the organs, bones, and muscles and put them all in the right places. I depend on the spiritual beings for guidance—and must remember to trust my inner knowing. As the person responsible for bringing humanity to this new world, I must present a clear vision. Planet earth holds much wisdom, as well as evil and darkness. I know I want to bring some books, especially ones that have shaped me, so future generations of Floredelis can learn from these great teachers.

Beryl wondered if Jocasta had asked for help from other people. It seemed like she only asked for help from the spiritual world. How could Jocasta think she could do everything or even think of everything without help from her fellow human beings?

January 25: I went to my first writing class today. It was me, a bunch of young college students, and the teacher. His name is Hamilton. He has a mellifluous, deep voice and large, strong hands. I stayed after class to talk to him. He asked me why I had signed up for his class—probably because I was the only grown-up there. I told him I wanted to write a book but didn't tell him what about. He offered to help. I must admit I found him attractive. That's something I haven't felt for a long time, and it scares me.

March 16: I finally told Hamilton about Floredelis. I think he believes me. He said he would help me write the book. He said he would be my first follower, that he would follow me anywhere. I think he used to wear a wedding ring, but I didn't see it today—and I don't want to ask him.

July 16: We finished the book. We took it to the copy shop and made a hundred copies. Ontihaponati tells me where to leave them around the city —in parks, libraries, at bus stops, places like that. We printed my phone number in the back of the book so people can contact me. I can't believe we're doing this. I think Hamilton is falling in love with me. We've spent so much time together these past few months. We even meditated together, and he was able to connect with Ontihaponati. We made a short trip to Floredelis—just a few hours—so he could see for himself. I want to fall in love with him, but I don't know if I can ever do that again. Will I be able to leave my past behind when I move to Floredelis?

Hamilton—the father, the Thirteenth. He was right here in the journal. Why wasn't he part of Floredelis' history? She remembered him saying, "Don't forget me." She remembered his tears.

She kept reading.

Before leaving, I recovered ninety-eight of copies of the book. Mostly, they were brought back by those who found them, those who will come to Floredelis with me. I destroyed all of the books I found. I wanted to destroy all of them. I don't like the idea that any mention of Floredelis remains in the old world. Hamilton kept one that he wouldn't let me destroy. I don't know why. But we are here now, and that's done.

The next couple of pages were blank.

I recently came across this old journal. I am old now, and death hovers over me. I've finished writing the Book of Jocasta. It contains the story of the beginnings of this world and sets out many important principles to guide future generations. I chose not to write about my personal life or my past there. But I fear that someday violence will come to Floredelis, that someday my memories of the old world might be helpful, and so I write here trusting that someone far in the future will find this journal if it is needed. I hope that never happens.

Beryl closed the book. That time had come. And she had found the book. She rubbed her matted hair. Ava left a comb and scissors by her bed, planning to cut out some of the knots later. But Beryl couldn't stand it any longer, so she took the scissors and started cutting. She looked at the growing pile of knotty hair. Good riddance, she thought.

Brother Earth walked in. She hadn't seen him since she had returned, although Ava told her that he had reattached her finger and sat with her while she was unconscious. He smiled and touched her head. "Most becoming, although it could use a little trimming in the back." He gathered up the loose hair in his hands. "If you don't mind, I'll put this outside. The birds will like it for their nests."

Beryl nodded, and Brother Earth threw the hair out the window. He picked up the scissors.

"May I?" he asked.

"Please," said Beryl. She turned her back to him, and Brother Earth trimmed her hair. When he finished, he took Beryl's injured hand in his large green one. He looked into her eyes and said, "You have been through a lot. I'm sorry for the pain you've suffered.

"You found Jocasta's Journal," he said, putting his free hand on the book. "I haven't seen it for many years. The Grandmothers gave it to you?"

"'Gave' isn't the word I would use, but, yes, I got it from the grandmothers."

"Have you read it?" Brother Earth asked.

"I started today."

"Jocasta came to me when she was old," Brother Earth continued. "She brought this journal with her. She said she needed to write about her life before she died. She never told anyone about her life before Floredelis. She stayed here for the last year of her life and finished writing this book. She gave it to the Grandmothers to keep until it was needed."

"Brother Earth, I haven't read all of it, but it seems like the story of an ordinary person who was unhappy before she came here and made some mistakes, too. I always imagined that Jocasta was different from the rest of us."

"You're right, Beryl. I think Jocasta wanted the recipient of this journal to know that she was a regular person who faced some of her challenges with courage, wisdom, and a connection to the light of spirit, while other challenges were met with fear and perhaps even foolishness. I think she also wanted you to know about the old world to help you understand the violence that humanity is capable of.

"Despite her mistakes and flaws, Jocasta created this new land. But she never really trusted other people and created some of the structures of your society based on her fears. Jocasta realized her error toward the end of her life but didn't have the courage to tell anyone, so she wrote about it instead. Now is the time for change, and the journal is one tool that can help."

Brother Earth looked deeply into Beryl's eyes. "Beryl, you're not the same person who arrived here a short time ago. You have grown in strength, courage, and wisdom. I am very proud of you."

It was true. She wasn't the same. She realized that she had learned and grown—largely through her own mistakes but also with help from her friends.

Before he left, Brother Earth suggested that she get up and move around a little. He told her how to get to the library. It had a comfortable chair where she could sit and read.

Beryl got out of bed. Her legs felt stiff and weak; her whole body felt stiff, but after the first few steps, it felt good to move. She took Jocasta's journal to the library. It was a warm sunny room with a fire in the fireplace. She sat with her back to the fire and the sunlight shining in a puddle at her feet. She found the page where she had stopped.

I don't know if it's possible for humanity to live without violence, but I hope and pray that we can in this new world. Only time will tell. The world I left behind is filled with violence. People hurting each other and injuring Mother Earth. I don't know how much longer that world will survive. It seems impossible to change the path that humanity has taken there. With the portal between the worlds closed, I suppose I shall never know.

The weapons humans developed to torture and kill each other are numerous and horrifying. I hope that future generations here never know about weapons that can kill a man from so far away that the bearer of the weapon cannot see his face and that they do not know the horror of the earth exploding beneath them and fire raining from the sky. Is humanity capable of living in peace?

I've experienced much violence in my own life. It's painful to think about it, even after all these years and even though it's a world away.

In coming to Floredelis, I happily left the old world behind. But I know that the past doesn't disappear, and I fear that my past hides in this society that I created and that my unresolved pain lives in the structures I created and will cause problems someday. With that in mind, I relate an experience that is too horrible for words. I tried to leave it behind, but it remains with me every moment of every day.

Much of what I write won't make sense to Floredelians, but rather than give a detailed explanation of things from the old world; I hope my reader will understand the essence of what I write. I fear if I stop to explain all the details, I'll never get through this. And I want to get through this as quickly as possible. Now I'm just avoiding what I've set out to do. Enough! Here goes:

Back in the old world, as a young woman, I was an attorney, a keeper of the laws. I had a beloved husband and a seven-year-old son. I worked at the State's Attorney's office, which is a place where we prosecuted people accused of breaking the law. Justice was elusive in this system. Sometimes the guilty were punished, but sometimes they went free, and sometimes the innocent were punished for crimes they didn't commit. I worked long hours, and Ed, my husband, cared for our son, David.

After a long day at work that dragged on into the evening, I came home. Much to my surprise, I found three police cars and an ambulance parked in front of my house, with their red lights flashing. These vehicles indicated an emergency. I sat in my car, trying to see what was happening, paralyzed with fear. Finally, I gathered my courage and rushed over to see what was happening in my house. One of my neighbors, my friend Sarah who I walked with on the weekends, grabbed my arm and hugged me tight. I wanted to go to my family, but she wouldn't let me. She told me something horrible had happened. Ed and David had been shot. Someone heard the shots and called the police. The police told me that I couldn't go inside, but I ignored them. I walked into my house.

Ed and David lay on stretchers, covered with blood and holes that ripped their clothing and bodies. The kitchen floor was covered with blood, their blood. There were bits of my beloveds everywhere. Even on the sandwiches they must have been making for dinner. I sat on the floor in shock. I knew some of the police officers from work. They told me I needed to leave.

I was compromising the crime scene. But I couldn't move while my family was still there—I knew this was the last time we'd ever be together. The ambulance left to take their dead bodies to the morgue.

Sarah took me to her house and helped me wash off their blood. She gave me clean clothes. I stayed there until my parents came and took me to my childhood home.

We found out later that a man I had prosecuted and sent to prison had been released and blamed me for everything. That's why he killed my family. I wish he had killed me. The last I heard, he was going to be executed, but I don't know if that happened. I didn't want that to happen. It's a horrible thing to kill another human being, even one who has done unspeakably horrible things.

I stayed with my parents for a long time. I couldn't face the world and felt too frightened to be alone. They took care of me as best they could. I never returned to my own home. After about a year at my parents' house, I knew it was time to start my life again. But I couldn't return to work as a lawyer. Instead, I got a job at a large corporation. I processed papers. I spoke to few people. No one knew about my past. But I couldn't leave it behind. I remembered it and still remember it every day. I hope no one in this new world will ever experience anything so painful. I hope we can have true justice and support those who are in pain. I hope that in this new world, we will live by the principle of nonviolence for all beings. And I hope that every child can laugh and play and listen to their dreams—and grow up to live them.

Beryl felt shocked, but she kept reading. As she neared the end, Jocasta's handwriting became larger and messier.

***Love and joy**—Love and joy are the strongest forces in the universe— and the most healing. If we can remember how to laugh, we will be much closer to overcoming adversity. Children are the best sources of love and joy. We must protect our children. We must allow them to run and play and spend time with their families and friends. When we face challenges in life, it is good to spend time with children. We must never burden the children with our troubles but rather allow their joy and wonder to* *permeate our beings so we can remember who we really are. Treasure every moment; it will never come again. I wish I had lived my life differently. I wish I had spent less time working and more time playing with my family. I miss my little boy every day. I blame myself for his death and the death of my husband, even though I know it wasn't my fault.*

This is the hardest part for me to write. There was a man who helped me, who helped all of us, come to this world. If you are reading this book, you will not have heard of him. His name was Hamilton. He loved me, and I led him to believe that I loved him, too. I wanted to love him, but I don't think I could love another man after I lost Ed. Because Hamilton loved me, he helped me gather the people who started Floredelis. Because of him, I was able to start a new life in Floredelis. When he imagined our life together here, I listened and smiled. I didn't tell him that I knew we would never live together. I told myself I wasn't lying, but I was. When we arrived in Floredelis, I made myself very busy overseeing the beginning of this new world. Ontihaponati tried to help me, told me I should let him into my heart, both for myself and the future of Floredelis. She told me that he left a pregnant wife behind. He never told me about her. I never asked.

I couldn't stand it when he touched me. I sent him off on many missions. I guess he finally realized that I wasn't going to marry him or live with him because the last time I sent him away, he didn't come back. I asked Ontihaponati if he was alright, but she wouldn't answer. I felt relieved that he was gone and put off sending out someone to search for him. Everyone knew he was in love with me, but no one knew how badly I treated him. Hamilton, I am so sorry. Floredelis, I am so sorry. It seemed so right to have twelve followers, like the months of the year or the signs of the zodiac, or the apostles. But he was the thirteenth. Well, actually, he was the first. What have I done?

51

The morning after Ava's and Tobias' wedding, the strands begin weaving together

The Tapestry of Life: Life is both beautiful and complicated. In the Old World, many cultures had myths about goddesses who were weavers-- Spider Woman, the Fates, the Norns. They all wove the fabric of life; they connected the physical and spiritual worlds. We are all part of the same tapestry, woven together, even though most of us can't see the whole picture.
From The Book of Jocasta

Beryl hadn't been in Brother Earth's realm for long, but it felt like a lifetime. She looked at the bright red scar that circled her little finger. She thought about Jocasta's journal and its sad story. She thought about Ava's and Tobias' wedding, watching them place the plain gold rings on each other's fingers. Ava had married. The night before, Beryl escorted Ava while Andrew walked Tobias down the aisle to Brother Earth's throne, where he performed the ceremony. They had danced and feasted late into the night.

*

Randall woke up inside a tree. His clothes ripped, and his body covered with cuts and scrapes. But he was alive and safe, at least for the moment. He was saddened by Fain's violent, senseless death and Eugene's injury.

One thread in the tapestry of had been cut, the blood of an innocent man spilled. Fain was dead. The people of Xantalon mourned the loss of their new friend. Otto, paralyzed with grief, accepted Eugene's offer to stay with his family. It didn't really matter where he was. He'd lost everyone he'd ever loved.

Eugene gathered the people together so they could decide how to deal with the murder and support Otto, and each other, through the shock of Fain's death. They wished that their king and queen and watchers would return home soon, safe and sound. No one had heard a word from them since they left.

*

At the same time, Solomon's men, who had returned with blood on their hands but without Zorina, listened to a long harangue about their worthlessness and how Solomon didn't know why he bothered to take care of them. They were lucky he was a compassionate man, caring for such worthless good-for-nothings. They all listened; they had nowhere else to go. It seemed like years since they had been home, although for most, it had only been a few months. They missed their wives, parents, children, or whoever they had left behind or lost. The days when they were clean, shaved, and sleeping in a warm bed at night felt like a distant dream. And Fain's murder haunted their sleep and their waking. Some wondered what would happen when winter arrived. It would be too cold to sleep outside or even in this cave. Solomon had promised their work would be finished before winter settled in. Even today, he told them that, despite their incompetence, things were proceeding as planned. They didn't know what the plan was, and he didn't explain. He didn't mention Fain's death—no one had mentioned it to him, and he didn't mention that Zorina hadn't been rescued, although they all knew. Instead, he strutted around, gazing over their heads into the distance as though seeing the future. The men hated him more and were more afraid to leave than ever.

*

Beryl sat down to breakfast with Ava, Tobias, Andrew, and Brother Earth in the tree castle's indoor dining hall, the outside air too cool for humans to sit in comfortably. A cheery fire blazed in the fireplace, and although the sky was gray, the room looked bright and sunny. Beryl wondered what had become of Lucas. She hadn't seen the real Lucas since right after she hit him with her crystal. Even though she didn't like or trust him, he was a human being, and she hoped was alright. Brother Earth said he'd locked Lucas in a room in the tree palace. Apparently, any of the doors locked if Brother Earth wanted them to. Beryl was too weary and confused—and trying to process her own experiences— to ask more about him.

Her friends, the gnomes, would come to say goodbye soon. She had come to love them and appreciate their silliness, wisdom, kindness, and courage.

A bowl of porridge with wild blueberries and cream sat before her. She poked it with her spoon. Brother Earth encouraged her to eat. She half-heartedly took a bite. She guessed she was a little hungry after all. Without even noticing, she finished her bowl and then the second one that was placed in front of her.

Brother Earth touched Beryl's chin. He turned her face toward him and looked into her eyes.

"Beryl, you haven't been chosen for this task because of your physical strength. Many are stronger than you. You have been chosen because of your golden heart and because your intuition is strong and true. You will have to rely on both in the coming days. Try to hold your center no matter what happens. You have already proven that you are capable of doing so under the most difficult circumstances. The gifts from your friends and family may help you." Brother Earth handed Beryl her pouch. She hadn't seen it since she entered the hill of the Grand-mothers. She wondered why he had it but just kept listening.

"But the gifts that will really help you are the ones inside you. You won't see me when you return to your world, but I will always be near and watching over you. I will help you as much as I can, as will my people. Ava will travel with you for a while but will need to return here soon. She has some work to do on Mother Earth's loom—to repair the damaged fabric of your world. She also has some reweaving to do in her own life." He smiled at Ava and then Tobias.

"Beryl, remember, you will never be alone." He touched his forehead to hers and looked at her, turning his head from side to side. Mama A used to do the same thing to her when she was younger, saying, "You have one long eyebrow that goes all the way from one side of your face to the other." It looked like that with Brother Earth too, and it still made her laugh.

Beryl wondered if he knew that Mama A used to do that. He winked and smiled. Then he kissed her on the forehead. "Come back soon, child."

"I would love to," said Beryl, "and thank you for everything." She thought of many other things she could say, questions she would like to ask, but said no more.

Buttercup and Ivy peeked in through the window. Beryl hugged Brother Earth and went to the door. The two gnomes waited with their wheelbarrow.

"Will I be able to see you when I return?" she asked the gnomes.

"You might if we let you," said Buttercup, trying to look gruff.

"I've seen gnomes in Floredelis," said Beryl, "but I don't think they were you."

"You are the only human child we've seen here, but now we must escort you to Floredelis. Come sit down. You too, Ava. For once you pass through the portal, you'll be too heavy for us to pull."

Beryl put an arm around each gnome and squeezed them. "I'll miss you," she said. "I'd like to give you a gift before I leave." She felt inside her pouch for the stick from King Jyrym. She pulled it out. the stick rolled out of her hand and landed on the ground, where it became indistinguishable from the many other sticks.

"Oh, my," said Beryl. "That was a special magic stick, but I don't think I can find it. I'm so sorry."

She looked about to cry. The gnomes looked at her disappointed face, and both began crawling around, collecting sticks. They looked so sweet and funny that Beryl couldn't help smiling. They each collected a handful of sticks.

"Do you recognize it?" asked Buttercup as he and his brother held out the sticks for Beryl to examine.

"Oh dear," said Beryl. "They all look pretty much the same. I don't think I'll ever find it."

"I think the best thing is to try them," said Ivy.

Buttercup continued, "Then you can see if we found the right one."

"Alright. I guess I can try a few. Maybe you did find the right one. My stick points in the direction you need to go next."

Buttercup handed her a twig. It looked darker and shorter than she remembered. She held it flat in her hand and asked, "What direction will get me back to Floredelis?" To her surprise, the twig twirled around and pointed to the right.

"Yes," said Ivy, "That's the way. Can I try?"

Beryl handed him the twig, and he gave her the twigs he was holding. He held it flat in his hand as Beryl had done and asked the same question, but nothing happened. Beryl didn't understand. She held on to one twig and put the rest down, so she could demonstrate.

"Let's do it together. Maybe you didn't get the hang of it."

They each held the sticks in their hands, and Ivy repeated each word after Beryl. But much to their surprise, the stick in Beryl's hand twirled around and pointed while Ivy's stick remained motionless.

Ava watched quietly until Beryl looked up with a look of such puzzlement and dismay on her face that Ava swallowed a laugh and gave her a quick hug. "Beryl, the stick that Jyrym gave you was a teaching tool. He probably picked it up on the way to your house. The magic isn't in the stick; it's in you. Your heart knows what direction to go, but sometimes your thinking interferes. Does that make sense?"

"Sort of," said Beryl. She began looking through her pouch again.

"Beryl?" said Ava.

"I want to give a gift to my friends, and a non-magic stick isn't a very good gift."

"On the contrary," said Buttercup. "It's a gift we'll treasure. May I keep the one in your hand?"

"But why?" Beryl asked, handing him the twig.

"It will help us remember that we, too, know which way to go, even if the stick doesn't spin." Buttercup continued. "And it will remind us of you. Right, Brother?"

"My brother is right for once. This is a precious gift. And since there are two of them, we can each keep one close to our hearts always."

"Don't get all mushy, brother. Ladies, hop into the cart. We haven't got all day," said Buttercup

Ava and Beryl climbed into the cart, and the gnomes picked up the handles.

"Wait," said Brother Earth. "Before you leave, I have something for both of you." He brought out two cloaks covered with swirling colors.

"They will just look brown in your world," he said. "But they will keep you warm and provide some protection and camouflage. Blessings on your journey."

"Are we going back to the well?" Beryl asked

"There are many portals between our worlds," said Ivy. "We're taking you to one closer to where you need to go."

"And one that will be easier to go through than the well," said Buttercup.

The two women sat warm and snug in their cloaks. Beryl wanted to soak in all the beauty of Brother Earth's land. She repeated to herself what he had said to her this morning, so she could remember. She wondered what would happen next. She ran her finger around her scar.

She had been through so much already. She wished she could just have a few days to rest. Ava put a hand on her knee. Beryl placed her hand on Ava's. She wondered who would help her after Ava left. She hoped she would know who to trust and who not to. She hoped she had learned from her mistakes and from Jocasta's, too.

Lost in thought, Beryl was startled from her thoughts when the cart came to a stop.

"Crawl into the hollow in this tree," said Ivy. "You'll soon find yourself in the woods of Floredelis. Ava will recognize the place."

"Thank you, dear friends, for everything," said Beryl, hugging the gnomes one last time.

"Yes, thank you for your kind care, gentlemen. And give my best to your mother," said Ava.

"We will, indeed. She enjoyed the wedding last night. She loves dancing."

Ava turned to Tobias. "I will return soon," she said, "my dear husband." She held him close. "Andrew, I will see you soon, as well. Look after your father while I'm gone."

Everyone exchanged hugs. Beryl took one last look at the gnomes as they trotted away with the cart, arguing about who was working harder. She got down on her hands and knees and squeezed through the hole in the tree. She heard Ava behind her, scraping and scuffling.

The hole hadn't looked deep, but Beryl crawled a long way in the narrow, dark passage. In a few minutes, she saw light in the distance It seemed harsh and dull compared to the light in Brother Earth's land. She crawled out into the woods of Floredelis, although she didn't recognize the place. Ava emerged just after her and looked around. Ava stood up and began walking quickly. Beryl followed, practically running to keep up. When Ava paused, Beryl panted, "Where are we?"

"This is the heart of the forest, a powerful and sacred place. We can rest here."

Beryl sat on a fallen log. She noticed that Ava's cloak looked brown, as Brother Earth had said it would. In fact, Ava and her cloak seemed to become part of the log she sat on. Beryl looked at her cloak. She stood up and twirled. The cloak reflected the shadows and colors that surrounded her. She was almost invisible.

These woods didn't look that different from Brother Earth's woods, and yet they felt really different, denser somehow.

Beryl and Ava heard rustling, and both turned toward the sound. A man, dirty, ragged, and covered with scratches, emerged from the trunk of a tree. He put his arm up to shelter his eyes from the light and then started as he saw Beryl and Ava.

Beryl and Ava were also startled. Beryl's heart beat faster. He looked familiar, although she didn't think they'd met.

"Hello," the man said. "I wasn't expecting, that is, I mean...You're not tree people, are you? You look like you're part of the trees?"

Beryl smiled. "We're human," she said. "And you look like a human who could use some help."

"Who are you, and what brings you here? And where is here?" asked Randall, for that is who he was.

Beryl wondered if she should trust this man. The familiarity and strangeness of him frightened her. She rubbed the scar on her little finger. Without thinking, she picked up a stick and laid it in her hand. It spun, and she wished the stick would tell her what to do. This man did have striking blue eyes, also somehow familiar. He didn't look dangerous. He looked like he could barely stand. Beryl looked at the stick again. It pointed right at him.

"My friend is a healer, and I'm her pupil," said Beryl. "Would you like us to clean those cuts? Some of them look pretty nasty."

Randall looked at his arms and legs. He saw his clothes.

"I'm sorry," he said. "I look rather frightening. I had quite a night last night. I don't always look like this." He sighed and shrugged his shoulders. "But let me introduce myself. My name is Randall. I come from the Temple City."

"You're Randall?" asked Beryl. "You don't look like a dangerous criminal who wants to capture me. My name is Beryl, and this is Ava."

"I mean you no harm, ladies. Besides, I don't think I could hurt anyone right now even if I wanted to. I'd be grateful for your help."

Beryl dropped the stick and found a small cloth in her satchel onto which she poured some water. Ava gathered herbs for a poultice to put on the bigger cuts.

Beryl told Randall, "First, we must clean these cuts. I'm sorry; it will hurt." Randall leaned his back against a log, eyes closed. Beryl knelt beside him with the wet cloth. "Your forehead looks pretty bad. I'll start there."

As Beryl leaned in, Randall opened his eyes. Beryl's face flushed. She wished the cloak made her face invisible. Now she recognized those eyes, blue like the ocean. Randall was the man from her dream, the one who would introduce her to Beryl.

"It's pretty bad, huh?" asked Randall.

"What? Oh, yes, it looks pretty bad," agreed Beryl, still looking into his eyes. "I wonder if Ava will want to stitch it up." Randall closed his eyes. Beryl forced herself to focus on her task.

"I'm lucky I found you," he said.

Beryl wondered if it was luck. It couldn't be a coincidence that Brother Earth sent Ava and her to the place where Randall was. As she cleaned the cuts, Randall kept wincing.

He said, "When I was a little boy and got hurt, my mother always told me a story while she cared for me. I don't suppose you know a story—to distract me?"

Beryl thought telling a story might distract her, too. She chose one of her favorites, "The Frog-Prince, or Iron Henry."

The story felt so alive in her that she could almost see it. Randall, too, pictured the princess with the golden ball and the frog knocking on the castle door. He gasped as the frog hit the wall in the princess' bedroom and smiled when the spell broke and the frog regained his human form. But his favorite part was when Iron Henry came to take the prince and princess home, and the three iron bands he had placed around his heart broke one by one as his heart expanded in joy.

Beryl's hands continued their work while she spoke. When she finished the story, it took her a moment to remember where she was. She was surprised to see two tears leaving a trail in the dirt on Randall's face.

"Did I hurt you?" she asked

"No, I believe you healed me."

52

Two days earlier, in the Temple City

Jyrym and Lillia sat in their cell, waiting for something to happen and hoping against all reason that it would be something good. They had been sitting for days. They'd examined the walls countless times. They wondered if Dr. Hami had forgotten them. Twice a day, a guard brought them porridge or thin soup, a little bread, and water. The food, tasteless and lukewarm, was better than nothing. They ate. They took turns pacing. They probably could have opened the door with magic, but guards always stood outside their door, so they wouldn't get far. Perhaps Anne and Beatrice would find a way to set them free if they hadn't been caught. They sat silently, their four hands clasped together. They didn't feel safe speaking openly here, but they knew each other so well that they often didn't need words.

As the sun arched toward the middle of the sky, two guards came in and told them it was time to go. One of them grabbed the queen's arm and pushed her. "That won't be necessary," she said, pulling her arm away. "I'm quite willing to walk."

These guards couldn't be much older than Beryl. They wore smug expressions on their smooth faces, but Lillia knew their expressions masked fear. Lillia and Jyrym wondered what they feared. The guards escorted Lillia and Jyrym to the Council room. When they entered, Lillia and Jyrym couldn't see in the bright room after being in the dark for so long. When their eyes adjusted, they saw no one sitting at the elaborately decorated council table. The High Priestess sat in her ceremonial chair at the far end of the room. A council member sat on either side of her. This must be a criminal hearing.

Lillia hadn't seen Jenna for many years and barely recognized her. Her face looked pale, her eyes vacant. Her short gray hair stuck out all over her head. Her robes looked like she had slept in them. Jenna had been Lillia's favorite teacher. Lillia felt shocked, even though Ava had told them what bad shape Jenna was in. Lillia rushed forward and kneeled before her. She took Jenna's hands in hers. They felt cold and dry. Her pale gray eyes pointed toward Lillia but didn't seem to see her.

"Jenna," said Lillia. That was all she got to say.

One of the council members signaled the guards. They grabbed Lillia roughly, pulled her to her feet, and pushed her back by Jyrym. As they pulled her away, Jenna squeezed her hand and pressed something into it. It felt like a small piece of paper. She squeezed Jyrym's hand and passed him the paper. He scratched his head, and Lillia knew he had put it somewhere safe.

Lillia pulled herself up straight. "I am Queen Lillia of Xantalon, and this is King Jyrym. I demand to know why we are being treated like common criminals."

Selene, who sat to the right of the High Priestess, spoke. "You are not common criminals," she emphasized the word "common" with her shrill, harsh voice. "You are accused of high treason and betraying the Temple Council."

Jyrym spoke, "What do you base these accusations on?"

"You harbor sworn enemies of Floredelis."

Lillia and Jyrym stared at the woman in amazement as she looked out the window and continued speaking, "You are harboring Zorina and Randall; is that correct?"

"Zorina is a prisoner in Xantalon, and Randall has been staying with us."

"You see, Jenna, I told you they had turned against us. I ask that they be publicly executed to set an example to all who disobey our laws."

Lillia and Jyrym looked at each other. They were speechless. Executions went against everything Floredelis stood for. Even imprisonment went against the principles of non-violence on which Floredelis was founded.

They watched in amazement as Jenna nodded her head but said nothing. The man on Jenna's other side raised his eyebrows. He wore the colors of Exeter province, was of medium height and build, and had brown hair and a long, curled mustache that he twirled constantly. After a long silence, he cleared his throat, "Doesn't that seem rather harsh, Selene?"

He said the right words, but without feeling,

"No," shrilled Selene. "Our world is in danger. We have chaos in the streets. We must show the citizens of Floredelis that we remain in charge."

Her voice softened. "Perhaps if you give us Randall, we could punish him instead."

"What do you mean?" asked Lillia

"You try our patience. Where do you hide him?"

"We're not hiding him."

"Randall, the most dangerous criminal in Floredelis, is the leader of the Pied Pipers. They have sworn to destroy our civilization. He is a murderer. We have searched for him for many months. Perhaps he'll turn himself in if we announce that those who have sheltered him will be put to death."

"What say you, High Priestess?" the man asked.

"I will take it under advisement. We'll reconvene tomorrow at this same time."

Selene's face turned bright red, and a vein above her eye began to throb visibly. She looked like she wanted to say something but didn't.

Lillia and Jyrym looked at each other dumbfounded.

"Will there be a hearing?" asked Jyrym.

"There is no need," said Selene. "You have already confessed; we only await the decision of the High Priestess as to the sentence. You may make a statement tomorrow if you wish. These are dangerous times, and I am shocked and disappointed that you have abused your power and turned against the Council."

"Guards, take them back to their cell," said the man on Jenna's left.

The guards, four this time, returned them to their cell. On the way, they discussed who would take the first guard duty and who would have to stay overnight.

"Is it possible to get a blanket and perhaps a mat for my wife to rest on?" asked Jyrym.

"Sure, why not," said one.

"Thank you," said Jyrym. "Your kindness is appreciated."

"I'm sorry this is happening," said one of the new guards. "You seem like fine people."

"Shut up, you idiot," said another. "Be glad it's their heads and not ours. And don't let Selene hear you talking like that, or we'll have one less person on this side of the door."

A guard opened the cell door. Lillia and Jyrym entered, and the guards locked them in. A few minutes later, the guard brought a thin mattress, two pillows, and a warm blanket. He wouldn't look at them; not easy in the small cell.

"Thank you, young man." Lillia stood beside him as he put the blanket on the floor, so he couldn't avoid looking at her when he stood up. "Your kindness is much appreciated. What is your name?"

"My name is Craig," he replied, looking away.

There was a shout from the hall. "Hey, get out of there. Selene is coming."

"I've got to go," Craig said.

Lillia smiled kindly at him. She heard the door lock and the sound of clicking heels coming toward the cell. Selene exchanged a few words with the guards, and two of them left with her.

Lillia and Jyrym set up the mattress. They had a loud conversation about how Lillia needed a rest after this stressful day. They sat down and pulled the blanket up to their chins. Jyrym, his back to the door, pulled the paper out of his shirt. He unfolded it and read it in the dim light as Lillia watched the door.

"Dear Lillia," it said, "I am being held prisoner and used to do the will of a group of council members who would destroy our society. They gave me drugs to make me ill, but I have stopped taking them. I am pretending to still be in their control. Please help me. Tomorrow I will pronounce your death sentence. Pretend to faint. I will send my physician to care for you. He will help. Please destroy this. Let us work together for the highest good. All my love, Jenna."

"Do you think this is real?" asked Lillia. "It looks like Jenna's writing. I remember it well from the voluminous notes she wrote on my papers. But it doesn't sound like her."

"I don't know, but we might as well play along and see what happens. I think we could get out of here if we needed to." As they whispered, Jyrym tore the message in two, and they each took half and tore it into little pieces. Jyrym stuffed the pieces into a mouse hole under the bench, making sure none of them stuck out.

As Jyrym pushed the scraps into the hole, tears rose in Lillia's eyes.

"Oh, Jyrym," Lillia whispered, "How can this be happening? How could such terrible things happen in Floredelis, and we knew nothing about it? I feel like I'm waking from a dream into a nightmare. What was I thinking when I said I wanted to retire? Floredelis needs me, needs us. And Beryl is so young. How did we end up prisoners? We have done no wrong. And a sentence of death? It goes against everything

Floredelis stands for. What will become of us? What will become of this wonderful land?"

She rarely cried, but she let her tears fall. Jyrym held her for a long time, rocking her in his arms.

"My beloved," Jyrym replied, "I have no answers. Maybe we were under a spell. That wasn't the real Jenna we saw today. Something terrible has happened to her. We will find our way through this, though. We will live to tell this tale. I can feel it in my bones."

53

A few days after Lillia and Jyrym were captured, in the Temple City

After the king and queen were captured, Anne and Beatrice returned to the woods. They stayed there for several days while they tried to figure out how best to go about freeing the king and queen. They spent one day walking back toward Xantalon City to get help before deciding it would be better to look for help in the Temple City. They also needed food soon, as they'd brought only enough for their journey through the woods. They knew enough of the plants in the forest to forage for nuts and berries, but still, their stomachs had begun to rumble for want of more satisfying food.

They decided to enter the City through the main gate, hopefully unnoticed. They hoped to find their old friend Ian. He had been an apprentice chef at the Temple when they were students. Beatrice had been Ian's friend and confidant, and best man at his wedding. They had seen Ian and his family occasionally since then. Beatrice and Anne believed they could trust him and hoped he might be able to help them find Lillia and Jyrym.

They waited with the other travelers until the gates opened just before dawn. The two women pulled up their hoods, looking like many of the other travelers who came to see the sights and seek spiritual counsel. The guards seemed satisfied with their explanation that they had come to sightsee. Once inside the gate, they slipped down a side street and hurried towards Ian's house. They saw him walking just a block away from his house, head down, apparently lost in thought.

"Excuse me, sir," said Beatrice. "Can you tell me how to get to the nearest Inn?" She pulled back her hood, so the gray morning light shone on her face. Ian smiled as he recognized his old friend.

"I can't talk now. I'm on my way to the Temple to prepare breakfast." And then more quietly, "Please wait at my home. I'll be back after lunch. Theresa is home with the little ones. She'll be happy to see you. Please don't go wandering around."

"Thank you," said Beatrice. "We'd like nothing better than to spend a little time in your cozy home."

Beatrice pulled her hood back around her face, and they went to Ian's house and knocked on the door. "Ian asked us to wait for him here," said Beatrice when Theresa cracked the door open.

Theresa looked at them suspiciously. She looked behind them to see if anyone else was near, but they were alone. Most of the city still slept. "Come in, then," she said. Beatrice and Anne stepped inside and pulled back their hoods.

"Oh, my, you are a sight for sore eyes." She hugged her old friends tightly. "Your hair is full of grass. Did you sleep in the woods?"

"For a few nights, but calling it sleep may be a bit of an exaggeration."

The two visitors removed their cloaks. The house felt warm and cozy.

Theresa said, "You must be tired and hungry. I long to ask you a thousand questions. But they'll wait. Come sit down, and I'll bring you breakfast."

Anne sat near the fireplace. "Some food would be welcome, and then perhaps we could rest; I'm exhausted." Anne rested her head on Beatrice's shoulder.

The house looked the way they remembered. They sat in the great room, which served as the kitchen, dining room, and living room. It had two bedrooms, one for the children and one for Ian and Theresa. The smell of coffee brewing reminded Beryl's parents of time they spent in this house before Ian had married. He'd always liked his morning coffee. He told Beatrice that he wasn't a morning person, but he had to leave before dawn to start the day's baking. The only way he could get out the door that early was to drink several cups of strong black coffee. Theresa brought out some delicious-looking sweet buns. "We always get great leftovers," she said, giving them each a bun and pouring their coffee. She added milk to their coffee and took some baked eggs from the oven. "I made these for the children, but I have plenty more, and they won't be up for hours. They stayed up late last night with their father. He loves to tell them stories of the old days. In fact, last night, he told them the story of how we met—you play a big role in that story, Beatrice. I can't believe you're really here! But I'll be quiet now. Please eat, and I'll get a mat so you can rest by the fire." She put the mat they kept for overnight guests by the fire and brought out a warm feather comforter. She rubbed her eyes and said, "I think I'll rest a little more. I always get up and have breakfast with Ian. It's the only time we have to ourselves, but it's good for me to rest when the children do—they keep me busy. I doubt any of us will get much rest once they wake up."

Anne and Beatrice didn't need to be asked twice. With their stomachs pleasantly full, lying together by the warm fire under the soft comforter, they fell asleep.

54

That same day, in the Temple

On the Sacred Circle of Life: "Let us offer thanks and praise for the circle of our days." So begins the poem "The Canticle of the Sun by St. Francis of Assisi." Life is a sacred circle. The creator, the Goddess, is at the center. A circle has neither a beginning nor an end. Like King Arthur's round table represented the equality of all who sat around it, so our Council table represents the equality of all citizens of Floredelis. Let us give freely of our gifts and receive what others offer to us. This is the best way to celebrate our sacred community.

From The Book of Jocasta

Dr. Hami thought things were going very well, despite a few glitches. People were easy to manipulate. They told you exactly what they wanted. Solomon wanted to be admired for his great wisdom. Selene wanted Solomon to love her. The high priestess had been a little more difficult. He knew she felt attracted to him the first time they met. He pretended he wanted to rekindle their relationship when he returned, but romance no longer interested her. She wanted only to serve her people. He wasn't interested in romance either, not with an old woman who had ruined his life, but it should have been an easy way to get what he wanted.

Jenna had been distraught when the people in the city began dying from a strange illness. Lucky for him, she blamed herself. She had no idea he brought the illness with him, although that was Ontihaponati's fault, not his. He had been ready to die and certainly hadn't expected or even wanted to return to Floredelis ever again. His illness spread quickly through the Temple City. Sadly, it spread no further. He had a bottle of ibuprofen, which, although it did nothing for him, miraculously cured those to whom he gave it in Floredelis. But supplies were limited—he only had one bottle. He gave the medicine to those who could help him. All the other deaths were icing on the cake.

Being weighed down with guilt over the deaths of her people, and being very trusting, when Hamilton suggested Jenna try his tonic to build up her strength, she did and soon became too sick to resist him. His subtle suggestions that she bore responsibility for all those deaths didn't hurt, either. Through her, he had gained control of licensing the practice of medicine—to prevent another disaster like the great illness from happening again.

On the downside, Solomon had botched things up when he was supposed to make that silly girl—Zorina—queen of Floredelis, and then he'd disappeared. Ava and the other little twit of a girl, Beryl, had disappeared too. And Lucas had disappeared, as well. He felt a little sad about Lucas, who felt almost like a son to him.

As he sat musing about all these disappearances in the sitting room in the Temple, as the day faded into night, he heard someone enter. He squinted his eyes to focus better. Yes, Lucas had returned. His heart beat faster. He was glad the boy still lived. He looked thin and tired but still remarkably handsome.

"Look what the cat dragged in," Dr. Hami remarked. Lucas gave him a blank stare. "Where have you been, my boy? I haven't heard from you in a while."

"I've been to hell and back. For you. I hope you appreciate it."

Lucas told Dr. Hami what happened to him after he arrived at Ava's house, leaving out the part about Beryl clocking him on the head with a crystal. "That girl, Beryl, insisted that they not put me back in the rock, and they didn't know what else to do with me, so they sent me back to you."

Dr. Hami rubbed his beard thoughtfully. He wondered if the lad had been drugged. His story didn't make any sense. But he was in Floredelis, and that didn't make any sense either.

"You look like you could use a good rest, my boy. Why don't you go home for a few days? Here, take some of this tonic; it will help you regain your strength."

"I will take a rest, but not the tonic. I know you too well for that."

"Smart lad. Well done." Dr. Hami laughed.

A few hours later, in the Temple City

Beatrice and Anne woke up three hours later to find three pairs of big brown eyes staring at them. Those eyes could only belong to Ian's children. The oldest boy must be eight years old by now and had Ian's long eyelashes. The middle one was a girl with golden-red hair that fell over the sides of her face as she leaned over and stared. She was about five, and the youngest couldn't have been more than two. He had his mother's dark curly hair and pale complexion. Beryl's moms smiled at the children. The last time they had seen Ian and Theresa, Matthew, the eldest, had been a baby. Anne sighed. Beatriz looked at her.

"I miss her, too," she said.

They wished they could see Beryl's bright green eyes staring at them, as well. But they didn't have much time to contemplate.

"Where did you come from?" asked Matthew.

"We came out of the woods this morning," said Anne.

"You look like you came out of the woods; your hair is all full of burrs and grass," Samantha said to Beatrice.

"Sam, that's not polite," corrected her big brother.

'That's alright," said Beatrice, "She's right." Beatrice put her hand to her head. "I don't suppose you'd like to help me get them out? I'm your Aunt Beatrice. I haven't been to the Temple City since Matthew was a baby. And what's your name?" she asked the little one.

"Zachary," he said. "Are you really Beatrice? Then you must be Anne. I heared a story about you." He stared at them with his mouth open.

"It's not polite to stare," said Matthew.

Theresa came out of her room. "Children, don't bother our guests. They're tired. They came a long way to visit us."

"They are certainly no bother," said Beatrice.

"No, they're quite delightful," Anne agreed. She pushed Samantha's hair behind one of her ears. "But seeing them makes me miss my own little girl. I wonder where she is."

Samantha spent most of the morning patiently picking the bits of plants out of Beatrice's hair while Anne played a card game with the boys.

They kept the children occupied while Theresa prepared lunch. They ate, and soon after, as the children were about to take their naps, Ian arrived. The children jumped all over him in their joy to see him. He took them to their bedroom and settled them down for a nap. Then he joined his friends. He ran his hand through his hair. He sat down heavily in a chair by the fire and motioned for the others to join him.

"I am so glad to see you. It's been a long time," he said. "But I suspect you're not here for a social visit. What brings you to the City?"

"Ian, we are very glad to see you," said Anne. "But you're right; urgent business brings us here. We came with the King and Queen of

Xantalon. The Temple guards captured them as we tried to enter the city through the back gate. We must help them. We hoped you might know something. Can you help us?"

"The four of us came to the City," continued Beatrice, "looking for answers. Our Beryl disappeared several weeks ago. We don't know where she is. And now, with the king and queen captured—we just don't know what to do. We haven't been able to contact Ontihaponati for some time. Something is terribly wrong."

"This is a strange and dangerous time," Ian said. "I've heard many stories, but it's hard to know what to believe. My good friend Randall headed for Xantalon with one of your queen's men a few weeks back, carrying a message from the Council. We heard that Randall killed the messenger and disappeared into the forest with a gang of followers who rampage through the cities in the outlying provinces. I don't believe that Randall would murder someone. We are both part of the Pied Pipers. We wanted to help set things right, but we never advocated violence.

"I heard that your king and queen were captured by the temple guard. Just today, they were brought before the Temple Council and accused of high treason for sheltering Randall and a young acolyte, both supposedly enemies of the state." Ian paused. "I also heard.... I still can't believe it, but I heard that the Council recommended they be punished by death. The high priestess is supposed to give her decision tomorrow."

A long silence followed.

"Randall and the girl were staying at the palace," said Beatrice when she found her voice again, "But there was nothing treasonous going on. Even if there were, we don't kill people in Floredelis."

"It gets worse," Ian continued. "The High priestess is not well. I—and many others -- believe that someone is drugging her. No one sees her without Selene or Jacob by her side. She hardly eats anymore. I cook her favorite dishes, and they return untouched. She looks terrible. She only repeats what Selene or Jacob say. Dr. Hami, her personal physician, is never far, either. I don't know where he came from, and I certainly don't trust him. I wouldn't be surprised if he were behind this whole thing."

"Someone is circulating stories that the Pied Pipers want to overthrow the Temple Council and take over the government. It's a lie, but because of the rumors, the condition of the High Priestess, and the unprecedented actions of the Council, people live in fear. The Council offers rewards to people who turn in members of the Pied Pipers. Any accusation of wrongdoing or association with the wrong people usually results in the person being arrested, imprisoned, or banished from the city. The Council doesn't even hold public hearings because we are supposedly in a time of great danger, and the Council must act quickly to protect the people."

"I can't believe it. I had no idea things had gotten this bad. Anne, perhaps we should leave Ian and Theresa's home. I don't want to put your family in more danger," Beatrice said. Anne nodded. She was thinking the same thing.

"Don't even think it," said Ian. "We are all in danger, and something must be done; we can't go on living like this, but we must help each other. My sister Gabby, who lives out in the country, will take the children for a few weeks anyway. She'll pick them up tomorrow morning. They can't even play outside now, and I certainly don't trust them to talk to anyone. You know how little ones are—they repeat everything, including 'my father told me not to tell anyone....' Well, you know."

"Maybe together we can find out what is really going on and help the King and Queen and Randall—and all of us. Luckily, I'm a good cook. They must suspect my sympathies at the Temple, but no one has said anything yet."

The next day, in the Temple

> *More on Children: "The best way to make children good is to make them happy." (Oscar Wilde) More than anything, young children need to play and be included in the work of the house-hold. Children long to be part of our world and to understand how it works. When very young, they won't work with an end in mind but for the sake of doing. Process, not product. Young children learn through imitation and thrive in an atmosphere of warmth. Our job as adults is to be worthy of imitation.*
> From The Book of Jocasta

The next day, the guards brought Lillia and Jyrym back to the Council room. Only Selene, Jacob, and the High Priestess sat in the ceremonial chairs. Jacob had returned the night before without explaining where he'd been or why he had returned, except for a private conversation with Dr. Hami. When the council members asked Lillia and Jyrym if they had anything to say before the court passed its sentence, Jyrym could not stop himself from saying that they had done no wrong and demanding a hearing before the entire council.

Selene, her voice grating, told him the Council had empowered them to make these painful decisions in this time of crisis, and his request was denied. Then the high priestess sentenced them to death, to be hung in the public square on the morrow. It was not difficult for Lillia to let herself fall to the floor. She let the shock of Jenna's words flow through her, and her knees buckled. Selene called for the Temple physician, Dr. Hami. They wanted Lillia to be in decent shape for the execution, for they intended to make an example of her.

"Take her away," sneered Selene. "I can't stand the sight of weakness."

Two guards carried Lillia out. One held her under her arms, and the other grabbed her ankles. The men laid her on the mattress in the cell. Jyrym hovered anxiously. When the guards left, she opened her eyes. He felt relieved. He hadn't been sure she'd been acting.

They heard voices in the hallway, a key turning in the lock, and saw a man walk in. His white hair and white clothing glowed in the dim light. Lillia opened her eyes but lay still. The man bowed slightly. "I am Dr. Hami, at your service. I understand the lady has had quite a shock. Let me have a look."

He felt her pulse and listened to her heart. He looked into her eyes and felt her hands and feet.

As he put his stethoscope on her chest, he picked up the queen's stone that hung around her neck. He held the warm stone in his hand and looked at it lasciviously.

"Beautiful," he said, pulling gently on the chain.

A wave of revulsion washed over Lillia, and she thought she might vomit.

Dr. Hami laid the stone on her chest and patted her hand. "I have something to make you feel better, my dear," he said, pulling a small bottle out of his pocket. He removed the cork. "Have a little sip," he said. "It will make you feel better, I promise."

Lillia turned her head away. Did Jenna really trust this man? He handed the bottle to Jyrym. "Let her rest for a few minutes, and then give her a sip every hour. I'll check back later."

The doctor touched the stone on her chest again, then stood up and left.

"I feel better having a locked door between that man and me," said Lillia after his footsteps faded. She took the bottle out of Jyrym's hand and sniffed. It smelled foul but not like the nasty-smelling herbs that

Ava sometimes used for healing. It smelled like herbs meant to cause harm. She wondered if the doctor gave the same medicine to Jenna. "We should dispose of some of this. When he returns, I'll act like I don't have a brain, like Jenna, but I am not giving that man my stone." She tugged on the chain; it felt strong.

She leaned against Jyrym's chest, and he put his arms around her.

"I'm frightened," said Lillia. "I wish we were home. Will we ever see Xantalon again?"

"I hope so, my love. I'm frightened, too, for Floredelis and us. I keep hoping this is a dream, and I'll wake up safe and sound in our bed with you in my arms. I hope Beatrice and Anne escaped."

"Me, too."

"If they did, they will do what they can to save us. And I wonder about Beryl—I feel like she has an important role to play in all of this. I hope she's alright."

Jyrym rested his head on Lillia's lap. She tangled her fingers in his hair. They sat silently for a long time. A guard brought the usual nasty porridge, but they didn't eat. The last of the light crept out through the window.

"We should eat," said Jyrym, picking up the spoons.

"I'm not hungry, and this food is disgusting. If this were your last meal, what would you want?"

They heard the guard change. Then they heard footsteps and knew Dr. Hami was returning.

He walked in carrying a lantern, which he put on the bench.

"How is the little lady?" Dr. Hami asked Jyrym. Lillia felt the hairs on the back of her neck stand up. She stared at him blankly. He looked at her and nodded, making a sympathetic sound.

"She seems quite calm since she took the medicine," said Jyrym.

"Good, then it's helping." Dr. Hami looked at the bottle. It was half gone.

"I'll bring some more in the morning," he promised. "This should be enough to last the night."

He bent close to Jyrym and spoke in a coarse whisper. His breath smelled of bad digestion. "The high priestess asked me to assist you. I will return before dawn."

Jyrym looked grim. This doctor stunk through and through. He nodded his head and said, "Thank you."

"Until then," said Dr. Hami.

After he left, Craig came in.

"Don't trust him," he said, "and I wouldn't take any medicine he gave you. He works with Selene and Jacob. They want to turn the people against you and prove your guilt by catching you trying to escape."

Lillia said, "Thank you, Craig. I haven't taken any of this so-called medicine. I didn't believe for a moment that he wanted to help us. We must find a way to thwart his plan without getting anyone else hurt or worse."

"I have word from your friends. They are well and working for your release."

"Thank you; you are a good man."

"I'll be outside your door all night. Knock if you need anything."

That same night, in the woods

The daylight faded. Randall built a fire. Beryl sat on the mossy ground, deep in thought. She closed her eyes, trying to find her calm center, but her mind kept whirling. Ava had returned to Brother Earth's realm and her new husband. Before she left, she showed Beryl the road leading to the Temple City. Beryl had cleaned and bandaged Randall's wounds using the herbs Ava had gathered. She still wondered if she should trust him. She couldn't even think in his presence. She thought about how good it felt to be close to the dream Randall. She thought about Lucas and how much she had wanted to be near him, too. She remembered all those men in the Hill of the Grandmothers. How could she follow her inner guidance when her insides felt like cake batter being vigorously stirred? She heard Randall sit down next to her. She took a deep breath, opened her eyes, and looked at him.

"I hope I'm not disturbing you," he said.

"Not at all," she said.

"I thought you might like to eat, and then perhaps we can talk. Come and sit by the fire. It's getting chilly."

She followed him to the fire, grabbing her cape on the way. She hadn't noticed the cold until he mentioned it. He offered her a bowlful of hot soup and a hunk of bread. Beryl saw no pot on the fire and wondered where the food had come from, and the bowl, too, for that matter. "A gift from a friend," said Randall, reading her thoughts.

She hadn't seen or heard anyone nearby. Still, the food tasted delicious, and she felt grateful for a warm meal at the end of this day.

"I would never hurt you," Randall began uncertainly. "I...well, I have the feeling that we need to work together to fix this mess—in Floredelis, I mean. The tree people saved me twice when I was injured and in danger in the last few weeks. They told me Mother Earth needed my help. They make delicious soup, don't you think?"

Beryl smiled and turned to face Randall. He looked at her, his eyes wide open, waiting for her to speak.

"Randall," she said slowly, "would you hold my hands and, well, I need to feel your energy. I don't know how to explain it, but please trust me."

"I do," he said. "I always trust my gut feelings about people, and I know you are both good and powerful."

He reached out his hands. Beryl's hands looked small next to his. His hands felt warm and safe. She closed her eyes and startled when a bolt of heat flowed from his hands into hers and traveled through her entire body. She opened her eyes. Randall sat quietly with his eyes closed. Her heart pounded like a drum. Did he really not notice? She took several long, deep breaths. She remembered what Brother Earth said about staying centered. She pictured Brother Earth in her mind and saw him smiling. He liked Randall; she could tell.

A peace settled over her and a certainty. She felt Randall's courage and goodness. He wasn't an initiate, yet she felt his power. She remembered Jocasta writing in her journal that everyone had spiritual gifts. In fact, Beryl realized, Jocasta never mentioned initiates. Where had they even come from?

"Oh Brother Earth, Oh Sister Moon," a voice within her startled her out of her reverie. "Bless this union, for from it shall come peace and renewal."

Who spoke? She opened her eyes and realized Randall was looking at her. Her face flushed, but she didn't look away, glad for the darkness. They gazed at each other, the firelight reflected in their eyes.

"Blessings on our work," said Randall.

"Blessings," repeated Beryl, her voice barely audible. "I need to sleep now. Let's discuss our plans in the morning. Perhaps our dreams will bring some guidance. I still have no idea what we're supposed to do."

"Me either," said Randall, "But I feel we could do almost anything together. Good night." Randall withdrew his hands. Beryl had forgotten that she still held them. She blushed again.

They slept, one on each side of the fire, in the clearing in the woods, well sheltered and watched over by Brother Earth and Sister Moon, who did indeed send them dreams.

That same night, in the Temple

> *On Dealing with People in Crisis: Just as the child requires loving guidance, so does the adult who has lost his or her way. People can be treated with firmness and honesty and should always be held accountable for their actions, but they should also always be honored and held with kindness and compassion, especially when they seem least to deserve it. We all have difficult times in our lives. These allow us to grow and learn. There is no shame in needing the support of others.*
> *From* The Book of Jocasta

Jyrym and Lillia lay down, although neither of them slept. Somewhere in the middle of the night, they heard Dr. Hami outside their cell saying he wanted to attend to the lady. They heard Craig fumbling with the keys and mumbling loudly about how the best thing for people when they didn't feel well was rest. Lillia felt sure Craig intended to give them time to prepare. She and Jyrym sat up. Lillia checked to make sure her pendant was tucked inside her top.

Dr. Hami came in, holding a lamp near his face. The light of his lantern was bright to their eyes. He drew so close to Jyrym and Lillia that they could smell his sour breath.

"We have little time," he said. "Come with me. I will tell the guard that you, milady, need medical attention and that I am taking you to my office for treatment. I will say that you, Jyrym, will not leave the

Queen's side, which I'm sure is true. Then I'll take you to a place where friends are waiting to help you."

Before Lillia could speak, Dr. Hami said, "Oh, and let me give you this." He pulled a small dark bottle out of his pocket and offered it to Jyrym. Jyrym scowled and didn't take the bottle.

Dr. Hami offered the bottle again. "It is poison, in case, in case...." He paused again and then blurted in a loud gravelly voice, "In case you find yourself in dire straits, there is enough for you and your lady to kill yourselves." He paused and wiped a line of sweat from his upper lip with the back of the hand holding the bottle. "Should the need arise," he finished.

"Thank you for your thoughtfulness, Doctor. But we won't need this. It's against our beliefs to take our own lives, no matter what the circumstances," Jyrym replied.

"And Dr. Hami," said Lillia, "We will not go with you. We're staying here."

The doctor held the light close to her face.

"I see the queen hasn't been taking her medicine."

"No. I don't need your medicine," she said, not trying to conceal her contempt.

"I only thought to ease your pain, madam," said Dr. Hami, bowing his head obsequiously.

"I am quite capable of handling my pain," replied Lillia.

"Of course. But we must go. Time is of the essence. The others are waiting."

"No," said the queen loudly. "We will stay here."

Craig opened the door. His dark form filled the doorway. "Is everything alright?" he asked.

"Yes, thank you," said Jyrym. "The doctor was just leaving."

"Oh, my dear fellow," said Dr. Hami to Craig, "I have orders to bring these prisoners to my quarters for treatment. They refuse to go. Be a good lad and help me out."

"My orders are to keep them in this cell. You have no authority to change my orders."

"But the high priestess said...."

"She didn't say anything to me. They stay."

"I see. You will be in a great deal of trouble when the high priestess finds out. What is your name?"

"Craig."

"Well, Craig, I see there is nothing for me to do but be on my way. I'll leave this bottle here in case you change your mind." He held out the bottle to Jyrym and then to the queen. When neither of them took it, he put it on the bench and left.

Jyrym handed the bottle of poison to Craig. "Would you keep this? I'd rather not have it in here."

Craig took the bottle with him and put it on the floor next to his chair outside the door before locking the door again.

Jyrym and Lillia lay down again, still not sleeping, wondering what the rising sun would bring. But the night held more adventures. About an hour after Dr. Hami's visit, they heard screams from the castle court-yard, followed by shouts and footsteps. What on earth had happened, wondered Lillia and Jyrym. Craig asked Lillia and Jyrym if they were alright. He had no idea what was going on.

Then they heard the sound of men running toward their cell.

"Craig, why are you sitting there when your prisoners have escaped?" shouted one.

"What are you talking about? I just checked on them. They are huddled together and wondering what all the ruckus is about. And so am I. What in the world is going on?"

"The high priestess is dead. She's been poisoned. Selene found her. She said Dr. Hami took the prisoners to his office to care for the queen. She said that the king hit the doctor over the head and stole a bottle of poison. The queen poured poison into the Priestess' cup, and she's dead, and the queen and her husband have disappeared." All of these words tumbled out in one breath. Lillia and Jyrym heard everything.

The high priestess dead? Unbelievable. Thank the goddess they hadn't gone with Dr. Hami.

Craig scratched his head.

"Utter nonsense. Look for yourself. I've been here all night. Dr. Hami came here about an hour ago. He wanted to take the queen with him, but I wouldn't let him. He didn't have the authority to take custody of the prisoners as far as I knew."

Silence, again.

"Well, go and look for yourself."

The door flew open, and five temple guards pushed into the room. Jyrym and Lillia sat on their mat. The men stared at them, their mouths hanging open. They looked rather comical, but this was no time to laugh. The men stared for another minute, then walked out the door without closing it behind them.

"Well, if they didn't kill her, then who did?" asked one. The silence that hung over them held the answer no one was willing to say. They all knew. They knew before they found the king and queen in their cell. None of them wanted to tell Selene what had, or hadn't, happened.

59 ▌

That same night, in the woods and the Temple City

In the forest, Beryl and Randall slept soundly. The moon had set, but the sun hadn't yet peeked over the horizon. Suddenly, Beryl sat up straight as an arrow. If it hadn't been so dark, and if anyone had been looking, they would have seen the color drain from her face.

"Oh, no!" she exclaimed.

She walked around the fire, now just glowing embers, and kneeled next to Randall. She put a hand on his shoulder and said his name softly. He didn't stir. She grabbed both shoulders and shook him.

"Randall," she shouted.

Randall woke to see Beryl's frightened face only inches from his own.

"What is it?" he mumbled.

"We must go to the Temple City immediately. Queen Lillia and King Jyrym are in terrible danger. Please. Let's go."

She told him about her dream-- the king and queen had been sentenced to death. They were to be hung at dawn. She had seen that man again—Hami. He held the queen's jewel in his hand while the bodies of the king and queen swung from gallows, side by side. She knew this dream was real, a portent, and not a projection of her inner darkness. Oh, why did she say that part? Did he believe her?

Randall looked into her eyes. He felt her hands still squeezing his shoulders. He had never seen a more beautiful sight. He put his hands on her cheeks, pulled her face down to him, and kissed her lips, very gently. She froze for a moment and then kissed him back but sat up suddenly and stared. On his chest sat a large green frog that hadn't been there a moment ago.

"Beryl, I am so...Are you alright? Hey, where did that come from?" Randall picked up the frog. He looked at it in the gathering light.

"What on earth?" asked Randall, still looking at the frog. Beryl noticed the frog wore a tiny golden crown on its head, just like the frog in the story. The frog hopped away. They looked for it, but it had disappeared.

Beryl started crying. It was all too much. Randall put his arms around her. She put her head on his shoulder and let the tears come. When her sobs quieted, Randall said, "Beryl?"

"I'm sorry," she said. "It was so wonderful—the kiss, but then the frog and my dream. It's just that...I'm so afraid...the king and queen and everyone, they need us, and I don't know how we will save them or make things right. We may not live through this, and that may be the only kiss I ever…" she stopped as the tears welled up in her eyes. She didn't want to cry anymore.

"Don't say such things, Beryl. We'll come through this together. We'll know what needs to be done when the time comes, and we'll do it. And you will get many more kisses. In fact," he held her closer, "I'll give you many more myself if you like—when this is over."

Beryl put her hand on his.

"I'd like that," she said.

"We'd better get going," he said. He threw dirt onto the remains of the fire, stirred it, and they gathered their few things. Beryl pulled a bit of bread and chocolate from her sack. "We ought to eat something. I have a feeling this will be a long day. Is it far to the Temple City?"

"If we walk quickly, we should get there mid-morning. I don't suppose you feel like telling another story?"

Beryl thought a story was a good idea as long as it didn't have a frog in it. She chose a funny story, another of her favorites, "The Golden Goose." As they walked, they felt as though Dummling, the three sisters, the parson, the sexton, and the rest were trailing along behind them.

*

The gallows stood ready. No one had any idea what such a thing even looked like. The builders found a book from the old world in the library with a drawing of a gallows, and they worked from that. They built it on the platform used for celebrations in the square, only now they'd prepared it for a horrible sacrifice. The builders knew what they were doing was wrong but were afraid of what would happen to them if they didn't. Besides, they were just following orders. They finished at about the same time the High Priestess died and Beryl woke from her dream. When they heard Jenna had died, some thought that it was good she didn't live to see this day, even though she had ordered the executions.

*

Craig found Ian in the kitchen. Ian prepared a lovely breakfast for the king and queen, although he doubted they would be very hungry. He also gave Craig a message to deliver. Craig took both to the cell. He nodded at the guard on duty, who let him in and then closed the door behind him. Lillia and Jyrym sat on the bench. Craig knelt before them. "Ian prepared a special meal for you. Please try to eat." The king and queen moved so Craig could put the tray down between them.

Still kneeling, he said, "I bring word from your friends. They know of your plight and are prepared to give their lives, if necessary, to save you. Others, including myself, will do the same. Take courage."

Queen Lillia placed her hand on his shoulder. "Craig, we don't want anyone to die on our behalf."

"Queen," Craig looked into her eyes. "It's not only for you. The future of our world is at stake. These people will destroy many more besides you to gain control of Floredelis. I don't wish to die, and I hope to live, but this is worth risking everything for. When Jocasta founded Floredelis, she proclaimed it a world without organized violence. I don't know how we've gone so far astray, but it must stop. Now. And it will."

"You're right. We must stop this evil, no matter what the cost. Thank you. You are a true guardian," said the Queen.

60

Early the next morning, on the road to the Temple City and in the town square

On Heart-Centered Living: If you are still alive, then your work isn't finished. We all live many lives, reincarnating many times, and we come into each one with a purpose, with lessons to learn. The truth opens your heart. I know that sometimes that hurts. It may cause you more pain than you know how to process. Allow the pain to work through you. Allow yourself to experience your pain—and all your other feelings—without judgment. If you are on the path of the heart, you will eventually feel yourself softening and opening; you'll experience peace. If you keep bringing your consciousness back into your heart, you will find your way.

From The Book of Jocasta

As Randall and Beryl hurried toward the Temple City, and Beryl reached the part of the story where the thirsty man drank all the king's wine, they heard a horse approaching. Randall pulled Beryl into the bushes. At his touch, a surge of heat shot through her but falling into the brambly bushes quickly distracted her from that. Randall peeked out and was startled to see his horse with Solomon on her back.

"This should be interesting. It's Solomon." He smiled at Beryl, still tangled in the bushes. "Watch this." He offered her a hand. She took it, using her other hand to protect her face from the branches.

They watched Solomon urge the horse to go faster, but the horse kept plodding along, paying no attention to the man on her back.

Randall whistled. The horse stopped dead in its tracks. Solomon flew over the horse's head, flipped over, and landed on his back. Randall threw his arms around the horse, Cherry Blossom. Beryl could see they were quite fond of each other. Beryl stepped out of the bushes and patted the horse. They heard a groan and looked over to see Solomon trying to stand.

"I wonder if he's badly hurt," said Beryl. They walked over to Solomon. He didn't seem to recognize them. Beryl bent a little closer and smelled alcohol on his breath. "Even if he is, I doubt he feels much," she said.

"How fortuitous that you should find me here," said Solomon, his speech slurred. "I seem to have fallen from my horse. Could you help me get up? I have an important appointment at the Temple this morning."

"Come on, then," said Randall. He gave Solomon a hand up and helped him to the side of the road. When Randall let go, Solomon staggered a few steps back in the direction from which he'd come. "He doesn't seem to be hurt too badly," said Beryl.

"I think we'll get to the City in plenty of time," said Randall, looking at Cherry Blossom.

"I—uh—don't know how to ride," said Beryl. They heard a loud thump and turned to see Solomon lying in the path again. By the time they walked over to him, he was snoring.

"Cherry Blossom is gentle. You can sit behind me and hold on. But first, let me fix her saddle. She hasn't been very well cared for." He adjusted the saddle and stirrups and whispered something in the horse's ear, his face against her neck.

"There now, let's go. Jump on up." He helped her onto the horse and climbed on in front of her.

*

All the citizens of the Temple City had been ordered to attend the public hanging. Most did not want to, but the temple guards knocked on doors and herded everyone into the square. Everyone knew the high priestess had died during the night. Rumors flew through the town about how she had died, but the people who knew the truth kept it to themselves. Whatever the real cause, people mourned her death. Jenna had been well-loved for many years before everything went wrong.

Fear permeated the square. Many knew Queen Lillia and King Jyrym from their student days. All who knew them or knew of them liked and respected them. And the premeditated violence about to take place terrified them—just as Selene had intended.

Temple guards brought Jyrym and Lillia to the platform through an underground tunnel usually used by actors for performances or to bring food for the feasts from the Temple kitchen. Selene had pictured the moment in her head. Guards leading the chained prisoners through the jeering crowd to the waiting scaffold, people shouting and throwing stones or rotten fruit at them. Selene believed that the story of the Queen murdering the High Priestess the night before her scheduled execution would seal the town's hatred of the traitors and ensure their support of Selene and Solomon and the "new order." But things hadn't unfolded as planned, so Selene decided at the last minute not to have the prisoners pass through the crowd. She wanted to accuse Craig, that interfering twit, of the murder, but too many people knew he was nowhere near the high priestess' chamber. Also, the bottle of poison that Dr. Hami said he left in the prisoners' cell had turned up in Selene's room. The servant who found it had her family threatened if she breathed a word to anyone.

Selene wondered where Solomon was. That man would be late for his own funeral. This was more important than his funeral; they were creating their future and the future of Floredelis. He was supposed to address the crowd. He had been framed as the hero who captured the evil Randall and thwarted his attempt to destroy Floredelis. He was to be the first High Priest, and they would rule together. Once in power, Selene planned to get rid of Dr. Hami, for he knew too much.

Craig stayed with the King and Queen that morning. He and three other guards accompanied them through the tunnel. The king and queen seemed calm. They held hands as they climbed the steps onto the platform. When they appeared on the platform, the crowd fell silent. Lillia had assumed the entire council would be present, but she didn't see any of them. Selene and Jacob remained inside the Temple. As she looked sadly at the sea of people, she noticed two people pushing their way through the crowd toward the stage. They wore brown wool traveling cloaks. Could it be Anne and Beatrice? She squeezed Jyrym's hand and leaned toward him to let him know. She felt him look as he squeezed her hand in return. She knew he understood. He always did. How lucky she was to have shared her life with him. But this couldn't be goodbye. "I love you," she said, kissing his unshaven cheek.

Lillia and Jyrym stood on the platform for a long time, surrounded by the guards, including Craig. Never had she been in such a silent crowd. She could hear the sound of the nooses flapping in the breeze high above her head. After a while, the people in the square grew restless. Some tried to leave, but the Temple guards blocked the entrances to the square. When did the Temple acquire so many guards, Lillia wondered.

Selene, still in the Temple, climbed the steps to the watchtower. She could see the square from there, as well as the road into town. She hoped to see Solomon hurrying into the City just in the nick of time. She didn't wish to speak to the crowd. She knew she lacked charisma and that her voice grated. And Solomon, she thought, was handsome and charming. She tried to remember when she had fallen in love with him. It seemed like she had loved him forever. She wondered if he knew. He thought most women found him irresistible. But he always went for the pretty young ones, not the more mature, intelligent women. She would show him the error of his ways. If only he would come. She watched the crowd grow restless. She would lose them if something didn't happen soon.

With sudden resolve, she walked towards the stairs. She paused by the mirror, patted her hair, bit her lips, and pinched her cheeks. She told her reflection, "I am a woman of power, a leader of my people. I've always gotten along without a man, and I don't need one now." She strode out of the room.

"Where are you going?" She'd forgotten Jacob was there.

"I am going to get this thing over with," she said. "We can't wait all day. Come on, and grab a few more guards on the way. We'll give them a good show."

She marched briskly. The day as she had imagined it flashed before her. She and Solomon standing before the people, bringing justice, and instilling fear. The people begging them to save their beloved land. She and Solomon would agree to be their humble leaders on the condition that the people follow their commands without question. They required complete trust and obedience. She and Solomon, and Jacob, too, she supposed, as highly evolved people, knew what was best for everyone. They would be like good parents, kind to those who obeyed, stern, and quick to punish those who didn't. The people would stand in awe of them and fear crossing them lest they end up like the King and Queen of Xantalon, who hung by their necks for all to see.

Damn that man. She could do it without him. In a few minutes, Selene and her retinue climbed onto the platform. Selene, who was quite short, had to shove her way through the guards surrounding the prisoners to be seen by the crowd. She ended up at the front edge of the stage. She was afraid of heights and so, after looking down, took a few steps back, bumping into a guard as he tried to avoid her heels. She wore a bright red robe and looked rather like a ripe tomato. She looked around expectantly and cleared her throat, ready to speak, but the people kept talking. Surely, they recognized her importance. She whispered something to one of the guards. He called the guards on the stage to attention, and around the perimeter of the square, the other guards snapped to attention as well. The crowd's mood shifted, and they became silent again, edging closer to the platform.

"Good people of the Temple City," Selene's voice sounded as melodious as a screech owl's. Lillia and Jyrym visibly grimaced at the sound. Selene noticed and thought she saw others in the crowd doing the same. Nonetheless, she was in charge, and she would continue. She would punish those who didn't appreciate her later, after this execution was finished. She hoped the guards were watching the crowd as she had ordered, noting who opposed the Council's decision.

"Good people," she repeated. "This is a sad day, indeed, for Floredelis. Our beloved high priestess has crossed the rainbow bridge and returned to the spiritual world. We will miss her dearly, but I know she will always watch over us." She felt satisfied with that part. She thought it sounded like something Solomon might say.

"It is also a sad day, dear people, because we have been betrayed by those in whom we placed our trust." She stepped aside so the people could see the king and queen. She had hoped for some booing or cat-calls, but the crowd remained silent. Lillia looked serene and beautiful, and Jyrym looked like a man who faced life and death with courage. They held hands and listened. She hated them with all of her being.

"These people have betrayed us. They tried to destroy our way of life. They must be punished, not only to stop them from doing further harm but as an example to anyone who would do the same."

Lillia saw, out of the corner of her eye, something happening behind the gallows. She felt sure Beatrice and Anne were there. She heard a shuffling noise behind her. Selene must have heard it, too, for she paused and turned around. Dr. Hami, looking as though he had not bathed for some time, his white clothes covered with splotches of dirt, made his way toward the front of the stage. Selene, upset that her moment had been interrupted, said in a loud whisper, "What are you doing here?"

"As the official temple physician, I come to officiate. I will pronounce the prisoners dead," he smiled and nodded his head at Lillia and Jyrym, "when the time comes." Lillia saw him looking at her chest where the jewel nestled beneath her blouse.

"Carry on, Selene. Don't mind me," Dr. Hami said without looking away from the queen's chest.

Selene tried to remember what she was saying. Flustered as she turned to face the assemblage, she became even more flustered when she saw a horse making its way through the crowd. At first, she thought it was Solomon making a grand entrance. She felt relief until she noticed the girl sitting behind him. Who had that rascal brought this time? But as the horse and riders came closer, she saw that the rider in front was taller, slenderer, and had more hair than Solomon.

Lillia's eyes widened in surprise when she recognized the people on the horse. She looked at Jyrym and saw a smile playing around the corners of his mouth. She didn't know what it meant, but she felt overjoyed to see Beryl, and Randall too. She hoped she would live long enough to hear the story of how they came to be here, together. When they arrived at the platform, the crowd cheered as Randall lifted Beryl onto it and jumped up after her.

While all this was happening, Dr. Hami grabbed the queen's stone, intending to pull it off. The chain held strong, and he pulled harder. Selene yelled at Dr. Hami, although no one heard her over the cheering. Selene tried to pull Dr. Hami away from the queen, but he wouldn't let go. Beryl and Randall watched, unsure what to do, and then Beryl knew.

"Kiss me," she said to Randall.

"What?"

"Remember the frog? There's no time to explain. Just try it—unless you have a better idea."

She kissed him, looking around to see what would happen, but nothing did.

Randall understood.

"I think you have to mean it," he said. "See only me, like in the woods."

She looked into his eyes, then kissed him again. She felt the magic. Something was happening. She looked at him. He winked and looked at the queen. A single golden feather floated through the air and landed on her head. The Doctor still held onto the queen's stone. Beryl knew the kiss had worked—it created some kind of magic. Dr. Hami felt something, too. He tried to let go but found his hand stuck fast to the stone, which still hung around the queen's neck. The queen looked surprised. Dr. Hami seemed to be stuck to her, and she realized that Jyrym also couldn't let go of her hand. They certainly couldn't hang them in this state.

Randall took Beryl's hand and walked over to Selene. He heard his name murmured throughout the crowd. Beryl squeezed his hand. They both looked out at the townspeople.

Selene looked at the crowd, too. She told the guards, "Take them to the gallows. Hang them. Now!" Craig came behind Dr. Hami and grabbed his arm to get him to let go of the queen, but he stuck to Dr. Hami. Selene didn't understand what was happening. She wanted Dr. Hami to let go of the queen.

"Get away from her, you fool," she hissed, grabbing his shoulder. But when she tried to pull her hand away, she realized her hand had stuck to Dr. Hami, and she couldn't let go. Soon, the guards, the king, the queen, Dr. Hami, and Selene were all stuck together. The people realized something strange was happening. Randall looked at the group on the platform behind him and started to laugh. The queen shuffled across the platform, and everyone followed. Soon, the entire crowd laughed. They laughed until they cried. The group stopped in front of the gallows. The people fell silent again.

Randall spoke. "We have been deceived by those whom we trusted. People stand before you now who used the power with which we entrusted them for their own gain. And I am not speaking of the good King and Queen of Xantalon. These people have tried to blame good people, like myself and Lillia and Jyrym—and many of you. They have used us."

Shouts of agreement came from the crowd, followed by shouts of anger. Some cried out that they should hang Selene and Dr. Hami. In the midst of all this, Solomon staggered into the square, his clothing ripped, covered with leaves and bits of branches.

"It's Solomon."

"Kill him, too." They grabbed him and dragged him onto the platform.

"Stop," called Beryl, but no one heard her.

"Brother Earth, help me now. I know you're with me," she said quietly. She raised her arms. A storm cloud gathered above the square, although on the other side of the city wall, the sun still shone brightly. A lightning bolt flashed directly above them, followed by a loud crash of thunder. Everyone fell silent once more, looking at the sky and the girl who seemed to control it. As she lowered her arms, the wind picked up, and the clouds dispersed. Beryl wondered if anyone else noticed that the cloud was shaped like a man. She recognized the Thirteenth and, for once, was glad of his presence.

"No," she shouted. "We will hang no one. Killing won't solve our problems. Yes, they should be punished, but if we meet violence with violence, all we will have is more violence. Our society is falling apart not just because there are corrupt people in power but also because we didn't take responsibility, we didn't speak up. We held our own darkness secret. We must work together. And we must deal justly with those who have done wrong, even if they did not do the same for us. I have brought back new teachings from Jocasta." She pulled out the book, holding it high in the air. Then she turned to the queen and removed the golden feather from her hair. As soon as she did, everyone was released from their stuckness. She held the golden feather in her palm. It lingered for a moment, then vanished.

Lillia hugged Beryl. Jyrym did the same. Lillia asked Craig if he would take Solomon, Selene, and Jacob to the cells. The guards led them away through the tunnel for their safety.

Anne and Beatrice pushed through the crowd and climbed the stairs to the platform. They hugged Beryl in a sandwich. "We untied the knots and loosened the bolts. The whole thing would have fallen apart before they had a chance to use it," said Anne, gesturing at the gallows. "But thank goodness it didn't come to that."

The guards had disappeared from the entrances to the square. The people talked excitedly, drifting off in groups. It seemed like the thunderstorm had cleared their minds, and the sun's return woke them from a long dream. No one knew what would come next, but they felt like themselves again for the first time since before the great illness.

When the crowd cleared, Ian invited everyone left on the platform back to the Temple kitchen for a celebratory feast. Their work had really just begun, and the death of the high priestess remained to be grieved, but for now, they needed to celebrate this victory. And they did.

61

The next day, in the Temple

The next day, a group visited Ontihaponati. They found her wrapped in layers of black wool, which someone had slashed to create an opening about the height of a human. They unwrapped her and saw that the crystal had split in two.

"Jyrym, what happened?" Lillia asked.

"I don't know, but can you feel it?" He held Lillia close. She rested her head on his shoulder, still touching the stone.

"Yes," she replied. "I feel her heartbeat. I wonder if there is some way to heal her."

Selene fumed in her cell, the same one Lillia and Jyrym had occupied. She wished they'd locked her up with Solomon. He had to be nearby, but she hadn't seen him since the debacle on the stage. He'd ruined everything. Yet she longed for him. She had heard guards escorting more people into the cells. They must be full by now. A guard took her out for a walk in the garden every day, but she never saw any other prisoners —or anyone except for the guard. She wondered how Jacob fared.

Ian prepared meals for the prisoners, and she had to admit that they treated her more kindly than she had ever treated her prisoners. The guards barely spoke to her, but one told her that Lillia and Jyrym had agreed to rule the Temple City for now. She shook her head. They were all fools. Someday they would beg her and Solomon to save them. She hadn't decided if she would say yes when that day came.

The Council members who weren't arrested offered to resign, but Lillia asked them to stay until they could be replaced. Five had been found drugged and sleeping in their beds with no memory of the last few days and were shocked to hear about the death sentences and Jenna's murder.

Dr. Hami was not among the prisoners. He had disappeared during the chaos that ensued after he was unstuck from the queen. Three people saw him run through the Temple, find Lucas, and head toward the great stone. They saw him cut open the fabric covering Onti-haponati. They saw the great stone split in two and watched Dr. Hami and Lucas disappear into her. They followed.

Ava, Tobias, and Andrew found themselves in a terrifying place after they passed through the stone. The gray air smelled dirty, and large buildings almost reached the sky. They stood in the middle of a great multitude of people, probably more than lived in all of Floredelis. They lost track of Dr. Hami and Lucas for a moment. Ava, not wanting to lose her companions, grabbed both by the hand and held on tight. They had arrived in Jocasta's world, Times Square, New York City, to be exact. Ava saw flashing pictures made of lights everywhere. She felt dizzy.

But she remembered why they had come. They must find Dr. Hami. Lucas looked as confused and out of place as they did in their gowns and tunics, so he was easy to spot. They pushed through the crowd toward Dr. Hami and Lucas.

People pointed and laughed at them and pulled out little boxes with flashing lights. As Ava, Tobias, and Andrew approached, the crowd parted for them.

"Look, there are more," said one person.

"Hey, are you in a show?"

"Where did you get your dress?"

Many questions and a lot of flashing lights confused the people from Floredelis. Dr. Hami tried to pull Lucas away, but Lucas didn't move.

"Come back with us, Lucas," Ava said, grabbing his arm.

Much to her surprise, Lucas sat down and started to cry. She put her arms around him. Hamilton didn't know what to do. Two men wearing uniforms and what Ava now recognized as guns on their belts approached them.

"We'll need to see your license," one of them said to Tobias.

"What?" Tobias asked.

"Your license to perform on the street. You have one, don't you?"

Dr. Hami spoke up. "Yes, we have a license, officer. It's right here in my pocket." He patted his side. "Oh, dear, I left it in my pants back at the theatre. I'll get it right now."

One of the uniformed men spoke. "Fine, go get it; just get out of here, and don't let us find you here again without a license to perform."

"Yes, thank you, officer," Dr. Hami said with a smile.

As the officers left, Dr. Hami glared at Ava. "Let go of him," he said. "He's mine now." Ava let go of Lucas, who still leaned against her.

"I take it we can't stay here," she said. "This is your home, Hamilton. What do you suggest we do?"

62

The days following Lillia and Jyrym's rescue

After they uncovered Ontihaponati, Lillia contacted the queens and watchers in the provinces. Many of them, as they recovered from Dr. Hami's hypnosis, remained befuddled and shocked to hear what had happened. She asked them about their food supplies, wanting to ensure that everyone had enough to get through the winter. Because winter would soon arrive, her request required some urgency. Lillia sent messengers to the forests to tell the Pied Pipers and the others living there what had happened and to encourage them to return to their homes before winter set in. She assured them that, although they would be held accountable for any crimes they had committed, they would be welcomed home. Their homes would be returned to them if they had been confiscated and all back-due taxes canceled.

Beryl didn't want to see anyone after her display of power, not to mention her very public kiss. She felt exhausted and embarrassed, even though she had helped to save Lillia and Jyrym. She feared what people would think of her or expect from her now. She especially didn't want to see Randall. She wouldn't be able to bear it if he didn't like her, and she didn't know what she would do if he did. She spent her time alone in her room in the Temple, reading Jocasta's journal. Her parents and the others gave her time and space.

After a couple of days, though, Mama B knocked on Beryl's door. Beatrice had hardly seen Beryl since that day in the square, and while she knew Beryl needed some time, she also needed to see her daughter. A lot had happened since they sent her off to Ava's house.

Beatrice waited, but when Beryl didn't answer, she opened the door and saw her daughter lying in bed and reading Jocasta's journal.

"Beryl, how are you?"

"Oh, fine."

"I know you better than that. Please look at me."

Beatrice sat down on the bed, and Beryl looked at her. "I just want to be normal. I want a normal life. I want a family and a home. I want to bake an apple cake."

"You can do whatever you want."

"Who would want me? What if I got angry and turned them into a toad?"

Beatrice swallowed a smile. "Oh, Beryl, you don't understand your power. You are right; you must be careful how you use it. But you can learn. There are teachers who can help you. I'm not sure that I know what "normal" means, but remember, everyone has powers. Perhaps not as visible as yours the other day, but each person has some gift they bring to the world, something that makes them different from the rest of us. And each person gets to choose how to use those gifts—or not."

"Mom, I think I'm falling in love."

"Yes, and he's in love with you, too. He's worried about you. Me, too." Beatrice took Beryl's cheeks between her hands and kissed her forehead. "I love you so much, Beryl."

Beryl began to sob. Beatrice put her arms around her, rocked her gently, and stroked her hair as she had when Beryl was small. When she finished crying, Beryl rested in her mother's arms.

"I didn't know if I would ever see you again," Beryl whispered. "I was so afraid."

Beatrice held her closer. A tear rolled down her cheek into Beryl's hair.

"Mom, I have this book written by Jocasta. It's her journal about her life. I always thought that she was better than the rest of us, but Mom, she was an ordinary person who had a really hard life. She made some big mistakes, too. She cut herself off from everyone and tried to do everything herself. I don't want to do what she did."

"It's the one from the town square," said Beatrice. "I recognize it. How on earth did you get the journal?"

Beryl told her the whole story. Beatrice cried when Beryl showed her the scar on her finger.

"Beryl, I had no idea you'd been through so much."

"I think this journal came to me now for a reason, Mom. I think the people of Floredelis need to know about Jocasta. She was not the highest of initiates or even a priestess. She was a regular woman who used her gifts and her pain to bring our ancestors to this wonderful place. But we don't need initiates to tell us what to do. We need to figure out what to do together. We need to reconnect with Jocasta's dreams and use our dreams to guide us. Let me read this part to you. It's near the end:

"We are all longing to go home to some place we have never been....
Somewhere, there are people to whom we can speak with passion
without having the words catch our throats. Somewhere a circle of
hands will open to receive us, eyes will light up as we enter, voices will

celebrate with us whenever we come into our own power. Community means strength that joins our strength to do the work that needs to be done. Arms to hold us when we falter. A circle of healing. A circle of friends. Someplace where we can be free."

These wonderful words were written by a contemporary of mine named Starhawk. She beautifully defines what it means to have a home. I have worked so hard to create this land, but as I come to the end of my days, I regret that I never really let anyone know me. I regret shutting love out of my life; I regret not making this place the home of my heart. I never told anyone the stories I have written in this journal. It has been a lonely journey for me, and too late, I realize that I am responsible for my loneliness. I wouldn't let anyone hold me. I held myself apart. And more than that, I fear that I have held myself above others, not thinking I'm better, but letting others think that I was so I wouldn't have to be vulnerable, to protect myself from being hurt again. I hope those who come after me can learn from my mistakes. I pray that Floredelis can be a home like the one Starhawk described. I hope I can give you the chance to have what I sought but never found."

Beryl and Beatrice sat quietly for a few minutes, arms around each other, then Beryl said, "Hey, Mom, is there anything to eat around here? I'm hungry."

Beatrice smiled. "That's my girl. Come to the kitchen. Ian has been saving some special food that he hopes will tempt you to eat. You'll make him very happy if you do."

Lunch was finished, and it wasn't yet time to make dinner, so Beryl and Beatrice found the kitchen empty. Many of the council members, priestesses, and students had gone home for a couple of weeks. Trees released their leaves, letting them flutter to the ground to make a blanket to keep the earth warm during the winter. And the farmers were busy harvesting the crops that hadn't been destroyed or stolen. With the small harvest this year, those who knew the forest were teaching others where to find berries and hidden fruit trees, as well as other edible plants. Despite the air of uncertainty, people worked together, remembering the joy of living in community.

In the quiet kitchen, Beatrice watched Beryl eat a big slice of chocolate cake with vanilla icing. She poured her a glass of milk, still warm from the cow. Beryl felt so hungry she thought she could eat the entire cake. She noticed her mother looking over her shoulder and turned around. Randall stood in the doorway. Her face flushed. She wanted to run away or crawl under the table and hide. To make it worse, she wished she felt some other way.

Randall couldn't decide if he should leave or try to say something.

Beryl turned back and examined her cake very closely.

"Hello, Randall," said Beatrice. "Would you like a piece of cake?"

"No thanks. I was looking for Ian, but it doesn't look like he's here." He looked at the back of Beryl's head as she continued examining the crumbs on her plate and turned to leave.

Beryl took a deep breath. "Please join us," she said.

"Alright. That cake actually looks pretty good." Randall smiled.

He sat next to Beatrice, who cut him a piece of cake. She gave him the milk pitcher and a cup.

"I have some business to attend to. I'll see you two later," Beatrice said, practically running out the door.

Beryl's face flushed again. "Mom," she said, her voice shaky. Beatrice paused at the door and smiled at her, but her eyes were steel, and Beryl finished, "See you at dinner."

"See you then." Beatrice left.

Beryl and Randall both dissected their cake, their eyes glued to their plates. Then, at the same moment, they looked up and said, "I...you...."

They laughed until tears ran down their faces. Randall told Beryl he had missed her. She tried to explain how she felt about her powers and her fear of what people would think. She especially worried about what he would think of her, and she wondered if she could only use her powers with him. The way they had worked together was wonderful and scary. Randall put his hand over hers, which still fiddled with her fork. Her hand fell still at his touch.

"I think you're wonderful," he said. "Amazing. I'm so glad I know you. I think I understand what you're afraid of. I always felt different from the other children when I was little. And I just wanted them to like me."

Beryl looked at him for a long time. "Will you...would you...I would like it if...."

Randall knelt by her and kissed her gently. She looked into his eyes, the color of the sea.

"I am alright now. Thank you." She stroked his hair. She wondered if everyone felt different inside and worried if others would like them. Then she decided to enjoy the moment.

"Let's go for a walk," she said.

"A walk?"

"Yes, you can show me the Temple City. I've never been here before, and I haven't really seen it yet."

Hand in hand, they strolled through the city. Randall hadn't planned to take Beryl to the square, worried that it would be difficult for her to return there. But she asked him to take her. She walked to the foot of the platform. The gallows had been removed. She looked up at the stage for a long time. Randall watched her.

"We did it," he said. "We did it together. And not just you and me, but your moms, Ian, Craig, the King and Queen, and many more."

"And Brother Earth and the tree people, too."

"Let's go out to the woods," suggested Randall.

"Just what I was thinking," replied Beryl.

"I'll get Cherry Blossom," said Randall, watching for her reaction.

Beryl smiled brightly and said, "Oh, yes."

She made Randall promise to teach her to ride some other time. He willingly agreed and said he knew just the horse for her to start on.

With Beryl riding behind Randall, they soon arrived at the forest's edge. Randall remembered racing Eugene there. He wondered if Eugene had recovered and hoped he and his family were safe and happy. Beryl slid off the horse, and Randall followed. After a short walk into the woods, they arrived at a clearing. The circle of soft green grass was surrounded by trees that blazed with glorious red, orange, and gold leaves. Randall tied Cherry Blossom's reins around the saddle's horn and let her graze. They sat on the ground beneath an old oak tree. Randall told Beryl about the tree people and how they cared for him.

"Do they help everyone who needs help in the forest?" he asked,

"I've never heard of such a thing, so I don't think so."

Beryl told Randall about her time in Brother Earth's realm. She pulled Jocasta's journal out of her bag. She had kept it with her ever since she got it. She opened it and was about to read to Randall when some dust fell into the book. She brushed it off and closed the book to protect it. They looked up to see where the dust had come from and saw what looked like a small branch wiggling above them.

"Acorn," Randall cried joyfully.

Acorn stopped wiggling and waved. "I'll be right down."

Acorn pushed and wiggled and then, with a small pop, flew out of the hole and fell straight to the ground, landing in front of Beryl and Randall. Randall thought he might be hurt, but Acorn straightened his hat, then stood up and bowed.

"I thought you called me," he said.

"I'm very happy to see you," said Randall. "I was just talking about you. This is my friend Beryl." Acorn stared at her with his eyes wide open. He reached up and touched her hair which was short but still wild.

"Oh my, she is most beautiful," he said to Randall, not taking his eyes off Beryl. "You are to come with me."

"Where are we going?" asked Randall.

"It's a surprise, but I think the beautiful lady will recognize the place."

He led them across the meadow to another tree with a hole in the trunk. He walked right in, but Beryl and Randall had to squeeze. They crawled through a long tunnel and found Ivy and Buttercup waiting with their wheelbarrow at the other end. Beryl hugged them and told Randall, "This is Brother Earth's realm. And these are my friends, Ivy and Buttercup. Hop in." Beryl climbed into the cart, and Randall followed.

Soon they arrived at Brother Earth's tree palace. Now the leaves looked like hammered gold. They sparkled in the sunlight, and when the wind blew, they made a sweet tinkling sound. The sight took Beryl's breath away.

"Come right in," said Buttercup. This time, the door led directly into a room with two thrones. Beryl and Randall gasped as they entered. Each throne was carved from a whole tree, with branches with multi-colored jewel leaves dangling from them, forming a canopy over the two thrones. The room itself was round, like the tree. Delicate tapestries hung all around, shimmering with scenes of fall. The pictures changed as the tapestries moved in the breeze that danced through the window-less room. Beryl hadn't seen this room on her first visit. She was so busy looking around now that it took a moment before she saw Brother Earth. He looked browner than when she saw him last and very happy. Next to him sat a beautiful woman, round and full-figured, with rosy apple cheeks and hair even wilder than Beryl's. It was orange and red and had leaves and maybe even birds in it.

"Beryl," said Brother Earth. "Welcome back."

"Brother Earth, I'm happy to see you. This room is so amazing that I forgot my manners. Hello." She curtsied and looked curiously at Brother Earth's companion.

"This is my bride. You know her as Mother Earth. When you were here last, she was working in your world, but she will stay with me until spring."

"How wonderful to meet you," said Beryl. "This is my friend, Randall."

"Yes, we know who he is. Although we haven't formally met, we've been looking after him. You have both done well, and we wanted to thank you," said Brother Earth. "And we have an invitation for both of you. We would like you to join the Council of All Beings. You would be the only human members besides Ava, who has been part of our circle for many years now."

"What is the Council of All Beings?" asked Beryl and Randall together.

Mother Earth answered, her voice like the singing of birds and the wind in the trees and the splash of raindrops in puddles and streams. "Dear children, the Council of All Beings is an ancient gathering of representatives of all beings living in this world. It was formed long before humans arrived. We weave the threads that form this land and celebrate the turning of the seasons. Most humans can't see or hear us. But you can, and we have chosen you. We would ask that you participate in our meetings and be our liaisons to the human world. In return, we will teach you to use your gifts, your magic. I hope you will consider joining us."

Beryl and Randall smiled at each other.

"I would be most honored," said Beryl.

"Me, too," said Randall.

"What do we do first?" asked Beryl.

Brother Earth replied, "For now, return to the Temple City. Help repair your human society. Share Jocasta's journal. We will come to you when the time is right to begin your instruction. Soon you'll be able to travel between the worlds alone, but until then, Acorn will be your guide.

"Take back this elixir. It will heal Ontihaponati." Brother Earth handed Beryl a small, full wineskin. "And take these pendants as a symbol of our alliance."

He placed matching gold pendants over Randall's head and then Beryl's. The branches of the white gold tree embossed in the center had jewels for leaves.

"Brother Earth, where is Ava?" Beryl interrupted. She missed Ava and hadn't heard anything about her since they parted in the woods.

"Ah, yes. Do not heal Ontihaponati until Ava returns, or she will never be able to return to Floredelis."

Beryl opened her mouth, but no words came out.

"Do you understand?" Brother Earth asked. Beryl nodded her head, and Randall asked, "Is Tobias with her?"

"Yes," Mother Earth answered, "And his son, Andrew, and Lucas, as well. Now you must return to your world. Remember, no matter where you are, we are always with you."

The winter solstice

> *Ontihaponati and the closing of the portal, continued: It felt like hours, but I'm sure it was only a few minutes. I heard a baby crying, but no one else stirred. Everyone chose to stay. I put my hands on Ontihaponati. She glowed pink and gold swirled together now—perhaps the most beautiful color I've ever seen. I thought there would be a loud sound when the portal closed, but it felt more like an ill wind had stopped blowing. Even though we were crowded in the cave, a fresh breeze ruffled our hair. As one, we raised a cheer. We were now the first citizens of Floredelis, for better or worse. And our work had just begun. But what joy we felt. We had been granted a new beginning, a return to Eden.*
> *From* The Book of Jocasta

Eugene had recovered completely. His wife was expecting another child. As much as Eugene had loved his family before, he loved and appreciated them even more after his close encounter with death. He felt honored to be trusted with Xantalon's rule until Lillia and Jyrym returned. Zorina and Otto continued to live with his family. Both had much healing to do, and they seemed to find it with his family just as he did.

The cities and provinces of Floredelis celebrated the winter solstice with quiet joy and hope for the return of the light. In Xantalon City, people gathered at the palace with candles and wound through the city, stopping at each house to light a candle. As they walked, the children led a song of the returning light. Everyone returned to the palace just before dawn to eat breakfast together before going home to sleep.

In the Temple City, the winter posed more difficulties. They had plenty of food. But the people mourned the death of the high priestess, questioning the role they had played, directly or indirectly. They mourned the numerous deaths from the great illness and the cruel plight of many survivors. The night of the solstice brought bitter cold, but everyone met in the town square. It was the first time they had gathered there since the day Lillia and Jyrym were almost hanged. Many cried, their tears freezing on their cheeks. Someone started singing a children's song—

"The light within shall never die,
The light in me is clear and bright,
Though the night be long
And comforts few
The light does glow in me and you."

Everyone joined in, their voices swelling with hope as their hearts beat with sadness. The temple guards distributed candles to everyone. Lillia and Jyrym emerged from the tunnel, each carrying a lighted candle. The Queen lit Randall's candle while the King lit Beryl's. Beryl lit her parents' candles, and everyone passed the flame until all the candles were lit and the square glowed golden.

"Follow me," Ian said to the people around him. Hundreds of people followed him through the tunnel into the Temple's great hall, decorated with fresh, fragrant greenery. Star-shaped candle holders nestled among the branches. Everyone put their candles in a star candle holder, and the large room twinkled.

Ian and his helpers brought out steaming pots of stew. The people served themselves and sat on benches at the long tables that filled the room. Ian served sparkling cider he had made from the fall harvest. They raised their glasses in a silent toast and drank. They finished the meal with sweet honey cake. Ian sent food from the feast to the prisoners, too. The candles burned low, and new ones lit as everyone returned home by candlelight.

After the solstice celebration, in the Temple

As everyone left with their candles, Ian started pushing a cart of dishes toward the kitchen. He saw Andrew, looking gaunt and pale, coming out of the kitchen. Instead of his usual happy, open expression and easy stride, his eyes darted all around as he plastered himself against the wall.

Ian looked Andrew in the eye and put a firm hand on his shoulder. "Andrew, what on earth...."

Andrew shook his head slightly. "Come with me. To Ontihaponati's cave. We're back, and Ava needs help."

Lillia, Jyrym, Anne, Beatrice, and Beryl were close by. They all hurried to the cave. Craig went to find a stretcher.

When they arrived, they saw Ava lying with her head cradled in Tobias' lap, both covered with blood. Beryl could barely breathe when she saw Ava bleeding and unconscious.

"We must seal the stone quickly. Beryl, Ava said you would know what to do." Tobias said.

Beryl stroked Ava's hand and didn't respond.

Anne touched her shoulder. "Beryl, do you have the elixir Brother Earth gave you?"

"Oh, yes." She tore her eyes away from Ava and removed the wineskin from around her neck. Everyone watched.

"Now?" she asked

Tobias nodded his head. Beryl's hands shook as she removed the stopper. She looked at Ava and at the giant broken crystal. Brother Earth hadn't told her how to use the elixir. The wineskin didn't hold nearly enough liquid to pour onto the crack in the stone. She felt Tobias staring at her; she heard the urgency in his breath. Her heart pounded, and beads of sweat formed on her forehead and the back of her neck.

She remembered how Randall had told her to focus only on him. She wished he was here. He would know what to do. She took a deep breath and focused on the crystal. She remembered the gnomes in the crystal garden, how they sang to the stones. She closed her eyes, felt Brother Earth's presence, felt the stone the gnomes gave her warm against her heart. She willed herself not to notice everyone watching and waiting. She didn't let herself wonder what would happen if this didn't work.

She took another deep breath, held the bottle out in front of her, and let the melody flow through her. She felt as though the crystal gnomes were singing with her and through her. She still wasn't sure what to do with the wine bag, but it began to warm in her hands. She closed her eyes and kept singing the song she didn't know. The sack's contents floated out like mist, covering the crack in Ontihaponati. The bottle emptied. She kept singing, eyes closed.

She heard a sound like thunder but didn't stop. The song still sang through her. With a creaking sound, the split rock grew back together, starting at the bottom and working its way to the top. When the healing was complete, it made a loud popping sound which startled Beryl into silence. She opened her eyes. Ontihaponati had become whole again, although she had a scar where the split had been. It reminded Beryl of the scar around her finger. Mama A put her arms around her. She felt weak and shaky. She let her weight rest against her mom.

Anne whispered, "You did it."

Craig and Randall arrived with the stretcher. "Who's this for?" Craig asked Tobias, who still held Ava, who now stirred in his arms. They followed his gaze and noticed Dr. Hami sitting in the shadows beside the stone, holding Lucas in his arms.

Dr. Hami said, "Please help. He is gravely injured."

Ava woke up. She felt dizzy. Although her head was still bleeding, she knew her injury wasn't serious.

Craig and Randall looked to Ava first.

"Shall we help you first?" Craig asked.

"No. I'll be alright. I just need to wrap my head," Ava replied. "But I fear Lucas needs immediate help. I want to check him for myself."

Tobias tore a strip of cloth from his shirt and wrapped it around Ava's head. He helped her crawl to Lucas. Lucas had a hole in his chest much like the one she had seen in Eugene's chest, and his blood kept flowing out of it. She asked Tobias to remove Lucas' shirt and tear it into strips. Ava pressed some folded strips against his wound in the front and back, with Tobias' help, and tied some strips around his chest to hold the bandages in place.

She spoke so quietly that it was difficult to hear. "Please put him on the stretcher. He needs immediate care if he is to have a chance. Very gently."

As Craig and Randall moved Lucas to the stretcher, Ava tried to stand up. She almost fell over. Tobias and Jyrym supported her. Dr. Hami sat slumped on the floor. Beryl looked at him. He looked unhurt, at least physically, but seemed unable to move. Beryl sat next to him as the others left with the injured.

"Are you coming, Beryl," her mother asked.

"I'll be there soon."

Their footsteps faded away. She looked at the empty wineskin in her hand.

"I wish I had some elixir that would make you whole again," she said.

Dr. Hami's eyes flashed with anger. "I would give my life to make Lucas whole again. It's my fault he's dying. It's all my fault."

Beryl followed his gaze down to his hand, which held the curved black metal, the gun. It looked the same as in her dream. Dr. Hami weighed it in his hand.

"Lucas tried to shoot me with this. I think he lost his mind when he found himself in that other world. Ava tried to stop him, but he hit her on the head with the gun. When he did, it went off, and he shot himself." He held the gun at his temple. "I was the one who was supposed to die. I wanted to die. I still want to."

Beryl inched closer to him, her heart pounding with fear. A story would help, a quiet voice inside her said, but she couldn't think with that metal thing filled with death so close. She remembered the sound of it roaring in her dream. She didn't want to hear it again.

"You came back," she said.

"She brought me back, this crazy stone. She won't let me die. She won't let me leave. This is the third time she's dragged me back here. What does she want from me?"

He pointed the gun toward Ontihaponati. Beryl saw the shadow of the Thirteenth against the stone. She felt his love for his son; she felt his guilt for deserting him. She looked back at the gun.

"Hamilton," Beryl said. "Please give that thing to me."

When she said his name, the barrel of the gun turned toward her.

"How do you know that name? Hamilton is dead. No one calls me that anymore."

"Hand me the gun, and I'll tell you. I've known you a long time, although we have never met." Cautiously, Beryl reached out her hand. Hamilton's arm tensed, but she kept going. She touched his hand and felt it relax. He lowered the gun to his lap.

"It won't work without these." He opened the chamber and removed the bullets. He handed the gun and bullets to Beryl. She took the bullets from him, but her hand refused to grasp the dark metal, so he placed it on the ground between them.

Then Beryl knew what story to tell this man, a story she knew very well. He needed to hear his own story.

"Once upon a time," she began, "in another world, there lived a little boy named Hamilton. It was a harsh world filled with fear, violence, and hatred. He loved his mother very much but never knew his father, who he believed had been killed in an accident before his birth. He didn't know his father had gone to a new world, seeking a new beginning, a new love. He didn't know his father regretted leaving his wife and unborn child, but only when it was too late to return. Hamilton had a golden heart and wanted to make his world a better place.

"He wanted his mother to be happy instead of always sad. He could heal with his touch, but he couldn't make his mother feel better. He found a book hidden in her room one day. It had his father's name on the cover. It told of a place of peace, prosperity, and joy. The book said his father was moving there to begin a new life and invited others to join them. Hamilton told no one, not even his mother, that he had read the book.

"One day, he found himself in this land where the air felt alive and the people pure and joyful. He tried to find his father, but no one had even heard of him. He brought back herbs from this magical land, hoping to heal his dying mother and others, but they didn't work. When he told his mother about his visit, she thought he had found the book and wanted to torture her with stories of Floredelis. The herbs he brought back only hastened her death and also killed another woman he tried to heal. People thought him insane when he told them that he had brought medicine back from another world; they locked him away, and destroyed his medicines.

"After that, he stopped trying to help. He used his healing ability to attain wealth and power. He resented and used those who trusted him. He thought they deserved what they got if they were too foolish to see the truth about him. Actually, he no longer saw the truth. His memories of the joy and magic of Floredelis and his life before were so poisoned that he blamed that place and her people for what had happened to him.

"But Ontihaponati did not forget him or his father. In his moment of direst need, when disease consumed his body and hatred his soul, when the law of the land was about to call him to task for the wrongs he had committed, that magical crystal, who still loved him and still saw his golden heart, brought him back. She healed his body but not his soul. He wrought evil on those who sought to help him. He hadn't intended to infect people with his disease, but when it happened, he decided to use it to get revenge. Ontihaponati knew that her land was already diseased. Hamilton, the son of her beloved, also named Hamilton, merely brought to the surface that which needed to be healed. He was a very effective catalyst. The violence and hatred that rose to the surface hurt her beyond measure. In fact, it broke her heart. But she knew that she must allow time and space for healing. As a crystal being, she experienced time very differently than humans. They'd only lived in this land for the blink of an eye.

"Still, she loved Hamilton and brought him back for a third time, knowing the magic of that number, a number of transformation and balance. This time she believes that he will unchain his golden heart and, perhaps, live happily ever after."

"I'm tired," said Hamilton. "I want to go to my room now."

"I'm tired, too," said Beryl. "Come, I'll walk with you."

Before she left, Beryl put her hand on the great crystal. She felt On-tihaponati's strength flow into her. She wondered if Hamilton would really find healing. She hoped so. She hoped that Floredelis would find healing, too.

65

A new year

The End: In every ending is a new beginning. And so, dear people of Floredelis, my story has come to an end. But the story of Floredelis is just beginning. I can't even imagine what wonders the future will hold here. All my love and blessings to you, my beloveds. I may be gone, but my heart will live forever in this place.

From The Book of Jocasta

It was another beautiful day in Floredelis. Beryl sat in Tobias' house, admiring the mosaic floor. She spoke with Ava, who, except for the bandage around her head, looked like her old self. Even after all they had been through, Tobias and Ava were giddily happy. Andrew was recovering his good cheer. It looked like Lucas would recover with time. Hamilton had not left Lucas' side since their return. Some wanted to put him in a jail cell, but Beryl convinced them that he had nowhere left to go and no one left to hurt. Beryl felt a strange kinship with this man whom she had dreamt about for years. She hoped his story would have a happy ending.

Beryl read to Tobias and Ava from the Journal she had brought back from the hill of the grandmothers:

So, I come to the end of my story. But really, it is only the beginning. If you have found this journal, the darkness I sought to leave behind has found its way into Floredelis. I hope this journal will help in the process of healing. Despite all the darkness and evil I have seen in my life, I have also seen much good. I believe in the basic goodness of humanity. I believe Floredelis can succeed. Perhaps it won't be a utopia, as I once hoped, but it can be a healthy dynamic society where all humans and all beings work together. Never forget Brother Earth. Work with the Council of All Beings. Work together. Love each other. Love yourselves. Forgive and forgive again those who err, especially yourselves. Together you will succeed. All my love to you, whom I will never know except in my dreams.

And so this story ends, and so it begins.

I am blessed to have so many people (and cats) in my life who support me as both a human being and an author.

First, I want to thank my family. My parents, Morris and Helen, have been amazingly supportive of me in so many ways on my winding path through life. My dad passed away early in the Covid epidemic, but he still inspires me with his kindness and wisdom.

And my daughters--Gabi and Rachel--have taught me much about life and love and art and everything. And, of course, my brothers, Marty and Andy, who are two of the best people I've ever met. Thanks to all of you for your support and for believing in me, and for just being you!

My lovely writing group always supports me and makes me laugh, too. Really, what more could you want? Thanks, Blake, Michelle, and Carol. And SCBWI has been a wonderful source of community and learning about this writing path.

To my Waldorf colleagues--especially Nancy, Laura, and Christine, my guardian angels--thanks for everything.

And to all the teachers who have guided me along the way. I appreciate you more than you'll ever know.

Thanks to my friend, roommate, and partner in art--Colby. Thanks for being my friend and supporting me in whatever I set out to do.

And last but not least, thanks to all the children who have given me courage, inspired me, and brought joy and wonder into my life every day--those who I've been honored to know as a teacher and mom--and all of Rachel and Gabi's friends who I have gotten to watch grow up from adorable children into amazing adults.

And, of course, thanks to you, dear reader, for joining me for this adventure!

Susan Bruck
Sunshine Lady Photography

Susan, a dreamer and lover of fairy tales, is a meditation coach, veteran Waldorf educator, and artist, as well as an author. Through all her work, she strives to inspire children and grownups with a sense of wonder, hope, and a reminder of the healing power of imagination. She is an active member of SCBWI, ALLI, NOCO Writers, and a graduate of the Children's Book Academy, the Institute for Children's Literature--plus colleges and law school, too.

Dear Reader,

Thank you for reading Beyond the Land of Dreams. I hope you enjoyed it.

As an independent author, I rely on your support to spread the word.

So if you enjoyed the story, please share your experience with others. And if it isn't too much trouble, I would really appreciate a brief review on Amazon--or anywhere else you like to leave reviews.

Many thanks for your support!

Love and blessings,

Susan